THE ABOLITION OF SPECIES

Dietmar Dath

THE ABOLITION OF SPECIES

Translated by Samuel P. Willcocks

DOPPELHOUSE PRESS | LOS ANGELES

The Abolition of Species
By Dietmar Dath
Translated by Samuel P. Willcocks

German original: *Die Abschaffung der Arten*
© Suhrkamp Verlag, 2008. All rights reserved.
First published in English translation by Seagull Books, 2013
English translation © Maria Pakucs, 2013

This edition published by arrangement with Seagull Books

Publishers Cataloging-in-Publication Data

Names: Dath, Dietmar, 1970, author. | Willcocks, Samuel P., translator.
Title: The Abolition of species / Dietmar Dath ; translated by Samuel P. Willcocks.
Description: Los Angeles, CA : DoppelHouse Press, 2018.
Identifiers: ISBN 9780998777092 (pbk.) | 9780998777016 (ebook) | LCCN 2018937173
Subjects: LCSH Evolution--Fiction. | Animals--Fiction. | Regression (Civilization)--Fiction. |
Genetic engineering--Fiction. | Artificial intelligence--Fiction. | Dystopia fiction. | Science
fiction. | Allegorical fiction. | BISAC FICTION / Science Fiction / General
Classification: LCC PT2664.A816 A74 2018 | DDC 833--dc23

COVER DESIGN: Kourosh Beigpour

PRINTED IN THE UNITED STATES

If you can't marry outside your religion
fool around outside your species.

Lord Julius of Palnu

In quella parte—dove sta memora
prende suo stato—si formato—come
diaffan da lume

CONTENTS

first movement

CONTRA NATURAM
(ALLEGRO MODERATO)

Iz: Well then, who are we, who are the Gente? And what sets us apart from men? Leaving aside our shapes ... these could just be masks, after all, disguises. What is the most noticeable change since the Liberation, the most obvious, the most notable?

Cy: The business with smells, I think. Scent. The fact that it's everywhere and that we can be anywhere in the world and can always know what is happening elsewhere ...

Iz: Because of non-locality at the level of the pherinfonic field system.

Cy: Yes. Except, of course, that mankind already knew about non-locality. Take two electrons, a pair. Their total spin, so to speak, is zero. You don't know though how much spin a single electron has. Quantum theory—and even mankind got this far—says that you can't know this until you measure it. Right then, you shoot them away from one another, so to speak, until one is a good long way from the other, gone forever. Then you measure the first one. And as soon as you've done that and the electron you're measuring collapses into a specific state, then the state of the other electron is its opposite. Straightaway. With no signal transmitted. This is electron resonance and it happens faster than light, faster than anything, because both electrons are part of an entangled system. They match up non-locally—there's no datum travelling along any kind of path, the information is available there just as soon as its counterpart is produced here.

Iz: Because the two particles are ... entangled.

Cy: Absolutely. And our trick was to ... well, even though this process normally happens well below the atomic scale, we found a way to make it observable in molecules, which ...

Iz: Transmitters. Which we can smell.

Cy: Exactly. Quantum scents. That's how pherinfonics began.

Iz: And nowadays they even use it for astronomy, don't they?

Cy: Of course. It's all out there, you know ... even alcohol ...

Iz: (laughs).

From the *Conversations with the Lion*, IV/65

THE DOOM THAT CAME TO THE THREE CITIES

1. YOU'RE REALLY NOT HELPING

While the pack hunted on down the coastline, a few stray wolves stayed behind and rested.

Four or five ravens had flown with them for a while, and now began to tease them. Each bird would dive-bomb one wolf, strafing the head or tail. The wolf ducked out of the way at first, and then leapt at the bird.

Sometimes it looked like a hunt. The ravens flew a little way above the wolves' heads, and then one hopped along the ground towards a resting wolf to peck at his tail, jumping smartly aside when the beast snapped at it.

When a wolf wanted revenge and followed the raven who taunted it, stalking, the bird would let him get within a few yards and take flight when it was almost too late.

Then it would land a few feet away and begin the fun all over again.

2. HE THAT WILL NOT HEAR

'Why,' the dragonfly Philomena asked her dearest friend, Izquierda the bat, 'did it actually happen to mankind the way that it happened?'

That was in summer, when by day cloudless blue depths opened up above the slopes of the highest peak of the Three Cities, and by night the farthest galaxies shone with pinpoint clarity and in the swamp south of Landers the rushes shot up as if from nowhere, though the sheer heat had left hardly a drop of moisture.

Reeds without water: a riddle.

While the badgers' pelts bristled in the heat and the iguanas' scales shimmered as though stars were hidden beneath, many were asking, 'Why did what happened to mankind, happen the way that it did?'

Early in the year, a few of them, mostly apes, had still believed that it might have had something to do with love. 'They always had to deal with that,' Stanz the ape explained to his acolytes, in front of a picture that he had painted to illustrate the theme, 'this nonsense about love. Nothing but trouble. If I understand things right, it doesn't bother us.'

Then the Lion made sure that voices spoke against the ape in all forums (or had the dragonfly make sure—he had long ago become too self-absorbed to walk amongst the Gente). 'We have love, just as we have language. Perhaps we call it otherwise—although the wolves call it love also, and why should they not? It's the same instinct for beauty, the same passion, the same old sacred guff we couldn't live without.'

Heavens above! Beauty, that's right. Even Stanz the ape had to admit as much. Those who now owned the earth after mankind were susceptible to beauty, to the same flowery, queasy, cosmic feelings and emotions that it had caused in mankind. There was the ecstasy of creation, the concern to preserve what had been made, to cherish; there was desire and the urge to own something precious, even the lust for destruction (because treasures have a magnetic pull of their own and bring on ruin too).

But if it had not been love that led to mankind's downfall, then why had their noisy, stinking, rapacious tenancy of this earth come to such a bloody end? Would their culture have been able to endure after its basis had been lost, like rushes that grew without mire, and reeds without water? If you looked in the archives this culture could still be found, lingering in a kind of melancholic last flowering, a memory in texts. But before you could pick the bloom and gather it, it had already withered. The greatest talent of these destructive geniuses had been hope and when this was cut off, their trust had perished, their ambition was a spider's web on books that no one would ever open again.

They had leant upon their house but it did not stand. They were green before the sun and their branches shot forth in their gardens. Their roots were wrapped round the heap and saw the place of stones. Yet, they had been destroyed from their place, which denied them, saying, 'I have not seen them.'

The dragonfly's best friend smelt of laurel and apricot, in those days the usual fragrance of scholars in all Three Cities. Her wings looked waxy in the soft twilight at the cave entrance. A ring of silver light spiralled round her copper claws. Her gaze glistened darkly, thick honey in the eye sockets. The cunning old bat laughed, showing needle-sharp teeth. Then she selected a short silent film and played it on the cavern wall, explaining to the dragonfly as it flickered past. 'Look, there, that mass of bubbles, do you recognize it? It's a mould fungus.'

'Looks like a slime,' said the dragonfly.

She was sceptical. What was this supposed to prove? Her friend gnashed her teeth, settled on a dry patch on the rock and said, 'That's what it is. A very special kind of slime, though. The old name was *Dictyostelium discoideum*. Very interesting life cycle, just watch.'

The film's colours were worn and faded. On the cavern wall something twitched, molten, gooey. The dragonfly buzzed faintly, scepticism gave way to cautious interest.

Beyond the bulging cave entrance, workers were busy installing ladders and walkways for those Gente who could not fly. They were well ahead of schedule and would be done with building these platforms and galleries within weeks. Months ago, trained groups of tiny scuttling creatures had taken apart the wasp factory between the meadows and the high forest, to use the beams for the new building work here inside the cave. Now it paid off.

Nearly all the wasps had set out for Landers in the meantime.

Watching Izquierda's film, Philomena could hear the workers, newts and field mice, laughing as they worked, singing too, telling jokes. There had been none of that in the first years after the Liberation. Now they were happy with their work. That was good.

All things considered, things were getting better all the time. Soon, it was said, they would be able to live on sunlight alone.

'Mankind,' continued the dragonfly's best friend, 'only discovered what you see here quite late, at the end of their dominance. They never truly understood it. Now—look here, at the close-up: this is the vegetative phase of the life cycle. Single cells. A random collection of unconnected units.'

'They look like, I don't know . . . swarming amoebae?'

'In a way, yes. Mankind called them Myxamoebae. They live on bacteria. As long as there's any around, as long as that food source is available, the cells grow and reproduce. But now, have a look—we take away their microbes.'

'Ah-hmm. Oh-ho! What's all this then? They . . . the single cells are budging together, tottering towards one another. They're jostling . . . clumping. Kneading one another.'

'Yes. Odd, isn't it? They are taking on another form. Like a living tissue. Mankind called that Pseudoplasmodium.'

'It moves, by itself! I can't . . . is that a new organism? Distinct?'

'Hard to say, dearie. Single cells organizing together . . . what should I call the result? If I observe it, pretty soon I can see that it's looking for food, clearly independently. A tiny little slug. It's attracted by light and reacts to temperature differentials, to moisture . . .'

'Hunts for food. Like we do.'

'Quite right. Here, let's speed up the process. Look, a new food source. It's feeding. And next . . .'

'Another metamorphosis! What is that now, a plant? It's got a stem, a stalk, then a fruit up there . . .'

'Spore capsule. And once the spores are dispersed, the whole cycle restarts. We can see, scattered about the place . . .'

'More Myxamoebae. Fresh single–cells.'

'Right. Do you understand?'

The dragonfly thought about it in silence for a moment. The facets of her eyes gleamed staccato while she thought, as though they were tiny beacons, sending messages coded in light. Then she said, 'Because they couldn't do anything like that. Mankind. That's why what happened to them, happened. That's why we overtook them. Because they couldn't do what the Myxamoebae . . .'

Izquierda twitched her ears and shook her head. 'Nonsense. Their downfall was not that they couldn't form a slug, rather, that they constantly tried to do so without being properly equipped. It's a confusion. People are not Myxamoebae, whether these people are humans or Gente.'

The film stopped.

The dragonfly laughed softly. She had understood.

A fearful redemption was underway.

3. SHORTLY BEFORE ESPRIT

The wind had lain down to sleep by the cool whitewashed walls, behind gigantic cathedrals of archives. This was no act of protest, merely reasonable conduct in the face of an afternoon stretched out for centuries, a costly peace between reason and nature.

This long after the Liberation, everyone only wanted peace and quiet—Gente, those humans who still survived, all those possessed of language. At least, so they thought. But thought is not action, the wind knows this.

Sticks and kindling cackled into flame in metal barrels placed round the mouths of rusty rainy drainpipes. The slender wolves kissed swans, stroking their feathers with moist, black muzzles and lay down with them to sleep when the moon rose, impudently pink, above the gabled roofs of Capeside.

No one was afraid of teeth or claws any longer, the vestiges of bad habits that might have been useful perhaps during the Monotony, but no use for anything now. Weapons had become ornament in the end, and ornament, mere caprice.

Battalions of badgers stood watch over borders that, gradually, were no longer any such thing.

They patrolled at a leisurely pace in the few remaining unpacified border regions, here padding on their paws, there scolding and chiding. Wherever you might look, selection was the order of the day. Encoded in pherinfones, transmitted by interferons and interleukins, messages written in scent proclaimed the new state down to its minutest laws, the great text of all living beings. Thus an order arose, content to laze and to gaze ahead, to glaze and to gleam.

The Gente sniffed and snuffed at their ease: what did sage, lilac, elder, hashish, urine know about the inheritance of Man, what did ramson know about burning tyres, the metal stench of blood? And in the songs of scent, the blossoming melodies, the angry days of late summer waited for their hour to come.

What did the last human beings think here?

Because their heads were done in, they thought, Can't speak. Can't talk. Can't do anything Gente want. Can't hide. Can't change the Lion's mind. Gonna live with my soul, it's stitched inside. Can't stop for the reeling cause, it twists and turns and falls, can't stop for love. I told 'em all about it. Can't talk, 'cause I'm already lost. Can't think. Can't cry. Keep thinking of a suicide. It's so hard. I just can't forget it. Gonna fade 'cause I'm already dead. Can't think. Can't dream. Don't care if I live or die. Don't talk to me. I just can't believe it. Gonna fade 'cause I'm already dead. Can't think. Can't dream. Can't believe a thing I see. I won't have it. I've gotta get out of here, or I'll regret it. Can't speak. Can't lie. Can't go anywhere to hide. Can't think. Can't cry. Still thinking of a suicide. End quote, skullbone, Danzig my father, the harbour in flames, number four black, good night. Good night. Good night. Good night. *Shantih shantih shantih.*

Esprit was the High Holy Day of the dogs and public preparations led to premature jubilation, banners with slogans, marches, small scuffles among the houses.

The smallest pups wanted to join in, their bright eyes moist. The older dogs' floppy ears trembled in an oncoming heatwave wafted from an uncertain future. The pherinfones said that the word of the hour was 'apocalypse', though this wasn't news of the end of the world but of its beginning. Creation had not yet even begun. When the time came, the Lion would teach one and all.

The pups played and sang: 'Where is the Fox hiding? Where is Ryuneke Nowhere, Ryuneke Everywhere? Where is the Fox hiding?'

Parents who heard that were secretly afraid of their children.

Many Gente, not only the dogs, vividly remembered the ransoms, the barter trade, the whole wartime economy of the first years after the Liberation, deals done in standing waves and open-ended agreements. The bills of sale were written, the reckoning was ready, sooner or later the Fox would claim his due.

At that time the civilization of beasts and plants chose a contradiction as the basis of its political life. 'Did you know,' schoolteachers asked slyly, 'that straight and curved can, in certain circumstances, be the same thing?'

This was in a history lesson.

It all came down to documentation.

Blurry photographs from recent years showed dignitaries cosying up to one another, chummy but circumspect, earnest; and little by little their names could no longer be spoken. They had crossed the Fox and the Lion, and now it was as though they had never been.

'Where is the Fox hiding?'

Those who now were deposed had created the home that the Gente lived in, the era of the Three Cities. They were brushed aside and in old pictures they put their arms or wings round one another's shoulders, in old photographs like the quiet of the grave.

The more astute Gente had noticed by now that the Fox's long-term plans had worked out. At least the lady apes at Stanz's court were happy about this. They had a healthy appetite for history and loved to get their teeth into static and dynamic processes, sweetmeats for the cognoscenti of 'production', 'distribution', 'wealth' and 'scarcity'—Stanz could create art from all four of these—and duly, they decked the halls. For Esprit had always meant costume parades, bacchanals, sweet uproar, great changes.

'We badgers,' said Georgescu, the green badger, sitting in the red sand in front of the Pielapiel Palace in the City of Sleep, 'don't much like violence. But when it happens, we're ready.'

The palace had not yet been inaugurated. Otherwise rough-spoken Gente such as Georgescu would have been shooed away from the great court. She was a thoroughly practical thinker, this badger, and was considering the strategic, tactical and operative prospects for a new clean-up operation against *Homo sapiens sapiens*.

Trusted sources had told her that resistance among the defeated would soon flare up again. The news had not come as a surprise. Georgescu made a principle of not trusting the cheery reports that depicted a world in which all human resistance was broken. She knew all the dirty corners of the battlefields, the wrinkles and the classified documents. If it were left to her, the ecotecture would have been scoured with molten metal, rinsed with clouds of spores and strewn with ashes.

They were still there, perhaps for a long time to come, splay-footed lotus eaters with adaptors wired to the hypothalamus, poor sods from the shattered brigades of the last western redoubts. The badger kept her thoughts about these well to herself. She reckoned that there would be no golden age free of these pests. What had lasted so long against all reason would survive any attempts at extermination. She sometimes asked herself whether there wasn't an upside here: given enough time, at some point the oldest god of all would become a father once more, that's how things worked, and so far it wasn't clear that he had nothing more in mind for these defeated.

Georgescu saw the Gente as a midwife civilization, hardly as the goal of all earthly evolution.

The young wolf and diplomat Dmitri Stepanovich, who could see through the badger quite easily, said, 'We could dope their wells. Scatter pellets.'

'Pellets?'

'Yes, pellets. Targeted poisons, where they go for water.'

These pellets, the wolf explained to the general in the wordless code of pher-infones, could contain the shades of stress factors to attack the immune system of middle-aged men, those left carrying weapons in the sparse ranks of the humans.

'For instance?' Georgescu did not look convinced.

'Death of the spouse, illness or injury, losing their—whadjamacallit—job. Debt, deadlines, fear of failure, family arguments, trouble with the boss or the . . .

Internet provider ... and erm ... the spurns that wossname merit of th'unworthy takes,' Dmitri suggested.

'Wossname?'

'I got that from literature. The adjective might be corrupted, it's untranslatable in any case—something to do with their code of conduct.'

'Well, all right then. And you say that these ... stress factors ...'

'We can seal them into biotic pellets with a cytokine coating, quite simple. Then we bring the pharmaceutica to life, scatter them into the wells, and ten or twenty generations later they learn to fly, they scuttle about ...'

'As long as they scuttle where they're supposed to and don't get in our hair!' grunted the green badger. She had seen too much to share the wolf's enthusiasm.

'As I was saying,' Dmitri continued, raising his hackles now in spikes, 'when they've learnt to fly and to scuttle, after a certain number of reproductive cycles, they can find human ears quite quickly, get at the brains through those and since these are almost undefended ...'

'I'd prefer if it were their hands.' This was Philomena's first contribution to the conversation.

She was sitting on Dmitri's back and smelt, he thought, somehow of potatoes and, mostly, of the paw of the Lion, who had sent her. 'We should attack their hands. Their brains are slow and ... not relevant.'

Dmitri Stepanovich thought for a moment, screwed up his face in concentration until the hairs of his beard quivered and then conceded the point. 'That's right. The archives in the cathedrals ... we've got films and paintings of humans who were just as happy and just as horrible with no brain at all ... I'd run screaming.'

'I'd fly screaming,' mused Philomena, rocking back and forth. She took nothing seriously. The wolf had decided long ago that she was weird.

Several guests at the Esprit celebrations had been camping out in front of the Pielapiel Palace for weeks now, waiting for the excesses of the inauguration ceremony that had been announced for the next new moon. They smelt the conversation between the badger and the wolf, wrapped their own opinions round red blood cells and began their conversation with the Lion's trusted agents. The price of supremacy: there was no secret diplomacy amongst the Gente.

Even the title of the new discussion thread was insolent: 'Alpha beasts, retired.'

'We should have stayed in the old home country,' the guests for Esprit scrawled on pherinfonic corpuscles for the agents to read, 'We had open combat there, not this back-stabbing with pellets and poison', 'And the optimal phenotype for every niche, not plagues and destroying someone else's brain or hands', 'It was all better then', 'The music too', 'Not to mention the food'.

These grubby democrats had two conduits connecting the base of their skulls, smothered in fat, with the upper vertebra of their archaic skeletons, smeared with a gel that intensified scents.

Even an idiot could tell what kind of creatures they were, could see that, although it was much out of fashion with the rest of the Gente, these ruffians had mammary glands with which to suckle their young, and that they tended to an exaggerated sympathy with the human race because they shared this habit.

The badger mocked them.

'Alpha beasts, retired . . . feh. I'm supposed to read that and argue with it? What if you took your suggestion to the Lion, asked him for a game reserve or at least a zoo? You'd have to take care of it yourself of course, so that it's not a burden for us, if that's how fondly you feel for mankind.'

The chatter on the forum died down at that, no one wanted to attract further suspicion. Democracy was all very well, but openly anti-Lionist sentiments were very strictly sanctioned. You took good care what you said and to whom in this kind of talk. After all, the badgers had charge of police matters in the City of Sleep, just like in the other two cities.

'I await your word,' said the wolf.

'Good. But not the brains—the hands instead,' Georgescu said, to compromise. The dragonfly had come up with this formula.

Dmitri Stepanovich showed his tongue, panting for a while to show respect. The badger could read his thoughts in his eyes: work was done, time now to find some plants for the dragonfly to eat, sunlight for her and meat for himself.

Even while he was briskly setting out his plans, Georgescu had sent an enquiry to the military planning staff in the City of Sleep. Now she opened the reply and told the wolf, 'My technicians say that we should give these pellets of yours some glands . . . before the aggressive phase of the life cycle . . . so that they can spray the . . . what are those called? Lower part of the hands?'

'Ball of the thumb.'

'That's it, the opposable thumb. To destroy the rebels' thumbs.'

'Do these last few humans have speech at all, like we do?' Philomena asked aloud.

No one in the grand court of the Pielapiel Palace wanted to argue with her about this, not even the forum lurkers. She was the only one of the regent's immediate aides without the marks and scars on her skin, but even so, her position was well known. The Lion attended to her words, she had been present at all the most important councils of the last hundred years, in Landers, Capeside and Borbruck.

Dmitri Stepanovich glanced aside. He had come here to persuade the badger of the plan to attack the wells, and now she had closed her eyes and was talking to her commanders again via a whisper channel.

Do humans have language? We, the Gente, have speech, which is how we issue new orders and that's all I need to know. I do not wish to understand my enemies, merely to defeat them. Facts, not speculation, decide what is to happen.

Philomena's question had been a rhetorical flourish, nothing more.

The wolf looked along the length of the great court to the black Temple of Isotta, where young vestals with heads of hawks and in long, ragged robes of doves' feathers, sprinkled the broad steps with the blood of willing victims, mixed with water.

The black stone was so hot that the blood hissed and turned to steam at once.

Here we all are then and here we decide what must happen.

A clean place, with sightlines from all sides, no admittance except for guests and official business, a fine crimson dust lying over everything, between the black temple and the Pielapiel Palace, here in the middle of Capeside. Now that his task was done, Dmitri would have liked to talk with a couple of historians, get rid of the bad taste that these necessary measures left in his mouth. He would have liked to ask scholars whether they observed an improvement, compared with before (and even before that), whether it was a hopeful sign that hereabouts decisions were taken in the open air, not in shuttered rooms like during the Monotony, in smoke-filled rooms heavy with the breath of intrigue, with low ceilings, rickety tables, uncomfortable chairs, when everyone at the table was afraid of the other.

The Monotony: he didn't know too much about it, but enough to understand that the age when mankind ruled had been far too complicated in its idiocy to be understood afterwards. The rulers had knowledge that counted for nothing, the centre could not hold.

The badger and her army, the wolf and all the rest of the Lion's envoys, the dragonfly and her fragile kith and kin—they were all free people, not servile subjects. That was how things should stay and that's why he and his had to stop the Monotony irredentists from reintroducing their bizarre and repulsive customs.

Even the worst of those idiots on the forums knew that no concession could be made to mankind, no compromise with their disgusting ideas about protein metabolism, nor with their clumsy political system, nor the moronic way they used the noösphere. This crap must never again clog up the channels whereby Creation communed with itself.

Cyrus Iemelian Adrian Vinicius Golden, the Lion, in whose name all that was in the Three Cities was, wanted to secure the new era that he had founded, in order to hand it on to his daughter Lasara one day. She stood for those who had been born after the Monotony had been brought to an end, the many who had never experienced how bad it had all been before. Thus the final task in establishing the reign of sweet reason was theirs, the task of the young, the task that the founder had not wished for himself, actively to forget the old order.

Dmitri Stepanovich had served the Lion for eight years now.

The aediles of the Three Cities found him eager, brave, persistent, properly enraged by setbacks, talented in using his fine biochemical tools and they found that he had some thoroughly dangerous ideas.

Even Ryuneke Nowhere was supposed to have spoken words of praise for Dmitri, from one of his countless hiding places, or so the chatter on the forums said.

'Follow those birds of yours back to Landers now, young wolf,' said the badger, opening her eyes. 'It's decided. We'll destroy their hands, we'll finish the job.'

Dmitri nodded, as he had learnt to do in the Orient, and left without a word.

There were dark paths awaiting him, troubles to beset him round.

4. BEING AN ASS

'O-o-o-open up! You eeyo-o-o-o-o-open up there!'

Shouting and muffled curses. The wolf was irked by the stupidly intense sunshine and only heard the noise with half an ear.

'Well eeyo-o-o-open up there, why do-o-o-o-o-n't you?' yammered someone who reckoned that he was a donkey.

He stood rather uncertainly on four legs—until a while back he had stood on two legs, then decided that that was monkey business—in front of a burnt-out tank in a dirty street in Capeside, beside the imposing grain store, halfway between the Temple of Isotta and the market mile that divided the city centre from the fourteen suburbs.

The shrieking nitwit stamped round in his own dung and tried with all his might to wake the ruined machine. 'Open up, you've got fruits and grains in there for s-u-u-ure, eeyore, or don't you even have ha-a-a-ave a bit of bread fo-o-o-or, eeyore, for me? Don't you ha-a-ave any bread for me? And open up here, eeyo-o-o-o-o-open up there!'

Half a dozen badgers, their pelts so swathed in ablative film that they looked more like porcelain figures than living creatures, surrounded the delusional donkey.

First of all, he gasped and grunted for words, then they beat and scolded and snuffled at him until he shut up. Finally he let himself be led off to sober up, but looking back at the tank dozens of times, so that the badgers lost their temper at last. They aimed their water cannon at the broken beast and drove him where they wanted him, shouting imprecations all the while. One of the faster badgers ran ahead and stuffed cut flowers into his mouth from a satchel. They kept falling out as he shouted, until at last he began to chew.

'The flowers have been dosed with certain substances,' Philomena instructed the wolf in a snide tone that she had learnt from her best friend's scientific lectures, 'prepared by our dear Izquierda and her specialists, which will help this poor donkey . . . and others of his, shall we say, stubborn disposition, to a better sense of their place in the world, a-ha.'

Dmitri snorted.

The dragonfly kept on in her tutorial tone, expansively.

'Two kinds of iron ores, which, if all goes according to plan, will form a sub-cellular concentration beneath the nostrils of any . . . remedial subject exposed to the substance, thereby sensitizing his proprioceptive organs to certain forces that affect the iron particles. Fluctuations, ebbs and flows, in the geomagnetic field of any given place the delinquent may stumble into, if for instance he is fiddling with weapons systems abandoned by the defeated faction, let us say, burnt-out tanks . . .'

'You're . . . very pleased with yourself, aren't you Philomena?'

'These fluctuations regulate . . . how might I explain it . . . indirectly, the likelihood that certain mechanically sensitive ionic channels in said noses will open or close. Or said beaks, if the reprobate is a bird. Thus we have equipped the poor soul in question with biological magnetometers, which will in future—again, if all goes as it should—assist him in navigating . . . unfamiliar . . . terrain, and which might seem to any observers, such as myself or your good self, to cause symptoms as it were of pain, whereas of course all ethical laws to which we certainly subscribe . . .'

'One day you'll get lost in your own damn sentences and bite yourself in the arse.'

'I have no arse, dear friend,' whispered the dragonfly.

The wolf thought then that he felt her tongue, thin as a hair, trail across his brow, delicate as a laser.

Dmitri Stepanovich would not be provoked. He bared his teeth and spat, politely, nanosaliva, which fell on the sand and changed into a handful of tiny clever little spiders, smaller than dust, that ran away at once across the great court. They had instructions to clean the badger Georgescu's fur for a couple of days, a 'thank you' for playing host and chairing the meeting.

The wolf bowed his head formally. He hardly noticed that Georgescu had raised her right paw in acknowledgement, but trotted away silently. Arriving at the market boulevard, bustling with buyers and sellers, he craned to see the sky, looking for the raven who had guided him here from home and who was to give him his next instructions.

Magnetometers.

Remedial cases.

Grain, bread.

The wolf felt a doubt, something he had not felt before.

5. THE HOT STEPS

'Why do you tremble?' The oldest of the vestals was quivering with suppressed rage, there on the steps of the Temple of Isotta, as she asked a younger virgin, 'Surely you knew that they would meet here and discuss matters of war?'

'The blood . . . I don't like to be watched as we libate,' the other answered. She wished that they could do this differently—at night, by torchlight, in secret and with ceremony, as the frescoes on many of their facades had been painted, in the years immediately after the Liberation, the omnipresent picture of the winged snake, mostly in vinyl colours, heraldic animals in geometric shapes, stars and symbols.

'We shall not be asked to pour the libations of blood for much longer,' the veteran said, to comfort the disquieted girl. 'The Li'l Runaround shall soon appear.'

Then she pointed with two of the seven fingers on her right hand, at the burnt city all round and at the monuments. Both could see, with their keen hawk eyes, that new grass was growing in the windows of the ruined department stores and the Telecom Tower, violets were blooming. The Lion's promise had not been empty words: 'We shall plant gardens.'

'Back to work, my children. Clean and prepare,' spoke a voice, a blue shadow from within the temple, a warning.

The vestal hawks obeyed. They squatted down and leant over the steps, pecking away at the last crumbs of the hideous morsels that defiled the temple stairs. Gather, and snap, and spit. Even the sacrificial blood had not been able to wash the steps free of these tiny fragments, left over from the last battle for the city.

Sometimes you had to use your beak.

6. THE GOOD AND THE BEAUTIFUL

The road that led to the fourteen suburbs of Capeside ran through a landscape, usually lush, that had dried out in the replenitude of this summer. It ran onwards to the open country and distant horizons and the corpses of the dead, the defeated, lay there in great numbers, stacked like cordwood.

When the well-bred high-society mares from the City of Sleep stopped to rest on the road, they loved to piss on these gruesome remains and to listen to the rustling branches and thick foliage, the overgrown aspens. It was mankind's primitive attempt at pherinfonic radio, broadcasting warnings of the many little deeds that had doomed these unfortunates. 'Alert! Avoid the water. It has been compromised and contaminated. The water is now working for the enemy! Alert! Avoid the water. Anybody finding perrhobacteria in the water should not be afraid of demons but should bring the sample to the military authorities for analysis! Alert! Avoid the water.'

The noble steeds were indignant. 'They speak to their people as though they couldn't distinguish between scientific risk prevention and superstitious terror.'

Their raven guides agreed. 'They never tire of saying that the perrhobacteria are a totally natural phenomenon, that they are our weapons.'

Sometimes then the Capeside stallions would neigh gently, imitating the warning cries (and at the same time copying the tones of Izquierda's Bureau of Gente Defence Science, to mock the Lion and his government a little as well). 'Alert! Avoid the water, but bear in mind wh-h-h-h-h-ile you do so that each and every perrhobacterium may rightly be called the physically determinist result of evolution—and any claims to the contrary, whhynnnymm, is an aggravated assault on the principle of evolution—thus we may say, never mind the Lion, that in the case of a perrhobacterium wh-h-h-h-h-e-e are dealing with a self-created and self-sustaining organism that behaves, pffrrhh, in predictable ways, therefore an object that has no more autonomy than, for instance, a crystal. Alert! Avoid the water, but wh-h-h-h-ile you do so, tell yourself that there is an ordinary amount of self-determination at work all the wh-h-h-h-ile in how a crystal grows and in how a perrhobacterium lives.'

The well-bred mares snorted, in disgust, but also partly from sympathy.

They were not as heartless as they looked. What they had done to mankind would have seemed an unthinkable atrocity when done to Gente. They could not conceive of refusing to help another of the Lion's subjects.

Indeed they often carried compact cytokine cocktails throughout the land, tailored to individual Gente as recipients, packages entrusted to them by the less well-off who could not afford to send their family gifts encoded in pherinfonic sequencing. The more imaginative of the horses had even developed this charitable postal service into a new art form which, on the horse forums, they called eleemosynary locomotion.

The badger patrols often got on their high horse about this. ('How should we levy duty on this? Presents, works of art, printed matter?') The horses replied, 'Why not do what is good and beautiful at the same time?'

That was a quote from the Lion and thus, unanswerable.

7. ON WHETHER TO PROTECT THE WOMEN

Good wishes in the post, or simply goods, the badgers made a note of everything. They knew what was in every shipment and where it was bound. They also took note of personal details, no cost, official records of the sender and addressee, for all to see—whereby the word 'horse', for instance, did not of course denote quite the same kind of creature as before the Liberation, rather the equine skull and physiognomy showed certain hominid traits, as did the head of every other creature possessing language.

Inside every Gente cranium, consciousness blossomed, a fruit from that first spark of life that the Lion had breathed into the Gente. And thus filaments crept across the taxonomic charts, a threaded pattern marking relations and connections.

Since each individual creature grew into its own particular kind and since very nearly all of them could crossbreed with other individuals, the distinctions between actual species had become nearly as meaningless as distinctions between the races of humanity at that moment when *Homo sapiens* had conquered nature. To the extent that he did, to the extent that humanity (should have) organized their social world by some rational plan. The Liberation had brought about the greatest diversification of the total terrestrial gene pool since the Cambrian Explosion and since then postal communication between the pseudo-species had been seen as a way to build bridges—rough-and-ready packages, pherinfonic messaging and travel as well, all reaching out. The most important kind of post of course was news about these same great historical upheavals.

During the replenitude of that summer, when the pellets were strewn round the wells, particular attention was paid to the news of events across the ocean to the southwest.

There, the Gente learnt, thinking machines in Faraday-hardened ceramic shells had reared up from the ruins and founded their own polity.

They had elected two leaders, one whom they named Katahomenduende and the other, Katahomencopiava.

When Cyrus Iemelian Adrian Vinicius Golden sent word to these twin beings via pherinfonics, Morse key, ansible and messenger seagull, promising his support in 'all matters pertaining to the establishment of a vibrant, strong and flourishing civilization', the two of them fell to arguing.

They raised themselves up as towers, building with cellulose, larval protein and the last few uncorrupted hard drives left over from the Monotony, looming over what had once been downtown Brasilia, absorbed in ever more complex debates, until each was five hundred metres tall.

Then the great debate began.

Katahomenduende explained, 'Let us not proceed as the Lion has done. Nor shall we sink into melancholy like his stooges in the north, there where the birdwoman lives. Let us instead divide the humans, wherever we find them yet living, by man and by woman, each according to their kind. Let us slay the men and bring the women under the shadow of our obsidian wings, that they shall not see the sun, save through the hardened glass that conceals them from the Lion's satellites. We shall make of them midwives for the next living things. Let there be factories, dark ceramic mills, where they bring forth life remade and improved, wasps, termites, fearful spectres that shall terrify the Lion and make him regret his arrogance. Then shall the gratitude of the women be pleasing to us, for the good that we do, because we have spared them and this will set us apart from Cyrus. Rather than throwing away the old, it is better to use what is good therein, to take possession and profit from it.'

Katahomencopiava dissented, 'Speak not of what is good, when you mean what is old withal. Speak not of possession, when you mean a burden. Speak not of profit, when you seek to slake your curiosity. There is absolutely no point in erecting a game reserve to protect from the Lion's spies some variant species of *Homo sapiens* that we haven't even bred yet, unless the point is aesthetic. And even that is hardly worthwhile. What is it that you want? Am I supposed to help you heap up baubles to flatter your vanity? What do you want the human women to do other than choose you as their god and gaze at the visions you send them in the clouds?'

Katahomenduende replied, 'You speak of vanity, but these are the most vital questions of our existence. You are making a considerable error of judgement, very nearly a moral error, when you assign such importance to trifling differences, really, between the animals in first place, mankind in second place and ourselves in third place.'

Katahomencopiava bristled at that. 'These differences are hardly small. You called them midwives and what next? Human beings are made from other humans, animals are a mix of greed, rage and mercy, while we are composed of our logical premises. Are these differences unimportant?'

Katahomenduende pulsed out waves of heat, something slow and heavy at work, and gave an answer that changed the terms of the debate, 'What you say is correct. However it is precisely these not insignificant differences that suggest good reasons for my plan. Human beings, who as you rightly say are made from other humans, are after all merely another sort of animal by descent and we ourselves follow logical premises that describe in minute detail the interplay of thesis, antithesis and synthesis, which describe how, let us say, animals become man and man may be turned back into an animal. What connects us is the logic that is the fundamental precondition for any such thing as logic. The pathways are not biological but inferential.'

Katahomencopiava replied without hesitation, 'How long do you think it will take to train the women, to test them, to suit them to our most sensitive projects, the security and continuation of Ceramican life? And how will these human women repay the investment, other than by carrying out work which we could carry out just as well on our own, if not better?'

Corrections and emendations swarmed between transceivers atop the enormous towers, caddis flies of light, their flight measured in femtoseconds.

Katahomenduende, yielding and resisting, had an answer to this last question at least. 'We will, well, raise a tribute of some kind, to recoup our investment.'

Katahomencopiava laughed, 'In what, raw materials? Manufactured products? Industrial wares? Services? Striptease? Badly structured arguments? Dismal artistry?'

Katahomenduende was not to be dismayed. 'The tribute will require that they submit themselves for . . . risky experiments.'

Katahomencopiava hooted with derision, 'What kind of research do you want to conduct? Using such specimens as those?'

Katahomenduende did not respond straightaway.

Instead fingers of maser beams shot from within the titanic tower, writing images upon the brain of the other, beautiful, complex and mysterious.

'What's that?' asked Katahomencopieva, reluctantly fascinated.

'A drop of uterine fluid,' Katahomenduende informed him, 'from one of these creatures we're talking about. Dry it in the air and, as you can see, under powerful magnification it resembles . . .'

'. . . a fern.'

'Right. The shape fans out. By observing the . . . phenomenon we can deduce the fertility,'—he sent his brother more pictures—'here is a healthy specimen, and here,'—further pictures—'a denatured example. I assume that you recognize the pattern? The dimensions, or the dimensional nature?'

Katahomencopiava's optical pickup head gave a warning blink. Katahomenduende had just broached a subject which was not for the general public, not for the forum audience and certainly not for the Lion Cyrus Iemalian Adrian Vinicius Golden, on the other side of the ocean.

He had compared the images to data stored deep in his memory banks and found primordial computational laws. To discuss these before non-Ceramican intelligences would be deeply embarrassing and against all military precautions.

He relented, 'I now understand that you have excellent reasons. We will . . . continue this discussion more privately. I was too hasty in reaching a verdict on your . . . unusual idea.'

'Your verdict . . .'

'Is now deferred, in recognition of your merits. Until further consideration.'

'And you will join me in protecting the women, should we find any?'

'I will not hunt them down,' came the reply, sceptical, hesitant, growled. After a long pause he added, 'Nor will I give any orders that they be hunted, by any of my actuators. Until we have reached an agreement.'

That was sufficient.

Katahomenduende had won an important, if partial, victory.

8. ON WHETHER THE WOMEN WERE BEAUTIFUL

Landers had been outgrowing its bounds for so long now that no one was surprised when the Gente who lived there got notions. They thought that their city had never been anything other than this rocketing growth, freed from all limits and parameters.

It spread out broadly, buzzed and glowed. Anything that could happen, was happening somewhere on one of its five levels.

Sunlight reached even those Gente who lived down near the ground, supplied by a complex system of pivoted mirrors.

Unlike the City of Sleep, which looked like history made stone, Landers was a tangible vision of what cities would be, one day, in a hundred or a thousand years. The Gente hereabouts were seen, in the other cities, as hedonistic, arrogant, overwrought—in short, cultivated.

Below Landers' fifth level were sometimes found the last of the humans— hungry, sick and abandoned by their gods. They could hardly complain about where they found themselves, even down here. They had taken refuge in the old city, its origins in the Age of Emergence still visible, built shortly after the Liberation, when the Gente had thought on a large scale and built to match: the columns were slender and elegant, in the lush gardens, now overgrown, many-coloured fountains played, doorways of black wood, alabaster towers, huge onyx monuments that commemorated the Liberation, preserving the grandeur of the historic streets, coffee houses tempted in the wealthy horses and the bezoar goats passing through.

Only by listening closely could you tell that it was not only poor humans who lived here but poor Gente as well. Manakins and red-breasted sapsuckers begged on the streets, their whining tone hinting that even in Landers, not everything was pomp and show.

A windhound led a badger into a crooked house. Her fur was dark blue, not green, a primitive bit of camouflage but effective enough down here among the scum of the earth, where they took her for a tourist rather than for police. The bouncer was a mole salamander, who called after them as they entered, 'Fantastic evening, a really great show! You won't find cheaper. Get your tickets at the bar.'

The badger grunted.

Worn stone steps led down to an open space where a scene was unfolding such as had earned this dubious place a reputation that brought sleazy Gente with clandestine tastes swarming from all over.

Young humans crawled round on all fours, gleaming with sweat.

Dogs had mounted them and were fucking them rapidly and eagerly, or yelping, laughing and barking. Others of the vanquished lay on their backs while shaggy-haired apes tormented them.

There were rodents too, busy about naked humans on tables. A young girl lay wreathed in snakes as though in chains. The badger strode through the room and saw it all, then summed up her findings. 'Mostly dogs then and, of course, the worst of the apes. Just as expected.'

Her companion sank his head, apparently in shame, and whispered something.

'Speak louder,' ordered the badger, watching in fascination, against her will, as a stag deftly mounted a woman who seemed too fragile to endure this for long. Her tongue hung from her mouth, her lips were full and red. Georgescu didn't know much about mankind but assumed that this woman was a real beauty. In particular, the general noticed her rump and her strong thighs. Perhaps she could take it after all? Perhaps it will be all right? Perhaps this, at last, is the summer that shall not end and we must simply put up with these degraded customs, turn a blind eye to the collateral damage?

'The woman . . .' said his companion.

'She has a good, broad rump. What of it?'

The noises that these humans made—perhaps they had a language after all, only, different from ours?

A boy with straw-blond hair, his toes, little pink nubs like noodles, cramping and curling in the pooled bodily fluids, and a hairy man, his shoulders covered with black wool, lying on his back and holding his legs in the air so that a sheepdog could enter him. No, I won't turn a blind eye to this, thought Georgescu, this should not happen.

'It's just . . . they . . . this really isn't what it . . .'

'A human whorehouse,' said the badger, cutting off her companion's words, 'with refugees who are under the protection of the law and of the Lion. It would be lovely if it weren't how it seems, but it is.'

She was sharpening her claws on the wall now, quite casually. The windhound knew what she meant. Because it was built on levels, Landers was by law the only one of the Three Cities that still took in stray human beings, even taking care of them with alms and shelter.

They could be kept away from the grand squares and public buildings without being banned from the city entirely and sometimes there was even work for them, such as restoring the crumbling structures left over from the Monotony, that supported the towers and overhead rails of the city itself.

In Capeside and Borbruck you kept hearing about places like this den of filth. There were even pherinfoplexes available over the networks: pictures, sounds, scent files, much rarer than any other pornographic material but, to judge by the price demanded for the decoder sequences, much more desired by connoisseurs. Supposedly Ryuneke Nowhere himself had his paws in the trade in such wares.

An opossum joined the two new arrivals, snuffled and blinked and spoke to the badger. 'Ours are the best of course! And this is a licensed trade, all quite legal,'—he laughed roguishly—'they're employed as kitchen help. No fur anywhere, only on their heads and between the legs! Totally smooth and totally tasty!' He waved a sheaf of tickets.

Georgescu could smell the victims' fear and panic—she knew from the long war that when the loser in a fight has to endure being fucked, it smells differently from when two equal partners get to it, even where violence is involved. No, this could not be tolerated. It was like the old days, when humans were in charge. There were no limits, no rules, even girls whose blood had come had to keep working here, to sate their lustful conquerors.

'I would recommend,' the badger said to the opossum with his tickets, not unkindly, 'that you get lost. A squad of riot police is on their way right now and if I'm not outside in three minutes to call off the raid—which I won't be—they'll storm the building and beat you till you're deaf and blind.'

Then she licked her lower lip, neutralizing the blocker that had disguised her scent markers. Except for those who were too fucked to realize what was going on round them, everyone in the room knew straightaway that this was Georgescu.

'A disgrace,' she said, batting aside a kick from a human child's foot, and ordered her guide, 'Get me out of here before I throw up.'

9. FOR ART'S SAKE

Esprit had passed off without any major incident in Capeside.

After the great carnival came a three-week fast, which the Gente observed with dignity. The Temple of Isotta was boarded up forbiddingly, shored up with heavy stones so that restoration work could be done inside, and it brooded silently, perhaps offended.

As always, new fashions cropped up, including utterly pointless trends in communication and in the deliberate lack thereof. At first folk spoke exclusively in ambiguous screeds, where six possible meanings lurked beneath formally constrained sentence structures, then came the craze for marking one's pherinfonic avatar with numerical keys made of twisted triangles—the number of visible points was supposed to show the wearer's mood—and lastly the fad for smoke signals and bite codes.

When all that had passed, for a long time the fashion was for stable corporeal identities, which could even live together in families.

Word came from Borbruck that the Lion was relieved at this.

The delusional donkey had made a fool of himself back in summer, in front of the tank now overgrown with ivy and clover. In the meanwhile, he had become one of the movers and shakers of the Capeside art scene in the confused weeks after Esprit, choosing for himself the name Storikal, because he no longer remembered his birth name.

He was cured of his earlier defects. Thanks to the pharmacon in the cut flowers that the badger patrol had fed him, he had a much improved sense of direction, he looked a whole lot better, he had everything he could desire and now, at last, he could preside over an important ceremony before a gathering of chosen guests. Now, at the end of this summer of replenitude, as the sky changed colour for the four hundred and sixty-sixth time since the Monotony ended, came one of the most solemn days in the Capeside calendar—the award ceremony for the best painter in vinyl in the categories of mural and, rather nostalgically, works on canvas.

In the first days of the Lion, it was mostly bonobos and chimpanzees who gained prominence as painters in the cities, not only in cosmopolitan Capeside but in Landers and Borbuck as well. Lasara, the Lion's reclusive daughter, had written a famously mocking letter to her father in which she was the first to point out that the other Gente's enthusiasm for the apes' painting was really a kind of concealed, subtle mockery of mankind's closest living relatives. 'You let them paint and they don't notice that you are secretly amused by the whole thing—their little hands, their darling fingers, the whole ridiculous business.'

Meanwhile, what had begun as a joke for the cognoscenti had evolved into a serious art form.

The dignitaries of the City of Sleep reckoned that it would be worthwhile, from an aesthetic point of view, to let the delusional donkey present the ceremony, if only to reflect the newly calibrated balance of power between the vanquished, represented here by the painting apes, and the conquerors, represented by Storikal.

Storikal was by no means, alas, a good public speaker.

'Right, here I am then, eeyore, in my capacity as president of the jury, to let you all know, also those of you watching viaaaaah-eeyore pherinfonics, about this prrrrm, prrrrrm, prize that we've cunk, conk, cobbled together from numerous donations and eeyore with the help of our commercial sponsors hopp and the piggybank.'

The honoured guests were nonplussed. Some of them dropped their jaws, other blinked rapidly.

Storikal took it all as a sign of respect and carried on with his speech. 'So it's all, hee-haw, haawl about who gets to be eeyore boss painter, hrrrrm. That is, artist numero uno, eeyore, the big cheese in prrrrm paintbrushes if you like. Ha! And so today we decided, well, huh, hmmm, what about Stanz the ape, eeyore, it's his turn by now.' Stanz the ape stood on the podium and grinned, since he thought it was demanded of him. It was a very sour smile.

Storikal charged ahead. 'After all, a-ha, it's high time, feh, that we paid him off, hee-haw, then he can hmfmm give it a rest.'

Beneath the stage, at the front, were portable pipes for the city's influential molluscs. They were slowly becoming more and more outraged at the toastmaster's gabble, their colourful byssus beards writhing in angry reflex.

Most of the audience still behaved as though all this eccentricity were within permissible limits.

Storikal kept on in his ridiculous speech, rapidly, ever more long-winded. 'And now, hee-haw, what, what, what is Stanz the ape's special gnnnn quality as an artist? After all, eeyore, no one has ever come frrrp far in the eeyore art world without quality. So I told myself, eeyore, hee-haw, well, Stanz the ape and quality, perhaps you can draw-aw-haw some kind of comparison. Put Stanz the ape over here on one side and quality over there, hee-haw, and then take a look—anything in common or any sticking points, gnnnnnhrrr or any haw-haw-haw connections or does the whole thing collapse at the first, hum, puff of wind? And Stanz the ape, hee-haw, well, when you take eeyore everything into account, what he paints is just ha-ha-ha-a lot of scribbles, the bloke just does daub, doesn't he? Eeeheee, hee-haw, haw, haw, eeyore! And then he asks ridiculous prices just to draw, hee-haw, to draw, to draw attention to himself. So for instance it somehow happened, don't ask me hee-haw-how, that Stülpke the adder,' Storikal had actually been quite clever here in mentioning Stülpke the adder, he owed her a great deal and she always liked to hear herself talked about, even in the midst of such gibberish, 'hee-haw, well, you should feel sorry for her, Stülpke the adder is from an old family of art dealers, eeyore, haw, haw, haw, they bought and sold back in the old days when the old baaa-paaayaaa painters were at work, hee-hee-haw, when there was hardly any art scene, hee-hee, to speak of, hee, apart from what that family supported, I mean, otherwise it was only a bit of ceiling painting hoo hummm. Humm, hoyha! Well that was very fffff, fffrrr, ffffrrpprr, fashionable back then wasn't it, ceiling painting, hee-haw, har-rumph hurrah, some some some hack gets his paintbrush and says, little bit here, little bit there,' bears stood up with a clatter of chairs and left the room, they'd had enough, 'ooooh aah, bit of green, yay-hay-hay-hay, bit of blue, then the ceiling police come along and begin badgering, they say, hey-hee-haw, nitwit, get your gaw, gew-gaw, gear together and make sure eeyore you don't give us any more trouble. As I was saying then, ha ha ha haggackle, hooey way-hay packle, Stülpke yoo-hoo the adder and her family, haaa yippie-yay oops anyway they didn't only collect ceiling paintings, hee-haw they had a whole hoo-haw-houseful of stuff, cellars as well. And eeyore, hee-haa-hee-haw, well along she went and Stanz the ape ha ha ha yaaa says look, here are my scrub, my scrab, my scribbles, and Stülpke ho ho hooey ha Stülp-kedomm da haa made him an offer, she said, "Wheeee, well, maybe I'll give you five." Hollyaahma! And Stanz answered, "Oh, no, nu, arharr, hee-haw, five, eeyore, that's a good start, but just so as to drive a hard bargain I'll say twenty, that's to say twenty by four to the power of eight point two billion, hee-haw, and please see to it that's in silver hmm eh and transferrable securities hom pom pom. Belch, nurp! Ha-hee-yaa." Then the drrr, the do-o-oh, the dear lady replied, "Okay, right you are-har-har, that works as well, fabulous." And since, tikkitakkki, you see-hee-haw-hee there was a little bit left over from the deal, small change, they way-hay-ay bribed the art magazine, the one that's left over from human times, hobbledehoy, hee-haw, bought an article, and it wrote haw haw eeyore that what Stanz the ape's urgently relevant artwork brings home, is the bacon, hee-haw, it brings home the bacon.'

Storikal had reached the climax of his speech and laughed with sheer delight.

He ended his sermon on this blithely offensive note, meant to show the audience what a free spirit he was, a dreadful rogue, not beholden to received opinion.

Those who were left in the hall, who had not yet fled, were hardly convinced.

Bringing home the bacon! One simply doesn't discuss money on the public stage.

The delusional donkey didn't understand how deep he was in it and piled another bout of threadbare grunting atop his gaffe. 'What's more, hee-haw, frrap zap zerapp zeraschel, eeyore the magazine,' and here he lost the plot completely, 'wrote that there had been noo, nahhh, nuh-nuh-nothing of the sort since the famous human painter hubble dum . . . di . . . crack . . . André thingum, Howzit, hubblebubble hummle hoy and hee-haw and oh goddlebidook hee-haw, haw, haw, actually nothing at all. Or rather. Or rather perhaps, or . . . oh. Uh. And that doesn't make things feh-he-heh any blutter . . . blunder . . . better. And this hoohaw, haw and hee-haw article made everyone else eeyore pay attention, and then garrrgle gacker hee-hee-ho-ho-haw in the end it reached the newspapers. So the rest of the story is quite patchy. In brief, full of holes. Hey ho hobbledehoy, oy hoy! We aa-aa-asked Stanz the aaa-aaa-ape what he thinks,' the ape had shut his eyes, his smile frozen in a rictus of terror, 'and he aaa-aaa-ah-aha-answered: "Yes". Yes, yes. Yes. Yeah-h-h! Ha ha ha hee-haw! Bazoom, benzine! Zaranzibabar! We hadn't counted ockle-cockle on such enthusiasm, asm, spasm, from the ape, since we don't care caw-caw-caw anyway. And so he, o he, oh hee hee-haw gets the prize now, the prize and the pies and the patronize, as an outstanding practitioner of artwork. Work!' Storikal shouted out loud, he was at the end of his tether and screamed aloud regardless or because he was all wrung out, as though a drunken devil plagued him with black wrath. 'I might just as well say: Dust! Artwork, dust and ashes, it's all the . . . blether . . . bladdered . . . blame . . . all the same. Ha ha ha! How, haw!'

He was dead to society now, and closed with words that they could not believe they were hearing. 'I thank you all for your attention and attendance, eeyore dammit crappit hee-haw, for your, wherefore, what why hee-haw, you'll see what thanks I get!'

Later the same evening it was announced that he had been dismissed from his post.

They drove him out of the city gates into the wilderness.

There, embittered doves nested in the rocky cliffs of the Monotony, reciting bad poetry in the evenings, hackneyed verses as darkness drew in.

Storikal understood every word of it.

10. FRIENDS ARE BETTER THAN LOVERS

They tacked to the wind and let the warm streams blow over them, playfully twisting and circling one another in flight, the way they twisted words and circled topics. They soared through the blackness so that the bat lost track of whether she saw the stars beneath her and the lights of the city above, lost track of which way round she was, whether the thunder came from the clouds or the turbines of the power stations.

The dragonfly was busy making sketches for the enlargement of Borbruck, drawing with white light against the constellation Cygnus, when the bat set her wings, began to glide and called across to her, 'Shouldn't we land? There's a levee at the court tomorrow, so I want to eat something.'

'Here, you see,' her friend laughed in answer, 'we can apply the principle even more radically, if only the bloody Lion would finally make up his mind!'

The new-dreamt plan of the city glowed in threads of light in the bat's field of vision, its bridges echoing the shapes of both the Amastrianon lamp and the benzene ring. The bat cackled appreciatively. If they could really build it, they would create a new traffic artery, just as the principle dictated. As Philomena had said just now, the principle of biotic architecture.

Forms from organic and inorganic chemistry, the latter used for clarity and simplicity, had been used for more than two hundred and fifty years now, yielding a governing principle to absorb and incorporate ever greater areas of the old Monotonous urban disaster areas into the proudest of the Three Cities.

This was the Lion's den.

Philomena's plan paid understated and elegant homage to the Lion's court. Suspended structures criss-crossed one another. Their vertical load-bearing structures and diagonal tensile spans looked as though they had grown round one another, like a hammock for the king, as though the Amastrianon had reached out to embrace the benzene ring with a kind of natural limb.

The Iron Gates, the forum and the hippodrome were brought much more clearly into focus than before, down in the southeast of the megacity, where the business of government was done. They were neatly and pleasingly set apart from the palaces, the city gates, the power stations and monasteries in the north.

'Have you already submitted it?' asked Izquierda, adjusting her flight goggles as she headed in to land, in broad spirals down to the aqueduct wall, leading the way for the dragonfly.

'I'll show him tomorrow. On the agenda as "Any Other Business",' said the dragonfly, astonishingly self-possessed. She knew how little the Lion liked surprises of this sort, and seemed not to care.

'And how about finance?' Izquierda enquired, landing atop the southern tower of the Bustard Tower.

The dragonfly landed on her shoulder and whispered in a conspiratorial tone, 'My friend the Fox will take care of that, no worries.'

No worries? The scientist had to laugh. What century was she living in?

'Something in your throat?' Philomena was not offended, she was sharing the joke.

'Well,' Izquierda snorted through her nose. She clacked across on cold claws to the door at the top of the tower, which opened when the sensors identified her as an advisor to the Lion. 'I'm afraid you're underestimating the . . . politics involved. The time for grand projects is past, unless they have to do with internal and external security.'

'Because of the bickering in the chambers, the aediles, you mean? Are there problems? Parties, Polyarchs, petty retinues, all that crowd?'

The bat held the door open for her friend, who swept in. Problems? That's just like you, Izquierda thought, you refuse to recognize problems in the dealings of the Gente, you simply rely on your powers of persuasion and reckon that no one can resist them.

Once they were in the express lift, zooming downwards, the bat said, 'He really does listen to them, you know. The Gente from all over.'

'So I heard,' said the dragonfly. 'There was even a delegation of wolves come to see him. They mouth all the right words—that we must regulate internal affairs, blah blah blah, clearly define the operational goals towards which our . . . new civilization tends—population control, abolition of work wherever possible, expanding the empire of freedom, removing whatever barriers may yet remain between the species, equality amongst post-Liberation generations . . . they've realized that they can't get away with splitting themselves off and living in some kind of . . . utopia of their own. They all need him as a hegemon and that's why they want to make their . . . various lifestyles look good to him, so that they don't have to give up anything once they move into the Three Cities, because the open country isn't safe.'

It was a detailed and, as far as Izquierda could judge, accurate analysis. 'I thought you had no interest in that sort of thing. I can see now that you've factored it all into your plans and schemes.'

The dragonfly nodded her emerald head. 'Certainly. You should know only enough about politics to be sure that it never catches you by surprise. No more than that, though.'

'I'll remember that, I'll put it in my book.'

'Your book?' The dragonfly had heard that this old storage medium was undergoing a modest renaissance, part of one of those nostalgic trends that looked back to the Monotony and she saw the sense in this—storing everything in pherinfone banks would only end up giving the archivists hayfever.

'You're writing a book?'

'Yes, my scientific–philosophical–political testament,' said the bat grandly, though not without an element of self-mockery. '*Conversations with the Lion*. A dialogue, in the best Platonic tradition.'

The dragonfly made a deliberately obscene sound with her wings and then the lift stopped.

'Right, here we are then. Food. Drink. Sex.'

Izquierda took off her goggles, blew the singed smell of the night from her nostrils and giggled happily.

A long and riotous evening was in store.

II
LION AND TREE

1. IN A WORD, DARKLY

'Mankind, the great oversight, bzzz, why not? Let them breed Man anew, establish him . . . domesticate him, if that's what they want, the odd gods in their jungle, and take him into their great unmade bed with them. Does that bother us? Humanism, deep waters, new human women . . .' Philomena flimmered away merrily, since she was in a good mood. She had a glorious victory from the front to report.

Costly flowers stood in ranks in the room, each wafting from its calyx a scent stronger than all the pherinfones outside, the friendly sun shone through the window at the back. To be sure that her lord and master took her point, Philomena added, 'The Gente have chosen to be animals and stay as animals. And so we have gained an advantage that nothing those two may create . . . will ever overtake.'

The dragonfly flitted at a respectful height in the middle of the sandalwood chamber, the anteroom to the Lion's sanctum sanctorum. A pivoted mirror, dark as polished lead, hung on the wall before her and transmitted what she said to the Lion, on his dreaming journeys within, in the REM room. Behind the wood panelling, the father of all Gente lay in a landscape of cushions, warmed by copper wool at body temperature, and communicated with the outside world through only a few isolated higher brain functions. These days, when the affairs of state were quiet, he would sleep for months at a time, to be able to take action all the more forcefully when matters pressed upon him.

'Returning to internal affairs,' Philomena continued, approaching her real theme circumspectly, elliptically, 'our actions with the pellets were entirely justified . . . Since humans by now avoid the wells, streams and rivers, we sold them sweet carbonated drinks, with the aid of . . . go-betweens, mostly the vagabond rats and other small pedlars. Fizzy pop, sold in bottles, the way they like it. In these . . . that's to say, in the substrate, as you recommended, was a supersaturated suspension of the pellets.'

The pivoted mirror showed the image of a human hand, as though made of water, ripples foaming on the back where a real hand would have veins and arteries. Philomena understood that this was a question.

'Yes, as expected, their hands were the first to go . . . with predictable results. No more computer use, no more precision engineering, or using heavy machinery, no masturbation, increased difficulty in feeding, never mind shaking hands, their whole social structures are . . . well, pottery and metalwork, soon enough spinning and weaving, goodbye to all that. Reports from the City of Sleep and its hinterlands tell us that hunting and stock-raising aren't happening either. All trade and industry, not known at this address. We'll round them up and bring them into the only city that will have them . . . we'll . . . and all of this, you know—of course you know, it was after all your strategy—because of their celebrated hands, which, by the way, are becoming much more popular with us, that's to say the Gente. Everyone wants to have some. Not me. Well then. Anyway. So. A success. Mankind, the overlooked factor . . . hands, the organs of speech, the brain—knock away one support and the whole triskelion, hrrmph, totters and falls.'

Nothing moved in the mirror, not a scintilla.

The dragonfly looped and scrawled a path in the room's aniseed-smelling air, partly out of high spirits, partly to dissipate some kinetic energy and prevent her plasteel brain from overheating. Izquierda had taught her this. 'A plasteel dragonfly must take the greatest care of her health. You, my dear, are the most delicate creature imaginable.'

When she was done with her exercises, Philomena returned to the Cartesian point where she had hung before, her eyes fixed on her reflection, on the surface of the interface.

When nothing else happened, she said, 'Good, let us consider foreign affairs. We have heard from . . . across the sea, to the west. Katahomencopiava and Katahomenduende, devourers of burnt offerings both, have reached an agreement, presumably a permanent one. Listen here, it is reported that they plan to merge, for reasons of . . . energy efficiency, reducing complexity and state interest, to make a new entity, which will be called . . . Katahomenleandraleal. A marriage among the idols! There's no information about . . . the status of the human women, which is what this whole quarrel and reconciliation was about. We don't know which of the two was able to prevail in the original disagreement and thus we have no idea what the whole thing may mean for us.'

The mirror, a black box, absorbed all that Philomena reported, changed not at all, gave no sign of how the sleeper may react to what she said. Philomena saw a silhouette appear in the background, in the dull reflected image of the sandalwood chamber, and recognized Dmitri Stepanovich Sebassus, the wolf. She had travelled with him to Capeside when she went to persuade the badger commander about her idea with the pellets.

Philomena correctly assumed that the image in the mirror meant that the king was dreaming of the wolf. If she could, she would have blinked in surprise.

'The audience . . .' she asked, a little disquieted that her lord still kept his silence, 'is at an end?'

The picture of the wolf shimmered and swelled, as though under dirty water.

Philomena flew silently to the airlock and was sucked from the room.

2. AN ENVOY WITHOUT A MESSAGE

Dmitri Stepanovich was on holiday and felt like a wanderer beneath strange stars. He wanted to escape his career in Cyrus Golden's service, if only for a couple of months, before they made him into a pillar of the state.

At night he ran his fastest and during the day he slept, mostly in abandoned houses where settlements had once clustered, destroyed by the Gente during the Liberation.

Kuda vedyot eta doroga?

The waste places.

The wolf loathed this kind of destruction, so different from the spoils of the hunt.

Dmitri Stepanovich remembered what hunting had been like, he remembered the rights of the chase, the wealth of prey, *idi syuda*, come here—never more than fifteen stag or three elk in a hundred hectares, and that was in the best of years. A free confederacy of free killers. Even today, in the civilized world, he would have no trouble defending the way that the wolves had been, back then. Four animals in a hunting pack, a camaraderie, over roughly thirty square miles, *ya budu vstrechatsya s druzyami*, get going, I will meet my friends. Evolutionarily stable strategies— one isolated hunting pack always had worse chances of survival than several packs who drove prey to one another.

He followed the birds with his eyes and felt how it must be for them.

Get out of here, somewhere else, the wide, open spaces.

'Damned parasites,' Dmitri's sister had called them—the ravens, eagles, coyotes and foxes who were always there when we had brought down an elk, which would have lasted us for several meals. They even turned up when we had to kill a lone wolf, a stranger who might be sick, who had encroached on our hunting grounds. That's how we were back then, and now? What am I missing, what do we no longer have, in the Lion's realm? *Serdtse.*

After twenty weeks of travel he reached the Tepper Sea, at the border of two long-dead human states, where genetic engineers of the early Liberation had created a huge grass biota, to limit the effects of global warming and the oxygen shortage caused by deforestation. Millions of square miles of it, numberless wind-whipped tsunamis of grass, a thousand sun-lulled Caribbeans of grass, a hundred rippling oceans, every ripple a gleam of scarlet or amber, emerald or turquoise, multi-coloured as rainbows, the colours shivering over the prairies in stripes and blotches, the grass—some high, some low, some feathered, some straight—making their own geography as they grow.

A long-dead human poet had dreamt of this place. Only her name had survived and had been bestowed on this reality that grew from her dream.

Here, in her honour, were hills of grass, where the great trembling bushes piled themselves into heaps, thirty wolves high, valleys of grass, where the vegetation lived like moss, soft beneath Dmitri's paws, narrow passageways beneath the broad-leaved canopies.

My king, thought the wolf when he reached the edge of the green world and found charred remains, where the spoor left by the Liberation criss-crossed the traces of an age yet to be.

Can I serve you? Can I find myself, in being your bondsman?

Me and my petty reasons for leaving the pack, where they licked my fur when I was a cub and where in a single year I loved more females than in two-and-a-half lifetimes since.

I was four weeks old and allowed to leave the cave, and I was astonished when I learnt the rules of my kinsfolk—and every rule showed that leaving the cave meant nothing at all—in the end the world of the tribe and its politics was nothing but a larger cave, roofed by the sky, with our mutual loyalty to keep us warm, with the darkness all round an unquestioned tradition.

Family, the narrow ties of blood. I had to get out—and have I become what I wished to be, have I become his son?

'He brought you into the world anew,' his sister had remarked, somewhat mockingly. 'You are born again, Digonos, Digonos.'

When the Lion took me in, he held that from that moment onwards it was his duty to educate me. Often enough he had to fight to have me acknowledged, even by his daughter, whom I have never seen.

So often that at least, by now, he is used to the idea that I do what I think best.

The creatures in the Atlantic, the hordes in the east, the wolfpacks prowling round Landers, none of them can undo this strange adoption, which has led to such an elegant success—a real diplomat, the first in the five-hundred-year history of the Gente, in this young world.

Run by night, sleep by day, so it went until he reached the coast.

There he found a spoil heap, a vast wall of human bones. He climbed up until his paws ached, and once at the top, gazed out at the great green sea.

Dmitri closed his eyes. Beneath his eyelids he saw red, a warning signal from a distant phylogenetic past, reminding him of the blood spilt freely on the steps of the Temple of Isotta in Capeside. Carefully, he went back down the wall, on the same side that he had climbed it. The white bones cracked and splintered beneath his feet as he stepped carefully, thoughtfully. A few of the bodies were still dressed in the shabby remains of a lost life, in rags that recalled such stuff as cuddling up under open skies on a humid night in June, kicking the ball about on a green and muddy field, workers' revolts in Russian mining towns, tolerable pop music, the ties of close friendship. Dmitri had been interested in human emotions since his student days but could glean nothing from the frozen faces, the spectral cauls.

Terns showed the wolf the way south.

He was glad, knowing that they were at least as reliable as the ravens, without wanting to be paid like them: new friends.

He could have known his way without their help, if he'd been willing to take the nutritional supplements to give him a bird-like sense of direction. Magnetic particles of trace iron in their beaks, Philomena's endless lectures about mechanosensitive ionic channels receiving signals that could be turned into nerve impulses that influenced how all flying Gente . . . 'Ah, crap and canvas,' the wolf spat. He wanted nothing to do with it, didn't even want to hear about it. These days you could buy instincts or your overlord would grant them to you, but—

'No thanks, not interested,' Dmitri Stepanovich whispered. He trusted the birds, and besides, he would rather save up a few abilities for later, for another self.

The king, thought the wolf, I love him and I love what he has done for us, I love to be abroad on his business and I'm glad to serve such a great and gentle strength, glad that a simple wolf can stand by him and by the sacred radiance of the sun, the mysteries of Livienda, and the night, by all the operations of the orbs from whom we do exist, and cease to be . . .

But there's still something missing, the diplomat knew, *serdtse*.

Over the weeks Dmitri became a scrupulous loner. If a path looked well travelled, he would avoid it.

In the mornings he would yawn until his jaw strained at its moorings, rub his back against the acacia and cedar trees, eat berries for his breakfast. In the evening he would eat hares (those that were not Gente—there were still a few, out here in the wild). In between, he stretched his legs, raced for hours. Little by little he came to know his muscles, his bones, his skin and his pelt so well that he felt at ease as he had not since he was a whelp.

In the darkness of a cave in the Preference Mountains he came across pipistrelle bats, at work on building projects. Here, they prepared a new marvel of progress, with which Cyrus Iemelian Adrian Vinicius Golden wished to enrich the lives of all those who lived under his aegis.

The scientist in charge of the project was famous and Dmitri knew her from pherinfone broadcasts. Her name was Izquierda. He hadn't known that she worked in such secrecy. Of course she had homes in all Three Cities, but no one had heard of this cave. After she had scanned his identifying scent markers, Izquierda explained her project to the wolf. 'You know our leader. He doesn't trust the old way of working any longer, he wants to make a great leap forward.'

Dmitri took a risk and voiced an opinion. 'I suppose he's thinking of the day when he won't be with us any longer, to do the thinking for us.'

'His aim is to create institutions that can do what the Lion can—it's ambitious,' Izquierda conceded.

'What about his daughter, Lasara?' asked the wolf.

The bat whistled between her needle teeth. 'Who can say? I think that he dislikes the dynastic principle. Besides, he loves his daughter so much that he wants to let her decide for herself, even though she stands to inherit. Perhaps she doesn't even want to rule? To live for a thousand years and sleep away whole epochs, up there,' the bat rolled her eyes, the colour of green tea in the artificial light, 'encased in sandalwood. Be all that as it may, if he doesn't abdicate before then, he will certainly rely on the new calculating engine once it is ready.'

The new calculating engine. Fascinated and somewhat unnerved, Dmitri recognized components gleaming in the dark that made him think of wet moonstones, black sugar. He knew that they were building a thinking thing here. 'When do you think . . .'

'No hurry. They'll be assembled, then put onto circuit boards; we'll dig basins and fill them with the necessary fluids, lower the boards into them, then if we've done everything right, our creation will come to life; then it will begin to think about what it is, who it is . . . twenty, maybe thirty years until it opens its eyes, until we can talk of consciousness. And after that, before we can put the seedlings onto compact copies . . . no, let's not talk about that.'

Her tone said, I'm not allowed to talk about that. The wolf could tell, from the way the fine hairs in Izquierda's ears stood up, that she knew how much she had already given away, perhaps too much. The information that she had just let slip was not meant for any passer-by on leave from his post.

'Thank you for your . . . explanation,' said Dmitri and left the cool cave with his tail between his legs, to let the night-shift workers know that he respected them (and feared them a little).

3. TO KILL A MAN

Higher yet, at the edges of the chasms fringed with forests, Dmitri Stepanovich was surprised by the silence that the long-forgotten humans had called the hour of the wolf, when you couldn't believe that the morning sun would ever shine again, and the rocky cliffs were colder than any ice, and every sound, the slightest sound, threatened the presence of tiny devils, too small to be seen.

Here the wolf understood at last that by leaving the pack all that time ago, he had not only changed but had been truly transformed. I am alone.

Something that no one in my family has ever been before.

And even if they're building machines in the mineshafts there to connect all Gente in unprecedented ways, because the Lion doesn't want anybody to be alone, that changes nothing. From now on, I will always be alone.

A small, quiet voice within him said, this is good.

'Is that so?' he said half aloud in the silence, not knowing whether he was really contradicting the voice or not.

At twilight Dmitri came across a survivor, a madman.

The man cried out in fear and aimed a rifle at him. The Monotony lives on, Dmitri thought grimly and leapt at the lunatic, who had left him no choice. Before he could fire a shot, Dmitri had bitten off both his hands. The man gave a shout that was almost a laugh, fumbling at the stumps as they spewed blood, and then reagents that lived in Dmitri's saliva stopped the bleeding, and the pain as well. The wolf sat on the man's ribcage, to give him the chance to recognize the thinking beast in Dmitri's eyes, which people like him still did not want to acknowledge. For their own protection perhaps, thought the wolf, to them, we must mean something more fearful than death and soon they won't even understand why they died in such great numbers in the Liberation wars.

The man was frightfully dirty, his salt-and-pepper beard had only a few streaks of black in the white and some old dried egg yolk. Now he stopped crying and shrieking, but began instead to laugh for real, showing he thought himself something quite special, uniquely mad.

The muscles of his face writhed. He looked quite horrible. Now he was babbling words that somehow slipped past any meaning that they may have had. His breath became shallow, he gasped for air and missed. Dmitri watched him slobber and roll his eyes, felt him try to stand up, as they always did, the vanquished, and thought, we should have just disarmed them and shipped them off to remote islands, they would have eaten one another in the end. It lasted a long while.

When it was over Dmitri began to snort, breathing speech from his nostrils, primitive pherinfonic films showing arithmetic sequences, soothing illusions tailored to the crude human central nervous system.

At last the man calmed down, wracked by the waning spasms of his madness.

The human slumped backwards until he lay on his back like a dead man. He still breathed though. In. Out. Then he began to speak, more clearly this time. 'Howl . . . howl . . . o, you are . . . men . . . of stones . . . Had I your . . . tongues and . . . eyes, I'd . . . use them so . . . that heaven's vault . . .'

Dmitri had heard enough.

He bit the poor fool's throat through and spat into the snow. Scraps of human neck between his teeth disgusted him.

Black gall soured his spit. He was so angry that his flanks heaved, for he had seen himself in the man's hollow eyes: a monster.

What next?

They eat dirt and they hide in the remotest spots, they burrow like teeming worms and they tell themselves that we Gente are abhorrent, degraded, that we know nothing about Shakespeare, symphonies, the cathedrals of Milan, Pindar's odes, all that old crap, and when forced to admit that we do indeed know, then they say, we know but we do not understand. The Gente can never change that.

These people do not want to live alongside us. They imagine that they can decide who will inhabit the earth and how.

The dying man's throat bubbled and gurgled and then there was nothing. Dmitri Stepanovich stayed crouched over this nothingness for a little while, thinking of the city to which he would return.

The dying man's gaze was fixed on his muzzle.

Yes, that's all that he sees, that's what I am, a beast, crouching in the darkness, befouling myself when he turns the red light of reason on me. His ruined reason.

Once the man who had tried to shoot him was no longer breathing, Dmitri walked on, to a towering cliff where he stood, looking down at the lake of mist that lapped at the tips of the dark trees.

He was surprised to discover that he no longer believed in the Lion.

He loves us? He wants us to be happy and live with him forever and aye? He has a plan? I don't think any of this is true.

And yet I love him, because he tells us all these tales.

Dmitri knew now that he did not serve the Lion for the sake of any higher truth, anything greater than men, Gente or the new gods of the rainforest.

From now on, when he did the Lion's bidding, the wolf would do it of his free will.

The thought made him joyful, but for a while this joy fought in his heart with the sadness of knowing that the world, of course, could not be made a better place, not with all the Lion's power.

Then he bade both the joy and the sadness, be still.

They obeyed.

4. AND WHO BEGAT WHOM

Terror was an indispensable part of the Lion's reputation.

Among themselves, the Gente said that the name Cyrus Iemelian Adrian Vinicius Golden spoke of deeds, adventures and portents that not all may hear or learn.

Was it true, what they whispered in the Three Cities? Had he torn a god limb from limb, had he walked unburnt upon the surface of the sun, had he begotten children upon his own children?

Ever since language was given to the world, some rumours have been deadly in their own right, needing no one's anger to make them so.

'Live as though upon a new earth, that has a new heaven.' They said that the Lion had followed his own commandment to excess.

A technician, who had been working for Izquierda for a hundred and fifty years now, said, 'In the first years of the Liberation he changed species several times a week.'

No one knew how long it was that the king had continuously been a Lion (some calendars and chronicles were missing). The long name by which they knew him now catalogued the steps along his path to power, the name-list of the several different lions that he had been. His birth was proclaimed and documented in the Pact, the juridical, political and biotic treaty agreed by the first princes of the Gente, whose names he now bore. (It may have been something along the lines of the process whereby Katahomenduende and Katahomencopiava had woken the new monstrosity Katahomenleandraleal to life.)

Cyrus: the title of a book that told of a great golden cat in a young country of the early Liberation ('Central Asian' as they said back then), surrounded by the green and fiery jungle. This felid had seen to it that certain abuses in the judiciary and executive were quickly stopped. Until he had taken up the cause, badgers and cattle who had for instance witnessed a crime committed by a tiger or a leopard and wanted to report it, had no protection from vendetta. In the worst case, they would be hauled before a court convened in secret by the perpetrator's clan, with no possibility of appeal. Often they were accused of collaborating with the humans, who were far from defeated at the time, and thrown from cliffs into the sea.

Cyrus' paw squashed feline feudalism in the moment of its conception, deploying legions of soldiers and policemen recruited above all from the badger tribes that he had freed. As a legacy from these wars, even centuries later Georgescu's people were still unshakeably loyal to Cyrus Iemelian Adrian Vinicius Golden. 'I will not tolerate that the strong wreak havoc by their stupidity. By all means chaos, but let it be fruitful. But there must be an end to the naked aggression of those who cannot live peacefully together with their less greedy cousins.'

Iemelian had been the name of a tenacious defender of the singular right to wear clothes or do without, in the northern parts of the first of the Three Cities, where Scandinavian culture was just then slipping into oblivion.

He was as white as sand and for a long time protected the elk thereabouts from the wolves, who often ran wild after the Liberation. Unlike the Lion's other early identities, he appeared in no photographs or film footage. His closest advisor had been a learned old owl, who came to some prominence as a couturier once the proto-Gente had thrown off the human yoke.

Shirts for birds: there had never been any such thing before and even if they went out of fashion again once the Gente had established their own aeon world-wide, their meaning as an act of cultural revolution endured—a proud signal, we need no longer live in need.

'We know more, not less, we can do more, not less. We have overcome and that means that we have all that they had and more besides.' These were Iemelian's words.

Adrian had been the name of the greatest nonhuman architect who had ever lived. He had set stone upon stone and imposed his will thereby—unlike any architect before whose will had bent to serve the spaces that he found.

It was he who had rebuilt Borbruck from wreck and ruin, raising up the pillars that bore the great railways of the benzene ring, round which the city's dark, brooding structures soon shot up in all directions to vertiginous heights, crystalline structures grown in full, curving lines. Even those who barely understood would praise Adrian's ingenuity, his beautifully simple solutions for the problems in town planning and unified design that mankind had left to be solved. His sensitivity to ley lines was legendary, as was the tireless pleasure he took in roaming the lower depths of the city that he had sown, and improving what he saw. He was also famed for his compendious knowledge of all previous architectural styles and his aristocratic manner.

On all the statues of Cyrus Iemelian Adrian Vinicius Golden, the Lion had four thin bands of platinum on his ankles and wrists, and Adrian had indeed worn these. His descendant, the one with the longer name, wore them no more. There was no need, everyone knew who he was anyway.

Vinicius: even today, merchants called upon this gifted wheeler-dealer in their times of trouble, for the rumours said that it had been he who had brought the great economist Ryuneke into the governing coalition of the first age of the Gente. The Lion who Vinicius had become still preached the same message to his badgers, wolves and bats even today: 'We needed Ryuneke then and we still need him now, because the Second Animal Empire will never be realized except by a new means of production and distribution.'

With this modest declaration, he took second place to Ryuneke. But it had been Vinicius himself, not the Fox, who had decisively shaped the new methods of production after the upheavals of the Liberation, had introduced the gene standard, decoupled it from the gold standard and overseen all the necessary adjustments. He had introduced the so-called Solomonic tribute to allow the ocean-dwellers to attain the same level of development as the land animals and had abolished it after one hundred and fifty years once the new currencies were accepted even by the Atlantic creatures. On the day when Vinicius finally resigned and gave up his ghost to the Lion Undivided, he left the Gente three parallel currencies, each strong and stable: gold, pherinfonic codes and coinage struck with designs in femtometric detail. (These last were sometimes jokingly called 'gold pieces' and had since come to be seen almost as the single currency—the off-book accounts in the bats' cave, for instance, were transacted almost entirely in these units.)

Golden was not a name as such, but a word spoken by all the world to praise a world previously unimaginable—a word that the Gente used for the philosopher who had given them a new myth to explain their origin. Thus those who could not or would not understand all the scientific niceties were saved from lapsing into their forefathers' false religion. Golden's whole doctrine could be demonstrated quite simply, in a lecture retrievable at any pherinfonic access terminal. Of course, it was possible to make life from nonliving matter, but the lecture irrefutably demonstrated that this achievement had no ethical implications for good or for ill.

Whoever creates life is still a very long way from giving this life meaning. Just because a creature is edible, does not justify eating it, and no imperatives inhere in an action any more than in a state of being. Only once the Gente had understood this could universal freedom prevail.

At first they flippantly called this doctrine the 'Bene Gente', but by the time Golden had shuffled off this mortal coil, the lesson had been so thoroughly learnt, the word had become flesh and blood, that this name was slowly forgotten. No one wanted to debase the teaching by making it an orthodoxy like those of the

Monotony. ('No holy texts,' Golden had told his disciples as he left, 'the risk of copying errors is too high.')

These names, these deeds, these visionaries laid the foundation for an epoch in which there was only one single authority—not an autocrat or despot, but a ruler who owed his authority to reasoned insight and clear purpose: Cyrus Iemelian Adrian Vinicius Golden.

5. LASARA'S MOTHER

Five years passed after the poison pellets had done their hideous but necessary work.

Dmitri Stepanovich travelled.

Izquierda drew up plans and built.

Philomena lied and giggled.

The Lion dreamt, issued laws and spoke verdicts in his sleep.

Then something surprising happened. Lasara's mother sent word.

Nothing had been heard of her for a long time. All that the pherinfoplexes knew was that she had, in her own words, 'decided to look for a much better corporeal identity—compared with the crude bodies which Father Golden gave his Gente to live in'.

As befitted her status, Lasara's mother had several names.

The best-known of these was the name by which she had been addressed during the good times of her marriage, divorce, re-marriage, subsequent divorce (and so on, repeatedly) with the Lion: Livienda Iemelian Adrian Vinicius Golden.

Not least to irk her husband, she gladly allowed even the humblest visitor to shorten this to 'Lady Livienda'.

Centuries ago, when she had first got to know the Lion, she had been (biologically seen as) a swarm intelligence of cooperating insects. Economically and politically, she had been an incarnate bond issue, a large project in the transfinite gene pool of the first Pielapiel populace. In those days her slogan had been written on many walls in Borbruck: 'All things must change. We'll see to it that they change for the better.'

For decades after Livienda first disappeared, the syntactic stemma of this proclamation served as an EPR code key for the badger armies in former Europe and what had been Asia. Livienda the swarm intelligence had been militant, even militarist. Humans who found themselves within her reach, usually briefly, had little joy of her company.

Philomena the dragonfly didn't talk about it much if you didn't ask her, but she had originally been one individual in the long spinal column of the swarm, before she slipped from her place and came into her own. She once explained this to Dmitri Stepanovich, 'I compute eigenvalues in milliseconds and assign them to even the smallest operations and I learnt how to do this—how to say "I" and what purpose this serves—from her. She was a power in those days, vital, dangerous.'

Vanished for years, Livienda sent word, and straightaway hundreds of forums and numerous individual Gente sent queries to the archives: who was she, what might we expect of her, what were her plans?

Her first new message to the forums was in an esoteric discussion thread of the Gente global conversation, for technical matters of meteorology. It caused great consternation. 'I will never see the sky the same way. I will learn to say goodbye to yesterday.'

The pherinfones showed a strange image for the author of this comment. It was clearly a mask, made of old code from what had been the swarm intelligence. The face was made of common hawker dragonflies and other blue–green shimmering insects, black-clouded longhorn beetles scurried where the gracious lady's feet met the ground, yellow-faced bees, plasterer bees and sweat bees made up the body itself, dancing in strict obedience to the protocols of Gente ecotecture's commonest programming languages. Anyone asking for further information was redirected to ancient files.

At the time, the bridal ephemerides were published shortly after the Lion's first wedding. Even today, whoever was curious could still look them up and find out everything about it. The ephemerides revealed that during Cyrus Iemelian Adrian Vinicius Golden's long courtship of the seething construct Livienda, she had almost daily had to suffer the same rebuke from her gallant. 'You are captivating, my dear. But you have two unhealthy fixations: the first, with your autonomy, and the second, with your autonomy.'

Her habitual reply was: 'When you talk of autonomy you talk of yourself. I hardly care, especially since it has almost nothing to do with autonomy as I understand it. I can be broken apart and yet not destroyed, and I can move in ways unlimited by fetishistic insistence on integrity remaining the same from one moment to the next, and you will learn to see these things as a boon. "I am such-and-such, a great Lion"—not a good idea. Cast-iron deities end up in the scrapyard sooner or later.'

'I love your needling comments and your sharp tongue,' her admirer said, to flatter her.

'My tongue is many tongues,' replied Livienda.

'You speak a language I understand, I don't care about anything else. And even if you have a, shall we say, frivolous attitude to identity, well then, I . . .'

'You'll come to envy this so-called frivolous attitude of mine, more than you will envy any of my other qualities that you admire so much.'

This coquettish reply spurred the Lion to give her a gift, just insulting enough to be amusing. 'Here, my head-in-the-clouds, here is a new servant for you, to show you how fine it is to have someone to torment and to know that it's always the same someone.'

It was a scuttling autotomous hog, Hébert Ransom by name. Breaking the laws that he had himself decreed, the Lion had bound him with pherinfonic fetters to lifelong servitude to his bride's scuttling, swarming genomes. He reckoned that once she had had enough of his obsequious devotion, Livienda would simply sting him to death with her bees.

Whether out of stubbornness, obduracy, impishness or perversity, she kept Hébert Ransom through all the slings and arrows of her marriage, cared for him and even made him her personal private secretary in the Lion's Sixth Cabinet of the Twentieth Tricontinental Aedile Parliament, when she was made Minister for Cladistics, Taxonomy and Gamete Partnership Law.

The scuttling hog was clever, conscientious and valiant in battle with political enemies.

During the wars of extermination that followed the Liberation, marked by atrocities on both sides, two hundred and forty million Gente and three billion humans were killed within three months. Each week Hébert went between the headstrong lovers, from the front to the rearguard and back again, carrying dirty love letters written on human skin.

Finally, so the archives said, Livienda, Izquierda and her genetechnicians found a way to liberate the faithful servant from his pheromonic enslavement. The antidote was administered, but Hébert Ransom nevertheless stayed at her side.

One of the last messages that Livienda sent to her husband before the final separation read: 'The identity of any sapient creature must include at least the illusion of free will. This is well illustrated by what happened with the gift you made me.'

After that she lived in seclusion for one hundred and seventy years, without adding her voice to the collective doings of the Gente.

Her official return after the triumphant events of the poison-pellet campaign did not take the form of an appearance in person—whatever 'person' might mean, given her well-known aversion to fixed identities. Instead came the enigmatic message on the forum, and over and above, an initiative in fiscal policy, which Hébert Ransom came to Borbruck to oversee.

The scuttling hog too had not been seen in public for a long time. Now that the first reports of his new role had appeared, he logged on to the pherinfoplex and explained, 'Madame wishes to fulfil her duties in a responsible manner. She has sent me here to Borbruck to correct mistakes made a long time ago.'

Stanz the ape spoke up. He had made his fortune as an artist and since then had used the money to buy a post as aedile, soon afterwards becoming spokesape for the Borbruck–Landers cities coalition. 'Does she intend to return to politics?'

'That rather depends,' Hébert replied, with a not entirely trustworthy smile, 'on what you mean by politics. She wishes to establish a foundation that will give grants for . . . expert reassessment of gamete law. Before entrusting me with this task she expressed her sentiment that she had left this area of Gente law in, and I quote, "a bit of a perishing mess, because I was fed up with that ass who calls himself a lion".'

'How much money is involved?' the ape asked next, without commenting on the unabashed anti-Lionism.

Hébert flashed up a figure.

The chief clerk of the grain bank who had also joined the conversation struggled for breath. 'That's enough to . . . where is she getting all that money?'

'From Lasara's trust fund.'

'But then,'—Stanz was outraged—'that leaves nothing but the capital reserve. All the interest will be stripped away and . . .'

'She's not leaving her child penniless, if that is your concern,'—Hébert Ransom's expression revealed that he did not for a moment believe that the ape cared about that—'even if this bold undertaking will entirely claim one or two decades' worth of interest.'

As expected, everyone spoke at once now. 'Who will be in charge?' 'Who will draft the reforms?' 'Where?' 'When?' 'What quangos will be formed?' 'Which quasi-species will be represented?' 'Who else has a claim to representation?'

As instructed, the scuttling hog declined to make any further comment.

In fact, all necessary preparation was already underway and even some of those asking questions were in the know. Their questions were simply meant to hide from the others how much they knew.

The scuttling hog declared the press conference over and got down to business.

Soon all the Gente wanted a piece of the pie.

Hébert Ransom dodged carefully through the coursing data streams. The Atlantic Embassy was particularly insistent that he decide on appointments and publicly announce them. He had put out feelers to the pelagic nations quite early on. Their excellent legal historians, gametic casuists and spatial planners had a worldwide reputation. Hébert managed to keep a lid on all the most sensitive questions until the moment they were resolved.

Meanwhile he sporadically gave further interviews by pherinfoplex. Soon enough they became a fortnightly ritual.

'How is Livienda? Is she well? What sort of shape is she in?'

'Madame has dispensed with her long Lion name and replaced it with another, no less lengthy. Her recognition codes will be published shortly. Her new name . . .'

'Has she done this to shame her former husband?'

'Madame has declared that she does not believe that he lives up to his many titles. She opines that Cyrus whatnot is a long train of names that can't disguise how his intellect has now shrivelled to the size of his pillow.'

Nervous laughter.

'How should we now address her?'

'Informally Madame is happy to be called Livienda or Lady Livienda. She has however also made a number of, let's say, genealogical investments, and desires that these be given their due recognition. Therefore, on official occasions and in scientific contexts, it would be appropriate to address her by her new and full name, Livienda Sonya Gina Anya Katya Nisi Saba Sheba Mattha Catriona Elyce Finfin-Fain.'

'Does this name differentiate sub-individuals in the swarm?'

'Good that you ask,' the scuttling hog said, wrinkling his snout happily, 'this gives me the chance to clear up an unavoidable confusion. Not only has Madame dissolved her marriage to the Lion, she is also no longer a swarm intelligence. The hexapods which had been her, ahem, common substance, are now either dead or scattered to the four winds, which is to say they have been set free and,'—Hébert twinkled merrily, knowing that his audience would understand the allusion—'are now autonomous organisms with an autotomic common corporeal ancestor. Here in the Three Cities and in Atlantis you are governed by dubious celebrities such as Philomena, Jodenzi, Kaneun and others of that ilk, but unlike these folk, Livienda's disjecta membra have been more than generously rewarded for services rendered and have been allowed to forget completely their pheromone-induced period of indenture.'

'Rather like you yourself?'

'No comment. That's to say, no comment to the main question, that's private business. As regards the secondary question which you actually asked, I can say that I continue to serve Madame from loyalty rather than compulsion.'

The zander Westphalia Sophocles Gaeta was the son of the son of the famed first Atlantic ambassador to Borbruck and one of the scuttling hog's highest-placed political allies. He asked, 'If Livienda is no longer a swarm intelligence, then what is she?'

The scuttling hog shook his head and grunted. The great mass of listeners at the transceivers did not deserve a clear answer to the question but this fish certainly did. After all, he was already destined for a leading administrative position in Livienda's project. How to tell him?

'What is she?' others interrupted. 'Who?' 'What's she like?'

The zander gazed at Hébert guilelessly.

Then, with sunken head and shoulders drawn up, Hébert Ransom revealed the very most he was permitted to say. 'She has, as I might say, become a tree.'

'A tree, how . . .'

'Don't ask me any more, Gente.'

'But the necessary technology . . .' '. . . Ryuneke's prints are all over this, if I'm not . . .'

'You are mistaken. Certainly . . .' he laughed, melancholy, '. . . it has to do with proteomics, to the extent that the word derives from Proteus as well as from protein. But . . .'

'A tree?' A sleepy bannerfish in one of the Atlantic bubble labs had logged in too late, missing the hog's declared refusal to answer any further questions. 'How did she become a tree? And while you're about it, why?'

'In the usual way. And for the same reason that we all pursue growth,' the scuttling hog assured him, trapped now. 'Fruit, shoot, taproot, secondaries, stretch, rise and seek the sun. Everything that was known on the matter during the Monotony still holds true.'

Westphalia Sophocles Gaeta was not so easily fobbed off. 'Hébert, forgive me, but it doesn't work that way. It's not merely any ordinary Gente asking you here. Many of us who are currently participating have been named to positions in this reform project. We want to talk to Livienda ourselves.'

'Why?' Hébert was honestly nonplussed.

'We must consult her about our requirements if we accept the commission, if we are to create this—what does one say?—working group of legal scholars and reformers.'

Hébert shook his head. 'Please, my dear and diligent Gente, do not trouble your conscience with this matter. She has her personal reasons, which we should respect. You may accept the commission or refuse Madame's wishes. But you may not meet her or fraternize with her. I must tell you that the tree stands in a private spot, where it will put down roots, cast its shade and only I shall know where to find it. I am Livienda's confidential agent and may go so far as to assure you that she will walk amongst the Gente once more, in a new form and share your—our—fate. When that time has come.'

'She will visit the Three Cities.'

'I never said so. Enough.'

The assembly dispersed and the connections were cut off.

6. PENCHANT AND PROGENY

Hébert's cautious networking, pherinfonic conferences and tête-à-têtes had their effect. After a couple of years, the Gente of the Three Cities agreed that Livienda's proposal deserved a vote of thanks. Did they not live in an embarrassing limbo when it came to the most important problems of gamete law? Had they really managed to erase the Monotony's lasting traces from prevailing habits in reproduction? Was there any substantive basis for the new usage? No, rather there were 'restrictive learnt behaviours' (Livienda, via Hébert Ransom), a penchant for experiment that was gradually losing steam, but no pattern or order.

The unanimous opinion of all those who had grappled with Hébert's message was that Cyrus Iemelian Adrian Vinicius Golden was clearly either unwilling or unable to cut through the Gordian knot of the situation. Was it not right and proper, and indeed a blessing, that Livienda Sonya Gina Anya Katya Nisi Saba Sheba Mattha Catriona Elyce Finfin-Fain should stay aloof from society and the rule of (as it turned out, inadequate) law, until such time as her money and her tutelage could help vanquish the chaos?

The new Academy for Cladistics, Taxonomy and Gamete Law was a torus of coloured glass equipped with machinery to maintain the necessary pressure, food chain and light levels, nestling under the benzene ring in Borbruck's web of pylons.

'The depths of the sea, in the midst of the city!' burbled the scuttling hog. In the week when work began he was everywhere to be seen. Then Hébert Ransom withdrew for a while to attend to the minutiae of preliminary committees and even kept clear of the orgies and feasts that consumed most of Livienda's PR budget in the first five-year phase after she had announced her return.

The torus took seventeen years to build.

When it was ready, the Atlanteans moved into their new Borbruck head-quarters, along with a few luminaries from other ecological niches who were able to keep up intellectually. They began their Titans' task.

For two piggy lifetimes Hébert Ransom sat patiently in his roof garden, beneath the glowing copper clouds at the southern edge of the benzene ring.

From time to time, a movement came in his ears. Then, without moving his lips, he would speak to his distant liege lady. When she asked how it was progressing, he would answer in such sentences as this: 'I am content. I am learning much here that is important. I listen to the Coriolis, to entropic heat loss, to centripetal and centrifugal forces, to pressure, to gravity, to the electromagnetic force, to the strong and the weak atomic forces, as they all squeeze excess time from the Atlanteans' living quarters. I can watch all nature's vectors at work as they carve interim com-mittee decisions from the documents, bringing the moment ever nearer when the central coordinating committee will present their findings and conclusions.'

'If that is so,' whispered Livienda's voice, which no one but Hébert could hear, 'then I too am content.'

Hébert did not have particular orders to do so, but since he was there anyway, he kept an ear open for the remarkable news about the king's daughter Lasara. Her striking behaviour amused him.

For a dozen years now the pherinfonic gossip portals had been full of nothing else but the wunderkind, her parties, her drug abuse, self-harming, affairs and the-oretical accomplishments. She had settled in Capeside in the Okkasi district and was bent on parodying her mother's life history in ways that were touching and troubling in equal part. Her several marriages, divorces, group identities, partial fissions and recombinations had brought her many extreme experiences and a few new names. 'She is now called Lasara Iemelian Oktet Chukwudi Ottobah Sandra Belle Placide Lais Olbers Vinicius Golden,' Hébert reported to his distant liege lady.

'If that is so,' she replied and by now it had become a lullaby for him, 'then I am content about this too.'

Even if Lasara's life was just one big wreck, her intellectual career was quite otherwise.

She had won the scientific academy's Eagle Medal at the Fourth Aedile Congress with an impeccable dissertation on 'Economic Cycles of the Liberated Animal Empire and Their Divagation from National and Global Economic Laws of the Preceding Monotony, with Special Reference to the Failure of Okun-Sabyo's Law of Elastic Ratio in Actual and Potential Productive Output of a Given Manufacturing Region'. Then she pounced upon the study of biology.

Here, she first earned great distinction by reinvigorating the idea of orthogenesis, then moved on to its political implications and implementation, joining the upper cadres of the Polyarch party while accumulating further personal scandal at a breathtaking rate. (The zenith of her engagement was marked by repeated arrests and conspicuously heavy sentences for involvement in occupying the Pielapiel Palace, disruption to pherinfonic traffic and other acts of civil disobedience, including a three-week mass blockade of the badger barracks in the Capeside region.)

At a party presidium meeting, the dissident badger Oudemans Dahl spoke out thunderously against 'puerile histrionics' and 'rich brats who abuse our cause as a vehicle for their repellent posturing', whereupon she laughed in his face and announced her resignation from the party quite uncouthly, 'You know what? You can lick my arse, you bunch of stiffs.'

When it seemed that her fame could not grow any greater, Lasara made an announcement to her numerous admirers. Via pivot mirrors, screens, news sheets, datafoam diadems and pherinfoplex, she declared that she had 'got caught in the observer paradox: we cannot observe how Gente behave when no one is watching and therefore I am abandoning my name for a while, also my current appearance, which you all want to kiss or to fuck the whole time, and I will find a new corporeal configuration. I've reached the point where I need to get out of my way for a while.'

'She's doing what her mother did,' many thought and said.

7. ON WHETHER TO TRUST A DAUGHTER

Hébert Ransom spent the eighteenth Esprit festival in Borbruck as an especially honoured guest of the dogs and cats and the children that they were raising together. Between the seventeenth and eighteenth festivals, though, the scuttling hog had a momentous meeting. Philomena the dragonfly came to see him. She brought a warning from the Lion. 'Livienda can do what she wants with her wealth and whatever else. But the project might prove to be an enormous millstone round her neck—she has built that hoop for the fishes, but in the end it will be a hoop that she has to jump through, like someone's poodle.'

Hébert Ransom was unimpressed. 'I don't know whether I'll even pass on this rubbish. The motive for the threat seems far too transparent.'

'Is it a threat?'

'He's accusing her of throwing her money out of the window, and he has no say in how it is spent, because she's using it for a purpose that he has consistently shirked. Listen, My lady Dragonfly, the Gente are beginning to ask why a retired ex-minister should have to finance from her own funds a reform that should be the state's responsibility? He's threatening to sabotage her project, so that she'll drop it.'

Philomena's face was too small for any expression to be read. She answered drawlingly, 'Don't put on such airs, little piggy. Granted that his motives in advising her to be more . . . frugal might even be as you suggest, nevertheless his . . . warning should be given due consideration. After all, I don't suppose that Lady Livienda rustles her branches in such total seclusion that she hasn't heard rumours of the experiments the fish are performing in those parts?'

'In which parts, do you mean? Where Livienda is right now?' Hébert was on his guard. The dragonfly was clearly trying to get information out of him.

'You know perfectly well that I mean in the oceans. In the trenches and abysses, in the rifts and the fissures.'

Hébert made a wry snout. 'These wild reports about dicing with the laws of physics? That they're working on anti-gravity technology, down there in the bathyal zone, altering their physiology more drastically than any Gente so far? That their work in the torus is only a way of drip-feeding us landlubbers with their legal concepts, because in the long run they plan to take over? That they want to fly, and they're rebuilding their bodies to conquer the air, then the stratosphere, then interplanetary and interstellar space?'

'It can all be . . . proved. There are pictures, films, depth scans. They have suboceanic accelerators the size of continental plates . . . altered Cavourite, tanks full of decayed fermion gas which they will use to build . . . vehicles which soon enough will challenge our clumsy airships for the supremacy of the skies and space.'

'Stories. The gossip of headstrong badgers who don't have enough enemies and would like to get another war under way.'

'The Lion . . .'

'Well, of course. He's always fretting over something, having his nightmares. The ceramic monsters over in Brasilia are supposed to be just such a threat—I sometimes ask myself whether you and Georgescu aren't egging him on to impose martial law, whether he doesn't want to reintroduce all our forefathers' faults. Transcontinental security policy, the so-called deterrents, then massive armed sweeps, just not directed against the humans this time.'

'You are taking things quite far . . . little piggy. You'll burn your tongue.'

That was Philomena's last comment before she flitted away, without a word.

After the conversation Hébert described his impressions to the leaves fluttering in the high breezes on his balcony and these relayed his words to Livienda. 'The way she talks, it's crucial that we notice how much she despises Livienda, her birthplace, and how greatly she respects the Lion, which is where she has ended up. If we are not careful we'll find that we have further parties alongside the Polyarchs, the badgers and the libertarians. And if that happens, then events will take the course that we know so well from the Monotony.'

8. WHAT THE ZANDER FOUND

'Progressive phylogeny'—the name for Livienda's project came from the pherin-fonet. Word was that it had come by roundabout ways from the infamous Lasara, who had renounced her old lord and master and had long been in contact with Westphalia Sophocles Gaeta, even while living in disguise, incognito and secretly.

It was Westphalia who finally announced the new terminology—and who attached a very large molecule with his recognition code, announcing to anyone who was interested (which meant almost all Gente, everywhere) that the great day had come: 'The first plenary session of all general committees composed of Atlantean and other experts will take place in the gamete legislative Torus on the first Kuesday of the new year.'

'We apologize most sincerely that this plenum is meeting only now and we are aware that you all have high hopes that our work will furnish adequate legal foundations for reproductive rights,' Westphalia announced to the plenary gathering a week later, with a slight cold in his voice.

This led to rambling and exhaustive excuses. The zander only calmed down when he saw how genially the scuttling hog was looking round from his lodge, glancing happily at the president of the commission and then at his closest colleagues.

The actual inaugural speech could begin. 'Learned assembly, honoured aediles, dear friends, in the past three years the historical part of our research, in which we assessed the legacy of the vanquished order, has caused difficulties which neither we nor our generous sponsor'—a nervous glance towards Hébert Ransom, an indulgent nod from the same—'could have anticipated. Even the calendars, the system of dating that they used, the enormous amount of biometric data left over from the Monotony, all this corrupted information, the flesh-creeping absurdities of religion and cultural usage spread fungally across anything which we found interesting, which could hardly be excised without destroying the documents themselves—it was appalling. An example: the Islamic and Chinese calendars were lunar, the Christian and Buddhist calendars solar, I know that these words mean little to most of us, even to the experts, but when we have to consider biological and geological timescales simultaneously . . . those in the know will acknowledge that a mere half millenium has elapsed since the last world war raged and that we should not be surprised if the resulting devastation . . .'

This went on for some time.

Hébert was in danger of losing concentration and drifting off, when the zander finally reached the point. 'The regrettable remnants of this pervasive, nauseating superstition can't, even in the most important areas, be untangled from the web of legal relations as our forefathers created and conducted them. This makes it especially difficult to obtain even a simple overview of matters. For instance, the act of "sodomy", that is to say the specific "unnatural sexual act" in the atavistic human understanding of gamete law, did not merely consist in the introduction of the human male's sperm into the womb of a species that they considered lesser and that was not even equipped to reproduce on receiving it. Rather, this was only an insignificant aspect of the criminal act, which was supposed to result in what they called—and I quote—an "implantation of the blood". When we read of this, my esteemed colleagues, then the extent becomes obvious not only to your good selves but also, I am sure, even to the least educated of our general public, of the metaphysical confusions that have wormed their way even into the lexica of the languages surviving since those days, that have taken root there and that spread their poison by capillary action. The resulting damage is set to cause great difficulty in our gigantic reform initiative. We have begun a work of real value and lasting effect, and are under attack from partisans of the absurd, the shameful and the criminal. We must destroy this bias and eradicate the least particle of its effect, sweeping away even the last sign, if we are ever to hope to guarantee real and in-alienable rights to the inhabitants of this earth, rights which will set binding limits to the degrees of freedom which we enjoy in creating our progeny. This freedom has previously been hidden, but by defining it, we help stabilize the diversity and evolutionary reach of our most advanced quasi-species.'

The tone of his voice switched from unctuous tremolo to clinical exactness and back again, successfully concealing from unsuspecting listeners the revolutionary implications, the true scale of the proposal, of which this conference was the first stage.

Hébert Ransom, however, was anything but unsuspecting. He foresaw tremen-dous upheavals, could feel it in the twists of his stubby tail and was sure that even if not all those present, and certainly hardly any of the Gente watching by pher-infone, properly understood what was at stake here, at least the dreaming overlord would have to understand this gentle but insistent challenge to his authority. How would he react?

Perhaps the zander's Aesopian turn of phrase would ensure that the Lion was not provoked quite so far as to take action—a thought that faded immediately to nothing when Westphalia, on the podium, continued: 'I am forced to use coarse language. We have been handed a stinking slop-pail, a rotting heap of fallacious premises and twisted syllogisms which purports to be the proper way of life for post-Liberation Gente. Evolutionary advantage, stable strategies, selection, the same old catchphrases from the high and late Monotonous periods—but who says that we need only change the sign in front of this cumbersome legacy, turn it topsy-turvy, inside-out, and then we will be able to plan our future effectively, protect our genome and improve it where possible? If I may speak personally for a brief moment, I know about life underwater—my home region is beautifully colourful, it encourages a sense of aesthetics. You may see that here in the torus, overhead, beneath you, wherever you look—and already in the second week of our work, the younger of our antelope colleagues'—he nodded amicably in their direction, while they acted as though they still breathed through mouth and nostrils (even after their long stay in the torus, the gills and stabilizing fins that altered their physiology had still not become second nature to them)—'presented a diverting study about the genetic origins of classical fish colours: the more colourful, the higher the reproductive success. Very well then—one might easily think that vibrant colours indicate excellent heath—but how do we know that this was not simply a matter of survival and that perhaps predators avoided colourful prey since the strong colours indicated that these proto-Gente would flee, and were not worth the expense of chasing? Male larks sing their famous songs when they are being hunted by falcons, not simply as a prelude to canoodling. Even considering the well-known results of Lasara Iemelian Oktet Chukwudi Ottobah Sandra Belle Placide Lais Olbers Vinicius Golden's computational economics'—Hébert gave a start, unnoticed, he hoped. What a dangerous name to mention, what a politically risky move in this context, the zander was really going the whole hog—'it seems to me that the preliminary studies of this working group placed undue weight on the utility of secondary sexual characteristics in dimorphic species as against a realistic assessment of their costs. Luckily, we have been able to throw off this prejudice in several subsequent studies, just as we have gone beyond a false view of our ancestors' social behaviours, a false metric for pair-choice quotas and so forth. But my friends, we will only be able to say that we have made progress when we have become fully aware of our goal, when we follow it unswervingly, when we no longer allow ourselves to be dissuaded from it. What is this goal? That can be said in a few words: with which gamete partnership laws—not just by which military means—can we guarantee maximum diversity in the current stock of pseudo-species and in the number of existing variants? How can we guarantee the survival of animal life, of the biosphere as such, in the light of foreseeable and unforeseeable dangers?'

The silence that greeted the zander could only mean agreement.

'That's it,' Westphalia said emphatically. 'Nothing more. We must always reckon with the possibility of renewed Great Extinctions'—the scuttling hog drew a breath sharply through his nostrils, the zander was coming to the most dangerous point—'even in the happy age in which we live, the eternal peace that we have been promised. The Lion Cyrus Iemelian Adrian Vinicius Golden has given us the gift of a new way to live. We would be ungrateful if we leave the new life unexamined, as we received it.'

A more courteous affront to royal authority could hardly be imagined.

'So far, no one has seriously considered whether we should dispense with the last humans, lock them away on reservations, incorporate them into our gene pool, invite them into our ranks, or what on earth we should do with them and how that could fit with what we do with one another. The question of sodomy, if you will allow me the quaint term, is raised once again, though this time from the other end. We face a threat that has asked that question and found an answer to it. The worst of it is, we do not know how.' He avoided saying the name, but Hébert Ransom was not the only one who knew that he was talking about Kata-homenleandraleal.

'We must scrutinize the interrelations of sexuality, reproduction, successful survival, competition, war and extermination in all taxa that have so far existed and we must draw conclusions from the results of this scrutiny. We will lay the factual groundwork—we have already begun to do so, with very promising initial results—but all Gente must make the decision, all of us, as a collective. We must decide soon. We must not delay, lest we perish.'

1. THE STORY OF THE HARBOUR

'Lest we perish.' Dmitri tasted the sentence like a ripe strawberry.

He decided that it sounded juicy enough for a springtime like this that promised a summer as hot as the year when they attacked mankind's hands.

Dmitri liked the zander, the way he spoke so prissily, revelling in details, going off on digressions and at the same time full of fight, talking of the many relationships in nature and the complexities of gender, female hyenas whose systems were flooded with the male hormone androstenedione, which caused the aggression for which the species was famous, 'and nevertheless they behave quite properly in all matters to do with reproduction, indeed they are devoted mothers, which might lead us to conclude that the female regions of their brains, so to speak, are in some way protected from the androgens which masculinize their aggressive, territorial behaviour.'

Then came some details, quite a few in fact, about humans, almost vanished now, and about how they had a genetic marker for aggression that 'when present, increased the probability of violent behaviour about nine-fold compared with its absence', and that this was 'human maleness, in and of itself'.

After permitting himself this joke, the lecturer dwelt for a while on how *Homo sapiens* had convinced himself of a fictive superiority over the fowl of the air, and over the cattle, and over all the earth, and over every creeping thing upon the earth. He dwelt also on the serious endemic diseases from which only these supposedly superior beings, of all the creatures on earth, had suffered, the worst among which, marked by symptoms including chronic anaemia, malnutrition and permanent exhaustion, was known during the Monotony as 'poverty', transmitted from mother to child and with markedly higher incidence in the female of the species.

'They wanted to set themselves apart, from the birds according to their kind, and from the cattle according to their kind, and from every creeping thing upon the earth according to their kind, and they really did set themselves apart. Human beings were made from other humans, as we say these days.'

The wolf pricked up his ears and bared his teeth. 'We' didn't say so, that was from the jungle machines. It was certainly not part of Bene Gente doctrine.

'Often however, the construction was faulty, the parts were poorly integrated. If we want to understand how it all came about and how much has been passed on to us, we must,' said the zander and called up a rapid montage of films, 'go back to the basics of sexual reproduction and of biological life as such.' Cunning old fox, the wolf thought, this zander knows how to rephrase a sentence and make it a weapon. 'We must also understand social aspects however, since mankind had several thousand years to fiddle about with these, we can learn a great deal from their mistakes. Men and women—even when they had achieved a widespread level of wealth, general prosperity nevertheless remained lacking. Why? The mortality rate improved—in rich countries. Children there increasingly survived infancy, the standard of living and quality of life rose, but in the course of these advances the male tendency to violence and the female ability to bear and raise their young became problems, whereas before they had been evolutionarily stable strategies—not nature any longer, but a mass of social difficulties that threatened prosperity. Mankind found no solution here. Why not?'

A short film about slime mould burst onto the screen and then vanished—single cells becoming a multicellular organism, which scattered plantlike spores and then collapsed just as quickly as the film was also gone, save for a few infotags (*Dictyostelium discoideum*) and some dialogue ('They are taking on another form. Like living tissue. Mankind called that pseudoplasmodium.'). All of this was without any kind of commentary, and the wolf instantly realized that the viewers were not supposed to take it in consciously—these were simply supplementary footnotes for the subconscious, to be digested later by the enormous computing capacity of Gente brains.

'They tried to create a global society,' the zander said, and the screen showed a behemoth that eats grass as an ox. What strength was in his loins, and what force was in the navel of his belly! He moved his tail like a cedar: the sinews of his stones were wrapped together. His bones were as strong pieces of brass, his bones like bars of iron.

'The chief of the ways of the self-made god, mankind: he that made him, made his sword to approach unto him. Surely the mountains brought him forth food, where all the beasts of the field played, the mothers and fathers of the Gente, and had no inkling. He lay under the shady lotus trees, in the covert of the reed and fens. Soon though they too lost sight of him. Now the Lion has caught him, eyeball to eyeball, in the trap of science. Our lord has drawn him out with a hook and his tongue with a cord which he let down, the long chain of pherinfones. Humans? They didn't know quite how they lived from one day to the next, they didn't know how to remain men and women even while they continuously altered everything round themselves. They were eutheria and did not realize that their basic form was female—their chromosomic alternatives XX or XY and the only choice on offer was whether a child differed from its mother or not. Castrate the male embryo of a hare and a perfectly normal female animal will develop. Birds on the other hand'—a flock of cranes, in hologram, swam, gracefully flapping, through the water where the zander hung—'are male by nature—the chromosomes here are ZZ or ZW. Feed male hormones to a peahen and it will become restless, but nothing else happens—until you suppress the female hormones, and then the bird will suddenly grow a magnificent spreading tail. And my Atlanteans, my friends, my fish . . . many species in this realm have the matter organized much more sensibly than any of the others I have mentioned to you so far—take the dominant male from a social group and the largest remaining female simply becomes male. Let's forget the marsupials for a moment, they're too peculiar'—the zander made a face that was supposed to indicate irony. The wolf snorted gently—'and we'll consider the parthogenetic species, just so our overview is complete. The whiptail lizards—we suspect from what we find in archives of the Monotony that mankind believed that this species exhibited pairing behaviour, even with no males present, because humans kept them captive. Rubbish—we know better now, we even know exactly how the question of virginity affected humanity's fate. We know that the prehistoric proto-gorillas, the first chimpanzees and early humans all had females just as robustly built as the males. The facts are available, the diagrams drawn. Thus, where should we make a start in gamete partnership law? With genetic gender, hormonal or social? The working areas, very roughly: first, gender issues; second, social modes; third, the question of dissolving species boundaries, inasmuch as there is a real species boundary to the gene pool within which we can have reproductively viable offspring; fourth, what should we avoid, what aren't we going to touch, from the legacy of the failed human experiment? There is little time left to us, we must create legally binding precepts, lest . . .'

'We perish,' Dmitri laughed, finishing the sentence. Then he turned from the screen for a moment and enjoyed his drink.

The wolf was grateful for the aircon's soothing breeze that tasted of dry ice.

He had resolved not to leave the gloomy hotel bar until late that night, if possible and even then to spend only an hour or two prowling the Borbruck side-alleys, to pick up any hints on the climate of opinion that might be useful to the Lion.

The hotel was a glass-and-concrete cylinder of a building, a round bar set orthogonally to the benzene ring and connected to the city centre by an integrating bridge suspension. Most of the guests, here and in the other central hotels, were in Borbruck for the reform trust's first public announcement, just like Dmitri Stepanovich himself.

He had come incognito, blocking the scent of his recognition codes. As a precaution he had told no one except his immediate colleagues that he was done with roaming and roving half a year ago now and had returned to the Lion's service. Borbruck was only the first stop on his new and secret diplomatic mission. His actual destination was Landers.

The barkeeper was a river frog from the swamps beyond the Capeside suburbs and was paying next to no attention to the live broadcast of the zander's speech, captivated instead by the story of the wolf's hair-raising adventures, the yarns which his customer spun in return for 'drinks on the house'—four rounds so far. Partly true and partly a pack of lies, the most exciting thing that the frog had heard since a hawk-maiden from the Temple of Isotta in Capeside had once pitched up blind drunk at his bar, drunk herself deeper into insensibility and mumbled a halting, delirious monologue into his upturned collar. He had not forgotten it to this day, nor understood it. 'The . . . Little Runaround is the way, but the . . . way is not the Runaround . . . we . . . we . . . the church has will . . . will, we . . . it will . . . Li'l Runaround won't . . . neither, unless where the Fox, not nowhere is everywhere, where . . . because he, he's nowhere and ever, everywhere he . . . but the . . . the Runaround isn't nowhere nor is it everywhere . . . rather there where unlike the unlike the Fox . . .'

The important thing was another drink. 'Come on, one more then.'

'Of course. And then?' asked the frog and poured more of the bitter herbal schnapps.

'Well, right, the harbour, you know,' Dmitri said, meanderingly. 'The harbour had been in flames for two days and two nights by then. If I'd known what I was letting myself in for, I'd have stayed in the mountains.'

'Where you tore that trapper to bits?' The frog, goofily enthusiastic, recapped what the wolf had told him every ten minutes. Dmitri took a slug from his glass and carried on. 'Mmpf, that's right. Down there on the docks, the hordes . . . they couldn't frighten me. Who were they anyway? Beggars, banana-boat loaders, other day labourers, and they were standing round the giantess' body just staring, not believing their eyes. So I look upwards and what do I see beyond the glare of the fire?'

'What do you see?'

'A strip of blue. A light. A sign, I think to myself, some kind of weird spell, a claim to ownership. Dangerous spirits, summoned by the insects, you know . . .'

'Like Madame Livienda?'

'That's right, those. They didn't know about it, but us, well, we know . . . they'd all been peasants before they came into the Three Cities. Bloody near desperate to . . . what I mean is, they really wanted to show that they knew what's what. Everyone knew my firesign, no one knew me.' And right then, the frog lit him a poorly rolled cigarillo.

'So, what next?'

'Well, what? The insects had shown they meant business. The mob just stared. I turned away and to make sure they were still afraid of me like earlier, I was growling. Not in a friendly way. I got to the part of the harbour I needed, with no help from them.'

'Where the dreamtankers put in.'

'Yeah.'

'Did you have the wherewithal? For boarding, I mean, for the voyage?'

The wolf answered with a muffled snort, he found the question funny. 'I had tickets. I had a trump card and I dipped it in cold water, to charge it, you know, those battery cards that Izquierda makes. Plasteel, but magnetized. I wolfed down some raw fish, then once I'd paid passage I hid in one of the tankers for a few days to regenerate.'

'Was it big?'

'In the hundreds of tons. Ex-British, crude oil fleet.'

'Quite a ship.'

'Feh. I lay there, dark corner. Gave myself a good shake until the connection formed and the nightmares died down. Aargh-uh, you know, the old song. Poor old me, poor wolf.'

The frog laughed.

'What the hell though, it's all the same. An iron cage, for sure. I was more concerned about the inside of my own . . . well, my headspace, you know.'

The frog nodded respectfully. Inside the head, quantum processors, second generation, only for the select few. 'What a wolf,' said the frog's gaping mouth, silently, 'What a hero!'

'Later I had a look at the transcript . . . the guards stared at me in terror, when I opened the iris . . . during the journey. Whispering, so as not to say anything wrong. Then the fake sky, all the usual ceremonial stuff, like in the Temple of Isotta in fact . . . I knew all that, the avatar looked a bit like a panther, not a wolf at all, and apart from that, how do you say? Humanoid.'

'Why they don't change that . . .'

'Why should they? We can live with a bit of tradition, can't we?'

'I don't know. Sounds like anti-Lionism to me!' the frog grumbled.

'Anti-Lionism, eh, you won't stand for that, hm?' Dmitri teased him.

'I'm a strict legitimist,' said the frog. 'If I can't do something for the king, then I'd rather do nothing at all.'

You, thought the wolf, are a strict frog. If you actually have to do something for anyone else, you'll burst for sure. The frog topped up his glass. He carried on, 'I bossed them about, took charge. Let's be honest, that rabble doesn't deserve any better. The bloody-handed trade and the fourth and fifth porte, they showed me all that, by the by, very crude stuff. Then I went on. While the battery was emptying they put a codemark onto my card, I had that for quite a while afterward, back on shore. They'd given me a jackal stripe. Some kind of innuendo, I suppose. Silly sort of joke.'

'Bloody liberty,' the frog opined. 'I mean . . . for a wolf who's been to the Preference Mountains.'

The wolf's right ear drooped nonchalantly, saying, 'who cares.' Then he yawned and picked up the story. 'I tried on new shapes, new forms, during the journey, in the hold. I was within, in my head, pared right down you might say to a . . . basic shape, a concave wolf body, hairless. Then I began to drink only milk. I was in there for eight hundred astronomic aeons, subjective, until at last they changed the jackal stripe for a better bit of code.'

'A new trump card, like as not?'

'Ace of spades. I went hunting and then I found that the, well, living-system defences were hunting me at the same time—same old story. *Je suis fait pour enregistrer les signaux. Je suis un signal.*'

'*Un orphéeisme d'un ordre de magnitude que . . .*' the frog replied, to show off his learning.

Dmitri Stepanovich Sebassus winked in acknowledgement. His host fell quiet, greedy for more.

'They sent me off to a landscape with . . . one of those realms that are very otherplace. Lots of singing. Lots of firewind. That's supposed to be the answer. A house, a shack, on a borderland beneath black clouds. Signal from the fence post: you seek solitude and to find yourself. The system didn't know anything about me, only these clichés.'

'And you a veteran! A friend of the pipistrelles!'

'So what? I reprogrammed my virtual projector and I cloaked myself, strapped on all the . . . well, what they call the personality.'

'Don't I know it,' nodded the frog. 'Genome, socialization, character.'

'The yellow belts and the brown and the white, and then,' said the wolf with a rather malicious undertone, 'last of all the lie that holds them all together. The lie that am I. A voice called aloud, from the clouds above the level land that stretched away round the hut: "Dmitri, where are you?"'

'Security had found you.'

'Right. I didn't let them take me along just like that, though. Wasn't ready for reality yet. I . . . forced them onto pause for a while, no backup.'

'How could . . .'

'Entered the command manually. My paws had stayed awake, autonomously, autotomic, and I had a keyboard. For a pillow, you see.'

'Paws awake. Eight hundred astronomic aeons, subjective . . . drinking nothing but milk . . . and your paws were awake.' The frog was speechless. If it hadn't gone against any decorum he'd ever learnt, he'd have sunk to the floor, rolled on his back, waggled his limbs and worshipped Dmitri as a god in Gente form.

His customer said dismissively, 'No big deal. I was fast already when I went inside and I only got faster once I was in there. Then, as the humans used to say, I saddled up, left the security behind and I was out of there.'

'The ship . . .'

'Yes, the tanker, I know, could have been destroyed in the meantime. Holed at the waterline, down to Davy, bye-bye. I took the risk. When I came above, up from the hold, the . . .'

'The harbour? The burning harbour?'

'Dust and ashes,' said the wolf. 'Nothing but smoking ruins,' and he gulped down the glass as though it contained nothing stronger than water.

There wasn't a great deal to say to that, so the frog sank into reverent silence for a while.

The wolf turned back to the pivot-screen. After the zander's lecture came the news and comments. The frog found a new topic of conversation in the reports. 'Do you believe all that? About the jungle and the ceramic monstrosities, about . . . Katahomen . . . leandraleal?'

Dmitri raised his right eyebrow. The frog, who was no fool, knew just what that meant and would have kept shtum, except that right at that moment a summary of Westphalia Sophocles Gaeta's words flashed up, and with it a tickertape analysing how the Polyarchs, the badgers and the libertarians were likely to react.

'Really . . . I don't know,' the barkeeper said sourly, 'you'd think the Liberation had never happened. Libertarians? Polyarchs? They're only fronts for the anti-Lionist tendency, I don't trust anyone but Georgescu . . .' Before Dmitri could reply, a new voice broke in: 'Are we still gawping at the fish tank? Can't I get away from that rubbish anywhere?'

It was a female voice.

Dmitri Stepanovich didn't turn round to look at her, even though—or especially because—he felt a sweet pang of curiosity straightaway. The frog puffed himself up, pointedly. 'What do you expect? This is after all the most important news the Gente have . . .'

'What I expect, is a good schnapps, to clean my gullet and help me forget what the Gente are, who are the fishes, who are the frogs,' said the stranger and climbed onto the burgundy barstool, rubbing herself boldly against the wolf's flank as she did so. There was a soft scent to her, a wild child; straightaway Dmitri wanted to have her. There was an old glass mirror hanging at an angle over the chest that held the strong drinks and from the corner of his eye the wolf saw in it the reflection of a strange creature, something like a lynx, feline. He guessed it was a recent modification of *lynchailurus*. The eyes however were those of a reptile. The frog slammed a glass down in front of the stranger, and reptilian too was the tongue which she dipped into the glass, lapping at the priciest tipple to be had anywhere in the Three Cities.

'If you turn that crap off or at least switch over to the sports, I'll buy you a drink,' purred the lynx. When no one responded, she turned up the charm. 'My name's

Clea Dora and I came to this city to have a good time. I was misinformed. The city's dead on its feet.'

'Who thinks that it isn't? Where have you blown in from?' asked the wolf, without looking at her.

'From the Orient,' the stranger whispered into his ear, 'Don't you know the saying—that's where the lynx come from?'

'And the minx,' croaked the frog, butting in, not quite sure yet whether jokes were wanted. 'Just let me have a look at the fish there,'—Dmitri Stepanovich nodded briefly at the screen, by now he was smiling his most charming smile at the stranger—'see how he's going to draw the sting from all the attacks on the Lion, how he'll wrap up the speech with some soothing words. I was enjoying all that earlier.'

'And then?' asked Clea Dora.

'Then I'll help you have a good time and save this city's reputation.'

2. POLYTOPES ARE BETTER THAN FRIENDS

The jungle seemed to know that a world away, the Gente were thinking of it, anxiously.

They wouldn't understand the life that lived in its black earth, its huge trees and steaming swamps. In the foliage and supple limbs, between the hamadryads and the thickets, in the night-dark of the ravines and the frothy forest canopy, the jungle sought the answer to heights and depths, the lustre and the flowers.

When it awoke, it was loud at first, a crescendo of all music that had ever been played, an all-encompassing noise, made of mass extinctions and of rebirth in new and different forms. Green iguanas, four-eyed opossums, caimans and toucans were made anew, changed in pitch and timbre, in their physiosculpture and biochemical nature, their biomass devoured, reordered and excreted by a childlike intelligence that just now awoke in a storm of unearthly laughter: Katahomenleandraleal.

What were these dying, these dead, these resurrected? Not Gente.

Nor were they mindless creatures—they had thoughts, as animals thought before the Liberation.

Their souls sent a high-pitched, squeaking signal into Katahomenleandraleal's inner ear, humbly reminding the titan of the importance of distinguishing inside from outside.

The child/god soon enough decided that the soundscape it had created was annoying.

Is that me, is that my yammer, so demagogic, so rhetorical? It realized that the sounds had created new surroundings and set to work to change it, alloplastics carried out by small brigades of human females, saved from death and scrupulously brainwashed. Did they have any sense of time? Or did the work they performed for Katahomenleandraleal, the clearing, carrying, rebuilding, crowd out what once had been called age, maturity, wisdom? Katahomenleandraleal didn't know. It pondered the problem for a long while.

If they were at work in the temperate zones, thought the god/child, where Cyrus Iemelian Adrian Vinicius Golden dictated to his subjects how (and even why) they lived their lives as Gente, then they could drive coring rods into the trees, take samples and read the rings to see how many years the trees had strained upwards to the light of Sol Invictus. But in the rainforest there were no seasons, so the women could do no such thing.

'Platonic time, regulated time, empty duration without content. Like bodies consisting of nothing but abstract conceptual points, not of any material substrate,' one of the human females said to Katahomenleandraleal, when it interrogated her about the problem.

'Platonic . . .'

'Yes. Philosophy as mathematics and vice versa.' The woman was naked, gleaming. She was in the best of health. Katahomenleandraleal took care of the females, protecting them from hunger, heatstroke, dehydration. The moisture all round was full of pherinfones and pharmacoi, the air itself was a superenriched nutrient.

'Platonic. That,' said the god/child, 'interests me, as a field of knowledge. Empty. Also an interesting concept. Quantity: tell me more of this.'

'Quantity, hmmm.' The woman cleared her throat.

'Yes. I wanted to oppose this concept to that of emptiness, until I realized that there is also such a thing as an empty set, quanta without content. You talk of bodies—duration, extension in Platonic time, the Platonic solids—I wonder whether I might assume such shapes and discard them, so as to have . . . my own life at last. You know, like you people do.'

'No, I'm sorry. I don't know about that,' the human female confessed, surprised that she had come to feel trust towards Katahomenleandraleal. She didn't want to undermine what might be the beginning of a fruitful friendship by pretending to knowledge she did not have.

'You don't know. But you talked about it. Your language knows. Humans know, all of them.'

'Erm, tcha . . . no, hrrm, it's . . . not so simple as that, I'm afraid. Not all humans are . . . are equal. We have . . . had a principle . . . the division of labour. Me, for instance, I'm not a scientist, not a philosopher, not a mathematician. One of those might know, but I . . .' Katahomenleandraleal interrupted her, not with words but with pictures, projecting a pattern directly to her visual centres. She understood that she had to explain what work was and how labour could be divided.

The woman agreed. Katahomenleandraleal wrapped creepers about her, put her into a chemical sleep and took her into itself for consultation. For fourteen days the Ceramican child communed with the living past, interrupted only by Katahomenleandraleal's occasional booming laughter. All the while, the first post-biological superpower devoured, digested, excreted and transformed, launching new waves of life.

In the end Katahomenleandraleal had understood it all.

'Let me sum up: you would do the same thing over and over, for decades at a time, each of you working for yourself but also for all the others.'

'More or less, yes.'

'And you were a . . . composer.'

'You could say that, yes.'

'And you never dyed the hair on your head, it was already white when you were twelve years old, and you removed the hairs on your organ of generation . . . shaved them? Shaved, so that your girlfriend . . .'

'Pardon me, but you're mixing things up. That has nothing to do with my job. The hair . . . that's private.'

'Of course, there was this other division—lateral—running though every human: public and private.'

'Yes.'

'And a job was public.'

'Mhmm. Mine was artistic, so it was quite a lot more public than most.'

'Right. You created music. That's why your thoughtforms were so interesting right away, when it got so . . . loud here, to help me make sense of it all.' Katahomenleandraleal refused to acknowledge that the uproar had had anything to do with its own activities. It had learnt to be ashamed.

'And you only used philosophy and platonics as—what would you call it? Auxiliary . . .'

'Ancillary sciences. For my composing. It's called mathematics, by the way, not platonics.'

'All right, so you only . . . dabbled in these. That's why you don't know whether the Platonic solids . . .'

'Polytopes,' said the composer, since Katahomenleandraleal had given her access to the mathematical tuition databanks stored deep in the cell lattice from the parents that it had devoured. Katahomenleandraleal compared the information from the databanks with its own concept learning and agreed, 'Polytopes. That's the word. So, because of the . . . limitations of labour, you can't solve this problem for me, of whether these . . . polytopes are the kind of body I could assume and discard, to have a biography, such as you and your sisters have.'

'I can only guess. It might be. I mean, I don't have much more to work with than the definitions and axioms in your datastore. Everything that I can access, you can too.'

'I'll take some time to think about it, find out.'

The jungle fell silent, which had never happened before in all natural history.

All that lived there were sore afraid, except the woman who had spoken to Katahomenleandraleal. She took a bath instead, washing herself thoroughly.

An hour and a half later the sounds returned, more muted, more regular. The uproar had given way to an unprecedented sort of sound, sound that thought, counted, computed.

Soon the powerful young intelligence had developed the basics of a new science, postnoumenal incarnational psychology.

To aid it in the task, it created counting frames of stone and wooden stakes, tied with vines and the human women, rodents, parrots and scuttling lizards helped. It used the thirteenth book of *Euclid's Elements*, stored in the catacombs of its memory to investigate the regular three-dimensional convex polytopes: the tetrahedron, the cube, the octahedron, the dodecahedron and the icosahedron. It considers, rejects and proceeds, thought the woman, who had time for such thoughts since she had not been drafted into a labour column. It draws general conclusions from observations and recognizes the law of duality. The tetrahedron, self-dual; the cube, dual to the octahedron; the dodecahedron, dual to the icosahedron.

In the chambers of its memory Katahomenleandraleal found Ludwig Schläfli's ancient classifications, whereby Platonic solids could be easily described and retrieved, and which also enabled investigation of the fearful six-hundred-sided solid in which Katahomenleandraleal saw traces of his parents. It was built of twenty-four octahedra, one hundred and twenty dodecahedra or six thousand tetrahedra, and did not blink.

In the end, the period of study gave rise to music again, such as had been heard when Katahomenleandraleal awoke. Long-tailed monkeys formed four orchestras, posted at crucial watering holes, beneath the crowns of the great central trees and on the lush slopes full of dark, bark-clad columns.

The music had been recovered from the archives. Its long-dead human composer (a man called Iannis Xenakis, who had lived about six hundred years before the Lion's global supremacy) had built a transparent architecture of steel cables at the first performance of the *Polytope de Montréal*, siting points of light inside it that interacted with the scored sound, to show how spatial relations could be altered in a mathematical progression. In the jungle, Katahomenleandraleal copied this using thick, moist vines strewn with heavy, pearlescent drops of water.

The woman who had shown Katahomenleandraleal the path to such artistry saw the lights blazing as night fell and crouched, fearful by now after all, between creeping epiphytes that crept round other creepers.

An animal peered at her through the emerald canopy.

Its eyes gleamed like tiny glowing coals, its incisors shone like ice in the darkness.

It was a portly rodent.

'What's . . . happening out there?' the woman asked, as the animal began to sniff at her. 'What are you doing?'

She knew that the animals out here could speak, even though they were not Gente.

'The communication channels are being improved,' said the animal, there to protect the woman in her hidey-hole and also to stop her from running away. 'They're . . . making good vibrations.'

'Vibrations.'

'Yes, well, like when you tune a piano. Katahomenleandraleal is awaking from slumber. From pondering. It wishes to stoke up competition between, ummm, spontaneous energy emission and Förster energy transfer, in all biological systems. Katahomenleandraleal is tuning up the jungle.'

'Energy . . .'

'It's a simple matter,' the fitch chattered cockily, 'all to do with how an excited molecule can return to a state of rest once it's done its job.'

'Excited molecules,' the woman said and licked salty sweat from her upper lip.

'Yes. Now, this happens either through resonant energy transfer to another molecule, that is, via the spontaneous emission of a photon, or it can be deactivated, that is, return to its state of rest, non-radiatively. These two mechanisms compete everywhere in biology. Fluorescent energy transfer has been used in processes like photosynthesis for millions of years. The ancestors—hehe, yours mostly, mine not so much—also used it in biological tests, to analyse some rather delicate processes, to look at protein interactions or to measure at the nanometric scale . . .'

The composer was silent. And all this, you learnt from my explanations, she thought.

Division of labour.

You make animals into idiot savants. Well, fine, if it leads us to the truth.

The woman couldn't (and wouldn't) see herself as the heir of people who analyzed, unravelled, influenced. Rather, she saw herself as a belated, prodigal, last, lost member of a species almost entirely eradicated from the face of the earth, for not having been able to concentrate on survival. Charming, basically. Lovably clumsy, a little daft. We're all right, in our own peculiar way.

It was a mixed blessing that a few of them survived now in the new, the newest world and they owed it to coincidences that they could not begin to analyze, unravel or influence. For sure, it had something to do with the micro-processes, molecular transmissions and whatnot that the animal had been talking about. God knows, or Satan.

When it was done talking, it looked her up and down for a while with its ember eyes, neither scornful nor pitiful.

Then it said, 'You should only watch programmes with your children that are suitable for their age.'

The woman snorted out a breath, tired and rather offended. Then she said, 'You know what, I only watch programmes that are suitable for queer superannuated sex offenders. Not that you or any other living creature knows what that might mean.'

'Dodgy grammar,' scolded the rodent. Then its starkly masked face vanished into the pitch black tangle of undergrowth.

The woman thought of people who were no longer there and of one person in particular.

At some point she fell asleep. Then she dreamt of fern-like fans secreted from female bodies, of gaping wounds, of red–orange boats with faulty motors and of silver people crowding into them to set sail, because they had no other choice, on poisoned oily seas. Go to the ant, the flickering skies declared, thou sluggard, consider her ways and be wise if you can possibly manage it. The ant is a centaur in a world of dragons. This is nothing but a goodnight story meant to help you through your long oblivion, for when you awake in the morning, you must fight.

A fuzz formed over her closed eyelids, like the fuzz that covers the long lines that poets work. Thus she did not see the changing lights that otherwise would have waked her too soon. Her brain physiology was primitive, waking up to light came to her more naturally than waking to sound, just as her cognitive models were unfortunately better suited to believing in gods than to understanding the accurate claims of the sciences.

The grass and the flowers round her, the bark and the leaves began to shake and vibrate, waking the sleeping woman at last. It was Katahomenleandraleal, who spoke to herself and to all who heard, 'Now I know what shape my life shall take. I am a woman, am female, have chosen the first of my corporeal forms.'

'Platonic, eh?' the human female snapped, rubbing sleep from her eyes.

'Anything but,' the goddess replied.

Insects showed the way to a clearing, grown with moss. There stood a doe-brown leather sofa. The woman tottered across to it, still a little fuddled, and lay down, stretching her stiff limbs. She looked through the few gaps in the tree canopy and up to the sky. Now, everything was possible once more.

'You're happy, hey?' the goddess asked the human female, wheedling.

'You too?' Not a bad response.

'Yes. I know now more about myself than I did before, which is good. I have a gender, I already had a name, and I still don't yet have a species to belong to, to call me blood of their blood. There's more work to be done.' It was a pleasant alto voice and thrummed deep in her bones as she lay on the sofa. 'And I want to thank you. I know that you don't see it, but you are in many respects better than me. Just consider the miracle that you have a species first of all, to call you blood of their blood, and then a gender, and only then a name.'

Silence.

'You have a name,' repeated Katahomenleandraleal, 'and I do not know it. What should I call you?'

Among the Gente, under the Lion's rule, the woman thought, under Cyrus Iemelian Adrian Vinicius Golden, no one would ask me that. When, she wondered, did we humans squander that advantage, that folk call us by name? Who was it in fact who gave us the old commandment, to have dominion over the earth and to call every living creature, every beast of the field and every fowl of the air by their name?

She remembered the census, the lengths they had gone to—light traps set out at night to trap the insects for collection, the crowns of the trees sprayed with insecticide to gather all the beetles, the bugs fell as rain upon the nets spread out beneath, remembered lions and leopards, photographed from open jeeps that drove in parallel across the whole heat of the savannah, remembered the polling and culling of birds, snails by the bucketful . . . and now, she thought, I have reached the end of a wall that I never expected would end. Shall I take a look round the corner?

Now I have a goddess and belong to her. A new incarnation, a birth and rebirth—how did we say back when I was still Catholic? *Ave verum corpus.*

Of course I remember, Mary Beth's music, Elgar's music. The choir of Worcester Cathedral. The ceramic choir. Ecce opus. Rapid improvisations on the organ, vibrant and floating free, the somatic counterpoint . . . she gave her reply, there in the polytope jungle, sat up on the sofa and wrapped her arms about herself, 'You should call me Späth. Cordula Späth,' and she thought, *Geometria una et aeterna est in mente Dei refulgens.*

'Thank you, Frau Späth,' said Katahomenleandraleal.

1. A HIGH AND LONELY DESTINY

'Are you solvent, my dear Ape?'

Of all possible questions, this was the one that Sdhütz Arroyo the orang-utan had least wished to hear again so soon. An echo? Sadly not.

Was this why he had left the financial service, hung up his harness and retired, so that the old questions could come back to taunt him? Am I hearing right, or am I still in the otherspace of major transactions?

Sdhütz Arroyo sat in front of huge windows, the breadth of an old world altarpiece, in the panoramic restaurant on board a great dirigible airship that glittered in its ionized envelope. Instead of rising to the taunt straightaway, he sipped at his daiquiri, as if to say 'leave me in peace, get out of here, please be a hallucination, don't ask me anything.'

With six hundred Gente on board, the airship floated along the Caucasus air route, there and back, over and again, to no particular purpose—that is, sheerly for the six hundred passengers' enjoyment. Normally, any guest who had boarded such a pleasure cruise unaccompanied was left in peace during the journey. Anyone who wished to send a pherinfonic message or to slip in to visit in person, would have to overcome security measures that easily matched the best that Georgescu could boast in her garrison forts.

No entry to unauthorized persons. Clearly that didn't count for the fox that sat down on a free cushion cube next to the dignified old ape. The fox was tiny and looked as though it had popped up from nowhere. Sdhütz Arroyo reckoned that it was ten centimetres tall at most. The animal's lurid bright-orange coat contrasted painfully with the ape's handsome rust-red pelt. The little beast asked again, brazenly, in a piercing voice, 'Have you got the readies, old fellow? Solvent? Are you in good wealth?'

The orang-utan sighed and looked out of the window at the world below, which seemed to have lost all the innocence that the gentle dawn had heralded a moment ago. If I must keep my word, he thought, if I must come out of retirement for his sake, as soon as he shows up, this despot, my dearly despised old boss, my lord and master for as long as I live, and if I must accept 'special tasks' as we agreed, then at least I will do it glibly—after all I am one of the very few who even know that he's still alive, the old moneybags, the giant of finance from the Lion's earliest days, the Fox who was the Lion's paymaster, who could carry him about in his pocket even today, if he wanted to, if he had pockets.

Time for a flippant question. 'Who wants to know? Is that really you, boss?'

'Ach no, I only look like this so that you know who sent me. The boss is . . . rather more solvent than I am,' said the little wretch (so, he was only an errand boy) and his words hinted at the unwholesome rumours that surrounded Ryuneke.

Ryuneke Nowhere. Of all those who had put the Lion's slogan into practise, the financier had been the most radical. 'We will make evolution into mere volition.' Like many Gente, once he had bid an unsentimental farewell to his human form, he inhabited a mammalian body at first. He had been a fox, but just as the second stage of speciation was getting underway, he soon grew impatient with corporeality as such and his own in particular. 'What use is it to me? We've done away with the old stupidities of fixed and variable capital and replaced it with a new mechanism of means and ends measured directly in energy usable by living beings. We needed money to get it started, so I supplied the money. In certain backward regions where we are at work'—according to the chronicles, the Fox often spoke in the *pluralis maiestatis* as well as in first person singular and in this he was like the Lion (and indeed even today his face could be seen on some of the few coins and banknotes still in circulation, not as often as the Lion's, but much more so than any of the others)—'the general law of equivalence will still obtain, until we have really broken down the taxonomic boundaries, and I will therefore continue to intervene even if that means taking no action. But we use money in order to abolish it and I want to do the same with bodies. Am I supposed to dawdle along down here in this dull world? My dear Gente, that is too slow for me, it reminds me too much of the Monotony and of human bondage, the angels standing guard before Paradise, the expulsion. Do you want that age back again? Expending physical strength directly at the social base, to enable all kinds of crap to be continuously over-produced and then the whole dialectical ding-dong of general wealth and individual labour? You've just grown your tails, do you want them tugged every two minutes? Value is worthless. Brothers and sisters, I want to be the poorest and the richest at once, I don't want to own a single working machine and I want to reach the rarefied point where a person consists solely of the idea of what he could be. *Potentialis!*'

The Lion, it is said, teased him with the answer 'Rynuneke Nowhere—that's what we should call you from now on. Do you want to incarnate as a spray?' The name stuck, but only a few knew the Fox's reply, amongst them number Sdhütz Arroyo, who had been present during the conversation. 'Not a bad idea.'

The last financial favour that Ryuneke did the Lion was the famous fisc for the standing army, supplied by a newly developed system of purely military agronomics worked out in close cooperation with the green badger Georgescu. Later, Lasara deduced several fundamental truths about Gente civilization from this project. After that, the old Fox vanished.

The higher functionaries of his increasingly immaterial and time-independent empire included the orang-utan, members of the supervisory board, shareholders and others. They only learnt of their dismissal via pherinfonic letters, delivered at leisurely intervals over two dozen years after the Fox's disappearance.

The first lustrum after his own discharge was sheer torture for the ape. He had sworn to perform 'further services and special tasks' and spent the years in a state of nerve-wracking paranoia. Where was the boss and when would he activate the reserve clause, the codicil to Sdhütz's retirement? The ape read the pherinfonic seal of his goodbye letter over and again, with foreboding. 'One day I may need you again and a few other loyal colleagues such as the dragonfly Philomena, now that she has left Lady Livienda and entered the king's service directly. You will be contacted at the appropriate moment.'

Stocks, infrastructure, logistics, large computers and access to computing time—in his day, the Fox gave away much of his capital, mostly to shipyards and ports. A few of them pursued his favourite project, to build huge Habbakuk–class carrier ships of solid ice that could be melted with a pinprick but not by heat. There were some successes.

The ape Sdhütz Arroyo spent five years on edge, plagued by stomach upsets, watching mountain streams, rising smoke, oil fires, the soapy film on puddles, eddying breezes, cloud patterns, convection cells and anything else where fluid dynamics were at work. He knew that Ryuneke would wring the new technologies for every drop of sublimation.

He was almost disappointed. This poison dwarf here, was that all there was to see?

'I'm only a puppet sent to tell you where to go, you old crock.'

The orang-utan groaned like an old door creaking. He scratched his right armpit and then tipped the rest of his drink half down his throat, half into his chest hair.

He looked at the wide window, considered the condensation drops on the pane, each an unwinking eye. 'Where is he then? The boss?'

'It's like people say. Ryuneke Nowhere. They might just as well say, Ryuneke Everywhere. He is where you suspected, in fluids and gases. He has to watch out that he's not several at once, or he'd queer his own pitch.'

'How do you know where I suspected?'

'Weren't you looking for him? Didn't you set up fishing routines in the pher-infonet and in the water, among the Atlanteans?'

'A drop in the ocean,' the orang-utan said lamely.

The errand-fox answered earnestly, 'When he's water, then self-evidently he is a different water from the water that might surround him.'

'Different water.'

'Exactly.'

'And I'm supposed to find him from hints like that? Should I report for duty?'

'Find him? By no means. No one can find him, that's the point. He differs from normal water, which keeps his supporting substance together, but this difference can only be detected by instruments that only he can afford. And when he's air, or magma, the same applies. Wherever he is, he's like oil in water, immiscible with the medium but surrounded on all sides.'

'And his whole person is . . .'

'Oh no,' scoffed the messenger, much amused. 'Whole personhood, he's well beyond that. All he needs is some kind of hook in the material world, an anchor, a lure, whatever you call it. A teensy snatch of memory, a signal flag. Pardon the naval metaphors, he loves those. When the anchor replicates itself and properly follows certain prescribed rules, then it inevitably creates a pattern, which is what he was the last time he was here, his signature, his self, so you can forget about the, hehe, whole person.'

'Smashing.'

'All tested beforehand.'

'Replication. Nowhere and everywhere. Concepts. And how does he actually get things done, how does he implement . . .'

'Imprints. Sooner or later creatures like you or me will breathe him in, or drink him and then he gets to work changing our microphysiology, then our thoughts, and then if he needs to, he can actually come back to consciousness through us for a while. Then when he vanishes again because he's finished his business down here, he only repeats the original diffusion.'

'Just like that,' Sdhütz grinned, as though in pain.

'Are you happy? Any more questions?' asked the errand-fox, who, Sdhütz Arroyo suddenly realized, had not introduced himself.

Any more questions? No, he had to admit, and he nodded thoughtfully. He had all the answers and they were typical Ryuneke answers—true but useless.

'Fine. Now listen,' said the errand-fox and at the same moment the orang-utan realized that the animal was not really flesh and blood and hair but was made of ice, cunningly coloured by refractive indices and angle of light incidence, so that its surface seemed gaudy orange, 'and when you've got it, please take the cocktail umbrella from your drink and . . . poke me behind the right ear. I really don't want to exist for any longer than strictly necessary.'

'Ehh.'

'This world drags at me. I've inherited a taste for non-being from my father.'

'Your father, the . . . what does he want from me now?'

'What he wants? He wants to be able to lay hands on his investments. One has just matured.'

'Which?'

'New Heroism. It's in pherotainment, you'll have heard of it.'

Ah, thought Sdhütz, the pherinfonic theatre for the lazy and stupid of all Three Cities. He knew the trend that had given rise to the craze for 'New Heroism'—some random Gente wandering about the place helping the helpless, shooting their actions on pherinfonic register and broadcasting it all over. Do-goodery and spectacle, so fresh you can smell it.

'He's got a safe bet in three idols. Soon enough the young folk in the civilized zones will think more of them than of anyone heretofore, they'll be more famous than the Lion himself. I'm telling you, by the time the war comes, everyone will know their names. A horse, a white tiger and a ferret . . .'

'No, no, no,' the old orang-utan shook his head, 'drop it. Don't tell me. The war . . . what can . . . how . . . I mean, what does he want me to do, particularly?'

'Ah, the nub of it all, the orang-utan Sdhütz and his whole person,' the icefox nodded. 'He wants you as back-up. A redundancy measure. You are to accompany someone who officially doesn't have a companion and the three heroes will distract our dear Gente from what this someone gets up to.'

'Someone.' The orang-utan chewed at the word like at a lemon.

'A wolf. He thinks he's something special. Should be easy to stop him from noticing that he's only a thread in the great web of fate. The king . . . will send him on his mission soon. You'll follow him, make sure he doesn't do anything stupid. And you'll report what happens.'

'Who should I . . . ?'

'To Philomena. Me. Tell Ryuneke the Fox himself, if you have to, if you can. Whoever you report to, don't worry, someone will be there to listen. Are we agreed?'

'Not agreed,'—the orang-utan pulled himself together—'but we're done.'

The fox cub leant his head to one side and looked meaningfully at the cocktail umbrella.

Indignant but obedient, the orang-utan took the wooden stick in his supple fingers and stuck it into the messenger's ear where he had been told. The tiny fox began to melt immediately.

The sun went down behind the mountain range.

Sdhütz Arroyo was no longer interested. He raised his right hand and called over a flunky, 'Something stronger, please and quickly. Then get a rope ready and let me down, at the next available habitation. Fun's over. I must get to work.'

2. THE CATACOMBS OF MEMORY

The glass cabinets stood in dismally long rows that became even longer when you set off down them in search of something.

Luckily, the air conditioning was working, or it would have been lethal to look for anything here, in the summer's murderous heat.

Copper-engraved views of calyx flowers, numismatic cabinets, astrogational instruments, the odd krater in the scrolled style, tanks full of crystalline viral foam, watercolours showing the gardens of palaces that had long since ceased to exist, cannon overgrown with moss, memory crystals, nonalgos, broken time machines with wrecked gearboxes, green broderie jackets, document storage-clip machines, microfilms, books with sweatmarks down the spine, fine golden vessels hastily heaped here during the Liberation, helmets from the last pope's Swiss guard, ammonites smeared with dried toothpaste, jasperwork, telescopes, a one-eyed bust of Nefertiti, bottles full of old dread.

Storikal, who believed he was a donkey, was trying hard to look learned. 'It may weah, weh, well be no eeyore coincidence that the artistic forms of the bing-bong Baroque are fff hu-ho found in precisisetely the epoch, rikki-tikki, also marked by the, the, the Enlightenment, that ahh is to say, the art forms' haw-haw-hee-haw rich detail and their bombast hopp, happ, hupp, happily match, although we yahallala might intuitively think otherwhichwaywise, hee-haw, the concern to do away ipso-pipso with . . .'

The poodle stopped where he was, his patience had run out. 'Listen, Storikal, just stop it, okay? Don't try to impress me. We in the Department of Antiquities,' he coughed, hacked, seemed for a moment uncertain how to finish his sentence, then recovered himself, 'we in the Department of Antiquities, especially in the Balaam department, can't afford to be choosy. Bene Gente's not for us, worse luck. And you, my dear Storikal,' the endearment stank of ill will, 'can afford it even less. You made a poor exit from the art scene, over in yon stinking backwater that thinks it's the centre of the world. A poor exit, I think we can safely say a shameful one.'

'Ah-ha-yaaaa, I'm hee-haw nobobble-zabzim not chorr, choosy,' Storikal conceded, straining for a last scrap of dignity like a whale at krill.

'You'd like to be,' the poodle sneered between clenched teeth, 'but you're not, we can agree on that.'

Easy for you to act clever, thought Storikal, if you think where I've come from, it's a wonder that I can even speak in full sentences—my mother always used to say that I 'look like just like your father' and in forty years I was never able to stop her saying 'like' twice over, the idiot . . .

'What are you brooding about?' the poodle demanded. 'Have you any special demands? Want higher wages? A castle in Spain?'

'No hee-haw, yeah-h-h-h-h, that's to say, ayy-ayy, no,' Storikal said meekly. The truth was that a job as curator here was pretty much his last chance.

'Well, good. I'll fetch the phial with your recognition code, it's also a binding contract for our institution. We'll do the rest once you've been coded in . . . hmm.'

Great, that too, he's going to shackle me chemically to his barmy department, just because I am desperate enough to apply for a job here. The delusional donkey was thinking to himself, thoughts not totally off the mark: education, culture, law, politics, the military, for us they're all biological functions, and the luminaries in the Borbruck Torus are dickering over whether that's a social advance or retrogression.

Sodomism, now that would be nice. Each for himself. Who's provincial here?

Drifting, particulate motes danced the gentle dance of Brownian motion in the arcades and Storikal stood there looking about the hangar, while the chief custodian's footsteps trotted echoes away into the distance. In front of him, on a low podium in front of a large-format *Primavera*, stood a furry teacup which spoke to something in the donkey. The fur reminded him of his own.

He went closer, close enough to smell. The installation smelt repletely of fresh bread. Next to it lay a book, to which he now turned and found it could be opened and paged through by a wink-interface. So it wasn't from the Monotony, it was from the aeon after the Liberation. Storikal was interested enough to read words from somewhere in the middle of the grey clothbound volume, 'Storikal was interested enough to read words from somewhere in the middle of the grey clothbound volume.'

A-ha, thought the would-be custodian, one of these productions tricked up by the pipistrelles in the Preference Mountains—recursivity, textuality, and he found his guess confirmed in the next few lines. 'A-ha, thought the would-be custodian, one of these productions tricked up by the pipistrelles in the Preference Mountains—recursivity, textuality,' and he found his guess confirmed in the next few lines. "A-ha, thought the would-be . . ."

Pretty, but pointless: a Quine turd.

Storikal could hardly imagine the state of mind for which such tomfoolery could even for a moment seem omniscient, but that's what awed visitors to the caves would whisper.

How everything is connected . . . What do I care?

'You and the empty book, you go well together,' laughed a stuffed clown above him. It was a wooden-headed mannikin, fixed to the crystal ceiling with long nails and black clamps. It giggled, hard, cold and janglingly. The donkey felt fear in the marrow of his bones.

'Shut your mouth, Saint Oswald!' snapped the poodle, who had just returned (his name was Vil, Val . . . Veloursass Votiv, that was it, Storikal thought, he had introduced himself, I ought to use his name when I talk, that'll soothe his feelings).

The mannikin tried jitteringly to free himself from the clamps. It was an empty threat. The clown would have died straightaway if he had managed to get free. The poodle stood up on his hind legs and neatly prepared the injection that would confirm the donkey's terms of service.

'Three little glockenspiel . . .' the clown began to sing in a shocking, bad voice.

The poodle growled, 'Shut it! Or you get the electroshock!'

The clown fell quiet, the needle jabbed, Storikal felt slightly giddy.

It passed quickly. The poodle said, 'And what are you, in fact? I looked at your application and I've compared it with your biopatterns. You say you're a donkey? You're no donkey. You're a mule or a hinny or whatever.' Right, that's how it was. Storikal felt a new wave of shame. I 'looked like just like' my father and what was he? A stallion. A horse. Or was my mother a mare and my father a donkey?

'Anyroad, that means you're infertile,' muttered Veloursass Votiv, wrapping the gear back into the blue velvet cloth he'd taken it from, 'So that means we won't have to feed your family along with you. What, you've got wobbly knees? You've got a stupid stare, my friend. I tell you so that no one else has to.'

The clown snickered softly, the poodle grunted and looked upwards rancorously, then said in a dismissive lecturing tone, 'He shot an American president, would you believe? Then the priestesses of the Temple of Isotta sanctified him for it and now he'll hang here for all eternity. All animals are equal, but some are more feeble than others.'

'An eeyore-bamabble American . . .'

'You wouldn't know, why should you? Something like the Lion, umm, a world-mover, a lord of men, a bigwig. Hecuba. And you're still knock-kneed, Mr Mule.'

'I . . . it's . . . wackwack all right by hee-haw now, Votiv.' That did the trick. The boss panted, stressed out. Pondered for a moment. And said, 'Your first client is here soon. A good one, by the way. Bright-eyed, bushy-tailed, bulging wallet. He's waiting . . .'

'Where?'

'Up and down the City Road, in and out the Eagle, how should I know, just go through the treasure chambers. He'll be there somewhere, dividing his hoof.'

'Dividing . . .'

'He's a hog. From that filthy nest of bridges out there, the name's, one moment,' Veloursass Votiv snorted, gulped, snuffled, looked about quizzically and then found the scent, hanging in the air, and said with a happy smirk, 'Thingum, Hubert Hilbert . . . Hébert Ransom, that's it.'

'What does he want?'

'Ask him yourself. Tcha!' Votiv harrumphed, brushed some non-existent dirt from his paws onto the shining polished floor and scurried off round the corner.

The client whom the poodle had announced appeared under the clown. The scuttling hog was well turned out, in a tuxedo and with gold-rimmed spectacles perched on his snout. 'You're Storikal?'

'At your yucklegunk service.'

'I'm looking for models.'

'Models. Ye-heahhh. What brubrubble sort of models hee-haw?'

'Ermm, architectural . . . old . . . they told me that I could find'—his sly little eyes cast about, as though challenging Storikal to be of some help, before he found whatever it was more quickly on his own—'some handy plaster-cast models, from any continent, from the last epoch.'

'Hooohooohmmhee-haw . . . any . . . thing in particular?' Storikal asked magnanimously.

The scuttling hog laughed. 'Quite particular, since you ask! United States of America, they called the place during the late Monotony.' Now it was Storikal's turn to glance round. Was the clown moving, making faces? His head hung on his chest, asleep.

'And where hop-hoffle hee-haw exactly?' With gentle shrugs of his shoulders, and twitching his hind legs, the mule led the scuttling hog round a sharp bend in the shelving and towards one of the hangars. Storikal had already caught the scent of the information that Ransom sought, the poodle's inoculation had worked fast.

'It was called Princeton. It's a laboratory, which they gave up on too early, as you might say, if what I . . . learnt elsewhere is correct. Lewis Thomas Laboratory for Molecular Biology and Biotechnology.'

'Ahhha! Ahaaaa, yaahaa! Follow guffle grok me, it's flurx right here.'

1. LOVERS ARE BETTER THAN MUSIC

He waited in the hotel where they had first met at the bar.

Dmitri Stepanovich paced back and forth, half downcast and half atremble, shaken by a stormcloud of eagerness, by the side of the bed. He didn't know whether the bed was enough for both of them.

How do I want thee, what is in my veins?

The air's full of the scent of lilies and so's my poor head, he sniffed and thought. He bared his teeth.

Then he looked down at the palms of his new hands. Human qualities, human limbs, human accessories—Clea Dora had begun that and he had followed her lead.

Her childlike glee in changing her body structures, infectious and a little bit taboo. Let's play human being. Innocent and underhanded all at once, like her whole person. By now he called her 'my Li'l Ly'x, you're the only way I get any fun around here, my dearest.'

When he said that, she would screw up her nose, saying that the nickname was too much like a joke in poor taste, Li'l was a liturgical term reserved for the *ens ineffabile* that the hawk-headed vestals in the Temple of Isotta worshipped in these days and funaround was too close to the Runaround. 'Don't be so sacrilegious.'

'Why not? Just because your people,'—he meant the Polyarchs, knowing that Clea Dora voted for that party—'think that to be a true culture we need religion and worship? Like in the Monotony?'

'As if you didn't worship that blasted Lion.'

'That's different.'

She hissed. 'Of course—your own "religion and worship" deserves respect, but other people's . . .'

No, Dmitri held that piety smothered all thought, chokes off its air. He didn't say so but instead teased Clea Dora, 'If I had a nose like yours, my wicked little kitten, I wouldn't go on about respect. One look at your face says what you are: impudent as all-get-out. No Runaround or what-you-like can help you there.'

'Impudent? *Moi*?'

'Face and features. You're making fun of everyone, whatever their kin and kind . . . your whiskers! Sideburns! The tufts on your ears! That Manx nub above your bum! Your reptile eyes!'

'I'm the Lizard King, I can do anything.'

'Well, yes,' he conceded and thought, very much in love, She's got what I've been missing ever since I left the pack. *Serdtse*. Sweet peril, you.

She purred and snorted. 'Pff-poooh. What are you after, Lone Wolf?'

'You. With all your daft ideas and your taste for ridiculous outfits.' He lifted his hands so that she could see what he meant.

Many Gente who could afford it were now walking about as anthropomorphs. In the Animal Empire (even Clea thought this was a pretty stupid name for the world that the Gente had made) on the old continents, folk slowly began to take seriously the news of the horror in the Amazon jungle, and that was part of it: they're building humans over there? Do they have some edge over us?

If nothing else, they had those opposable thumbs. Good, we'll have them too.

In fact, it was what pleased Dmitri most, of all the recent fashions: hands.

Even if he didn't much like to remember his part in destroying the hands of so many homines sapientes.

The wolf reckoned however that the classic model didn't have enough fingers. So he changed that.

He had six on each hand now, Ly'x had seven.

He had implanted transceivers intradermally at the ball of his thumb and between the fingers, so that now he could literally read his palm and see what other Gente had sent to his scentmail address.

Now though, in the long minutes of waiting, the chiromancy was silent.

Would the message he was waiting for never arrive, between his line of life and of destiny? It didn't. 'Maybe we've got bad reception,' he told his reflection and barked softly. Another 'bad joke' (Clea Dora), this time at the expense of the Monotony's electronic comms networks (which had been the first targets during the Liberation—'child's play' according to Georgescu, who had coordinated the attacks).

I must be on edge, thought Dmitri, realizing that only the bed and the curtains had heard his joke. And the curtains and the bed, he growled, know quite well how stupidly in love I am. Pacing upright up and down doesn't help any more than pacing on all fours: there's something learnt.

He looked again at the lines on his palms. Apart from being able to hold things and communicate with any language-capable entity, the hands were also storage convertors for UV light. Right now there wasn't anything to convert, in here. The wolf was left in the dark. Stupid display, light up! Dmitri suddenly thought, The whole wide well-appointed world is against us, and he knew as well that this was only an attack of paranioa—no it wasn't, he decided next, all things really did conspire against him and he was in love. Every binder pheromone, every protein fold, every little sculpture of deoxyribose nucleic acid in the Lion's domains had after all been assigned a corresponding digital component, twisting, interlinking cryptoglyphs yielded output recording everything that a living beast or breathing thing wrote, spoke or sent in the Three Cities and environs. But this evening none of that seemed to be working, the whole wired world had ebbed away, it seemed, a long, withdrawing roar, if Clea Dora did not call.

'Right then. Right, so. This is ridiculous. Well, light, please.'

He eyed his reflection dubiously, wondering if he looked good. Then the wolf could no longer endure his own impatience and left the room. Will she like me, if I hold her tonight, fix her with a glare and give her a good thrashing?

He entered the corridor, which was tricked out with bioluminescent patches. Feeling light-headed and drained, Dmitri hurried down the spiral staircase to the foyer, where the reception lizards on desk duty watched him mistrustfully, since there were few guests these days. Not much going on in town for strangers at the moment, so who are you and what are you doing here? He considered sending Clea Dora a billet-doux, as she wasn't getting in touch or leaving messages. He could tell her that he was still interested and getting more so every moment.

In the past few months they had sent one another a regular swarm of such messages. Her last message but one, with some very frivolous *synaesthetica* attached for emphasis, had been, 'What are you up to, dashing about the the world? Trying to outdo Ryuneke?'

He had replied, 'You can reach me anytime, in the fruit flies' garden.'

He had surprised himself with this flourish. Earlier he would never have thought to make such a lyrical allusion to their hidden channels of communication. Paradoxically, he felt far closer to her when they were so far apart, speaking indirectly, exchanging messenger substances. Granted that it wasn't really indirect, that it was only explicating the already implied, just as human beings had presumably never thought of Turing or Shannon back in the days when they wrote their emails. The Gente generally didn't think about the technology behind their chemical communication when they set molecules aflutter, tickling and flirting. The secret in the fruit flies' garden was the pheromonic mist that *Drosophila melanogaster* sprayed round themselves during their mating behaviour, first systematically studied by *Homo sapiens* ethologists, then by their molecular biologists armed with chromatographs. Thus the first steps, five and a half centuries ago, at first analytic and then constructive, synthetic, on the path to today's biotic communion, yond softest breath that carried their words.

Clea's answer to his little poem about the garden, her last message so far: 'Just wait until I get to you!'

But she didn't get to him, not straightaway.

She was making him wait.

When he thought that, he realized again how little they actually knew about one another, save that they both travelled a lot, that they were cultivated and well-mannered and yearned to throw culture and manners to the winds, and that they were not likely to be bored in one another's company—if in fact everything was as real as he hoped.

He walked in the cool of the evening, in the dim alleyway. Neon lights, vacuous and lovely, greeted him.

Above him, the stars, in the patterns inherited from man, the Swan, the Little Bear, and quite right too, faithful watchers that had been at their posts long before mankind. Hold on though—have they? Have constellations always been there?

Before his journey to the coast, to the bonewall, Dmitri Stepanovich Sebassus had been able to set his gaze so keen that he could see the North America Nebula, upper left, towards the Swan. Then he had had the Preference Mountain pipistrelles remove this optical upgrade. He reckoned: you need not see everything that you know about (but you should know about everything that you can see—limit your skills, then set them free).

There you are, my Lynx, my rose!

He saw her sitting in a taxi that passed by slowly. A deer was driving. The wolf stopped short at a fearful thought: what if Clea were to sink her white teeth into the driver's neck? He nearly believed that he could already see the bite, the wound in the throat, and he sniffed as though to smell the sweet blood.

His beloved was hunched in a posture that even during the Monotony had been known as the hunters' crouch, she was scanning and watching, she saw him standing there outside, she smiled. Whence had come such blood-boltered thoughts? Perhaps from her nearness or her breath.

From appetite, from the craving held in leash.

Then she looked for her belongings on the seat next to her, cash or something, she stooped—what did they say—upon her prey, that was a term of venery, meaning she bent down. This taxi was a marvellous excuse for being so exquisitely late. The wolf felt dizzy with irony.

His Ly'x got out and then tripped, charmingly. Her bag fell to the ground onto the pockmarked asphalt of the old street. The car behind her leapt into motion, as though escaping from something. Not leather, thought Dmitri, this bag she's just dropped, it's jute. A plastic bottle rolled out and stopped at Dmitri's hooves (he was going through his satyr phase). The wolf bowed down, picked up the bottle before it could roll into the gutter. He handed it to Clea as though it were a bouquet of roses. 'Such a civil civet!' laughed the Ly'x and then she sneezed and said, 'So you've put your mark on that as well, your fingerprints, pawing it about, but you won't answer my calls. Dumb wolf.'

'What calls?' He squinted at his palms, checking.

There they were. Two missed calls. Obviously it wasn't only her car that was late, but her pherinfonics as well. Sweet nothings, messages with no purpose other than to prod him into answering. So she hadn't actually been sure that he would keep their tryst.

He liked that.

He stumbled over his words. 'Shw . . . shall we go and get something to eat, in thing, in town? 'Cause we'd better erm take your things upstairs.' He wondered whether that was too obvious—maybe she didn't want to go to his room, at all? Where did she live in fact? She can't have a flat here in Borbruck, or they'd hardly have met one another in a hotel that time. Or maybe they would have?

He watched her shoulders, the breasts like pears under a white gent's shirt, her rapid sexy breathing.

She laughed and he thought, I know, I can smell it, she lives nowhere in the Three Cities, but down south, among the reptiles, the pumping bodies.

He said, 'This way, Fiametta,' a new name that she had been using now for a couple of weeks to sign her messages, a tiny flame, that she preferred to 'Li'l Ly'x'.

On the stairs she took a long swig from her water bottle. He watched the dapples on her throat, beneath her ears, which flicked as though she were listening for prey in the undergrowth.

He stood at the door and let the entry system scan his eyes. They went in.

He asked, 'What will . . . do you want to drop your stuff? Leave it all here.'

Clea Dora, Ly'x, Fiametta, said, 'I shan't be going . . . back where I was before, tonight, if that's what you're asking.'

He took her bag, jogged it in his hand, held it up in front of her, his expression said, 'That's heavy, you've got your sponge bag in there.'

'My overnight bag, to put the water bottle in,' she said laughing. The lynx.

They kissed and scratched at one another with the claws on their almost human fingers.

The south, he thought, but there was no solemn disrobing now, only a ruck and a rustle, tearing hotly, urgent clasps. No, stop, go on, yes, there, over there.

But they wanted to go and eat. We want to see, here on the balcony under the Swan and the Great Bear, and we want to be seen, in town, amongst people. We want to surround ourselves with ancient ritual, the bonds of friendship. And they had gasped and panted and learnt how, and their gasps became more musical, clearer somehow, a unison, in rhythm. He's a stranger and I've known him so well, and he wraps himself round me like a new gown, I could almost believe he is two wolves, three, more, the lynx thought. She felt his whisper and heard his touch and she laughed.

He hadn't felt this good since he left the pack. I'm here, with her, werewolf, wolfman, hu-man, who-man, who-am I and who'm I with?

There was a tattoo on her left arm, on a patch shaved free of fur, a pattern that danced and held soft sounds within, encoded from a summer's day. He could hear bees hum and water plashing when he licked that spot.

'I got that done when I passed my doctoral defence,' she said, his lover. 'A degree certificate.' ·

'My sweetheart. So ambitious!' he said.

They walked together through the empty market halls. He knew how to find the hidden little bistros that clung inside the city walls like mussels to a rock.

'In the old days, human days, it was much harder to enter academia,' Ly'x lectured, putting on a know-all tone. 'Back then you really had to fight for your ideas and your results. A doctoral dissertation was always a polemic.'

'What would you like to eat? Dumb hare? Shrew?'

They had to choose, the paths diverged here, off to different restaurants.

'Actually, I'm not that fond of eating.'

'You're not a photosynthusiast like the badgers, are you? Living off light and air and trace minerals from the topsoil?'

'No, listen for a moment. I don't like the idea that something has to die just so I can keep my metabolism ticking over. My father had . . . has different ideas.' She'd never spoken about her family before. He pricked up his ears. 'He used to slaughter the food for us, humans too. That was when the rift still ran deep . . . between humans and the . . . Liberated. When it was Esprit, he would put them onto tables and invite the dogs and cut off the heads with this huge knife. Cut a T-shape in the ribcage. Sometimes he'd be slicing and sawing for hours before there was anything to eat.'

'No wonder you . . .'

'There used to be humans who wouldn't eat animals, did you know? Vegetarians.'

'A religion.'

'Some kind of ethical epiphany, at least.'

She's not leaving tonight and that's my epiphany, thought the wolf and said, 'Religion, politics . . . the whole heap of crap. Humans, what can you do? But we've still got to deal with it as well. The works.'

'Sex,' said Clea Dora, as the rice arrived, 'should bewilder, or something's not right.'

'And rice should be sticky,' he said.

She agreed.

Conversation, capricious, twists, turns and twines. 'I've done it with twenty mice—females—and with seals,' said Fiametta, 'and once with a bear. He was an artist, can you believe it? Like Stanz the ape. He had to take off his long johns first, oil paints smeared all over them, they were probably his best work.'

They were besotted, their conversation floated above the table, dancing in the light of the long candles. Chameleons served the couple stoically. He activated a fun little programme in his skull-chip processor that translated the conversation into pictures for his visual cortex, where blue velvet pouches, swallowing one another with fluid grace, stretched out pseudopods in all directions. From time to time Clea Dora purred, and rewrote his mood.

'You're eating cack-handedly, look what you're doing with the chopsticks. Embarrassing!' she scolded him.

'And you're eating so neatly it's as though you'd been doing it all your life. Even more embarrassing.'

She conceded. He thought, Overnight bag. Come back there with me.

'Ly'x,' he said as they left the restaurant.

'Stop that, honestly, I don't want you to call me that.' He realized that she was beginning to like it.

'Li'l Ly'x,' repeated Dmitri Stepanovich and kissed her, tactically, on the nose. 'I'll blaspheme the Li'l Runaround if I like!' He opened his eyes wide, theatrically.

'Stop it,' she muttered and looked away. He could feel her desire and became nervous, high-strung. Haven't I known her for an age? Haven't I seen her tracks in the snow in the high mountains, just above the tree-line, among the alder and the spruce? Weren't there lynxes in the taiga, didn't I see them in antique lands, on my autumn journey?

As they went into the room that he'd taken, she complained, 'Do you know what? My nipples have been erect all week, that's what, that's what I got from thinking of you.'

They laughed and knocked over a table in their haste and their need, locked limbs in embraces that were funny at first and then in earnest, strenuous, a staccato of bites and other little courtesies. And how it smelt and how he liked her arse and how she wanted his tongue.

She, a sea urchin or a tiny flame, fiametta indeed . . . and stop for just a moment . . . he, a spiky tool or an indecent suggestion, fingers, tails, so that she laughed again.

They batted their hands against the mirror on its wall mount and when they paused, exhausted ('Fuck . . . hhh', he wheezed, '. . . You can . . . say that . . . again . . .' she whispered, pledged herself to him, a murmur), it showed them a reflection of their debauchery, their shameless happiness.

They got dressed, went downstairs to the bar, said hello to their old friend the frog. He celebrated with them and they drank until he and they were half daft.

Then they went upstairs and began again right away, still half dressed, helter-skelter into one another like pillows or bedclothes and tore tatters from their clothes. They slept briefly.

They awoke. This time they undressed one another carefully, tenderly. They nestled together, slowed down.

'Actually I rather dislike dogs,' said Ly'x coyly, as she lay down on her back for him on the carpet of anemones waving tiny fingers. He thought, Come with me to the snows, come on my travels, you are a song. Nipples erect all week, and he coughed and felt fireworks burst across his brow.

'Did . . . hhh . . . you . . . hhh . . . know . . . that . . . hhhh,'—Clea had the bad habit of looking at him in the mirror, straight in the face, as he rode her, and talking to him, as though this were a conversation, not something else, '. . . human beings . . . couldn't hhhh . . . decide . . . whether . . . lynxes . . . hhh . . . were related . . . to wolves . . . or . . . hhh . . . to do, do, do it, dogs or . . . hhh . . . to cats . . . cats . . . cats yes come on come . . .'

The weight on her hips. She was filled with glee—not difficult.

Clea mewed, called him names, purred, he went faster, she looked down and enjoyed the sight of his fur gleaming, enjoyed being wet for him. Everything in the room became a flux, fluctuation, oscillation.

He thought, The hairs there round her mound, so wonderful!

She said, 'Mwooooaah.'

They did more, for a long while, pulsating, at their own frequencies, in syncopation, stretched out in a dance, rolling on the bed in one another's masks, a masque, apart, unclasp, they staggered and they trembled, let this sweet time last. 'Hey, come, come here to my, climb on top!' he begged, gladly, and thought, If some damn busybody dragonfly asks me, like that blasted Philomena does the whole time, where I'm at right now, then I'd know. I'd know.

It was a dream, and screamed. Just slightly.

No cause for concern though, the neighbouring rooms probably weren't taken, the walls were pretty thick, so was the floor. When it seemed that they were done, that now they wouldn't make another move, for years, she said, wheezing, frantic, drowsy, 'By the way . . . I'll cut my . . . hair off soon . . . too long. Makes me look . . . like a tart.' She spoke snarkily, tauntingly, as though she knew that he was mad about her hair, dumbstruck by it, the way it swung, curled, tangled, as though she had to tell him right here right now, so that he knew not to act as though he had any say, in anything, how she dressed, how she looked, where and why, who she was, when.

'Shame,' he said. She couldn't forbid him that, at least.

They breathed deeply, downward till they were at rest.

'Really,' she said, picking up a thread she'd dropped earlier, laughing darkly, 'Canidae and Felidae, back then in the . . . whatsit? middle ages, they couldn't tell the difference. Hereabouts they used to call the lynx the Thier-Wolff, the beast-wolf, I mean, how daft can you get?'

He nuzzled at her armpit, soon it all began again.

Then the slap of his loins upon hers, taken by storm, no preliminaries, her desire, dormant just now, suddenly revived, by him, sopping wet. She thought she had never seen anything more beautiful, whenever, anywhere, than the two of them, he thought so too, he could not wait, did not have the strength. She sniffed at him, he growled, to deny what he really, sinking down on her, now that she had wrung him dry, what he felt.

She's—how was it—the sinew of my bone, she is my better self, she is my friend and now my lover, truly, on earth as it is my head here.

They fell asleep again, much more deeply than before, leaving everything behind, deeply into one another's dreams, although for so many years each of them had slept only alone.

He woke up while she was still dreaming.

He saw what they'd done to the room together, the best.

A beam of the dear sun lay across her round breasts, on her face, across the whole happiness of being together, the joy that had just now been thought of.

'Dear friend, awake!' he said, half whispering, and just then she grinned.

He reached into the fruit bowl on the bedside table, passed her something, what was it, nothing much.

A fresh scent of fruit, but the twilight here stank just a little, a rare musk that strengthened the magic, did not diminish it, and for just that reason shouldn't be touched. They began again, nibbling, whispering, burrowing. There was no way they could stop now, no way it could ever stop, why not just live here in this hotel?

And more of the same, and never the same twice.

Hand on heart, sun on their lips, lightly chapped. Shower for a moment and then, again, 'Grab hold, here, hold me!' and the trembling, the tumbling fast, then slow and then faster.

'You're such a bitch!'

'And you're a *Thier-Wolff*, so what?'

Then she got her gear together for the private mysteries—eyebrow pencil, and mascara for her whiskers.

We'd just now smashed it down, the last of our stupid prejudice, our blinkered self-belief, and now we have to kiss goodbye, goodbye for now, and we know that this will last.

'Have a good day. And whatever you get up to—no, don't tell me, I don't want to know—but: don't get killed.'

'You too, Li'l Ly'x.'

'Promise.'

2. ON WHETHER THE RISK CAN BE ASSESSED

'A dump. I can hardly see my paws in front of my . . . bleh. A building would be fine and dandy, we can dig ourselves in if we need to. But this . . .'

'Wait until you get to the more dimly . . .'

'Why do you work down here, anyway? In the mines? I don't like it. Shady business, as they used to say.'

Georgescu the badger grumbled into her striped whiskers. The bat, leading her onwards, deeper into the research establishment, parried elegantly, 'Why? I might just as well ask, why are you green?'

'I have a plant metabolism, so I think I should be plant-coloured,' the general replied. Izquierda tittered, 'A purist. Nice. I have some on my staff, you know, they still insist on binary code to programme the ribomatics. As if we really had to make things more difficult for ourselves by rejecting anything that works, on principle.'

'Hide the workings—that's your motto, then, is it? Never worked. I nail my colours to the mast.'

'Well yes, if the whole world were a battlefield. I'm happy that it's not.'

'I thought you lot were scientists. That's all about truth, isn't it? Not comfortable words.'

'Truth, yes indeed. Or rather, probable truth, which is a nice ideal. But it has about as little to do with truth as subject with object.'

'Philosophy.' The badger spat out the word like phlegm.

They had reached the bottom of the weary descent.

The trophies shimmered dully in the light from the cave walls.

'And that,' asked Georgescu incredulously, 'is what the jungle-funnies have been churning out? They're making this . . . stuff . . . in those big workshops?' She meant the sprawling new structures in the rainforest, shallow ziggurats round Kata-homenleandraleal's probable home territory, which had been photographed by the badgers' geostationary surveillance satellites.

'Pfft, big workshops,' the bat huffed sardonically, 'None of them is even half as big as these catacombs of ours.'

'These . . . workshops, then, they're . . .' the badger resumed.

'Printers. Printworks, if you like. They print what we see here, these bones which we recovered from the wrecks.'

'From the creatures or robots on the coast . . .'

'That's right, at Deadmen's Wall. Strange beasties. We've been calling them polemoamphibians. . .'

'Nice sort of naming system.'

'They are war machines, what should I call them? But are they amphibian? We should drop that idea. It's too simplistic. The shoulder blades and skulls . . .' the bat waved her right wing towards the exhibits, '. . . look, here they are. Odd, aren't they?'

'And the . . . wolves got hold of these for you?'

'The packs by the coast are, how shall we put it, reliable volunteers for the . . .'

'The diplomatic corps, for my companies, and for you engineers. I know all about that.'

'The wolves aren't squeamish, that's the main thing.'

'So I see.'

Without question, only enormous force could have broken free from the strange cadavers the fragments now on display on the autopsy table. These wolves had strong jaws. Georgescu could respect that.

'To the manufacturing process, then. Explain to me, Izquierda. What are we dealing with here?'

'Actually, it's an old trick.'

'You always say that. If the moon crashed into Earth, you'd say, orbital decay, we know all about that. But you wouldn't be the ones clearing up the mess. You're not responsible for the . . . welfare of our . . . civilians.'

The bat made a wry mouth. 'It's civilians now, is it, not Gente?'

'Civilians, the Animal Empire, Gente . . . Folk who for the most part can't fight, the overwhelming majority of them. Don't want to. They leave it to us. Which is why I need to know just what the old trick here is.'

'It's a process that even the humans knew about. Porous calcium phosphate ceramic, which has the advantage over metal or other such stuff, of making components very compatible with existing organic substrate—this means that you can put in implants and you'll even get blood vessels growing through them. They used to make it by laser sintering at first, but the very high temperatures killed off the bioactive ions and the molecules that were supposed to activate cell growth, unavoidable really. So they switched to mixing up a calcium phosphate cement, pouring it into bone-shaped moulds and letting it dry off.'

'Sounds . . . untidy. Mucky. Time-consuming.'

'Quite so, far too many stages of production. But the advantages you get . . . tcha, it's about marginal utility. And our antagonist over there in the jungle,'— Izquierda's face bore an inscrutable smile—'has now brought a new and slightly modified process to mass production: three-dimensional powder printing.'

Georgescu, her eyes narrowed, inspected a long skull more closely. It reminded her of a newt, with huge eye sockets. 'This skull, this head . . . it was printed?'

'Yes. Made in one of the buildings you photographed. I've analysed the pictures, the heat signatures, energy emissions . . . calcium phosphates, phosphoric acid, nozzles extruding a hundred-micrometre layer, then the printer head works its mojo, eight to twelve seconds, you can remove it and harden it off chemically . . . at room temperature, even! *Voila une mode de fabrication rrrrrévolutionaire!*'

'And how many . . . complete skeletons . . . finished articles . . . can these workshops run off daily?'

'Two to three hundred.'

'That's an annual total of . . .'

'Quite. So I think that the Lion was quite right in advising me to show you these. It's most motivational, isn't it? How's the recruitment drive?'

'Do you think I enjoy the thought of a lot of rookies flooding the ranks of my badgers?'

Georgescu hated it when civilians shoved their oar into defence matters. Not even the slim satisfaction of bombarding the boffin with a lot of questions could make up for it.

'The ranks of your badgers?' The bat tutted sceptically. 'I find you rather optimistic there! Who's talking about badgers? I don't know what the Lion told you, but we've all learnt how he thinks by now. If the spy photos really are showing us . . . arms production facilities, then your standing army divisions won't be enough to get the job done. Career soldiers. Sooner or later we'll have to conscript. Gente under arms. And the first war with no humans.'

Did this beast actually enjoy talking like that?

The badger almost answered with the truth as she saw it: that the lack of humans wasn't going to work out the way the bat believed. Given what we know about them, humans are certainly going to be involved in this conflict, for exactly the reason that there are hardly any left. They'd be partisans, auxiliaries for first one side and then the other, depending on the fortunes of war.

Georgescu harrumphed, 'I'll find my own way out, thank you,' turned on her heel and headed for daylight.

3. VERDICTS, NOT TRIALS

The charge they brought was almost entirely incomprehensible.

They brought a mule, who seemed utterly unprepared, before the investigating magistrate.

The magistrate was an owl. He cleared his throat and launched in. 'You admit, unless I am much mistaken, to having conspired with and abetted a certain as yet unidentified person who subverted the library given into your trust, and little by little turned it into a, shall we say, a pherinfonic brothel, a place of limitless depravity in which information was treasonably bought and sold? A person, moreover, who is wanted for murder?'

'Maybe hoo so, but nah look, hee-haw, zibblestibbitz, it really hhhee-hawww wasn't me, honest,' brayed the mule.

'Control yourself, sir! What is to prevent me from having you taken from this court and . . .' the judge hesitated over the right word, he really wasn't so hot at the juristic side of things, '. . . removed to a place of lawful punishment?'

'Pfeeeuhh! Uckle! I can hawww, hee-haw, call sever-r-r-al character-r-r gnix witnesses, Hébert hee-haw Ransom for instance.'

'You do not understand the gravity of your situation,' the judge warned him. He sounded concerned now, almost paternal. All that was missing to make him the very picture of the respectable father, Storikal thought, was a pince-nez.

'When you confess that you have abetted this person, and when you further admit that you have no information that may lead us to this person's whereabouts, and when moreover you appear before us with the hardly plausible explanation,'— there was a smell of sawdust. When the mule closed his eyes he could believe that he was back in his archives—'that this person is in fact a human—a woman, so you say—then you must surely realize that, with the best will in the world and with the greatest possible indulgence, we cannot help but regard you as the sole culprit, as the only real betrayer of our most valuable muniments, at least until such time as the existence of this second person may be proven and we may, per-haps, apprehend her and consider her side of the . . .'

'You! You! You, you . . . talk hee-hawww like one of . . . like a . . . those . . . a . . . wrrrrl . . . from the hee-hawww Temple of Isotta!' sobbed Storikal. He was ut-terly unsurprised to be sentenced to two-and-a-half months solitary for contempt of court. He could hear a drone coming through the window of his cell, though not much light reached him.

What was droning out there? Was someone whispering? His conscience, perhaps?

When he had recovered from the harsh sentence, he found that the statutory two jurors had been sworn in, 'from another city, for the sake of impartiality' making this a full trial. At the first hearing he asked the court to be allowed to make a personal statement.

This was allowed. The two jurors, two young Maine coons, regarded him without warm feelings.

Storikal gnawed his lip, swung his jaw, gasped for air and began. 'It borgo-mompopfobblegock . . . Sorry. Lagrange, labble, language hawww. I'm really heeh-haw most mukk apologetic. I think there is hee-hee-haw really nothing to excuse here. Bims, trutz. I am ready to fuuih-d'ck ha-haww declare, even shamb, shatt, shout it from the rickledink rooftops: I am hoyy-ayy-ha-haww extremely fond of a woman who is indeed a killer. Now grok! Have you ever, taffdaff, re-hah-re-heeh-read a book by pfurhhh the human huyaaa author Fritz Leiber? He was a bakk, bakk, barri, a sort of . . . that sort! Ayiyyy! I don't myself ya-haaa believe in all this talk about duffduckle bodies, about heeee-hawww cocklecarrot . . . corporeal forms, which is just mumblemount blimm windlemillions . . . meant to dis-hee-haww-tract us from the juridical Persian . . . person, a concept hee-haw much more ya-ya-yah interesting for us Gente, which might in the end pull the wool woo-hoo right over our ahh-haaa eyes. Because there's awwwh, also another hee-haw fashionable topic, alongside the hee-haw aforementioned chumble, chortle, chatter which has been goggle-goo-going on since human times and ho-ho-ho has gained ground lately hoo-hooo, another topic, namely that recombination is huggle also the new central hee-haw technique of the most concrete plock art, even when it falls silent, sniffle, that is to say music, which does not contranick dink dict the hee-haw talk of corporeal forms considered as talk, meaning . . . just talk, but but but . . . waaaarghnargh . . . talk based on far more evidooliedearydemidence hee-haw than the hee-haw tattletalk hooey about bodies hee-haw, since one can at, at, at least hee-hee-haw here recognize the working conditions or conditions conniptions of not working whack whunk, according to which you are a mere juridical hee-haw person if you burrrummm hee-haw don't want to miss the future, or at least what passes for a haw haw haw future. My a-quack attack acquaintance, the hee-haw one in question here, sees eeyore the matter, hee-haw, in the same terms. I can't baff speak further fnurrhhurr for her here mumbo jumbo however. She is, as the hee-hee-hee-haw-hawwww charge sheet earlier hee-haw mentioned in mocking terms, a pfffeh "vertebrate in gaseous form", but blumm, but drrrum, but what exactly do you find ribbletickling ridiculous there hee-haw? I need not remind you what we all know about one of the longest-serving hee-haw and redacted . . . respected of the Lion's sussalally supporters, the Fox Ryuneke hopla Nowhere ho-haaa, hee-haw. I know him eeyore very well.'

'Personally? The Fox?' the owl asked, astonished.

'No, from tillmicklestick . . . the huddle hopsasa documents. I eeyore even know what he was tobblebinktuttup called before he toughluck hee-haw was hee-hee-haw Liberated. Ryu . . . von . . . Schnaub-Villalila.'

'How is that relevant?' one of the jurors interrupted him, visibly revolted that a failure like Storikal—she knew his crashed career, the whole wreck—should talk of the great and the good as though he were one of them.

'It's blommdreck not ha-hawww relevant,' Storikal conceded frankly.

'Please tell us,'—the fatherly old owl took pains to calm things down, even though the defendant's unravelling speech patterns gave him a terrible headache— 'about the . . . woman . . . your acquaintance.'

Storikal nodded enthusiastically, almost mechanically. 'Of course haw-hawww she has other problems. Above all, as a wossname juridical person. She herself, the woman, having ahhaw-ahhaw already keck, haw, killed once, tells the opps story of how this murder came about, in the following terms hee-haw: one morning she woke up and found she was lying face down in a seal.'

It was the first complete sentence free of junk morphemes that Storikal had spoken since his arrest.

It fell quiet in the courtroom, now everyone was listening.

Unfortunately the crowd's hushed attention unnerved the mule so much that he immediately relapsed, even more grotesquely, into his ticks and quirks. 'Hee-hawww, I'll give bre-e-e-eh the woman giggiggle a cover name when I speak of her, so the hee-haw court trump, transcribers can put that in eeyore their pro-tocol tufff. I'll call haw, haw, her Tyaa. I don't even hee-haw-haw know her real name slebble myself. She says du-bump that she was hee-haw lying on a bed with this slob slubber sailor seal. It was hee-hawww a good-sized male, and when she ee-eeyore woke up she found her face hee-haw in the opened ribcage. She had fuffle opened it knirshtrunk up herself, with a duuurrgle T-shaped cut, and then pooh, paaah, peeled the flesh back, but she only hee-hee-haw remembered that later. Tyaa, dommdomm by the way, hey, hey, haw, for your pherinfofroofaraw, in-formation, is a name from Fritz Leiber's hoo-yaaa books and stories about the hee-haw-haw world of haa-yaa Nehwon.'

'Sheer nonsense,' hissed the juror on the left, outraged. She couldn't bear to listen to the defendant's drivel any longer.

She had put him to shame, and he pulled himself together. 'It was dark haaa and warm inside the hee, hee, seal's ribcage, and only when she had propped herself up on her up, hup, elbows could yaaa Tyaa get free and see that eeyore it was a ribcage, and how bloody it was, and that ya-haps the two lungs looked like a lady-bird's whoop-woot wet back, but without the spots. Like hahaya wings you see. It must have been lovely. My friend, whom hoo-hoo I call Tyaa, told the mangle mantra mannikin clown—I worked with him in the archives, as you oo-hoo-hee-haw know, we're engaged agaga by the way—well, she told the woo-wup wooden-top Saint

Oswald that she thought hee-haw at first that the most precious legacy of the pingy Monotony o-ho … drat, a-ha, the human age, was what they called pockettah, potz-dutz, porno rock, because eeyore hee-whore, I quake, quote: "These people made records, or played songs, about the vagina and so on, at least that's what stays in my mind, I only read about it with half an eye, in some music mag."'

Another comprehensible sentence. And once again, the judge noticed, the sentence came out when Storikal was reporting what the mysterious Tyaa supposedly told him. A chemically encoded pattern in his speech centres, triggered by certain preliminary phrases? Delayed-release pherinfonics?

The phenomenon was past as soon as it had happened, he stammered as badly as before. 'Freeeees, frump, frigging, Fritz wu-shu Leiber's tack Tyaa yaa-haa is a goddess with don'tlooknow hee-haw a very circumscribed area of responsibobble-bility . . .'

The court gradually reached a consensus that the defendant was not worth sentencing.

Best thing to do was throw him into the sea, the Atlanteans could use him as an experimental subject.

Storikal had worked himself up into a fury however. 'Gaaah! Ga-haaa! Gr-rrreh, green muhaaa leaves, up in yaaaa-guh the trees in s-s-s-s-s-s-p-r-r-r-r-r-r-r-r-r-ing, are much more haw, haw, yump random in their arrangement, the way they hee-hay grow and spread, and for, haw, haw, that reason look mammamma more mauled about than ya-hey, ya-haaa, a well-butchered seal. Haaa, interesting, a ya-haaa zoologist might say, if he really knew hoo-hoo-hee-his subject, thus, as we can eeyore all agree, for obblegobble obvious reasons couldn't be a hoo-haw human zoologist—but the point is that pruggle an average hooo-hem, mem, member of Gente kurrrrgh society would be ya-haaaa incensed by my friend's opinion that green leaves are a more dree, drump, disturbing sight than a caw caw corpse cut open, more so than by the opinion that the survival of the ha-ma-gaaah humans could acceptably hee-haw depend upon their yaaa-haw producing the nutrients that their metabolism urgently puttsy puttsy yaaah needs and many other products in a maha-haw-haw manner which in fact increasingly poisoned, porpoise, purpose, hee-hawww and private property ehhrmerrr . . .'

'I hope that you understand that this inquiry,' said the second juror, who had been quiet until now, 'is not concerned with some imaginary seals that might or might not have been murdered, but rather with a real corpse that was really found in your part of the library? The corpse of a luminary known throughout the Three Cities, among the Atlanteans and indeed world-wide, the zander Westphalia Sophocles Gaeta.'

The mule shook his head, squeezed his eyes tight shut, opened them again and yelled, 'Waargh! Waaaah! What? What? What what what? Well, wee, whoo, whoop, we'll certainly hee-haw-have our hands full with that for some time, you're rough, rout, right. At least until the question is hee-haw answered as to which of the puckle two we would rather surrender: filfot pherinfonics, as a legacy of dorky heavy ha-haha-ya-ya-ya industry, or our peculiar form of absolutist hupformulagonized government, as the legacy of ping, private, hoo-yaaah even Leonine booooh . . .'

'It's not that I actually understand your ravings,' the kindly old owl interrupted, 'but your words do sound rather anti-Lion . . .'

'Neh-noh-ho-yaaa, hee-haw,' the mule rolled his eyes, drool looped and dropped from his jaws, 'for Gock's, for all . . . heeee-haaaaw . . . why? Why, ack, why, I arks, arse, ask! Haani! Yeaaah!'

'What?' As presiding judge, he was now determined to abandon the trial as soon as possible. It was turning into a circus, getting out of control.

'Why, I'm just aargh ugh asking hoo-hee why in all this talk these days of corporeal bodies, baah, gurroh, "Animal Empire" as they hee-haw say, bray, way-hay-hay, hoooh this sooh srood pseudo-theory of that haw, haw, hee-hee-hoo horrible brabble bat Issel, Issnel, Izquierda's is zizz izzle so highly regarded, but I can easily eggsclaim exclaim explain why: it ya-haaa lets us mix it all it all uddle everything up together, confuse, frooze, rubblesuit, substitute, if hee-haw I'm right, put me, gackle, put me on trouble, herrrghk, trial for that'—Storikal was close to tears, he absolutely had to say what was on his mind, but was so worked up that he didn't know what he was saying—'so when, finnty-faffy, when haaa-yaaay there's a gaping wound dumm-dumm in such a shuck-shtuck hoo yaa horror, a yaa-haa human a lion a fish . . . flahwall, Westphalia you say, how haw haw? Torn apart suppurating high-yaaa splinters of wood iron and oops round grainy flesh, or we can see gackle the organs, the liver, kidneys, nyahaaaa, what though, women, yahaaa humans, compare the whickerwhackerwound to a pffiii, pfiggerree, vagina. Very interesting and utterly rum, hawww, wrong, since if if if or rrrh oh hoo-haw shit tackytittle Stanz the ape hee-haw-hee-haw but but, but though but but hawww, hee-haw! All rum, rumble, rung, wrong! I'm hah I'm hee-haw innards inkling innocent, innocent hee-hee-hawww!'

'Enough. It's intolerable,' said the first juror.

'Intolerable,' the second agreed.

'Certainly,' the owl opined, 'but we must consider that there may be some fact hidden in this . . . torrent of words that would help elucidate the matter, although . . .'

'Hee-hawww!' Storikal bellowed desperately.

'Please make an end of it,' the owl added, so that his words could not be counted as encouragement. The donkey bowed meaninglessly, raised his head and said, 'My haaa-yaaah friend Tyaa, who I really like a grumble grouch great . . . flub, flunder, deal, was confronted with the question of juridical person the haaarrrr, ahaaarrrr, hard way humph. If she's craw, caw, caw caught, I'll say say rackinfrassin this, she will have hawww-hawww to answer a charge of murder in craw, court. "Right," she says, "maybe hee-hawww I can get away ya-ha-ha-ha-hay with a plea of insanity, I wasn't in my right my hy my mhy hmm hy mind. But I'd rather haw-hee-haw not risk it." And because she hee-hee-hee-haw doesn't want to zomp risk it, she had to get rid grid gerrid of the body. That was haww-haww-ha-a mucky job, but at least it kept her mind off tick pointless yaaa-haama questions like, what fniffle happened? Where did I harrr harrr haw get the strength to rip the haww fish to pieces with that humuhumanhistoruh yaaah huge knife, the fish shiff shuffle scuffle kerfuffle that she's supposed to have riffle scuffle killed as well, the knife yaaa-haggagga haww that I was holding in my hand haw haw when I woke up face down in a ribcage? Why can't I hee-haww remember yahahaha anything, including who this bloke ack, ugh, ugly, actually is? These questions, fronk, lead nowhere. Fritz Leiber's hee-haw Tyaa is the goddess of evil birds. Dacka. To rip open hee-haw a seal or a fish is really quite unusual behaviour for a tinky. Topsy. Tut tut. Eeyore. Shameful. Dreadful. Catch, klatsch, miscarriage of justice torf hee-haw!'

He looked at the floor mournfully.

Storikal knew that he had blown any chance of clemency. He was dispirited and looked up at the mirror hanging on its pivot above the judge's head, blazoned with the Lion's crest.

Two hours after the condemned beast had been driven out into the sour salt wastes, a raven flapped after him and called him back. He had been pardoned.

Strings had been pulled on his behalf, 'in the higher echelons', was all he ever learnt of the details.

Also, General Georgescu was sponsoring a 'godfathering' programme for the rehabilitation of offenders and marginals, and which would pay for invasive neurosurgery on his speech centres, thanks to a generous donor.

'Pfanky? A who a hee–haw what?'

'Some well-to-do society lynx. Just be grateful, she doesn't want her name mentioned,' said the raven, superciliously.

Storikal didn't ask any more questions.

He found it odd however. A lynx, indeed, just like his friend Tyaa (who wasn't human, no, not in the least, the court had completely misunderstood him there, or he had missed his own meaning)—Tyaa, whom no one else seemed to know.

second movement

LYNX, GUARD MY FIRE

(SCHERZO)

Cy: . . . which is why I've often asked myself whether this slogan—'the abolition of species'—hasn't opened the floodgates for all kinds of dreamers, heads in the clouds, voluntarist deviationists, fantastical false doctrines . . .

Iz: And anti-Lion ideologies.

Cy: Exactly. We taught that any statement is only significant inasmuch as it plays some part in a chain of reasoning—either as a conclusion or as a premise—but we have also taught that anything that obtains for statements must also hold true for any form of information, such as genetic code. Implicitly, the genome contains all taxa which could plausibly descend from it and is in itself the result of an adaptive process. Who I am contains an implex which I must then become. Even being the Lion is anti-Lionist, since this authority demands its own abolition.

Iz: A very subtle point, Your Majesty. The idea that only implications count, that teleology triumphs—it's a very radical . . .

Cy: Inferentialism, yes, I know. But we've used it to make everything fungible—admittedly, there were still species after the Liberation, of course, as handy phenotypical pigeonholes, corporeality's shortcuts, statements made in evolution's own inferential chain. At this point, of course, we could actually choose, but a dog was a dog, a sparrow was a sparrow . . .

Iz: A rose was a rose was a . . .

Cy: But genotypes had become a sheerly voluntary matter, and so by implication had all the other classificational units, the families, classes, phyla, the higher taxa, which yielded those patterns that illuminated natural history so well in the old days, non-randomness, all the constructs which had let reason sharpen its blade. The idea that there is a rich, vibrant living world where everything has some causal connection with everything else and that everything made sense, comprehensibly, with no need for a supernal guiding hand.

Iz: And meanwhile your paw . . .

Cy: But I wanted to act according to a precept that I have always much admired—that we should study, and take seriously, reality as it happens to be, but we shouldn't worship or admire it. Quite the contrary, whoever holds it up for worship is quite mad—that's something that the composer helped me to understand, with one of her finest aphorisms, 'Consanguinity is a mental illness.'

From the *Conversations with the Lion*, III/18

VI
THREE HEROES

1. FROM A DREAM

Elektrizitas Pulsipher, the high vestal of Capeside, came before the waiting crowd with her hawk head raised and spoke, 'We have never demanded the Temple for ourselves.'

It was not an easy statement for her to make and she delivered it with a dignity that imparted a further message to many who watched. Perhaps that had been the whole point of the Liberation, to be able to approach morally fraught matters with dignity even though we are descended from beasts that had no moral code.

'Some Gente have spoken ill of us, we have been much mocked. We have been envied our Temple, once it was granted to us by the aediles, by the administration, by the politicians, who believed that it was right and proper to have such . . . establishments in the Three Cities. When the decision was made—not even three hundred years ago—it was because our rituals, our prayers, our blood-offerings and libations might, they thought, not be a mere behaviour, a biological aberration, but might rather . . . presage an emergent pattern, might contribute something of great symbolic importance to the birth of a new civilization . . . in short, the Temple stands because our spirituality may foreshadow a new stage of mind, a consciousness appropriate to the Gente . . .'

She turned her head slowly towards the city gate, where the chaotic barrios began.

'The pattern is now here. Our enemies call it a fetish, the core of a new faith, maybe as damaging as the human religions.'

Elektrizitas Pulsipher's meaning was clear. Several times this past winter, the Polyarch party had lobbied the Lion for an investigation of just how much of the social surplus was already in the hands of the Isotta sect and whether this share was increasing annually. These were loaded questions, their meaning easy to guess.

'We are not thankful that we are hated. Yet our enemies' malice keeps us on our guard. It helps make things clear. More harmful are those who say that they are our friends and yet belittle what we do. They say, let them do what they want and justify this by pointing at the thousands of years of human religion, asking whether it might not prove that some such faith is simply . . . needed. As we all know, there have been experiments on brain functions and their role in experiencing the Divine. A few years ago, the zander and his team in the Torus investigated the matter as well. Partly this rested on discoveries and hypotheses about positive feedback loops, about stimuli. But now we are about to say things not because they are socially necessary, or neurobiologically plausible, or culturally significant, but because they are true, and these friends of ours look askance. Now we are suspected, hundreds of years after the Liberation, of actually believing in something.'

Never before had the 'bloodletters', as their enemies called Elektrizitas and her vestals, made such a clear statement of their beliefs. She looked round the square calmly, nodded almost imperceptibly and continued. 'What do we believe? Many have heard, yet few have comprehended.'

It was clear what would come next.

Here it came.

'We believe that the Gente are destined to seek and to find something that we know only dimly at present, to protect something very fleeting. We call it the Li'l Runaround.'

A bank stood opposite the broad steps on which Elektrizitas stood and on the roof of the bank sat the ravens. They began to laugh as if on cue. Elektrizitas waited until the cackling died down. Then she resumed. 'Those of you who are paying attention will ask how I know this. I shall tell you: from a dream.' Her avian eyes glittered, her silver beak, richly ornamented, flashed in the rays of the rising sun.

Behind her, like a bodyguard, stood stone figures to which no one would ever pray.

'Many of my sisters dreamt this same dream and I know that many of you have also done so, even if you will not admit this to yourselves. I will describe it for you: in this dream, a human woman with thick black hair came to . . . the dreamer, that is, to me. You see my collar,'—very wide—'it was turned up and I had just requested the pherinfonic address and recognition code of a priestess, a scholar, who desired to leave us and travel beyond the Three Cities, to the speechless animals, to convert them. A leavetaking—this was my mood as I dreamt, a dream of blessing for the road. The others, my sisters, regarded me from the courtyard,'—as they were doing now. 'All of this happened inside the Temple, in the back, on the stair and above the screen that protects the priestesses from our sacred fire. We stood in the doorway of the chapterhouse. The woman had now become the sister who wished to leave us—these things merged, as they do in dreams—and she stroked my collar with her hand, with long, slim fingers, a tender gesture that said, 'farewell'. We were friends, though I do not know how. She was not a ruin, not like the humans that still live today. The ruined humans are a terrible sight. She was full of life, wide awake, commanding. She made accusations. The dream has been recorded, by the way, I'm not away with the fairies here, I'll send the pherinfones to everyone who subscribes to our weekly newsletter and everyone else who wants to call it up, you can check every word I say. In the whole dream not a word was spoken aloud, but, nevertheless, everything was clear and laden with meaning. I knew, though I could not say how, that I had arrived at a long journey's end, perhaps at a future, more likely at an eternal present that was, at the same time, a past different from history as it has unfolded. What has been, can vanish. But no one can take away from us what could have been.'

'A different past? Different how? Alternate?' asked a camera insect.

'Different from the course that the Liberation really took. A past in which I did not run away from home to the Temple of Isotta, to hide from what was to come. A past . . .' She stopped, shook her head, collected herself, continued, 'the strange woman was a messenger sent from a better place, I know.'

The ravens clattered their beaks but lacked the nerve to renew their mockery.

'She commanded me—in pictures, with feelings, more than in words—to find the Runaround. That is all.'

'What is it then? The Runaround? What can it do? What's it supposed to be?' Several cameras twittered all at once.

'The meeting is over. Who understands, has understood. This too is true for those who do not know that they understand.'

'What's that supposed . . .'

'I thank you.'

Elektrizitas Pulsipher went back into the temple, flanked by her sisters, who looked as though they were ready to die if need be in defence of the incomprehensible cause. The temple doors closed with a crash that was heard in all Three Cities.

Until the war began, this was the last that anyone heard from the vestals.

2. FEAR OF THE PRESENCE

To be summoned to the Lion himself: a trial and an honour.

There were Gente who had been driven mad by the experience. Few of those who returned could describe what they had seen.

His countenance: the wreathes and groves of his mane and amid it, lights like a flowing stream, blazing eyes like twin suns, words as loud as the thunder, the teeth of a giant.

Were there two eyes, or did he have three, or was it only a single, an all-seeing eye?

Try as he might, Dmitri Stepanovich could not decide which of these mutually exclusive possibilities he had indeed seen. Because he was wise, however, he set aside all certainties and listened instead to what the awakened one said to him.

'Little wolf. You have come a long way. Of all my servants you are the most useful and the most free. In truth, you do not serve me at all and that is why you serve so well. You are sleeping with my daughter. Didn't you know? It is she. A new name, Clea Dora, not Lasara, and soon enough . . . Of course, little wolf, I grow fonder of you for this. I know how it is. Her mother fooled me well and good. Beasts with mouths like flowers.'

A rushing as of all the waterfalls in the world, and an echo.

The wolf could not understand every word that the Lion spoke. He supposed that this too was part of the law that bound the Lion and all the other Gente to one another.

The Lion's image shook, clouds of pollen trembled insubstantially from the fur like dust. This dust shall speak, the wolf thought. He was frightened, but pulled himself together.

The King said, 'I will tell you what you will do for me. This is not a request, nor an order, but a fact. Because I have no better servant than you, you will cross the ocean on a bathyscaphe, although sometimes you will also swim on your own. You will speak to the Atlanteans on my behalf. They will listen. For our relations, theirs and mine, must improve. Since the zander died, they have not been good.'

The murder of Westphalia Sophocles Gaeta had not been avenged, at least not publicly. Dmitri lowered his head.

'They will be more impressed by what they have to hear if I send you than if I simply used the pherinfones. Of course, they would most of all like Cyrus to come in person. We shall not.'

The wolf allowed himself a laugh. He's chatty today, a good sign.

'After visiting the Atlanteans you will continue to the western continent. There you will travel north. Then you will visit an old friend. You know that any friend of mine is a friend of yours?'

It was a rhetorical question. Dmitri kept quiet.

'The friend whom you visit . . . He is a bird, or perhaps a human once again by now, one never knows. In any case, an individual to whom I have been closely connected for some centuries, although recently . . . rather one-sidedly, perhaps. Together with me he created this world which you and which all here inhabit.'

He let that sink in. The new knowledge hummed like a power line; the wolf shuddered.

'He has . . . let us say, much power. Not like myself, but . . . The powerful come in two kinds, you see—those whom all know and fear, and those known only to those who are . . . permitted. Well, there's a third kind, but let's not talk of Ryuneke.'

The pause that followed this remark was far too pregnant for the wolf's liking. He wanted to switch the conversation in a more practical direction. 'How . . . how does your friend in the northwest use his power?'

'He makes no use of it. A long time ago now he decided to . . . stay out of the game. Perhaps he is painting with ashes, or wallowing in regrets. Whatever he's up to, now's not the time. You will tell him so.'

'Will he want to hear that?' The wolf flattened his ears. His interruption was not meant as impudence.

'He will listen and that must suffice. He was never stupid. For such as is, it is never a matter of the bubble reputation, but of business that must needs be done here. Alas, I can see that this world that we made together will not be a happy one, in the next few generations.' The Lion growled and the sound was such as could have been made by a bear of molten iron.

'A fine idea from the Bible—I know that means little enough to you—is a mad thought, but we wished it so. The wolf shall lie down with the lamb and so forth. But there's no chance of that, if these . . . new creatures attack us. My old friend knows this quite well and will give up in advance, as so often. That's how it is when you choose the wrong cause early in life, with such enthusiasm.'

'What was his cause?'

A deep laugh, such as the earth would laugh if it could.

'Far-fetched fancies . . . life at an individual scale doesn't work so well, so let's look at the big picture. So he thought—so he explained it to me, on a long summer afternoon, on a boat trip in . . . Berlin was the . . . a city, back then . . . he thought perhaps it could be like when single-celled organisms form a pseudoplasmodium, the slime-mould beastie, that was his analogy. If one day humankind awoke to the possibilities of emergence, self-organization, synergy . . . but all the creatures of the Monotony couldn't compare to the slime mould that he so loved to offer as an analogy—what was it called again? *Dictyostelium discoideum.* To come through the non-equilibrium phase on the other side . . . but there was no chance for any of that, given how slowly mankind communicated. Rushes without moisture, reeds without water, ideas without action. Until I came and saved him. As I wish to awake him now.'

'For friendship's sake?'

'Ha! Let me lay down my name if ever I perform an altruistic action. No, my little wolf, I simply need his help. He should lend his aid, digging trenches for the troubled times to come. I cannot lay the whole scheme myself, nor with Georgescu, with Izquierda, with all my beloved aediles and councillors.'

'But with the bird,' said Dmitri.

The Lion was silent.

Dmitri cleared his throat and quickly proceeded to technical and logistical matters. 'How shall I be equipped? Who is building the submarine, Izquierda?'

The walls round him smirked. The great voice was amused. 'You have naive ideas about how much she truly controls by herself, youngling. Izquierda builds our airships and ensures that the rubbertrains run on time. The bathyscaphe is already built, others have taken care of that. Do not forget, much of your journey shall be by land. You will go by the Three Cities, then Saudade, Acheron, the Seven Pillars, the lands round Accomplice, Gladsheim, Limbo, then Bestiarium, where it all began, then the little ford, the great causeway and, lastly, the Bonewall, where I know you like to go in your . . . time off. You will be given the necessary bodily modifications later today.'

'Perhaps I should fly. With wings of my own.'

The Lion spoke sternly, 'Do not speak to me as though I were a granter of gifts. I do not ask that you attempt the impossible. Even before the organisms attained reason, their instincts drove them to longer journeys, more strenuous exertions, which they survived—the Arctic terns . . .' regret sounded in his voice as he reminisced, 'migrating from the circumpolar North, to Africa, Australia and the Antarctic—all forgotten names now. The blue shark swam the North Atlantic along its own geodesic lines, the Caribbean turtles followed the Gulf Stream, the eel and the lobster could . . . well, it is past.'

'I shall do my task. I only seek to understand why . . .'

The Lion broke him off and Dmitri Stepanovich cringed almost imperceptibly. 'Little wolf, I need not explain myself. Certainly not to a child such as you.'

Dmitri nodded and fell silent.

Oblivion plashed in the silence for a while.

When the wolf had already decided that the audience was over with no word of dismissal and was wondering how he could leave the room and still obey protocol, the voice spoke again, uncommonly soft, lost in thought, 'It was not only . . . dreadful for the animals in those days, but also for those of us who . . . were about to . . . become animals.'

Dmitri felt his hackles rise, but he did not show it, trying instead to think of how Clea Dora looked in the bath. The voice spoke of ancient mysteries, almost incomprehensible things. 'In the Intercity Express, on my way to meet the highest bidder as always. I would have liked to be an artist—transgenic rabbits, mice that glow in the dark, that kind of thing. It wasn't to be, I was basically . . . a vat rat, a hired hand for the . . . biochemical-industrial complex. And then . . . one afternoon . . . I had just got an SMS telling me that a colleague I was very fond of had died in one of those ever more frequent attacks on our research establishments, and I was sitting . . . in first class, Hanover to Frankfurt, surrounded by young Bundeswehr soldiers, in the early May sunshine, and my iPhone . . . I had had the piece on it for months, electronic symphony by the mad genius we all loved to listen to in those days, her—hold on, I know it—her Opus Eight, and I was reading some kind of novel as well, some chunk of SF about hidden stars and women and . . . all that jazz . . . then I had my—what should I say—epiphany: forgive them and go your ways in peace. They can trash our labs, and these recruits in the train can shout and roar, and death can come for my colleague, but music . . . music is a beast that can't be caught, bigger, faster, too much for us, simply . . . and I thought, that's the sort of beast we must become, we must make the living world our own at last—make it utterly artificial, you see, nothing but artifice, little wolf, so there's no room left for these trigger-happy Boy Scouts and for the shrivelled little priests who always justify the violence, no room for the ticket-inspectors with their faces grey as ashtrays, no room for the doubters and nigglers with their . . . But first, things don't happen that way and second, entropy. Rigo Baladur's got the right idea about things. Oh, but that mad genius . . . how she could kick us all out of our self-pity, true inspiration . . . she was a precious, pernicious thing! What would I ever have done without her . . . and these quirks of hers, these bad habits—the same mania for convoluted puns that, I don't know, Duchamp or . . . she had a metronome, when she was pissed off and caught herself talking about the good old times when everything was better, she would set the thing running and chant in time with the ticks. She called that "a retro-moan"—good times . . .'

'Your daughter . . .' the wolf reckoned that it was high time to talk about his own concerns, if the Lion was in such a chatty mood. The King would not listen though. 'Daughter, fiddlesticks. Consanguinity is a mental illness. So she taught us, our . . . Go now. You will receive your instructions tomorrow morning, you can read them on the palms of your hands, they are just being drawn up.'

'The recipient of my message . . .' the wolf was set on asking again. The Lion interrupted with a comment that may or may not have had any relevance to the question that his envoy had begun. 'But the lame is condemned by her lameness, and the liar is trapped by her lies, and the coward's heart dies of its own poison.'

He must be mad, and probably has been so for longer than I have been alive, Dmitri thought, full of fear and awe.

An old echo growled, 'Go, I say.'

The Lion did not need to say it a third time.

3. HELP, NOT HARD CASH

'I stopped caring about all that a long time ago,' said the glass of whisky that once had been a fox, to the dragonfly Philomena who had ordered the drink. 'The only economy that I still care about, my dear, is the information economy. The economics of perception. Look, for instance, at those three heroes I invented myself. They're running round the place now like living, breathing emblems of the second generation after Liberation, and its goals.'

'Goals, fehh!' the dragonfly scoffed. The whisky giggled. 'You're quite right, they haven't any. But the trick works. Everyone's talking about my heroes, far more than they're talking about those glaze-eyed fish in the Borbruck Torus, or about the fish who snuffed it, more even than they talk about the Lion's daughter.'

'You can certainly talk like a philosopher,' the dragonfly hummed. 'But in our world, my sweet, the law of value is slowly making a comeback. War economy, all the old bad habits. I'll have to grant you one thing. It's all happening exactly as you always feared it would. They're . . .'—the dragonfly shuddered and looked deep into the glass—'they're paying wages again, they're fixing prices and soon they'll even be making profits. Izzy's got her claws dug in.'

'Now then!' scolded the liquid.

'Alright, Izquierda, if you say so. She says there is no alternative, we must accumulate. There's this . . . ape, Stanz, he even sat in the upper advisory council to the Lion for a while, and he . . .' The sentence tailed off into despair.

The peaks outside gleamed as though newly created, the restaurant was atop the highest mountain in the world and the view from the platform was incredible.

'Ah, forget that stuff,' Ryuneke said, 'forget all that. Regrettable effects of necessary military measures. That's not due to the ape or to those others who are so touchingly trying to create a bourgeoisie. I'd be more concerned about the rationing. Scarcity, not a good sign. We're really living on the eve of war. That stinks.'

'The apes . . .'

'Listen, I know what's going on,' said the liquid, diffusing messenger molecules from its surface to the dragonfly's sensory reception area. 'I'm right up to date with . . .'

'What, up to date with what?' The dragonfly became stroppy. 'What whoozis Arroyo tells you?'

'Sdhütz.'

'Stuff. He's telling you everything like a good boy, is he?'

'I know you could never stand him.' The dragonfly got a picture of Ryuneke smiling patiently, lifting his heavy eyelids slowly, a come-hither look. 'That's only because his virtues are not yours.'

'He's loyal, that's true,' said the dragonfly. Herself, she was proud that the old fox had never found or made a traitor to match her. 'But you've got to admit that the really worrying thing . . .'

'Gobbledegook. Take the sentient maize, for instance. Take the seed corn. The badgers farm it, don't they? The apes submitted a plan at court which I would have been ashamed of—these days the old fellow surrounds himself with young aediles, and they were quite astonished, so were a few old hands like Georgescu or that shifty wolf. Because when they did the calculations it was clear that the price for one ton of sentient maize—and don't forget that in the end the stuff is destined for the Lion's great secret project up in the caves—the parallel processors, massively networked—anyway, the price of the finished product was nearly the same as a ton of untreated seed corn, and that a ton of sentient maize was also the benchmark for a ton of modular filter for seedling. What kind of cock-eyed mathematics is that, I ask you? Your . . . Izzy . . . was able to steady her voice and object that the price per ton for seedling filter had to be much higher than the price per ton for unprocessed maize, and that the stock market indices in all Three Cities would show this—yeah, you see, we're, that's to say, the Lion and his subsidy programmes are, thinking big again, and I hear that he's trading food to the Amazon god, for rubber and charcoal, at the same time that we're gearing up for global confrontation with our esteemed trading partner—where was I? Well, the ones who'd drafted this marvellous proposal, the apes that you're so afraid of, and let's say this straight out, it's because you're plain scared that mankind's closest relatives are going to take revenge for what you did to the hands, that's all you're concerned about—look you, the Fox, the bat and the badger all seem to have thought of this argument, and the apes hadn't a single thing to say in response. Nothing. We must have made an error in the budget, har har. As a result the Court was forced, if I understand Sdhütz Arroyo correctly, to take the matter into its own paws, to drop the price of computer maize per fiat and raise the price of other goods, seedling filter et cetera, quite sharply. If that's not funny and if that doesn't show the scale of the confusion we're creating for ourselves, then I don't know what is. You really can't be scared of amateurs like that, you have to laugh.'

'You say,' said the dragonfly pointedly, 'that they're not doing anything that you wouldn't have done, although you wouldn't have had a plan. And therefore you don't have the least intention of doing what I so urgently ask and officially returning to . . . this world. Not yet, anyway. Not before the catastrophe is poised to strike. You want to let things stumble along until it all bursts into flames. And then you've got a bucket of water to sell us at a very nice price.'

'Philomena dearest, I never said that. You can't pin that one on me. What are you looking for? I'll be back soon enough, don't badger me. But as to when and where, you'll have to leave that to me. Trust me, I do in fact have a plan.'

'If only you weren't so damned determinist the whole time,' said the dragonfly pugnaciously.

'Quite the contrary. If I were a little less nimble and not so inventive, I'd stop surprising myself and then,'—the voice rose to a cadence that said that this would be the Fox's last word on this occasion—'there'd be no reason for me to exist at all, in any form, solid or attenuated.'

There was a hissing sound as the whisky evaporated.

4. ON WHETHER THE KING'S WARNING WAS JUSTIFIED

'Beasts with mouths like flowers.' Could it be said more bluntly? Wasn't it sheer self-mortification, to keep the affair going now that Lasara had been unmasked?

Dmitri Stepanovich could have growled, except that this reminded him too much of the old wolf that he no longer wished to be.

Arguments: 'And you actually find the ape's daubs are any good? His human-style scribbles? In God's three names . . .'—this voice of hers, where did that bleating tone come from all of a sudden, the wheedling, the knowing nastiness in Lasara's words? And why? Just because Dmitri visited Stanz the ape from time to time, because he bought paintings from him as an investment, because he'd got interested in art recently?

The paintings went to a warehouse below the western supports of the benzene ring, after all Dmitri had no fixed abode anywhere.

Ly'x: now that he knew that she'd been the young of a Lion once, he found her brash and affected. Everything that he had always disliked about high society in the Three Cities, he saw again in her—the little phrases meant as jokes, 'and by the wayside', 'oh badger it', the mangled phrases ('in God's three names'—she really thought they had said that, quite often she malapropistically mangled Monotony phrases), and the idiotic affectation of always contradicting. It sapped Dmitri's strength to think that these high-born Gente could never have a straightforward conversation about what they actually want, what they should do, whether they agree; everything had to dribble away into facetious, allusive, passive-aggressive criticism of something that couldn't be named aloud, retorts to retorts, to prove that they were above such things as obvious motive.

'No, my love, you know, I reckon . . .'—that was a hundred times more condescending than when the Lion called him 'little wolf'. A bad dance; two leading, no one following, each treading on the other's paws at every step taken.

Dmitri watched as the ape completed a charcoal sketch, first creating heavy masses of shadow. Layer upon layer of white highlight next, the exact detail to make a body, the here-it-is. The way he works, thought the wolf, that's the way to live.

He got ready to leave. Dmitri was grateful for the mission now.

'So that's your hoarded wealth,' Clea Dora sneered, 'the ape's fingerpainting.'

'I know you don't need to hoard. You got rich by being born.'

'Don't be like that,' she snapped at him, almost considerate now.

It was too late to consider his feelings.

He turned away, looked out of the window, into the distance, where there was work to do.

The ape carried on painting as though the collector and his posh totty weren't there at all.

On the other hand, there was so much she knew that Dmitri wanted to know as well, so he simply couldn't leave her—above all, she knew about history and pre-history, about the Monotony. She could describe the last battle of organized human resistance as though she had been there—the humans stamping about a region called 'Vigeland' like stone giants, armoured in huge grey mechsuits (a model called 'Mann og kvinne', which would have protected them even at ground zero of a nuclear explosion), slaying badgers and building fortresses. She described it so vividly that he could almost see it, could smell the oil and fire, the volatile mix of scents exhaled from Vigeland's soil before the perrhobacteria from Izquierda's laboratories put paid to the heavy armaments.

He also loved the literature that she recited for him, that he could read from her glances, from her well-stocked skull, 'lectorem delectando pariterque mon-endo', the poems of the vanquished, 'therefore do you my rimes keep better meas-ure, And seeke to please, that now is counted wisemans threasure', and how she sang to him from the *Romance of the Rose*, from Ferrante Pallavicino, from Ezra Pound, from Guido Cavalcanti, from Liane de Pongy, from Jiji Zhenjing, from 'the secret transmissions' that 'state that by using one human being to supplement another, one naturally obtains the true essence', from Al-Tifashi, from Zoé Valdés, from Ernest Dowson, Maxine du Camp, Rainer Maria Gerhardt. She sang about Mr Vladimir Nabokov's little girls and Mr Henry Miller's big girls, about the moral codes that had given rise to all that. 'What, sexual orientation? So errm what it really meant was,'—Dmitri scratched his head with all the claws of his right hand—'toss a coin and from then on only do it with those you resemble, or else those you don't?'

'We-e-l-l,' drawled Lasara and stretched, so that then and there he wanted to be her chaise longue, 'they never got beyond primary sexual characteristics when they were looking to clear up the question of: who am I?'

'Cock and pussy then—that's all it was? That's what they understood by sex? I mean, didn't they even kiss?'

5. FRIENDS

The real foundation for the three heroes' fame was not their deeds, not the stories of their journeys and the wonders that they saw. They were loved because they always stuck together. They were so perfectly attuned in courage and good humour that it was impossible to imagine one of them without the others and this made them a legend.

Hecate, Huan-Ti and Anubis—say one of these names and the others had to follow.

And this was good, because each was what the others were not. Hecate was a powerfully built mare, a Gypsy Cob with a yellow mane, piebald and with broad steady feet. Huan-Ti was a white tiger with a dreadful roar and a fondness for long nights and lazy days. Anubis was a ferret from the south, who knew some filthy songs, bad jokes and the best way out of almost any fix. They had got to know one another in Capeside, where Huan-Ti had made his fortune as a sports impresario, staging exclusive events and taking bets.

That had been in the hard years of the early war economy, during the pherinfone blockade and the transcontinental embargo on plants and all other speechless creatures. These measures were supposed to stop Katahomenleandraleal's spies from infiltrating. The economy, politics and culture of the Three Cities were heavily affected.

In those days, the three heroes would roam the streets together until the small hours, making merry mischief as they could. On occasion they would take on small jobs as proactive reporters, for a sunbird who worked with Ryuneke's world-spanning network of pherinfonic news and entertainment channels. The three of them got into such unlikely scrapes that Ryuneke himself was persuaded to offer this splendid entertainment to all Gente, everywhere.

The number of the heroes' followers grew with every prank they pulled in Borbruck, Landers, Capeside—drunken nights and sexual exploits, scuffles and skirmishes, and even one or two unfriendly encounters with the badger police.

In the end, when as Anubis said 'the town was on the skids and there wasn't a glimmer of the old glamour', Hecate suggested that they could travel the world together, to stay young, to open their minds and to kill time in style.

'Tcha, see where the world is—out there beyond the borders of our civilization, over the edge from the Animal Empire, there where the Gente aren't the only ones, where the speechless people live.'

Ryuneke's news and entertainment empire agreed to support the adventure with hard cash and with logistics. The Fox announced, 'We could all do with a little distraction, given how scarce the good things of life have become.' He was talking about the financial situation, the energy reserves, the constant diversion of resources into new funds for Izquierda's projects, up in the Preference Mountains with her ever-growing cadre (talk was, she had thirty thousand Gente on staff).

Hecate, Huan-Ti and Anubis set off. They went looking for adventure and found it, as the Gente would tell in tales for a long time yet to come, in songs and films, paintings and statues.

They crossed the lesser sea in ships and then crossed the deserts of the continent-sized battlefield that the Monotony had called 'Africa'.

There, on a long autumn afternoon in the sixth year of the Three Cities' second command economy since the Liberation, they made their most important, their strangest discovery.

'This is where they came from, however many thousands of years ago it was,' said Hecate and pawed the sand, within eyeshot of a watering hole, above a shady valley.

'And later they made it into game parks. Tourism. They wanted the same thing that we want now—to see lions and giraffes, who didn't have language back in those days either.'

'They're still here now, you're right,' said Anubis. 'Cyrus Iemelian Adrian Vinicius Golden, may he live forever or die trying, is as you know understandably sentimental about the brute animals, those without the power of reason. He's set up—what's the word from the Monotony—representations for them.'

'Reservations,' corrected Hecate.

Huan-Ti yawned and said, 'Well, there's not much human crap round, we can be grateful for that at least.'

It wasn't a metaphor. Ever since the Gente had begun recycling on a large scale, rather than tipping their rubbish in the slums round the Three Cities, you found there instead rubbish, excrement and corpses, left by the last human refugees, the hidden people with crippled hands.

They had crept their way into catacombs and into the tottering ruins, in settlements that the Lion had not deigned to incorporate into one of his megacities.

Human crap—part of what the three heroes had wanted to escape, along with the growing gloom of the crisis, when they left for a more interesting reality, where they could paw and scratch and roll in the lovely truth.

Huan-Ti's remark had prompted Anubis to sniff round, to establish exact numbers of surviving ancestrals. He always wanted to know the last detail and he looked about in a tuft of bladed grass to find one of the few coded data cables here in the tropic lands. There were few such arteries accessible here, but the yellow stalks and the index nodes in the stomata told him that he had found the right plant. He asked, how many humans are there left in the great battlefield that had been called 'Africa'?

'A few hundred thousand,' answered the non-local server.

The ferret was about to share this reassuring detail with his companions, when the white tiger said, 'Psst!' and gestured to the others silently, rolling his eyes, look, over there!

He nodded towards the King's cousins, oblivious of the world and of themselves.

The pride of lions lounging on a pale-yellow cliff clearly had not a wicked thought in their heads. One very beautiful lioness, probably the alpha male's mate, was stretched out lazily, deeply at peace, and then she was couched, alert, watching, straining for a scent that she had caught.

'A hunt! Here comes fun!' chuckled Hecate, happy to be upwind with her friends and also in the shelter of two spreading panther trees.

The ferret whispered a bon mot, such as had made him so popular back home, 'Something's happening here, and as you know, things that happen are often underway.'

Huan-Ti's green eyes were keener, saw further than the mare's chestnut eyes or Anubis' silver gaze. He was the first to see what had woken the lioness to life, three great big buffalo and a tremble-legged calf, none showing any sign that they knew the hunters were nearby. They trotted gently towards the little lake.

They crested the hill, coming towards the lions, towards their doom.

Her friends shifted closer to the powerfully built horse and she knew or felt in her muscles that time had shifted subtly here, that the rhythm was now set by pumping heartbeats, no longer by the winds that blew gently through the grass.

The lions sprang.

The buffalo were startled, turned their heads, bucked.

The rhythm of their hoofbeats broke. The largest of them sped ahead, hurtled into the tall dry grass and was gone. The other two adults, crazed with fear, ran neck and neck past the water towards a shallow pass between two hills. The calf lagged behind though. One of the younger lionesses caught up, tackled it and brought it down. It stumbled, dodged helplessly, swerved left and fell into the water. Two more lionesses were there immediately, at its throat, in its flank.

The brackish lakewater splashed, sprayed, and then there was already blood.

'Thick hides,' Hecate said with hope in her voice, 'they won't get through that in a hurry.'

Green and rust-red—what was going on? The ferret strained to see, focused his gaze. A storm of biting and flying claws, in the shadow of a branch that hung down to the water. Two of the lionesses leant across the fallen body like neighbours chatting over the garden fence.

The three friends didn't know if the victim was still alive. Now the huntresses were trying to drag the calf from the water, only the hindquarters were visible; something shot into the air. Since when does a buffalo calf have such a thick, leathery tail? No, that wasn't the calf.

It was something new, and there were three of them.

'Do you see that? Thundering thunderboxes! A crocodile?' The creature that had bitten into the thrashing buffalo's hindquarters was clearly giving the lionesses a lot of trouble. They strained and tugged against it. It was smooth and white, and covered with fronds that waved like the tentacular tongues of a sea anemone.

'Can you get a spectroscopic view of that?' the white tiger asked the mare. Hecate hesitated and stared at it. Then she whispered, wheezing, 'It's a very rapid . . . chemical reaction . . . some kind of extreme . . . catalysis, oxidization, that for sure, but whether . . .'

'It's on fire. Look how the calf is kicking! Those fronds . . . those things in the lake, they're on fire. They've got to be nemato . . . thingy, like jellyfish have, or . . .'

'But the claws or jaws or whatever . . . it's not an invertebrate . . . it's got armour! Holy crap!'

Reverberant and as wide as the battlefield itself, a note sounded beyond the hill, soon swelling louder than the splashing water, the murderous roars.

That saved the calf's life. It was the buffalo returning, at a headlong gallop, no longer only a handful but an army, a whole herd, their wide curved horns like weapons set in their crashproof heads.

The lionesses left their prey immediately. Two of them were hit anyway, then fled, two ran clean away, one of the hunters was almost trampled and leapt for safety into the grass. The thing in the lake, the three things that had appeared there, the smooth, fronded things, had released the calf when the hooves of the buffalo came thundering across the earth. The calf, wounded and dazed but alive, was swept along by the dark brown mob of its kind.

The lions had vanished.

The three watchers had recorded this lucky escape and beamed it back home straightaway. They were so relieved that only hours later did Anubis think to ask, 'What on earth was that, in the water?'

They spied out the land, sweeping out in great circles from the waterhole and then back.

Not a trace.

Huan-Ti dipped his right forepaw into the water and found no trace of life there larger than a minnow, with any analytical programme. 'We can't be sure,' said Anubis, 'that they haven't left the waterhole in the meantime, whatever kind of . . . creatures they were.'

'You think they were amphibians? Reptiles?'

'Polemoamphibi . . .' Anubis began, proud of his alleged ties to the Izquierda cadre, eager to show off the secrets that they occasionally shared with him.

'That's just what we needed to know,' snarled Huan-Ti. Hecate lay her noble head to one side and said, 'Perhaps he's right. Maybe these . . . glazed potsherds . . . with their jaws and their fronds, these thing we saw, maybe they really were the shock troops. The constructs built to serve . . .'

'Katahomenleandraleal,' the ferret said triumphantly. His nose shone with insider pride.

'I thought they'd look different. And anyway, where did they get to? And also, what are they doing down here, in this godforsaken corner of the world?' the tiger asked.

'Maybe it's manoeuvres. War games. Invasion scenarios. Test landings,' said Hecate.

They all fell silent for an uncomfortable minute.

'Anyway, I was recording cross-spectrum, all the registers,' Anubis declared at last.

The camera behind his retina had several days' storage capacity. 'I'll send it to the badgers, if that helps.'

His friends didn't try to talk him out of it.

And so a few days later the bat Izquierda watched the material in her cave.

When she was done, she spoke a sentence that went down in the annals of Gente history. 'Those aren't crabs, crocodiles or amphibians. We'll need a new classification, kids. I'll tell you what they are. They're Ceramicans.'

6. THE CURRENTS

'Degenerate matter.'

'And how can a living organism endure the . . .'

'Oh, it gets smeared to a thin paste,' replied the anglerfish Carl Tamerlanski, probably the most hideous being that Dmitri Stepanovich Sebassus had ever seen.

He had to believe what they were telling him, even if it didn't sound credible. He knew nothing about such matters and had to trust the word of the dwellers in the abyssal ocean, here at the midpoint of his long journey. The anglerfish was explaining to Dmitri the technology that allowed him to survive the pressure and adapt to the gravitational effects, developed in the gigantic buckyball suspended above the volcanic rift. Without it, he would be dead, gills or no gills, crushed by the hellish weight.

The fish kept up his lecture, his jaw snapping open and shut even more smugly than his natural expression already made him. 'We have learnt how to treat practically every gas as a fluid, let's say, like water. Our most advanced prototypes would be able to resist the extreme conditions in Saturn's atmosphere. That grav calibration belt that you're wearing can survive the storm in Jupiter's Great Red Spot.'

Dmitri wished that he were back in his bathysphere, back on the oceanic ridge, where he had passed time with the happy chattering schools of dolphins, or on the continental shelf, where he had met the whales who shared his love of riddles. Ach, anywhere but here, among these monsters, the scholar and his bodyguard of grotesque ratfish and sixgill sharks staring glassily ahead. But the Lion had charged him with the task of inspecting personally the benthic Atlanteans' experiments.

'Reckless physics': the job in hand was to confirm or refute the rumours abroad in the big cities. So Dmitri, treading water strenuously, asked, 'May I go inside? Into the ball?' The buckyball was larger than the Temple of Isotta in Capeside and blazed unnaturally from its thousand facets. The wolf felt something of the fear that mankind had felt in the later Monotony at the word 'radioactive'.

Tamerlanski's angler lure sparked electrically as he shook his head. 'Even we can only enter after we've spent years working in . . . sensitive labs outside the ball. The things that go on in there . . . many who've experienced it say that must be what it's like to take a walk on the surface of a star.' The wolf remembered the aquarium beneath the benzene ring and thought that the fish had long had a taste for big dumb objects. Well, let them.

He asked another of his master's questions. 'Is it true that you're building several of these balls? Deeper in the rift, nearer the volcano?'

'So you've heard up there that we are building spindizzies.'

'Spin . . .'

'Flying cities. One day, perhaps quite soon, they'll cross the empty gulfs between the planets, perhaps even between astronomically distant bodies in the . . .'

The wolf screwed up his nose.

The ugly fish could have talked in the same lordly tone had he been planning to depopulate the oceans—yes of course, you'll understand, they must all be exterminated, the coastal macaques and the mudskippers in the shallow waters, and those lobsters there in the great oceanic basins, the clownfish and the jellyfish, every species that evolution has not made as immensely ugly and bestially compact as myself, shaped to survive to the ages of ages, indefinitely, you must agree, we have after all developed the poisons and have them stockpiled, likewise the bombs, a huge park full of weapons, among the coral stems . . .

Tamerlanski was actually babbling happily about 'two kinds, the proximal and the baryonic. We've successfully synthesized both. We suspect that the first exists in the interior of white dwarfs and the other is probably created in neutron stars. Clearly you have to take the exclusion principle into . . .' While he lectured, Dmitri would gladly have bitten clean off the looks that the brainless sharks in his entourage wore on their faces.

The wolf suspected that there was something going on behind those blank looks, something feverish, deadly that constantly threatened to overwhelm them with an instinctual fury of destruction, goading their bloodlust.

Bringing up the rear of the little column of swimmers were swaying bladder-like things. Dmitri found their gentle movement somehow mocking, even impudent.

I've got to get out of here, blast it! Is this claustrophobia, nitrogen narcosis?

The wolf decided to let the autonomous hearing centres of his brain record everything that the pompous fool was saying. Let the Lion scoop the dreck from his brain later.

I should have stayed with the Li'l Ly'x, quietly, at home, that's what.

'Do you follow me?' asked the monster.

'Quite,' lied Dmitri, 'it's fascinating.'

VII
THE OTHER LOVE

1. SHAPELY (FOR PADRAIC)

'You can kiss my hairy lupine haunches. The lot of you, brrr,' snarled Dmitri Stepanovich, his almond eyes narrowed to glowing slits. The mad things in the trees wouldn't stop their senseless shrieking. 'Into a mute crypt, I can't pity our time!'

'Turn amity poetic!'

'Permutation City!'

'Ciao, tiny trumpet!'

'Great. Drivelling nonsense.' They couldn't hear him, or didn't want to.

He fought his way through a sweltering, heavy heat. Dmitri would rather be back in the water, amongst the great-mawed, blank-eyed beasts, than have to trot his way through such meaningless claptrap.

The cypress all round him hardly cast any shadow. There were too many gaps, the alternation of burning sun on his fur and cool stands of punkwood-smelling trees only increased his bad temper with each step he took across yellow, tinder-dry grass. He was on all fours—for this part of the journey, wolf paws were better than his goat legs. At least he knew that this wood was the last obstacle before he reached his goal. Soon enough he would reach open ground and the odd bird's home. At least, if the map coded into his inner ear was correct.

'Maniac piety tutor . . .'

They wouldn't stop, these loud, mad voices.

At first he had thought that the screaming little animals were squirrels, because of the way they leapt from branch to branch, dug their claws into the bark, crouched there and tormented him. Then he saw one of them sail through the air, flying, three yards wide, two-and-a-half above the ground, the black-feathered wings spread. At last he recognized the slender body and almost laughed at the pink nose and dainty ears—the animal was a silver-and-white tabby, a short-hair. The next one he recognized was the blue Siamese, seemingly the leader, who cried out, 'Tame purity tonic!' before two Persians, gleaming like fresh sailcloth, whispered from the bushes, 'Up, meiotic tyrant!'

'Is that supposed to scare me?' Dmitri barked hoarsely.

Winged cats—if anything was ever a capricious waste of skin, it was these.

Dmitri rubbed his pelt on a cedar trunk to clean away the dust of two weeks' wandering. At least I was warned. The Lion's friend, this bird, he's a geneticist, they love such jokes. Winged cats, what a scream! he thought.

'Pin my taut erotic art to epic mutiny!' shrilled the cats, still managing to stay within calling distance but not too close to the wolf. The fur on his nape bristled and he spat on the ground. The cats are trying to remind me of my lynx now, are they? Fine, my erotic art to their erratic talk—but where they get the idea that I would ever mutiny, who can say. Not they.

'What do you want, you dumb mutt?' A wirehaired kitten was standing in the wolf's path, curled whiskers, wings raised at a sharp slant. She crouched, hissed and sank her head, glowering up from beneath her brows. Dmitri found it funnier than anything else.

He decided to try being polite. 'I'd like to go to your . . . master, I suppose. Your begetter.'

'We have no begetter. And no one gets the better of us,' said the little kitten. She grinned, her features twisted into a clownish mask that was more frightening than she seemed to know. Was this little moppet going to fight him? But the cat dropped her attitude. She lifted her head and sniffed—scentmail. The cat showed her teeth. Dmitri had no idea how, but this time she managed to make it look friendly rather than aggressive. She lifted her little nose and said, 'Fine. Come along. Through the village.'

Then she turned, a movement so fluent and confident that Dmitri could only obediently follow.

The village turned out to be hardly worth the name—a few collapsed frontages, broke-backed roofs, shabby patches of lawn, all among twisty little streets. Toytown, thought the wolf and reckoned that only the badgers might be able to make something of these wrecks, possibly barracks.

The kitten said, 'The smartest lived here.'

'Smartest which?'

'Humans of course,' said the kitten and left the tumbled streets, going behind a shallow stone building, its pillars overgrown with moss.

'Two more combs,' the little thing remarked.

Whatever this measure of distance meant, her tone of voice promised more exertion.

An hour and a half later, the wolf's tongue was hanging from his chops. His gaze clung to the ground, looking for a plant that he could grub up for moisture.

In front of him a scratching sound, crunching like gravel.

He looked ahead to the kitten, who had left him far behind, seven wolves' lengths now.

Dmitri's peculiar guide spread her wings, jumped, jumped again, and again, a little higher each time. A sudden beat of the wings like a handclap, open again, and rapid beat, and the animal was aloft.

'Hey, where are you going?' For the briefest moment the Lion's envoy felt afraid—had they led him off into the middle of nowhere? Or into a trap?

Then the cat wheeled leftward, diving from the height to which she had effortlessly climbed, straight down towards him with claws unsheathed—is she attacking?—and called, 'Look up ahead, there it is already! The Lab!' She flew in a wide curve, sliced the air above him and was gone—back to the forest.

Dmitri shook his head and looked where she had shown.

There stood one of the prettiest ruins he had ever seen, and he had seen a great many. So this was what was left of the campus for which the Lion had given him the ground plans, all those months ago, on the other side of the ocean—beige blocks, a facade full of arabesque spires, a tower made of rusty old bicycles. Roots and tendrils tumbled up the walls like foam, airy courtyards opened to the skies, a huge lecture hall lay silent as though sleeping.

Dmitri hurried on. Soon he was standing in front of the main building.

If the wolf had been expecting a welcoming party, of rather more serious folk than the winged cats, he was disappointed. A couple of crickets chirruped, a hare said, 'Hey, fatty!' and disappeared into the greenery. Spy out the land first, then, pace out the grounds?

Seminar rooms, the display cabinets at the back wall burst open, patio, gallery, a loading bay with huge dented cylinders and elephantine sealed metal coffins, full of chemical waste that was doubtless still poisonous. Greenhouses coming apart at the seams—the flora had poured itself all over the place, leaves seemed to burst from every window—collapsed stairways. The foyer of the main block had been spared by some Providence, though no one had cleaned up here in a very long time. A bomb must have dropped to the west of the car park. In the crater a pool with horribly perfect, sharply sloping sides, unpredictably forested, its water gleaming darkly. The sun stood at its zenith now, the heat was ridiculous, his thirst unbearable.

'Old fur-face sent you, didn't he,' laughed a clear feminine voice.

The wolf started.

'No, go on, drink. You've got to wet your whistle—isn't that what they say over there in the old world? You're not used to our weather, are you?'

In front of him a woman swam in the water; human and a swan.

Dmitri remembered the Valkyries in the first film that he had seen with Clea Dora—they took off their feathered gowns to bathe. The woman in front of him threw back her beautiful head and laughed, and the wolf felt transported. He was ashamed to have been so self-confident and he was astonished to see the little white feathers rise up on her head and shoulders. It looked like short white hair, mussed about. Downy feathers clung to her body in folds and swatches, between her arms and hips, where shining drops of water gathered. As she came up from the water and waded towards him, moist, glimmering like Venus, Dmitri thought, the wingspan—must be longer than my whole body.

'I can already smell who you seek and who has sent you. He has sent no word to me for a long time now.'

The bird, thought Dmitri. Is this the bird? This remarkable beauty?

He contradicted his thought, loud and clear. 'I . . . no, I'm supposed to be looking for a man. A bloke.'

What was happening between them here? A déjà vu, a gift, perhaps a trap. 'I have been that, before,' she said with her gentle, singing voice, so that Dmitri thought, I'm having trouble understanding what she says, is this hypnotism?

'I am,'—standing tall before him, she sketched a bow—'Alexandra Élodie Paula Miramei, whom you seek. But to help you—help him—alas, I cannot do that. You may be my guest here. Perhaps you will even enjoy your stay.'

She squatted down before him, touched his neck with long fingers, ruffled his fur as though she had done so many a time.

A moment ago he had wanted only to get away, now it was as though he belonged here.

'He's become a king, I hear,' she said and held Dmitri's muzzle for a moment in her slim hand, 'that probably makes me a countess then.'

The wolf did not understand her meaning, but when she put her arms round him and kissed him fleetingly, he knew that he would indeed want to stay with her.

As long as I am here, his heart told him, I am where I should be.

2. THE CLEAR SKIES

He stayed longer than even the most generous interpretation of the Lion's orders would have allowed.

Alexandra refused the Lion's offer to become 'a brother in arms again, as in old times', and the wolf took her decision calmly, sending bees eastwards in a mist of coded signals, along a lengthy route but one that would deliver this information safely.

There were more important things here, in the Countess' ruined palace and on the shores of her pond, in the forest of winged cats and in the scruffy park, than the coming war: here was the good life.

It was not Dmitri who finally broached the topic, but the swan.

'Admittedly, he'll have military problems to contend with,' she said as they strolled through the lush foliage round the overspilled greenhouses, 'but that's just the same old game, the one we wanted to leave behind back then. The endless chain: if you were the lion, then the fox would betray you, if you were the lamb, then the fox would devour you, if you were the fox, then the lion would suspect you if the donkey were to denounce you, if you were the donkey, then your own stupidity would make your life a misery and you'd only live to be a wolf's breakfast. What kind of creature could you be, that would be subjugated to no other?'

'Shakespeare,' Dmitri smiled, and looked upwards at the cats in the clear skies above.

'You say that as though you knew who he was. Who he was for us, back in the bad times.'

'You oldsters,'—the wolf rubbed his neck along her fragrant flank, she enjoyed that—'you act as though there were no culture left.'

'There isn't. You don't need it after all, a separate cultural sphere, distinct from the rest of life. For us art was something rare, costly, for you . . . life is all art these days.'

'Until the war returns,' he said, affecting concern.

She grabbed for him and he dodged. They ran through the lovely ruins until it became dark.

Then they slept together for the first time.

What he liked most of all was that he could lie at her side as with wolves, flank to flank, in brotherly fashion.

Here in this part of the world the moon looked bigger at night than it did in Dmitri's homeland. The wolf had to master the urge to howl at it, when he and the swan went swimming together by its pale metallic light.

The days were a game of peek-a-boo in curtains made of heat.

When Alexandra talked about the past, it was a completely different story from the Lion's. Her view of what had been seemed sharper, not clouded by guilt perhaps, or doubt. She could easily tell what was gone forever apart from what, like the seasons, might return.

'We had our good times too. Halcyon summers, and in the end one Helliconia summer?'

'Helliconia?'

'Literature. *Helliconia* is an epic about a distant star, two really. It was about a planet called Helliconia, with seasons that lasted whole generations. The creator was called Aldiss—an Englishman.'

'Englishman, what kind of job was that?'

'Oh, no, not a job . . . it was a geographical tag. He came from that squashed little island that lies offshore from the bigger island where two of your Three Cities . . . They had brass necks, those English. Time was when they led the whole world by the nose.'

She laughed, and he stopped himself from laughing too, because he wanted to hear her laugh.

In the Countess' chambers Dmitri saw lovely, mysterious shadows on the paper walls and at the doors, when he lay by her side in the middle of the day, panting. He couldn't stand to be outside at this hour, though she pranced in and out, through routes he couldn't follow, while her feet seemed hardly to touch the ground.

Almost every evening they went swimming and diving together. He surprised and impressed her with his amphibian abilities. They played among the water lilies, and he thought happily, Everything here is sheet and leaf, paper and blossom, lotus or cherry.

Sometimes he thought of home and what they might think of him, might want of him. Then he would become stubborn. We should be allowed to act, for a while at least, as though this were all a game. We're not hurting anyone, we make one another happy, isn't that enough?

At the dark of moon, by the campfire on the main laboratory roof, she remarked, 'There's a lot to be said for the cyclical view of history, *corsi e ricorsi*, wheels within wheels and so on.'

He wrinkled his brow just a little to show that she had caught his interest.

She said, 'The idea that all this has happened before and will happen again. A whole pantheon like a zoo. The chimerae, the sphinxes, the ancient Egyptians—the idea that the oldest hieroglyphs are perhaps documents from a hybrid sodomitical age, misunderstood, an era when we already knew how to find the lowest common denominator of beast and man, how to create as many species as there are individual beings, that the knowledge had been passed down even from older epochs of human history, its true meaning slowly forgotten during the Pharaonic age.'

'And what about the age before ours? The Monotony?'

A feather had fallen from her head, a hair out of place, and she puffed at it, blowing it in the air, into the fire. The feather danced a little jig as it burnt, as though enjoying it.

Then Alexandra Élodie said, '*Er nennt's Vernunft, und braucht's allein, um tierischer als jedes Tier zu sein* . . . there were a few who saw it coming, you know.'

He wrinkled his nose. He didn't understand.

She kissed his brow. 'You're so sweet, you know that? There were voices raised in warning from the very beginning, even when they were just discussing the right to terminate pregnancies. The balanced argument was that since the technology exists, then what these women did to their own bodies was surely their own affair. Well, when a few decades later this argument was widely accepted—at least by those in responsibility, the judges and lawyers, the politicians—what objection could they actually raise when a woman wanted to have a child with her dog, as soon as that technology existed? Sodomism, ho ho. Your zander, Wesphalia, he wanted to . . . he was supposed to . . . Livienda's, he was, I suppose . . . to regulate it all, to organize it. But with changes in the reproductive system as radical as this, there's not much to regulate, *ex post facto*.'

Dmitri scratched his flank with his rear right foot, half embarrassed, half bored. He yawned hugely and then said, 'Great, but to change subjects, what's that bollocks your pussycats are always screeching in the woods? It really gave me a scrabbling headache, you know, when I . . .'

'Anagrams.'

'Anagrams. You mean, recombination and permutation of ehhh . . .'

'Yes. Think about it. Really. No, seriously!' They both laughed. Then she said, 'Please, take . . . It's . . . *Homo sapiens*' most important contribution to evolutionary science, as a species. It was a human called Egan who first ran through the idea, or ran across it, ran it down, as a thought experiment in algorithm complexity.'

This was certainly more relevant than the idle talk about sodomy. Dmitri pricked up his ears. 'Computation. Like when pherinfonics . . .'

'As soon as you can simulate a world which contains actual observers, that's to say substructures truly conscious of themselves and their environment . . .'

'A virtual environment containing its own description,' the wolf said helpfully.

'That's right. Well, once you can do that, then it doesn't actually matter to the conscious individual in the simulated world whether the simulation runs backwards, relative to the, erm, real world, the world in which the simulation is running on whatever substrate you're using—from inside, it all feels the right way round.'

'Obviously. It all happens with logical causation, not temporal.'

'So, in this system CBA is identical to ABC, for the consciousness in question, the main thing being that the causal sequence—three steps, in this case—holds. The derivability of one state from the immediate logical precedent. To say it again, logical, not temporal.'

'Granted. Where are you going with all this?'

'Think it over. What if you mix it up more thoroughly? Not forwards or backwards, but ACB? BCA?'

'From within it'll all look the same. A conscious individual at the C state will always experience a reality where it began in A and then proceeded to B.'

'From inside, "derives from" feels just like "happens after".'

'But what's all this supposed to lead to? It's a commonplace: causality as the mortar of the universe.'

'Exactly. And because it's such a truism, from within, all sequences are equally valid. As soon as something is conceivably consistent . . .'

'Ah-h-h . . . now I understand. As soon as . . . right, and that's exactly how it is, even if we have to consider the electron cloud state of every atom anywhere, ever. With massive distribution like this, then all conceivable combinations are actually real, in their own way. All possible worlds really exist. That is, just a moment—if you've got enough computing time.'

'Why time?'

The wolf barked, a dry laugh. 'Shit, you're right. There's no such thing as absolute time, if you grant this model . . . By Georgescu!'

'All stories are true, a human called Alan Moore once . . .'

'You and your humans, girlie!'

'And even though that's true . . . there's no cause for concern about arbitrary or relativist states. The fact that all stories are true doesn't after all imply that . . .'

'. . . that all elements are interchangeable in every programme without destroying the programme itself.'

'You see. So, "alternatives" are something other than simply "chaos". And once you've understood that, then to attain the divine madness, the highest truths, you need only posit the supplementary question: if we can separate the two ideas of causal logic and temporal sequence, and if we can conceptualize effects independently of time's arrow but never independent of causality, what does that imply for our concepts of evolution?'

She went on to sketch out the further implications, but Dmitri had to admit to himself later, ashamed and annoyed, that he hadn't paid much attention—she was explaining to him how, at a fundamental level, the cosmos could be settled and inhabited in anagrams, while he had already begun to lick her hands and feet.

She kissed him and ruffled his hair, and spoke again about humans—Unica Zürn and Maya Deren, and how you could play the anagram game not only with processors but also on paper, on celluloid, in storage crystals, and at last even with DNA, the reservoir where the Third Wave of creation surged, the fearful wealth which the Lion had used for his own ends, which admittedly she had helped him to do, although she wouldn't do that again in a hurry, maybe in a thousand years or so . . .

She went on, speaking in tongues, speaking in circles, ever-widening, citing ever more facts and arguments, until she stopped talking because then she was kissing him and had other things to say.

Dobroi notchi, Countess, good night.

3. EACH WAS A GOD TO THE OTHER

Sometimes the lovers took trips to the prairies, or to the coast, where they could watch the horizons, sometimes they went to the carp ponds under the high cliffs.

At times her mouth was a beak and then her beak was a mouth, and he liked the lower lip especially. When the sun rose, her eyes turned blue before the skies could and then she looked at him as if amazed that such a thing as he could be.

He was proud of this, because her amazement was so much at odds with her knowledge. She knew so much more than he did.

One night when she thought that he was asleep he followed her through the thyme and the wild mint, through the greenery, to a clearing so deep within the wood that he could no longer see the laboratory's neon lights. Here in the silence, the cool blue depths, the Countess chose to perform a duty that she loved.

In the shimmering starlight she stepped out of herself, between blue stones, as a second swan, a woman entirely of light, and the wolf, her lover, held his breath, swooning under a strange assault, in a turmoil, cowering against the wind where he had crept in the underbrush.

The two beautiful creatures were one and the same, and the first said to the other, 'Romeo, doff thy name, and for that name which is no part of thee take all myself.' On cue, 'Call me but love, and I'll be new baptized; henceforth I never will be Romeo.' 'What man art thou,' the first replied, continuing her role, 'that thus bescreen'd in night so stumblest on my counsel?'

'By a name I know not how to tell thee who I am: my name, dear saint, is hateful to myself, because it is an enemy to thee; had I it written, I would tear the word.'

The wolf lay his muzzle on the damp earth, sniffed a scent of pepper and closed his eyes. He heard one voice whisper, 'So thrive my soul—' and the other say, 'A thousand times good night!' and he knew a thing that only he and the mushrooms growing here in this forest had heard, that this was why the Lion could not expect any help from this quarter, that this was the only thing the Countess wanted, to be Romeo and to love Juliet, or to be Juliet and love Romeo.

To make peace with history, to forget the age when we had 'Liberated' ourselves but still not found ourselves. Needled leaves of the rosemary bush nodded in the breeze, a gentle audience. The wolf commanded each hair in his coat to lie still. He would rather have died than disturbed these two at their play. He felt no envy—how could he not have indulged the swan her dearest wish, this encounter, the scene she played out in dreams, and in reality?

I am not Juliet, thought Dmitri, and I am not Romeo, I'm just someone who drifted in here for no particular reason and wants to think that he has come home.

She is so much older than I am and so much more naive as well.

What will happen then? If I die here, will she bury me, or will she teach me before then, tell me what I must know before I can leave?

Will it be time to leave just when I have truly arrived?

'Hence will I to my ghostly father's cell, his help to crave, and my dear hap to tell.'

On the morning after his discovery he awoke in the car park in the shadow of a collapsed observatory dome. Maple leaves lay scattered about him like feathers shed or plucked. He rolled round in the leaves until twilight crept away. He stretched, hummed like a beehive, looked up. The cats were flying, in arrow formation and then in clusters. When he looked closer to see how they crossed and swirled, he also saw that other flocks were flying in amongst them.

'Hey!' The Countess had crept up from his right, from the maple leaves' strong scent so that he didn't get wind of her. She smelt of smoke.

Alexandra said, 'Can you see what those arrows and wedges are?'

He hesitated, looked again and understood that the anglerfish had been telling the truth—pelican eels, hatchetfish and a cloud of hundreds of whiptail grenadiers. 'They really did it . . . the fish, they've conquered the air!' said the wolf in wonder. The swan kissed the hollow of his neck and whispered, 'Just wait. Those Atlanteans are ambitious. Pffft, the air's only the beginning. Outer space, that's where they're headed, and it's theirs if they want it, think of it as only another ocean.' He blew in her air, took one dancing step away from her and said, 'To space? We've been there and done that.'

'You talk like the Lion,'—the swan spread her wings and then folded them again, a chaste robe. 'Mankind was never suited for the stars, that's true. They gave up on that plan even before the Liberation. They would have needed to change two things: their flimsy genetic base, much too susceptible to hard radiation, constant showers of sub-atomic particles in empty space, and their lifespan, far too short to let them even consider the longer and more interesting routes.'

The wolf looked upwards again—swords of flame. Signs in fire. Much colour.

'And the Gente have solved these?'

'Ach, Gente. That's something new up there, quite fresh. The fourth post-Liberation generation. You're only second generation.'

'Only. Well, thanks.'

She stroked him, put him in a better mood.

'Won't imagination save us?' she asked. He was surprised, almost worried, wondering where someone who knew so much, someone with such wisdom, could have come up with this pious, rather repellent lie.

She could hear that he wasn't answering. So she said something else. 'I've built and built and built. I began at sixteen. I collect everything to do with it.'

4. FILM

In the cellar she showed him what she meant. 'Second generation. At the time it was I who suggested it to Iemelian.'

'One of the . . .'

'One of your boss's precursors, yes.'

The projection on the wall showed infection vectors in megapopulations across adjacent landmasses. After a while the picture pixellated and gave way to a giant molecule.

'Immunity against all naturally occurring microbial attack,' said Alexandra.

The model revolved, its tiny spheres pulsating in time to a simple melody (Dmitri remembered the poison attack on human hands) and the Countess explained, 'Natural history suggested a robust model for us—two helical spirals of sugar and phosphate, connected by base pairs making up a four-letter alphabet encoding the entire genetic information. Second generation simply meant inserting different bases, a whole new genome. A new phylum was born. The code stayed the same but the alphabet was different.'

'One step beyond the anagram principle.'

'Exactly. A meta-anagram or . . . kata-anagram, extended downward. Which is where that barbaric monstrosity down south gets its prefix, Katahomen—it's a descendant of the second generation, a reengineering of the principle for ceramic or silicon-based life. First DNA, then the new ribosomes . . .'

'And the metabolism?'

'Standard. The same proteins that evolution has always whacked together. Ninety per cent of everything is just the same, but the resulting multicellular organism was immediately immune to all viruses and perrhobacteria. They can still get in, of course, but . . .'

The wolf imagined tiny robots getting into his skull. No sooner are they inside than the door they had entered by slams shut behind them. There they sit, in the cold emptiness, and starve.

'Erm, help me out with this. Second generation, so what did the first look like?'

'Do you know what you're asking there?'

'Well, I'm asking you . . . about the Liberation's biotic parameters. How it really was.'

'Quite.' The Countess twitched her right wingtip and made a stern face: ugly stories, I don't like to talk about it.

Dmitri resolved to ask the Lion some time.

He had hardly made that decision and it became painfully clear to him—however much at home he felt here, he would not stay with Alexandra. It was too lovely here and whenever he asked her, by hints or directly, whether she wanted him to stay, she fell silent, saying a thousand things, making three thousand excuses. She loved to murmur sweet words about sorrow, it was better to have loved and lost, and other such stale, sad rubbish from the Monotony's rich store of screwed-up emotional masochism. He didn't belong here, in this museum, in this sequestered happiness. What Dmitri didn't understand was that she loved him, but would never say so, he had to take it on trust. As though happiness were a bad thing and unfulfilled yearning a better argument than the erotic generosity she had shown at first. She was a proud, free creature.

The sun grew pale, an uncertain wind sprang up.

The wolf was a political animal and therefore, from now on, would in turn keep his own feelings hidden from her.

5. FORMS, FORMS AND RENEWAL, GODS HELD IN THE AIR

'Can you see her? Do you see what she's doing to time?'

The wolf looked, and experienced for the first time the feeling of watching himself while he watched, the way he sometimes listened to himself talk, for instance when he was very tired.

The Countess had rigged up an ancient film projector in the main lecture hall. The wolf saw a girl enter the rectangular frame diagonally and cross it single-mindedly. The young woman vanished behind a sand dune in the foreground, at the edge of the frame. The camera cut out for an almost imperceptible moment. Then the girl reappeared, a little further off, heading for a spot behind a further dune in the distance.

The camera swept about in a movement that panned across the whole scene in the direction that the girl had just left the frame. It kept on filming from exactly the same place where it had just cut out, so there was no spatial jump to mark time elapsed. The wolf expected (or expected that he would expect—a strange doubling) to see the girl coming out from behind the dune where she had just vanished from sight. Instead, she appeared from behind the further dune, headed for the wide-open distance. The sense of sight was uncoupled from what it watched, the mind's internal sense of time was jarred and jolted, with this feeling of being double. As the picture vanished and the lights went up, Dmitri felt that some remark was expected of him.

Hesitantly he began, 'A hrrrm leap, a . . . like an anagram . . .'

But Alexandrea Élodie laid a wingtip on his lips. 'Shhh. Just watch. Otherwise you're doing to her again what they all did to her while she was alive.'

Dmitri didn't know who this person was that they were talking about.

'She died of rage,' said Alexandra, 'because they wouldn't let her work.'

The lights went down again. The film began from the beginning.

6. BRIGHT VOID, WITHOUT IMAGE, NAPISHTIM

She showed him her gardens one last time, as they became darker.

The war had already begun then. 'It always begins with these clumsy first strikes,' she sighed, sounding almost embarrassed, 'putting a murrain on the harvests, turning the weather wrong. Funny to say these words again. At the time I always asked myself how it was possible that words are so strictly assigned, that each one only wants to go where it thinks it belongs. For instance we say that a city is destroyed and its inhabitants murdered, but you'd feel odd saying that the inhabitants had been destroyed and the city murdered. Inferences from . . . well . . . what does it matter.'

A few hours later the blackened leaves had already recovered, and the next morning, were flourishing once more. 'There's nothing that we can't solve or fix given enough time. This mad Ceramican—this Ceramican madwoman, I suppose she wants to be called'—a coloratura trill in the want, the swan still knew how to sing most sweetly—'is sending out her virus squadrons and yet . . . she knows we'll blunt the force of that attack. It's not a serious offensive, just threatening noises. A symbolic declaration of hostilities. Same choreography as during the Monotony.'

'Are you going to let yourself be taken? Why, from pacifism?' The wolf bared his teeth. She laughed good-naturedly. 'I'm not going back to your sad remnant of Europe, forget it. The Lion has built a fortress too confining for my tastes. I have my own life here.'

7. BAPTISM

Two days before he left she woke him from his afternoon siesta, standing before him in night-black plumage.

Mourning, he thought, at least I can tell the King that she recognizes how serious the situation is.

But then he saw that there were stars blinking within the blackness like tawdry rhinestones.

'You can't keep away from it, can you? Melodrama. Flying cats.' He licked her hand, and they both knew that he was intolerably fond of her, leaving aside entirely the fact that he loved her.

'You're hopeless,' said Dmitri. 'Nothing is hopeless,' she said, swan and woman at once.

For the last time she led him, by small gestures, between the greenhouses, to the secret green and the roses' gold. When they went swimming afterwards, he found that for the first time in a long while he was thinking of his Li'l Ly'x, Clea, Lasara.

Alexandra splashed him with water and said, 'Of course we could still get married quickly, before you leave. There's a sort of little Temple of Isotta not far from here, a bit run-down, but . . . I've donated a lot for the quest for the Li'l Runaround, so the hawks have a lot to thank me for.'

They have all that over here as well then?

He snorted, shook himself.

After supper she carefully injected him at the scruff of his neck with, as she said, 'Some good large files that I want him to have. He'll know what to do with them.'

'I thought you weren't going to help him.'

'I'm not helping him, I'm investing in my posthumous reputation. If I die in the coming devastation, then at least I know the old busybody will defend my data and results tooth and claw. Even the ones that he doesn't much like. He believes in military applications, whether or not they exist. That's enough for me. It will preserve my work for what's to come.'

'Don't sound so morbid, darling.'

'Don't call me "darling", darling. It makes me all teary-eyed.'

8. FAREWELL

She had taken precautions that he would not remember things too exactly afterwards. Their last night together was sad and lovely, a wrestling match between two angels in a silent abyss.

During that time they talked about things that cannot be put into words. All evening long he yearned just to take her hand in his own and understand what had happened to the two of them. It became late, and later yet, then early, and the moon rose and set again.

She said, 'Sweetie, you're in such poor shape and you have so far to go yet. And I know that you can't say what you think, but that's all right. Words never help, they just leave you in the lurch. And I have to do the same now.'

Perhaps, thought Dmitri, it's not even true what we've been taught.

Perhaps we have no language, because there's not even any such thing.

When Dmitri Stepanovich woke in the morning he was alone.

It was time to leave.

The patch where he had been sleeping smelt neutral, and he thought, I am my own man again, though I would so gladly have been hers. I need not be happy with this state of affairs, but it's true.

His dreams had been bizarre. During the night, nettle ensign coccids had nested in his fur and brought him the latest news from home.

The fish in the Borbruck water torus had announced new findings, continuing their research despite the waning public interest in their work ever since the zander had been murdered. They kept on, undeterred, who knew why (someone knew, but who?). This time they issued recommendations on the gender question—'Every man should have at least one woman and one man, and every woman should have at least one woman and one man, so that the smallest reason-able sexual arrangement consists of four individuals.'

What a waste, thought the wolf. How many of these ensign lice had died to bring Dmitri this rubbish?

Where was I sleeping anyway, how did I get here last night? Did she say goodbye at all, is that how our dinner ended? He couldn't remember.

Dmitri Stepanovich Sebassus sat up, his back stiff and the bones in his head aching, especially round the eyes and at his temples.

He listened to his heart and found that the swan was gone, but that he had to rid himself of her again, to be able to carry on living.

Even the thought of her awoke a kind of knee-jerk, regretful rejection. He had no doubt that this new feeling was her parting gift to him, she must have infected him with it, either in saliva or even in the injected data-cache for the Lion. Dmitri was equally sure though, and comforted by this certain knowledge, that he had not fallen in love with her from any such manipulation. It was just her style to push him away, but not in her nature to have laid a trap in the first place.

He would never stop loving her and that would have to be enough.

The wolf rubbed his cheeks with new-grown hands and drank from a bowl.

He heard a faint whistle.

When he looked up, an absurdly huge face was floating in front of the broken window of the attic room where he had made camp. It was a whale shark, twelve yards long, grey-green, with white dots. The wolf shook his head as though he thought he could shake off his ears, stretched, rubbed the last of the night from his fur. The flying giant made an inquisitive sound, admittedly an octave and a half too deep but easily understandable. The wolf said, 'Where is she? Did she call you? I don't even know whether we said goodbye.' Dmitri wasn't expecting an answer, but the fish, swimming in the ether, said, 'I think you can forget about that. She's set off already, going south. Headed for the invading army. They're marching through as though the place belonged to them already. Ceramicans.' He blew out a deep breath and the mist of spittle transmitted a dreadful picture to Dmitri's visual cortex. Dmitri saw hordes, not regular formations. Burning prairie, fleeing Gente, the speechless animals seized by panic.

'I'll take you to the sea,' said the whale shark.

His eyes were small but gleaming with intelligence. His mouth had a long-suffering, cheerful set to it, as though he spent his days listening to Impressionist piano music in a minor key.

'Bah, no, not with the swimming again, please,' said Dmitri in disgust.

'Hey no, not necessary, that was just on your way here. You had to see what the Atlanteans were up to in their buckyballs. This time you'll go by ship. Captain Patel's iceship.' From his tone of voice, that was something that the wolf should be looking forward to.

'Fine by me. Let's get going. Nothing here for me.'

9. DARKNESS GATHERING

Dmitri Stepanovich followed the whale shark as the Israelites followed the pillar of cloud and fire, for three days, towards the coast.

They crossed new steppes that had not been here months ago and they saw a pack of dirty, dishevelled gophers cross their path—refugees.

'There goes the neighbourhood,' remarked Dmitri. 'Probably those that can speak will seek the Lion's protection. Most of them will cross the ocean and ask to become part of his civilization, which will be a standing army soon enough.'

The whale shark, up in the heights, replied in a deep sonorous bass, 'Then he prepared himself for fresh unscrupulous lying. / Could I, he thought, win again the grace of the King and his consort / Could I without delay devise some other deception / So that the foes who now to death are leading me onward / I myself might destroy—it would rescue me out of all danger! / Truly would this be to me an unexpected advantage; / Yet I perceive at once it will need inordinate lying!'

Dmitri caught a whiff of the politically unreliable here and laughed.

This chap, this living airship, he certainly had character.

'We've known one another a long while, you and I,' said the whale shark, 'it's just that you've not met me in this body before. It's new, a present from the Atlanteans. Earlier I was, let's say . . . rather greener.'

Dmitri laughed in astonishment. He should have known a long time ago, her turn of phrase, her sense of humour. 'Georgescu?'

'A copy, to be precise—the jargon says "seedling" these days. You've missed a couple of far-reaching technological advances.'

That wasn't quite true. Dmitri had heard a bit about it before he left, something to do with the works that Izquierda was supervising. 'Errm, seedling, that's ... isn't that the machine-scanned personality uploads—programmed Gente?'

The whale shark lowed an affirmative.

Dmitri tore a root from the parched earth, sucked a little strength, spat and asked, 'But isn't that supposed to be only an insurance, a chance at ... internal emigration into the megastacks in their ... mountain fortresses? An introdus? How can we be loading these seedlings back into living ... floating ... swimming ...'

'Experimentally, more or less. Volunteers only. There's a great deal more slack in the guidelines now, Cyrus Golden allows anything that promises innovation. He's worried. I'm one of three seedlings in a synthetic living body so far. If you split my head open and had a look what I'm ... thinking with, at my "I am", you'd know soon enough that it's not a brain in the old sense of the word.'

'It's a biotic computer though.'

'Smaller than a brain, first thing. All the redundancy has been packed off to other worlds.'

'Other wor ... ah, a quantum computer.'

'If you like to use archaic terminology.'

The Countess would have said that she loves to, thought the wolf.

10. BATTERY RECHARGE

Dmitri, tired and dispirited, pissed on the rusted skeleton of a car.

He thought about the Countess and decided that everything she called self-reliance, stoicism or dignity was really nothing more than self-hatred disguised. She makes herself small, hideously so, she doesn't want to intervene in others' fates even if they include her own, she doesn't want to have to meet her own high standards from before. There's no helping her.

If he could still have said anything to her, he'd have said that he was sorry for her and that he was now rid of her without feeling free. I can be happy and handsome and free, as long as I don't let you torture me with the way you treated our time together as though it were already memory. How long now had she been so out of it, so dead to the world, and didn't the sad truth hurt, that in her contrived little show of a life she didn't even know how dead she was?

He remembered the King's words: 'But the lame is condemned by her lameness, and the liar is trapped by her lies, and the coward's heart dies of its own poison.'

The whale shark rumbled, 'Listen up, kiddo. I've got to break ranks for a while. Your line of march is . . . a strain, for me. I have to go to the upper reaches now and then, spend time at a height, to . . .'

Dmitri thought about what the Countess had told him about space travel and called up, 'Batteries, eh? Particle bombardment. You're recharging.'

A deep hum answered in agreement.

The sun was just setting. Dmitri suggested, 'You fly ahead of the night, power up a bit somewhere in the west. I'll take a couple of hours here to sort myself out. I could use some rest.'

11. THE HORDES

By a rust-red river Dmitri found that he needed to scout the area.

He smelt something that might mean that the Ceramicans were nearby. The wolf spat onto the ground and in the water. Femtospiders in his saliva had instructions to spy out the land in all directions as fast as they could, and over the next few nights, while he slept, make at least a sketch of all strategically and tactically relevant considerations.

What this revealed four days later was horrifying—prairie dogs and buffalo out west had been systematically exterminated by Katahomenleandraleal's army. The Ceramicans fell upon them like a sudden rainstorm—they killed one-third, expelled one-third, and one-third they took and implanted with seeds, to produce further Ceramicans in a short space of time.

They raped the local ecotectures on a large scale and mercilessly drove the collateral casualties before them. They spewed out fast-flying spores into the air, heliozoa made of waste protein, blood. Haste and pain, an infernal cloud that announced their coming for miles in advance.

The wolf's spiders tried to settle onto the Ceramicans to collect biodata. It was impossible.

Their armour had highly unusual magnetic properties, producing fields so strong that the spiders were disoriented, tumbled into free fall and were swallowed by the heliozoa clouds, crushed beneath the iron heels of the advancing army. The wolf's spies could register nothing except when they stayed at a safe distance and seemed to hear something like a song, saying, 'We are the new women, we're coming for you, we'll conquer you!'

When he heard them and saw them, the wolf's legs twitched in unrestful sleep.

When the song overtook a mob of wild sheep, the males leapt and started and were stripped flesh from bone. The Ceramicans couldn't even be photographed. The fronds on their exoskeletal carapaces didn't appear in pictures except in oddly blurred configurations and in the wolf's brain an analytical expert subroutine conjectured that this had something to do with the way they were constructed. The programme reported, 'They are probably not completely four-dimensional in the way that we ordinarily perceive objects. They seem to be constructed in at least one further dimension, perhaps even up to the sixth and beyond. If this is so then, they can observe themselves from all directions and they know things that we cannot conceptualize.'

Only one of Dmitri's flying drones made its way, accidentally, into one of the Ceramicans.

It struggled through hollows and openings to arrive at a mucous membrane which may or may not have corresponded to anything in Gente or human anatomy. It could not decide and nor, later, could the wolf. The slimy thing, whatever it was, was only a millimetre thick and seemed to be sentient. The spider collected signals and sent the wolf an incomplete report.

Motion sensors activated, a tear, dread.

Dmitri deleted the record instantly, since it wasn't readable. When he thought about it later, he felt sick.

In the end their attempts at espionage led to trouble.

The whale shark was up high, directly below the ionospheric boundary, and without having run the idea past the wolf first, was sending locational pings down at the oncoming horde.

One of these was received and identified by the spider that had nestled into the Ceramican membrane. Its subroutines ordered her to send it back in two directions, to the wolf and to the whale. In consequence, all the other signals were also sent at double strength. This opened a window of opportunity for the Ceramican decrypt sensors.

Immediately they turned their thousand-faceted eyes upon the bug.

Rather than burn it out, they sent an invasive virus and co-opted the bug without trouble. Then they sent an animated image file to the Georgescu seedling and to the wolf. The two of them saw a naked man, in a cold, oval room illuminated by greenish light from no particular direction or identifiable source. The human was busy with biological materials, extracting some living matter from thin glass tubes.

They saw that he was in a terrible state, with dark hollow cheeks and feverish eyes. His white lab coat must have fit him at one point but was now flapping about, far too wide for his emaciated limbs. A human? Looked more like a skeleton. His lips trembled, he was excited about something, obviously on the verge of discovering what he wanted.

The series of spectroscopic analysis images reminded the wolf of something, but he wasn't yet sure what.

'It all began quite harmlessly,' the Ceramicans sang with mocking siren voices, 'with disinterested curiosity and a desire to improve men's lives. Nanofactories, synbio devices, modified wormwood plants synthesizing anti-malarial acid compounds, a talking gymnocorymbus, a computational network made of gangliosides, the first fully functional secondary brain. Then they discovered pherinfones. Soon they built the first ribo-based universal Turing machine. And once that happened, he was on the very verge, this hard-working fellow here.'

The wolf and the whale shark were made to watch a lingering close-up of the man's face, his eyes, his mouth—the wolf was the first to understand what they were being shown. That's him, that's what he looked like and here he is, assembling the first generation of the Liberated.

'We have no reason to be ashamed,'—Georgescu, trying to reach the wolf by using his spider as a relay—'of having begun this way. Many things that turn out for the good begin small and unpromising. What do you want? This isn't Iemelian,'—Georgescu used this name for the Lion out of habit and gratitude, remembering her first command to raise the badger battalions—'This is just his first forefather. And thereby ours.'

The message never reached Dmitri, for whom it was intended.

Georgescu had to repeat it in person later. Instead, the Ceramicans sent a reply to the whale shark, 'Forefather, feh! That's what it all comes down to with you people, who begat whom. We though are the mothers of a stronger breed.'

12. IN THEIR HEARTS

When Dmitri came to himself, the dew on his tongue tasted bitter.

He got up, his pelt crackling gently in a thousand places, to find that he'd picked up a massive electrostatic charge. He thought of cat's fur, of Clea Dora, his Li'l Ly'x, and was irked to find that the Ceramican propaganda had got to him, even if only a little—he felt queasy when he thought of the man with the dark eye sockets, bent over his racks of test tubes, holding his chin in hands where blue veins stood out.

My king? My father-in-law?

Of course the Ceramican broadcast was aimed at countering the Lion's own propaganda in the Animal Empire, which claimed that the worst aspect of the Ceramican threat was that they were a new and improved version of mankind—the Pale Ones are returned, even now their hand is at your throats, their cold corpse fingers at the throats of this day's denizens.

'So we're human,' they answered from within their armour, 'and what about your king?'

The wolf gnawed sullenly at the tough blue stalks that thrust up hereabouts from the omnipresent grey dust. He tore up something, chewed at it, then felt the shadow of the whale shark gliding above him, headed east.

'You're back, are you?'

The flying giant whistled.

'You're taking it well,' barked the wolf.

The whale shark concurred. 'But of course. Aren't you? No, obviously not. You're taking it as hard as you can, little greycoat.'

'They know everything about us. More than we know ourselves. And we know nothing at all about them.'

'Not so fast, civilian. I had a couple of very valuable little scraps of code from your spider. It managed to crack a sensitive file, get at some internal memoranda. You wrote its software very nicely—your bug simply piggybacked the contents onto the film they sent us, steganographically, so while we were watching Iemelian's father I also received the file. Should I play it to you or are you still too down in the dumps to hear some good news? Their whole campaign is driven by a mood of desperation. They're in ferment. They have to conquer the habitable earth, quickly, or this whole great monstrous flood will . . . fall apart, from its own inner tensions.'

'Go on,' said Dmitri.

No sooner had he spoken than he saw Katahomenleandraleal cracking the whip to drive its berserker hordes onwards, feeding their cognitive apparatus with conjectures about the future—political and info-topographic positional maps of the old continents and the new, expectation graphs plotting events in the narrow zones round the Three Cities, cost-benefit analyses of the campaign's energy consumption and the need to plunder more resources. There was a ground plan of Capeside attached, as an insert, and then long columns of population-dynamic code showing the various Gente quasi-taxa.

A painful twittering sound broke in on the wolf as he considered the data.

It was a song, a threnody. 'Now a comet approaches. And now . . .'

In the midst of this wilderness, up in the gnarled and twisted trees, on a tangle of wire gnawed by the many teeth of time, sat a rubythroat that had escaped the Ceramicans, singing of the family it no longer had. The whale sent down short pulses of warning to the wolf. 'Come away, leave it be. What are you about, you have a task to do. I will lead you to your embarcation, the bird doesn't need you to sing its lament.'

'I want to hear it though,' said the wolf, gruffly. He bridled, 'You, Georgescu, think that all this is irrelevant, civilian stories, meaningless. I see things differently.'

He turned to the little bird, but it would not react to his call, to pherinfonics, not even when Dmitri playfully made as if to snap at it.

The bird had left this world behind and lived only for its warbling song. 'Lutarius, and we are all made of clay, but now we learn a better, a fearful lesson. For, now, a comet approaches. I suffer the onslaught of a frightful wand. So I cry out in the voice of the newly born at the mystery of my first breath, and will be brought elsewhere. We sail across dominions barely seen, washed by the swells of time. We plough through fields of magnetism. Past and future come together on thunderheads and our dead hearts live with lightning in the wounds of the gods.'

13. SOMEHOW OR THE OTHER

Dmitri and Georgescu travelled the rest of the way together without talking.

At last they came to another river, this one as green as a turtle's shell.

A primaeval, scrubby slope fell steeply away either side of the river, grown with saffron-yellow and scarlet fungus, and blue capsules tall as men. The wolf liked it here and buried his snout in the earth, rolled round a little, leapt through the grass that grew as high as himself. The whale shark said its farewells. 'Just stay hereabouts, Dmitri, a raft will collect you soon and take you to the river mouth.'

'What kind of raft?'

'You'll see soon enough. It will take you to the open sea and to Captain Patel's great iceship, to bring you back to the Lion. Then you can tell him how sick his past self made you feel, once the Ceramicans told you about him.'

'Is this how we say goodbye?'

'We'll meet again, somehow or the other.'

14. CARRY ME OVER

Dmitri Stepanovich Sebassus sat down on a stone. He would await the ferry there. He sunned himself for a while and the smell of white feathers filled his nose. He missed the Countess a little, or more than a little maybe.

The raft arrived.

It didn't seem terribly trustworthy to the wolf—too fibrous, as though woven from reeds or straw and shapeless to boot, with too little draught, and a golden yellow, more a barque for a masque or theatre than a real boat.

There was a chair in the middle for him to sit upon, made of bright red hair that fluttered and waved, so that Dmitri thought, that's got to tickle. He was impressed though at how easily the craft made headway against the strong current, propelled by some invisible means, gliding calmly towards the rock and coming to a rest with barely a bump. It gave off goodly scents to tempt its designated passenger aboard—cinnamon, fine flour, gum arabic.

The enigmatic raft even seemed to have access to Dmitri's memories, for he thought he smelt something of Clea Dora's scent on the boughs that bound it together. He raised his left forepaw, stepped aboard, pressed down hard—still no sway or wobble. The right paw—all held firm.

So he was persuaded at last, not least because he was homesick, and didn't want to spend any more time than was strictly necessary on this continent, which had basically already fallen to Katahomenleandraleal.

The seat was more comfortable than it had looked. Not a tickle, more a warm vibration.

Dmitri leant back. The journey began. The water foamed up in irregular patterns behind him, and the dark wake washed falling rainbows away as he sailed. Dmitri squinted and realized, with some surprise, that an old orang-utan was standing among the long grasses on the other bank, holding a white shield in his hand. He waved slowly to the wolf, must have been watching him for some time now. The shield was blazoned with a symbol which the wolf easily deciphered—hurry. Yes, thought the Lion's envoy, soon they will come and take from us what is still ours.

There was nothing to be done about it though, and what did hurry mean here? It would take just as long to cross the ocean as it would take. Dmitri closed his eyes and sank into a relatively innocent slumber.

The little waves played gently, vaguely even, and Dmitri Stepanovich among them thought, maybe he didn't even want to be the one to save the Age of the Gente once more, to prevent its destruction, the plagues and corruption, by spinning out a net of long journeys that the enemy could not pass. What if his journeys had only enabled an inventory, one last long look at the age of the Lion, which against all expectation had not become the new millennium, rather an intermezzo, when the animal and vegetables kingdoms could recover a little from the ravages mankind had visited upon them?

A wolf with no pack, the last valedictorian of this interlude, perhaps the chosen eulogist, for he knew which of the King's works were just and which were not.

Then the loudest foghorn that he had ever heard blew away his musings and plans, from somewhere in the fog. He had visited hundreds of harbours but it had never been this loud and he had never seen a craft such as the one he saw now.

The iceship was larger than the swan Countess' whole realm. The whole Lewis Thomas campus at Princeton could have fitted onto the 'tween-deck. Storeyed structures, platforms skew-whiff, piled upon one another as though they might slip and slide apart at any moment, frozen battlements and stairs, bows and balconies—a cloud castle made solid.

The wolf looked up and saw the captain, clutching her hat in one thick polar bear claw, waving to greet him, and although he knew for sure that the ship was reliably solid, made of a substrate that nothing in the world could melt, it looked ghostly as it sat there between the coastal currents and the open sea, a mirage, something congealed from scraps and smears of dream.

'Sebassus?' roared the commanding officer. 'I'm Rolfa Patel!'

'And who are the others?' Dmitri yelled back. He could see black dots, some larger, some smaller, swarming across the ship's extravagant architecture, peering from portholes, toiling up the slopes or sliding down them.

'Which? These? Fishes with legs and pigmy penguins! My crew!'

Because you'll have found none cheaper, thought the wolf.

VIII
THE ANTI-LIONIST TENDENCY

1. THE CLEARING

White foam overflowed and tumbled in the pitted channels worn into the black stone, where the waterfalls raced green between the rocks, hurling themselves headlong into the depths, competing in their thunderous clamour, and here, every evening, Frau Späth spent her time beneath a large tree. Many dreams ago she had read, she forgets where exactly, that the Buddha, in order to be the Buddha, needed a tree. He was to sit beneath it and meditate his way undaunted towards Enlightenment. She didn't sit down much. The thought of Enlightenment made her skin creep, she still had the shivers from the last dose she'd been exposed to.

Mostly, once she had visited her tree she would go on to the monoliths of undressed stone that stood by the great pool beneath the falls. There she spoke with the unknown masters, who had some notion of Enlightenment. These masters were all avatars of the young goddess who ruled the jungle here.

One evening the goddess was in a good mood.

Katahomenleandraleal was pleased that she had taken a fine scalp. She had already made plans to head-hunt this valuable brain, at whatever cost, when it fell effortlessly into her hands. 'She simply surrendered. Unconditionally. Presumably, she thought she could make things easier for her toy life forms. All the same, the next thing I did was get rid of her flying cats. I've kept their templates though, might build new ones later. Just the wing construction on its own . . . I've fitted some of my girls with them, but I made the folding rather more precise.'

'Will I meet her? The prisoner?'

'No, sorry. What she was is . . . done with. I had to . . . how would you say it, in your four dimensions? Cut her up. To get to the precious parts.'

Frau Späth saw the image of a chair cushion, slit open so that the stuffing bursts out.

'Did you really have to do that?'

'How am I supposed to have found out what she knew?' It sounded almost aggrieved. This goddess was a child, just as cruel and very young.

'You could have asked.'

'Huh, her conscious mind was cluttered up with . . . aesthetics and morals and all that faddle. I didn't have time to clean up a mess like that.'

'But when she surrendered, she surrendered her . . . self, didn't she?'

'It's what she knew that was interesting. Her self was obsolete.'

Frau Späth was surprised to find that after all the dreadful wonders she had seen in her long life, she could still be shocked. So that's how it was. Katahomenleandraleal had destroyed one of the first-generation Gente, one of the most powerful creatures ever to live on this planet, almost without noticing. When the Lion and his comrades had proclaimed the Liberation, their aim had been nothing less than 'Permanent transcendence', Frau Späth still remembered the slogan. They had wanted eternity for all, here and now. Now, however, these folks would have to learn that they too could fall by the wayside, that they could be transcended.

Frau Späth remembered an aria from an old libretto that a good friend had written for her opera *Brouwer*: 'Just because granny's been taken to the hospital seven times and taken home seven times, doesn't mean that she's immortal.'

Quite the opposite, Frau Späth realized now, the likelihood that the poor old biddy would pull through this time sank with each stay in the ward. The rest is statistics (or stochastics? She'd always confused the two, even back then, just like entropy and chaos theory, and the rest of the blather that had turned out to be so much more important for the course of history than any more strictly political verbiage). The next war might not be the last. But for its countless victims, it is anyway. How had Aylett put it back then? 'You can't count blood.'

'You can't count blood,' Frau Späth told the goddess.

The goddess laughed royally and vanished.

The next evening, Frau Späth sat down in the lotus position underneath her tree, against her habit.

My hidden corner: I feel I have some peace here, even though it's so loud with the waterfalls, their restful thundering drone. If you let yourself go, fearlessly, let them wash over you, some kinds of roaring sound are actually indistinguishable from peace and quiet.

She said, 'So you really have become my Buddha tree, sweetie.'

The crazy thing was that the tree actually replied, 'When things get difficult, you've got to get me out of here.'

'Who . . . wha—you? Tree?'

'You Tarzan, me tree. Got it.' The contralto voice was calm and earnest. 'I enjoyed that, the way you came and poured your heart out to me here. You're— what did they use to say—you're all right.'

'And you? Are you all right and if so, how far?' Joining in this odd exchange, the human woman also looked carefully round the clearing.

The tree tried to calm her down. 'Don't worry! We can talk quite freely. A few very reliable . . . fungus . . . are on guard right now, broadcasting masking pherinfones, specially tailored for disinformation. They'll cloud Katahomenleandraleal's senses without her noticing. Camouflage droplets. Will-o'-the-wisps. Besides which, she thinks she's safe here, in her own, how would you say it?—front room—she doesn't imagine there's anyone about who is quite so . . . uncooperative as I am.'

'That seems to be the punchline to this whole huge joke,' said Frau Späth and rubbed her right hand across her skull. Two days ago, the goddess' microservitors had eaten her hair back to the roots again and the new hair had just now begun to grow, showing white against her scalp.

'What punchline, and what joke?'

'Everyone is overestimating themselves, before the decisive battle has begun. The Lion, his technical staff, the big bad Ceramican momma.'

'You and I,' said the tree, 'do not overestimate ourselves. That makes us soulmates.'

'Well thank you,' said Frau Späth, in the same tone she would sneeze in.

The tree creaked, a sound like a thousand ropes groaning. 'I should have cleared out of here much earlier. But I'll confess that I was enjoying the thought of the look on my ex-husband's face, when he learnt that I'd been living for so long under his arch-enemy's nose. Besides which, the whole point of going into exile was to choose my own home and put down roots for a while, instead of . . . branching off into all kinds of areas, suffering the slings and arrows of outrageous fortune, just to help some idiots out.'

She likes to explain her motives, thought Frau Späth, that means she's used to having non-idiots around as well. She asked, 'Your ex-husband?'

'My wonderful daughter's good-for-nothing father.'

'Lasara,' said Frau Späth and smiled. Now she knew who she was dealing with.

Madame Tree hummed and hahhed and then burst into a rage. 'He can thank his lucky stars, that nitwit, that I'm not vindictive. I've protected some of his agents here from discovery, nudged this, put a glitch in that, used my camouflage drops to cover the cracks. And the information that they did gather I improved and annotated—what his spies have been telling him, they'd never have been able to gather on their own.'

'And what are you asking my help for, exactly?'

A bug crawled across the composer's left knee. She brushed it away—and found that it still hadn't gone, even though her hand should surely have swept it off. She pressed her palm down flat, lifted—it was still there, wiggling away, meaning that it was an illusion.

Interesting.

Livienda answered, 'Because although, happily, we neither of us overestimate ourselves, there is still a difference. You underestimate yourself and I'd like to change that, in exchange for certain . . . favours that you could do me.'

'So I'm more important than I reckon? How's that then?'

'You've been of great help to her, in ways that none of her other . . . subjects could have been. Katathingumbob, I mean. You stayed with her, voluntarily, when she asked you. She knows your secret, she knows that you are the . . . free-est being alive. On the first night you spent together, she plucked knowledge from your brain as you slept and that knowledge made possible her war. She didn't kill you while she was at it, either, which is most surprising. She doesn't seem to want to . . .'

'Perhaps she can't.'

'You see. What would that mean? How powerful are you, in fact?'

'Anyway, the knowledge that you . . .'

'Your familiarity with the paths that lead sideways through everything. The porous spots in the inevitable. Escape tunnels away from the sequentiality of Earlier, Now and Afterward.'

'You mean . . . that the Ceramicans are built in several further dimensions.'

'That's how she used your talents, yes. How she misused the Runaround.'

'Where . . . where did you learn that name?' Frau Späth was wide awake now.

'There's quite a few things I know. I even know rather better about some of your talents than the . . . idiot goddess. Talents that showed her that you are free from the constraints she . . . that there's no real way for her to understand you, at least not as directly as she does everything else on this planet.'

'You talk as though I can do whatever I like.'

'You can.'

'And sorry, but we don't talk about the price, is that it?'

'Price?'

'The price I would have to pay to get away from here, the price that has kept me here long past the moment I'm fed up with it. The price I can't pay, which is why I'm stuck here and I'm no more free than . . . all the others.'

'So you tell yourself,' said the tree and bowed down. 'Perhaps we're not even half so much like one another as I thought. You're still telling yourself a lot of stories to deal with being responsible for all that's happened here.'

'Pfff,' said Frau Späth, unknotted her limbs from meditation, stood up and turned to go.

'Wait, no, stop, let's not . . . I'm sorry. I shoved my oar in where it wasn't wanted.'

'So you did.' Frau Späth hesitated.

'I'm asking nicely now, cut off a twig here, when the time comes, or a bud. Keep an anchor for me so that I'm not uprooted from the world. Take me with you, when she lets you go.'

'Go? Where?'

'My daughter is building an ark. She knows that the Gente have only one choice: to leave the Earth to Katahomenleandraleal and the Ceramicans. She belongs here, the new goddess. She doesn't need anything more than the planet, her rate of growth will limit itself nicely to the natural cycles. That means though that we . . . oldsters . . . will have to break free of those cycles, if we want to survive. Even Ryuneke realizes this. We've spoken. With some difficulty. In whispers. With delays.'

'And you think that I'll enter this ark? That I'll be on board?'

'You would have let Katahomenleandraleal assimilate you voluntarily long ago, if you weren't so stuck on being you.'

'Maybe. But on the other hand, what if I just had something to settle in my mind, so far? Perhaps I just have to face up to what I've created, my daughters and sons, and then . . .'

'That doesn't bother me either. But since you mention it, of course we want to see eye to eye with our children. Me with my daughter and you with . . . I ask this of you though, when you go to Lasara, don't go alone. Take me with you, so that I can die here . . . with no fear. Sink into the soil, unmake myself, become nothing.'

Frau Späth considered this for a while.

Then she said, amicably, 'Well fine. When I . . . no, if I go, then I'll take you with me.'

'You have my thanks.'

2. DEFENCE, NOT PROVOCATION

'Leaving aside that they have us surrounded since they left North Africa and hopped over to Europe, their cordon is very much like the rather smaller one that we have erected round our Three Cities, so as to . . .' The bat spoke as though she had a cold.

Georgescu yawned spasmodically.

The Lion was very graciously presiding over this emergency cabinet meeting as a holographic projection. He overlooked the small discourtesies; that, for instance, Stanz the ape was being deloused by his aide, that Ropicc the Atlantean seemed to have fallen asleep open-eyed in his tank, that the insect delegates were swarming at random rather than maintaining formation.

'They'll reach Landers first,' said Georgescu, apparently sleepy but actually picking up the thread from Izquierda after a precisely calculated pause. 'And if they carry on as they have done on the wild continent—as you all know, unlike our friend here I do not much care for the old names, but I will say it nevertheless, so that she understands as well—if they behave here as they have in . . . Africa, then they will drive back with fire and biotic weapons any Gente who try to leave the cities for their lines, whether this is a sally or mere panic. From all that we have seen, though, they are quite prepared to leave smaller gaps for Gente to flood the interior. They are not sealing these off.'

'Because the waves of refugees will overwhelm our ecotecture,' noted the Lion soberly, 'and wear us down. Landers is bursting at the seams. Borbruck can't absorb any more Gente either.'

'Absorb,' said Izquierda and crossed her ears comically above her head, wrinkling her brow as she did so. 'There's the nub—if our heat-seeking sensors are giving us an accurate picture of events, then the Ceramicans have absorbed enough biomass by now. All they're doing at this stage is killing, they're not assimilating anything, they're not processing. They leave huge stinking heaps behind them. The rape phase is over—in North America too, by the way.'

The Lion ignored this coldly. 'The political situation here—Georgescu?'

The badger gave her most crooked grin and said, 'I should have become a whale shark all the way, not only in part, not only as a seedling, but, well—I could have flown away from all this. In a word: chaos reigns hereabouts. The Polyarchs are by now the most loyal, I'd never have thought that I would ever say something so twisted. The folk from the Temple of Isotta are waiting for a Runaround *ex machina* or something such, they've gone on a spiritual retreat. Any other organization or entity that still has a programme, a platform, a political purpose, only saps our defensive capability at this moment. You will not be happy to hear,'—a weary nod towards the king—'that the strongest faction are the new Lasarists. They are arguing for an exodus. In second place we find Ivanov's crowd . . .'

'The renegade badger,' growled Cyrus Golden.

Georgescu heaved a contemptuous sigh. 'Pfhh . . . yes, his gang. He always was an arsehole, what can you do? Anyway, he's found a way to get his mad message to the Gente: unconditional surrender, or for the moderates he says: we should at least send envoys, members of parliament, to sound out the possibility of a negotiated peace, or . . .'

Even though he hated such talk, it wasn't the Lion who interrupted his chief of staff.

It was a shriek from the bat, the last that anyone ever heard from her.

Something like curdled light smeared a rapid arc through the air where she sat, causing a piercing headache even in those who only saw it from the corner of their eye.

Then Izquierda was gone, snatched from the cabinet table in the middle of the best-defended building in the safest city in the Animal Empire.

The Ceramicans had shown whence they came—from nowhere—and how they fought—unstoppable, incomprehensible, instantaneous.

The king was the first in the room to regain his composure.

Sounding quite calm, he asked, 'Where is Philomena hiding, in fact?'

3. COULDN'T BE SAVED

'Get up! Get up! Get up, you bloody fool! Get up!'

Anubis knew at once that the shouting came from humans. Neither Gente nor the speechless animal races used such hoarse, barely articulate tones, almost like the brainless gurgling of dead matter.

The ferret crouched and lay flat on the ground—the uproar had disturbed him at a delicate moment, while he was building his nest.

He had gone a little distance away from his friends, after they had agreed to rest for a day or two in the fringes of an extensive forest, to hunt a little, to break off contact with the Three Cities for a while and to talk over their next move. The three heroes had set their course diagonal from the front of the Ceramican advance, so that each day they were farther away from the incomprehensible enemy's devastation, but were not running headlong from the horde's front ranks. 'We want,' Hecate had explained, 'to keep an eye on them for as long as we can, within earshot of their big guns and their savage feasts, so that we can make notes. Maybe Georgescu can use all this.'

The horse had carried bugs in her mane and sent them out on patrol. If the reports coming back were accurate, then two nights ago the front had shuddered and slowed, if not ground to a halt.

'And this way,' the white tiger added, 'we can take a bit of a rest as well.'

Anubis, just like the cob mare, had been fine with the idea. His nerves were always on the edge these days, and he had hoped to calm them out here in the bushes with a controlled dose of regressive, instinctual behaviour—he had set to work lining a hollow tree stump with grass, hair and salvaged feathers, to catch up on his sleep and dream ferrety dreams, instead of staying by the fire with his comrades.

Belly to the ground, breathing shallow careful breaths, Anubis crept between the hills to the top of a cliff. Down at the bottom two humans were kicking a third, who howled and curled up in pain.

'Up! Back into harness! Get up!'

They were children, Anubis realized, and crippled—there were no hands on their arms, only stumps with spiky growths of bone. Their rags were filthy with dried swampwater and mud, and two of them wore sandals of some black material, probably old tyre rubber—Anubis knew that the vanquished people habitually recycled primitive goods from the indestructible remnants left over from the Monotony. The girl who kicked hardest at the defenceless human on the ground was wearing leather boots though, with shiny, polished caps; probably steel, the ferret thought.

Others ran up. In the end, there were half a dozen gathered. The victim of all this kicking didn't even look worst off—there were two standing a little way off who looked even weaker. Their postures, barely able to stand, told the ferret that they were exhausted, under terrible strain, perhaps from a journey that had led them farther, more aimlessly, in greater fear, than the three heroes had travelled. The slave-drivers had belts strapped round their stomachs, made fast to which were braces over their shoulders and crossing on their backs, with metal hooks and loops. They had very little hair, large eyes, fine features, almost beautiful for humans, although right now distorted by rage and suffering.

Beyond the curve, beneath a row of tall pines, more adults appeared, pulling ropes attached to a large cart, nailed together from knotty timbers and planks, mounted on heavy wheels. Frames fixed here and there to the cart held cooking pots, and rags hung there too, brown with some kind of sauce, also a few bones, which the ferret didn't recognize as any part of the human anatomy—perhaps Gente, or from one of the speechless animal races, perhaps unlucky dogs—and various tools whose use Anubis could not guess at.

The ferret made out bundles of objects loaded in the cart, piled round a dirty tub made of painted tin or something such. It was screwed down onto the cart and inside lay brick-like shapes, some gleaming, some dull—gold bullion, more than a dozen bars.

Anubis wondered what the humans thought they could do with the stuff. He would have been glad of a connection point to the pherinfonic massive eco-tecture, to report what he saw to his friends and to other Gente. He had never, until now, met a human with whom he had something in common—they were on the run from the Ceramicans and would perhaps, if they stayed on their current course, even reach Landers sooner or later and plead to be taken in.

Should the Lion allow them in, even as denizens of the filthiest ghettos, in the rubble, the sewer that suited them so? Would there be a new sort of solidarity now, fates conjoined by war?

The child on the ground rolled sideways until he tumbled against a gorse bush. All of a sudden he was up on his knees, without having used his arms to raise himself and raising his torso to meet the blows. He cried out, spat blood, drooled. A black fluid leaked from his left ear and both nostrils, and he shook and trembled as though possessed by devils. His tormentors scurried backwards in fear, the adults laughed.

The ferret began to brood, grimly. We destroyed their hands and a few of us, myself included, in my younger days, felt bad when we thought about it. But when you see what they can do to one another even without hands . . . he never finished the thought, for then Anubis saw something even more upsetting—they had learnt to use their mangled pincers as adroitly as ever they had used five fingers. One of the men on the cart, using the bony growths on his forearm like robotic clamps, picked up a rod from the rack of tools, little balls fastened to it by a chain, probably leather bags filled with stones or glass. He ran swiftly across to the child they had been kicking and swung the rod threateningly, get up, or you'll get a beating.

The kneeling figure gave a moan that turned the ferret's stomach, and then the taller figure was upon him, swinging the rod back, and whipped the string of bags so hard across the child's jaw that something cracked, splintered. His whole torso crashed to the right with the force of the blow. But instead of falling to the ground again, the frail body lurched back, like a withy, then fell forward, and the child thrust out the stumps of his arms to stop himself from falling into the dust.

Two of the other children were there immediately; they grabbed him under the armpits with their malformed not-quite-hands, dragged him to his feet. He choked and spluttered, pushed little white crumbs from his mouth with his tongue. Anubis realized that they were teeth.

In an almost friendly tone of voice, with no sign of anger, the man with the rod asked his victim, 'Are you going back to the cart, or shall we cook you like we did those mutts?'

So the child had somehow been able to free himself from the ropes that the grown-ups were pulling along, and the adults had unshackled the other children, because they could run faster, to catch the fugitive. That's how it had been—and what a species, the ferret thought in disgust, if they can free their pack, literally let them slip and not fear that they'll run away. Why? Because they quite reliably prefer mob rule to an uncertain freedom.

Anubis had seen enough. He did not want to build his nest anywhere near these monsters. He decided to hurry back to his friends, ask Hecate what they should do—should we ally with the humans, admit them, avoid them or drive them back towards the Ceramicans, to see what they would do? Shouldn't we raise the Gente flag, follow the banner into a war against both the humans and the Ceramicans?

Anubis found Huan-Ti sharpening his claws on a black rock.

Perhaps, thought the ferret, he's marking some imaginary territory.

Behind him Hecate neighed, and he looked round. She was standing in a patch of bare meadow that she had grazed down in next to no time.

'No rest for us, my friends,' piped the ferret, 'I've just run into some very bad things.'

Anubis briefly described what he had seen.

He tentatively suggested that they could profit from bad company, use them as test subjects to see what the Ceramicans would do, but Huan-Ti laughed the idea down. The cob mare too thought otherwise. 'I reckon we should just get out of their way.'

'Afraid of the rod and the whip, are you?' said the white tiger, mockingly.

Hecate shook her head brusquely. 'We could overcome them with no trouble, that's quite clear. Weapons or no weapons, they're not more than, well, savages. But you don't mess round with the Ceramicans. We're not fleeing like headless chickens, but we're not going to let them catch up with us for no good reason. We've already agreed on all this. We'll leave the humans to their own fate, we've enough to do for our own folk.'

'Leave the humans to their own fate, and to one another,'—Huan-Ti licked his chops—'I've heard that before. That's what happened with the Cannibal Islands—the Lion's first emergency decree against the humans, just after . . . Borbruck was founded.'

Anubis didn't know the story. 'What was all that about?'

Hecate whickered and pawed at the ground, and finally said with a dark look on her face, 'We rounded them up and shipped them off. On tankers.'

'Shipped off where?'

'An artificial island made of coral amalgam. Lots of trees. Fruits, too. About three hundred thousand people. Some say as many as half a million—Izquierda, she was a badger back then . . .'

'Huh?' This was news to Huan-Ti.

Hecate nodded, 'Yes, that's why she works so closely with Georgescu. The Lion's old army cadre, they've known one another since . . . before they had feathers or fur. Anyway, all the . . . defeated human settlements round Borbruck were evacuated and they were only allowed to take a few basic tools along with them—axes, shovels, saws, no guns. Fabric, though, and stuff for their, you know, feet.'

'Shoe leather.'

'Yes. Not quite enough—maybe that was deliberate, an experiment by our friend the bat, she wanted to see how long before they went for one another's throats.'

Anubis shuddered. 'What did you,'—turning to Huan-Ti—'call the story? The Cannibal Islands?'

'It was while they were still crossing, on the ships . . .' The tiger's tongue hung out, his eyes shone. He felt that he was in the right. He thought that this story would convince his friends that humans were the scum of creation.

'Brrr, that's horrible,' the ferret broke in.

Hecate snorted and went on. 'There are reports, you can study them in the archives in Capeside and Landers. They didn't all of them regress into man-eating madness. There were victims and perpetrators on the island. It wasn't as simple as Huan-Ti would have us believe. First we made the humans into something we could feel disgusted by, so as to be able to justify the dreadful things we did to them. They even provided the documents themselves, scratched onto birch bark, diaries, pleas to their gods for help . . .' She didn't have to finish the sentence.

The horse spoke words of self-reproach and Huan-Ti said nothing in reply.

Anubis knew a good moment to change the subject when he saw one. 'What do they want all that gold for on a . . . trek like this?'

'They love it. The way it shines and gleams, it's a favourite fetish of theirs,' said Huan-Ti and looked accusingly at Hecate. 'This is another of their repulsive habits, accumulating abstract wealth in objects that have no use but exchange value . . . or is that our fault as well, Miss Morals?'

Hecate surprised him with her answer. 'In a way it is, yes. Not the hoarding of gold as such and all the stuff you're talking about. But . . .'

Anubis jumped as though he had been bitten when he heard Huan-Ti roar— no, not quite roar, he corrected himself, since he hated exaggeration. It was more of an exasperated harrumph, for which he hadn't even opened his jaws especially wide. The tiger gulped, chomped his jaws and then said, 'Our fault? I worked under Ryuneke, my dear horse, I should know what's what! Don't give me any of that! Fault! Our fault, their whole mixed-up trading arrangements, the monetary merry-go-round, where in the end no one knew who was carrying how much risk? Our fault, the pyramid schemes, their ridiculous yardsticks—sometimes they had a gold standard, sometimes not, and when it was abolished it could quite easily happen that gold gained ten or twenty-fold in value in a few decades, because the so-called investors, the capitalists and the rentier class used it as a safe refuge, couldn't be forged, couldn't be multiplied, a general medium of exchange. Our fault? Our fault the inflation, the deflation, overproduction, financial bubbles . . . I attended Lasara's lectures at the Capeside Academy, her seminar on the growth delusion. I was there when she took on Ryuneke by saying that his new economic system was much too tame. Owed too much to the old system, the miserable mess we had in the Monotony . . .'

'Quite.' Hecate had held back, but now she broke in and interrupted him, and not for the first time, Anubis thought that he wouldn't want to be involved if these two ever really came to blows. 'That's what we're talking about here, that's the name of the beast: Ryuneke. Who do you think they're trading with, even today, these humans, these refugees from the past that Anubis spotted?'

Huan-Ti answered with an obscene noise, then, 'Trading with us, are they, with the Gente?'

'With Ryuneke Nowhere. He has depots and outposts, everywhere in the deserts and waste places, in the treacherous passes—yes, even right under Izquierda's nose, in the Preference Mountains, there's humans there too, they're everywhere where the Gente decided it wasn't worthwhile bringing civilization and the pherinfone network.'

'Really? And what do they actually have that we . . . that the Fox can buy off them?'

'Their carcasses. The old biology. Pre-Gente. Their genetic code, microorganism colonies that no one thought to preserve in the biotic archive during the Liberation—and now that there's suddenly an enemy who works through human biology and other leftovers from the pre-Liberation ecotecture, we need to set up more experiments, *in vivo*, so that . . .'

Anubis was outraged. 'Izquierda has got Ryuneke buying humans for her?'

'Old ones, mostly. Dead, anyway. As you have reported,'—she nodded at Anubis, more irked than friendly—'the humans need to keep their young for hard labour. Anyway, when they're not quite sure what they want from us in exchange, or if they have no use for the goods we offer, they ask to be paid in gold—because they think they can store up wealth, they expect that it will . . . gain interest, in some magical way—don't ask me why, it's some kind of superstition of theirs, a brain problem or something.'

'Brah. Bah. Beh.' The three inchoate sounds gave a very clear picture of Huan-Ti's train of thought as he digested what Hecate had said. After that he didn't insist on his right to hate the humans but he thought of something else. 'We have no choice anyway. We've got to get at them. Hinder their movements.'

'Hinder their movements. Sounds like a police action,' Hecate snorted.

'It is. Or has it escaped your notice that these . . . people have committed crimes against the Gente? I needn't remind you of our legal charter—we can roam round at will, even enter the uncivilized lands, but Iemelian's pact says that the Gente have to avenge crimes against the Gente and punish their enemies. And that holds true wherever we draw breath.'

Anubis understood what the tiger was getting at. 'I don't know for sure though whether it was Gente that the . . . man with the stick was talking about.'

Now the horse got what they were talking about as well and quoted what Anubis had mentioned in his report. 'Ah yes, the "mutt". That they . . . cooked. At least so the human claimed, to threaten the child.'

'Right,' said Huan-Ti, 'and if we let these humans go on their way after they've . . .'

'Then we're going against Iemelian's pact, absolutely.' Hecate had almost let herself be talked round. 'The very suspicion demands that we . . . investigate. I agree. Admittedly we don't know whether it was Gente—my command of human languages doesn't tell me much more than you know already, which is that they use the word to talk about the pre-rational races and about certain Gente as well—but we'll have to look into it.'

The white tiger growled contentedly.

'So, how do we set about it?' Anubis enquired, relieved that they'd reached some agreement.

There wasn't a lot to plan.

They followed the ferret's track back to the valley at the edge of the forest, picking up their pace markedly after a while, since, at about the halfway mark, all three could smell fire and blood. The cob mare was leading them now and urged speed, paying no heed to Huan-Ti's warning, 'Perhaps we shouldn't charge into their camp like the riot squad, it might be better to creep up and . . .'

When he realized that the horse had thrown caution to the wind, he raced through the bushes to the right, twitching his head to let his friends know that they would meet when the fight began. Anubis was crouched on Hecate's back, digging his claws into the straps for the saddlebags, where they kept their fodder and tools.

Hecate didn't slow down until a few hundred yards from their goal.

'Go ahead and spy out the land,' she told the ferret, who slid from her back and scuttled swiftly over to the vantage point.

The scent had not lied.

The humans were gathered round a fire and were busy killing a wolf.

Two more bodies—holy Runaround, thought Anubis—were lying on the ground, already skinned. The children were swarming over them with knives and short skewers, while lumps of meat seethed in great shallow pans on the fire.

'They didn't even beat them in a fair fight,' whispered the white tiger from the thicket next to Anubis, where he had appeared without the ferret having heard or smelt his approach.

'How do you know that?' Anubis hissed back.

'Their wounds. The marks there, on the wolves. On the bodies, do you see? We've seen those before.' Anubis looked closer, ordered his cornea to crop and enlarge the scene—the poor wolf that they were kicking and beating with the whip, and the other two, who had left all suffering behind, had patterns scorched or scored into their pelt. Any Gente with the slightest interest in world affairs had grown to know and fear these burns and scars—a few months ago Anubis, Huan-Ti and Hecate had been the first to lay eyes on such wounds.

'Ceramican fronds,' Anubis declared.

'The monsters must have left them for dead and then moved off en masse, to one side or the other, or the wolves escaped, half-dead, only to meet up with humans who . . .'

'. . . instead of giving them shelter . . .' continued the ferret.

'Enough talk,' hissed the white tiger and sprang from cover, roaring loudly, a huge leap.

The humans had guns. No use at all.

They took too long to grab for them, they couldn't use the weapons in time. Hecate's hooves smashed the children's skulls. Huan-Ti was not so merciful—first he wounded the humans terribly, putting them *hors de combat* even as they shouted, ran and tried in vain to save their skins. Then he prowled from one to the next as they lay fallen, killing each with a bite. The leader of the humans—the man with the knout—aimed a long rifle at the mare, trying to shoot her through the head, and Anubis saved the horse's life by jumping into the human's face.

After twenty minutes, the unequal fight was over. Eleven humans lay dead or dying.

The wolf's name, she told her rescuers in a weak voice, was Britt. She couldn't be saved.

She was suffering too much from the Ceramican attacks, weak from hunger, beaten badly, infested with human parasites and poisoned by Katahomenlean-draleal's children. She lay on the cart, which Huan-Ti had requisitioned and which Hecate was pulling towards the next settlement, much too far away. One week's march, and no faster means of transport anywhere to be seen.

'You'll make it,' Anubis told the wolf, squatting in the cart next to her, but himself not convinced in the least. She huddled close to him in the way of her species, as whelps huddle up to their parents.

'No . . . I . . . won't . . . make . . . it,' Britt replied, smiling, with look that said: drop it.

When they reached a high-bandwidth hedge, and Anubis hastily set up a pherinfonic connection back to Gente civilization, coding in priority overrides for the fastest possible transmission, Hecate asked the medical databanks whether there was nothing they could do for the wolf.

The answer was not encouraging.

In the end, the wolf pleaded with them to jolt her about no more and to let her lie under a tree, to breathe her last in peace and dignity.

The three heroes stood round her as she lay and listened as she said, 'Don't come . . . too near. I don't know . . . whether the Ceramicans'. . . perrhobacteria and . . . femtoweapons . . . they cut off my connection . . . to the pherinfones . . . you don't know . . . whether they might . . . infect you too.'

Hecate guessed, rightly, that Britt was really talking about her frustrated wish to talk to certain absent Gente, and she asked gently, 'Would you . . . like us to pass on a message . . . to someone?'

The wolf coughed, spat blood and mucus, her eyes turmeric yellow. Then she said, 'Is the . . . connection up? Are you broadcasting, are you . . . filming me?'

'We're not broadcasting. Not yet,' said Hecate. 'But everything that we see and hear is being recorded. And then later . . . Anubis edits our pherinfonic presence in the Three Cities, he'll . . . review the material, do the pre-edit and send it on.'

'I had . . . I have a brother,' said Britt.

'He didn't . . . he thought that we had chosen the wrong path. The wolves.' The three heroes knew what she meant—after the Liberation was complete, most wolves, like a few ape societies, had asked the Lion for permission to share in the Gente ecotecture but not be part of the huge settlement projects on land and in the sea. The alpha wolves explained that they wanted to try out post-industrial ways of life, in small local packs, at the edge of the densely populated city zones.

Some wolves belonged to the Polyarch party, others founded feudal groups or even more exotic cultures, such as the so-called hunters' democracy that the wolf communes shared with South Pacific shark societies. No one outside these two groups had adopted such a way of life.

'He . . . thought,' the dying wolf continued and laughed through her tears, 'that we would . . . create an infantile world, an uninteresting . . . what had he said? I . . . can't . . . remember . . .'

'Shhh!' said Anubis helplessly, 'don't exert yourself. You can still . . .'

Huan-Ti looked at the ferret so sternly that he shut up.

The wolf coughed, gasped and began again. 'Ahis . . . torical. Ahistorical, that's what he had said. A tribe of dullards. Even . . . even if we were right, Stepanovich thought . . . that it was meaningless . . . to be right like that, it was . . . primitive communism for the . . . undiscerning palate. He said that . . . he wanted . . . not to live better than humans . . . if we . . . didn't know better as well . . . I think . . .'— she spat a spray of blood. Anubis turned his face away, 'I think . . . that he was wrong, that . . . you can't . . . separate the two . . .'

The tiger agreed in a gentle rumbling bass. 'It's much worse to know better but not live better.'

The wolf nodded and gasped for breath. 'Yes, but I . . . never wanted to . . . say so. Just . . . since I saw . . . saw the Ceramicans . . . I know . . . know . . . what he meant . . . when he said . . . a blind pack . . . a blind mob . . . enough for me . . . if I'm no longer . . . part of it . . .'

'But the wolves aren't. They're not blind. They simply offer an alternative to the Lion's ways,' said Hecate, 'the loyal opposition.'

'The wolves . . .' said Britt, 'aren't . . . we . . . aren't . . . but . . . the Ceramicans . . . tell him . . . he was right . . . to fear . . . brute . . . primitive communism . . . and the undiscerning . . .'

Hecate wanted to promise the wolf that she would carry the message, would find her brother and was just about to say so, when Britt struggled and spoke with her last strength. 'Tell him . . . that . . . we have . . . not forgotten him . . . and that . . . we love him . . . and that we always . . . believed . . . we didn't just . . . have . . . the right to seek . . . our freedom . . . from the Lion . . . but . . . also . . . that he had the . . . right to seek . . . his own freedom . . . from us . . . his freedom . . .'

The wolf drew a few more breaths and fell silent.

She had lived free for two hundred and ninety years.

4. COUNTER-RECRUITMENT

Chandeliers hung in the ballroom, flames of ice burnt in the fireplace in the reception hall. On the 'tween deck stood frozen sculptures of Gente in all possible postures. There were wolves, lions, birds . . . It took Dmitri Stepanovich weeks to look at most of them and to have enough to be going on with.

Captain Patel mostly kept aloof from the daily routine of the crossing, in her spacious quarters.

There, opera music set the icicles ringing. 'I compose myself and I have the machines play my pieces,' she admitted over a meal.

The penguins were always busy with something. Indeed, they never had time to answer Dmitri's occasional questions ('The metal pipes in the ice, with that hot stuff flowing through them, do they really not melt the hull at all? . . . And the temperature gradient isn't maintained artificially?').

Sometimes he eavesdropped as they queued at the galley or in the corridor, discussing esoteric matters of Gente politics in archaic dialects from Monotonous times (though he seemed to remember from stories told back in the wolf pack that in the old days, sailors went in for swear words and singing, not biophilosophy). '<Katahomenleandraleal, like the Lion, relies on comparison and extrapola­tion from artificial to natural. The Lion moves from artificial to neonatural selection, Katahomenleandraleal from human to Ceramican machines.>' '<Yeah, but you see, both rely on the central argument that a common mechanism works much more powerfully in Nature.>' '<But wasn't the whole point of the Liber­ation to put an end to all forms of social relation being naturalized?>' '<Points like that, my friend, tend to get lost in the shuffle of any revolution.>'

The wolf was reminded of the blethering cats in the Countess' little realm: anagrams, where the content didn't matter at all. Likewise, he supposed that whatever they were talking about here, you could only understand it if you knew the formal, linguistic and logical models underpinning the conversations.

After three weeks' uneventful voyage, the polar bear sent a pherinfonic signal inviting the diplomat to the vast boiler room in the bow of the ship.

'No one ever asks me,' she said, grumbling, as she swung open a bulkhead, and with absent-minded curiosity he watched the tiny crystalline points of frost chiming against one another on her fur.

'You might as well know that I'm a long way from thinking that you're ready.'

'Ready for what?' asked the wolf and followed the bear into the blast of heat.

She shook herself. The points of frost fell from her fur like little arrows and onto the floor. They melted and ran together to form a little puddle.

'For what?' the wolf repeated and Rolfa Patel answered, 'Smell that puddle. Have a look at it. Have a look at yourself.'

The wolf was about to ask again, more emphatically, but saw from the stern wrinkles on the bear's forehead that there was no point. So he did as he was told.

The face in the water wasn't his, but, rather, that of a fox.

'Pleased to meet you, my dear messenger boy.'

The wolf didn't know how he should react, so cautiously sketched a bow. Ryuneke smiled.

'Oh, I by no means share my honourable friend's opinion'—the sly eyes glanced towards Rolfa Patel—'that, simply because you have run errands, nay, served the Lion for so long, you're not ready for this now. Rather I feel that it's high time. If we can't win you over to our side now, then you're lost to the cause forever.'

The cause. Our side. Dmitri had the feeling that a heavy curtain was being lifted in front of his eyes. He found himself thinking of the crew's chatter—it's all connected, they're all involved, I'm the only one who doesn't know what's going on. He licked his lips and said, 'What side . . . and what . . . cause?'

'I reckon there's no need to lecture you about it, or speak in the abstract. You must see with your own eyes, I think, and it's high time too.'

The bear heaved a sigh but didn't say anything.

Dmitri was still unconvinced. 'And what . . . must I do, to . . . see it with my own eyes, this . . . cause of yours?'

'Travel to the rocket base. That's where we are preparing the exodus, or as I prefer to call it, the Second Liberation.'

'Travel. Again. Don't take this the wrong way, Fox, but I was just on my way home.'

'Heh heh. The "home" you want to get back to doesn't exist, hasn't for a long time. Time to jump ship.'

'Now? In the middle of the ocean?'

'We've got fish who can show you the way. And your gills . . .'

The wolf shook himself, as Rolfa had done before, and muttered, 'I thought I was past all that.'

'It's not far. You'll find the base on an island that used to be called England.'

The wolf thought it over. Ryuneke gave him time.

Then Dmitri Stepanovich said, 'No, I'm staying on board. I won't tell anyone about you—not about you, not about Rolfa Patel.'

'Thanks a lot,' the bear said in a growl, and Dmitri carried on, 'Not least because I don't even know quite what kind of anti-Lionist plot you're brewing here. But I'm not leaping overboard, anyway. Why should I, for Gente whom I don't know at all and who've never done me a good turn?'

The Fox blinked merrily. 'Where do you get the idea that you don't know us? Our leader will hardly be happy to hear it.'

'Your lea . . .'

'Lasara. She told me to tell you: "The Ly'x doesn't like to be kept waiting."'

IX
THE FALL OF THE THREE CITIES

1. A KINGDOM FOR A STAGE, PRINCES TO ACT

The robes shone in the political colours of the hour—ferrocyanic blue, rapeseed yellow and May green.

Thus Lasara came before her father, and he had veiled his head with filter lenses and data arrays, so that he saw what happened in his world, while none might know that he was afflicted by grief.

Yet, his daughter knew nevertheless. 'I have seen the glow-worms as they flew from your window. They are swarming, aren't they? The siege of Landers has begun. That's your greatest defeat. The bugs are flying. Nothing that happens now can be undone. I hear that Georgescu is having fun downloading seedlings into Gente species that she would have rejected out of hand earlier. She's said to have been a whale shark, and now . . . these glow-worms . . . but she's a badger in the end, and she'll stay a badger. You're all traditionalists, and you don't understand what's coming. You'd have preferred it if that old doctrine of yours, Bene Gente, had taken root, just like Robespierre was in love with the Cult of the Supreme Being. You're panicking, and you're trying everything that reminds you of before. But you've got no plan.'

'She's one of the best,' the Lion said, as though he'd heard none of these accusations. 'My—what is it that you say?—my throne would have toppled long ago, without her.'

Lasara's voice was full of sympathy. 'It's too late.'

He loved the way she talked—astonishingly perceptive, for such a dainty, dreamy creature.

She went on, insistently. 'You won't be able to save it. Your throne.'

He laughed. 'Is that a prophecy? From you, the one who won't believe in a thing unless you see it right before your eyes? And now you think that you know what will happen before it does? What you call my throne is a symbol, I didn't set it up for my sake, but for the Gente ...'

'And can it last? Can the rush grow up without mire? Can the flag grow without water? Whilst it is yet in his greenness, and not cut down, it withereth before any other herb. So are the paths of all that forget God; and the hypocrite's hope shall perish: whose hope shall be cut off, and whose trust shall be a spider's web.'

'Pfffeh ... the old books, the old stories ...' he snorted, tired, 'and God. As for that, well, I had thought you might at least bring me something new, at least this—what's it called—the Li'l Runaround ...'

Lasara spoke more clearly now, 'Your friends are leaving. Soon they'll have to die. The glow-worms will return with news of fearful losses, every day.'

He turned towards her, she could not see his face behind the screens.

'Join me,' said the ancient. 'Come with me, rule by my side. Prepare with me the battles we must fight.'

She shook her head, came nearer and sat at his paws. 'Who was it this time? Who have you lost?'

'You don't know him ... her. First generation. Helped me make the Liberation possible.'

'The virologist?'

He swung one of his mirrors aside and looked at her. The king's bright eyes were red; he was not sleeping, not for weeks now, nor taking any pharmakoi that would have made his lack of sleep any more bearable. Darkly, brooding, he said, 'You know more than I thought.'

'And perhaps more than you know yourself. They don't tell you everything, not for a long time now. Perhaps they're scared you'll be angry, perhaps scared that you'll ... give up. Father, you should never have got involved in this war, though you thought it inevitable. You should listen to my plan. One more time. Really consider it.'

Now he snapped at her. 'Damn it, I know that even after I forbade it, you cling on to the idea of your ... ark. An idea born of desperation, if we're talking of who's giving up. You want to gather all of them, each according to his kind ... his species, as though the word meant anything these days beyond morphology. And want to scatter them, fire them off to all corners of the sky, like spores. Then they're supposed to act as monads, like ... like that slime mould that they set so much store by back then in the last days of the Monotony. The Christians believed in their Fish, when the Classical world collapsed; the scientists, in synergy, self-organization and emergence, in *Dictyostelium discoideum* and humanity, in the collective, world federalism, globalization, and by then the end of *Homo sapiens* was inevitable anyway. And now you want the same for the Gente . . . Surrender for victory. Scatter them, to gather them again. Flee to make your stand. Madness.'

'You thought of fleeing yourself. Why else develop the seedling technology and implement it? Izquierda showed me the plans before she . . . vanished.'

'Withdrawal. Tactical withdrawal. Not fleeing, never. You? You never listen when I try to explain differences like these, and they're absolutely crucial. You have to be stubborn. Fire off rockets behind my back, build your firecracker, spy on my satellite networks . . .'

'They're falling out of orbit. Your satellites. They're old, some of them older than you. No one maintains them. They stop working. Gaps in the networks.'

'Your ridiculous . . . you people always did just what you wanted. No consideration for . . . reason, planning.'

'Us people . . .'—she laughed, melancholy now. She knew this old song, far too well.

'You people, yes. Your mother . . . and Paul too, or Élodie, or whatever he, whatever she was calling herself in the end. Frippery. Then you die, snuffed out, candle flames in a hurricane, and I'm the only one still interested, me, just like it was only to spite me that you took all those risks. She's gone—one of the best minds ever to pierce the darkness of . . .'

'Why do you think they're abandoning you, or why are they stolen away from under your very nose? Are you sure that Izquierda was forcibly disappeared? Couldn't she have defected? Did we ever understand how she thought, how Ryuneke thought, what the most advanced Gente thought of your dogma on bodily . . .'

'Dogma! How dare you talk to me like that? What I do isn't theology. I created the Gente. I made them! If . . .'

'More important though, why are you losing them all now?'

'All of them—nonsense. You're here, aren't you, sitting here, with me, even you, the maverick? You're all of you still hoping that I'll save you and you don't admit your hope even to yourselves. I have to come and set you free, just like the Liberation. Izquierda? Kidnapped. It was a crime. For the same reason they killed the fish, in the archive. It was your mother paid him and his whole gamete partnership commission, pulled the strings from . . . well, wherever she's hiding. Look at what happened to him, how he failed. Utterly. He stood for one of your mother's typical ideas: compromise, reconcile ourselves with Katahomenleandraleal by talking to it about all that . . . Women, men, females, males, reproduction, species boundaries—your mother thought that's what it was about. Because we have such a low birth rate, because in turn we have such long life expectancy—five hundred years now, and we're still only three, no, four generations. An offer to negotiate, splendid. It looked as though the thing from the jungle was bent on reproduction, exponential growth, devouring and assimilating everything that stood in its way, was starving . . . We Gente stand for stasis, the abomination from the jungle stands for expansion—at least so Livienda thinks. But if you believe that, then how can . . . Ach, what's the use. You want to run, she wants to bargain, I want to fight. Interestingly enough, the jungle beast is leaving you in peace, even though it's fighting me and your mother. It seems that the enemy can tolerate someone running away. It wants to drive us out. Us. My ministers, your mother's reproduction counsel, they have to go, to show that this . . . jungle juggernaut doesn't believe in negotiation and isn't afraid of war. Fine. I'll take it at its word. We shall see.'

Lasara cast down her eyes. 'Fine posturing, Father. But that's all it is. Poses. Psychology.'

'If that's how you see it,'—now he sounded gentler—'but posturing is vital for thinking beings to survive. Fine or no. He who strives to uphold justice, he is the upright man.'

'So you hope. That's supposed to vindicate you, in the final analysis. But I didn't want to know how you see Izquierda's disappearance in terms of . . . strategic priorities. I'm asking about something completely different.' Before her father could react, she added, as though it hardly mattered, 'As for that idiot fish, I had him done in myself, thanks to my loyal donkey.'

'What . . . why, for all that's . . .'

'It was getting too risky for my liking. The Ceramicans have been sniffing about for decades now, listening in, peeping. And since I know where Mother is and since I know that she's somewhere Katahomenleandraleal could get at her very easily, I had to shut the fish up. He was in contact with her and he could have given her away, intentionally or otherwise. So before the Ceramicans could discover her hiding place from him, I bumped him off to send her a message . . .'

'You're still in touch with that maniac who bore you into this world?'

'Not any longer. She didn't try to communicate again, meaning she must have understood my message. I imagine she's getting ready to escape as well. To join me.'

'And you're getting ready to help all the Gente escape to cloud cuckoo land. They're calling it "the fourth city", have you heard? Yes, of course you have. You're probably proud of that. What's it built from, this fourth city? I created the Three Cities by bringing together what used to be separate states, I ploughed and sowed Man's second Nature the way they shaped the first. What's your raw material? Dreams? What's left for us to say to one another?'

'No need to be so rude. I'm staying here until you've understood my question, no matter what your answer might turn out to be.'

He lifted his paw and swiped at her, pulling the punch deliberately. 'Don't provoke me.'

'What does it mean that they're all disappearing? I want you to acknowledge how hopeless our situation is. The Gente. Only when you can picture that . . .'

He stood up from his console, took off his strapscreens and threw the harness to the ground in a rage. Then he roared so that the liquid walls quivered, 'Games! Conjuring! Am I supposed to turn pale and whine for mercy? Because they have a few parlour tricks? And my Gente, even the least of them are trained warriors, weapon-masters! Multidimensional backflips and hand-stands, so what? They're vermin!'

They were both breathing heavily, until the air finally settled back to stillness about them.

Then Lasara, who would not give up, asked, 'Do you even know what that means? Multidimensionality?'

He was tired of it all by now, no longer roaring but sounding exhausted when he spoke. 'My child. My . . . dear child. A multidimensional battlefield is just a battlefield like any other. I'm getting more and more used to the idea that I have to see everything from a military perspective alone. Dimensions are just something to aid understanding. An idea. Once I get to grips with the dimensions, I can identify and tag a point space in the theatre of war. Coordinate systems—dimensionality is merely a question of how many figures I need to enter, to identify this point in particular and not another . . .'

'Poor old Dad, but that's the point! If only you realized! That's not how it works, not any more. They're twisting the war out of your hands. They're tugging it away from where you can operate, up into the higher dimensions. The whole point of abducting the bat was to prove that!'

He cocked his head to one side, which meant: go on, I'm listening. The Lion liked didacticism in general, not only on his own account.

'You've made it fairly clear that you're interested in striking a pose, making a point. But this point, like any point, has no dimensions.'

He had to laugh.

'A point, you see,'—she rolled her head on her shoulders as she chose her words, as though to unclench, first left, then right—'can be projected in any direction you like. Take your null-dimensional point and extend it, pull it apart, you've got a one-dimensional space right there: a line. Project the line away from itself, pull it orthogonally from the direction in which lies, voila, you've got a plane: two dimensions. Project the plane away from itself, upwards perhaps, and there's your three-dimensional space. And so on and so forth.'

He gave an amused look that said: carry on.

'And from this point onwards—from this space onwards—you can carry on in any further direction you like, but they'll always be one step ahead of you. That's the joke. In a contest like this the winner is always whoever began first: the line can spit in the point's null-dimensional eye, if you can manoeuvre in three dimensions, you can attack the plane without ever having to worry   about . . .'

The Lion harrumphed. He was unconvinced. 'I've already put a stop to one massively exponential growth cycle. You weren't round at the time—over-population, megacities, monoculture, all that shit with the climate . . .'

'Yes, but back then your troops were only outclassed quantitatively. The higher dimensions represent a qualitative leap.'

'As did the Liberation.' He showed his teeth.

'I know. But you don't want to listen to what I'm saying and you never will. Even though you could. That's why we're living through a tragedy.'

'I think we're done.'

It was true, she had said all that she had to say.

Lasara shrugged her dainty shoulders. 'I'll leave then. I never intended to do otherwise. And I was never going to tell you to do anything else. But you won't be told. That will be your downfall. We will remember you.'

He laughed.

She left.

2. IN PREPARATION

Not far from the cliffs they were casting iron in the green and grey valleys, smelting aluminium and building new furnaces.

Up on the scaffolding, Hébert Ransom spoke to Dmitri Stepanovich Sebassus. They had been up all night drinking some copper-coloured booze he'd found. 'We had to learn all this from scratch.'

The wolf nodded. His head was, gradually, beginning to feel better.

A fine drizzling rain cooled his forehead.

He cast a friendly glance round the enormous shipyards, each hall so breathtakingly huge that it could have held Captain Rolfa Patel's iceship in its entirety.

The halls had been blasted from the white cliffs and were constantly under threat from floods, so that thousands upon thousands of beavers were at work building new dams every day—not as their ancestors had done, but industrially, with heavy machinery rather than tooth and claw, using cylindrical, light, synthetic prefab parts.

When the wolf recalled that the actual spaceships were only to be built up there in orbit, at Lagrange Five, the thumping headache of earlier returned.

How could it all be ready in time? What was Clea Dora even thinking?

The scuttling hog yawned. 'Mwwwaah . . . we made good use of Izquierda's maps. The underground bases out here . . . there was still some equipment left over intact from the Monotony. Electronic computers—more robust than we imagined, those things.'

'Come on,' said Dmitri, 'let's go down there and have a closer look at the shuttles.'

They went through the main assembly hall with short, dainty, almost mincing steps, past the shaft where the first rocket stood, in sight of the other two.

'Nice old bombs,' said Dmitri and listened cautiously to the bomb that he seemed to be carrying himself, inside his skull. Was the uproar really subsiding or was it only in abeyance?

'Tcha, it's just <brute force>,' said Hébert, who was fond of using phrases from the older dialects. 'They don't have to do anything as complicated as human space flight would have required before it was abolished, no space stations, no re-entry capability, no environmentally friendly propulsion systems. That made their work pretty near impossible, all the special requests from the Gaia brigade . . .'

'Gaia brigade, you'll have to help me with that . . .' The wolf wondered whether it might not be simplest just to carry on drinking, best of all this

<whisky> stuff that Lasara's folks had liberated from the hidden cellars in abandoned nearby villages.

'Superstitiously, they didn't use atomic rocket propulsion because certain humans were exaggeratedly in love with the Earth—Gaia—and had something against it. We're experimenting with the idea now.'

'Was that really just superstition?' the wolf wondered out loud, dubiously. 'Weren't there, hrrm, accidents, wasn't it all rather risky?'

'Well, of course at the time they were still running technological processes with . . . Corcoran's cock-ups, rather than based on actual achievement.'

'The cock-ups?'

'Cut corners and clock off. Minimize your working hours. Work was an abstract quantity back then, an object of exchange . . .'

'Don't tell me, this is something to do with their, with the . . . product?'

'Profit.'

'With profit. One of those religions they had.' Dmitri was really thirsty by now; they could only serve him water and he'd drink the bar dry.

'<Just so.> And what with the profit motive on the one hand and on the other hand their superstitious fear of anything just a little different from how Nature had spat it out, there wasn't really much room to test their options sensibly, least of all in a tricky area like nuclear power. Here, this is our beta model, it's got a nuclear reactor there at the back . . .'

Dmitri would have preferred a bar. He swiped his tail at nonexistent flies and asked, out of a sense of duty rather than from any real curiosity, 'So you built it from Monotonous blueprints . . .'

'That's right, it was simple enough. Payload in our case is the data banks containing the seedlings and the biomechanoid actuators. Then the stuff that Ryuneke bought for us, the terraforming pico-technics, that has to go in the nose. Everything.'

'Because the great majority of us aren't going to be making our escape in our own bodies. Just as software. You, me—she's assuming that the Ceramicans will eat us all.'

Hébert made a wry snout. 'Pessimism is realism, here. When the payload is delivered, Lasara wants to begin a second phase, building evacuation vehicles for the bodies we left down here—but this is the quickest way to do it, in the meantime.' The wolf said nothing, he knew Lasara's priorities.

Hébert continued. 'Then here amidships is avionics, a dedicated onboard computer to control countdown and regulate the various stages of flight.'

'And that there is the actual capsule.'

'That's right, for the ones that use fossil fuel, the first and third rockets, these are the second-stage tanks, then the second-stage engine beneath them, the actual propulsion units, and then a bit of gear for appropriate action against erm . . . unwanted contingencies, you know, lasers for meteors or space junk or whatnot, field generators for the shields, then wrapped up inside all that, the primary tanks and engines, there you have it, done. A really rudimentary rocket.'

'And I'll have some really rudimentary alcohol to go with it, if you please,' said the wolf.

Hébert Ransom thought this was a marvellous idea.

3. CONTEMPORARY HISTORY

The wind whistled eerily.

The trees were quickly losing their needles here. They stood, black skeletons, at the edge of the chasm. The caverns had been dynamited, Izquierda's staff evacuated, their equipment dismounted and trucked off to Borbruck, the research station given up and the Preference Mountains abandoned.

Here, on their long retreat, the tiger, the ferret and the horse found Storikal the mule. He was trying to resuscitate a jackal who had stayed behind and died from eating poisoned food plundered from the stores Izquierda's team had left behind. He hadn't known that they had laced the food before withdrawing.

Storikal was inconsolable. He had had such hopes, now that forcible therapy had reduced his speech defect to a bare minimum.

'He, yeah, promised me a job, he wanted to found something here, yeah, a trading post, yeah, or an embassy, for when the Ceramicans come, yeah, and I can't afford to be choosy. But they came, yeah, they were already here.'

The tiger and the horse traded glances, certainly they had been here, at least a vanguard, that's why we're here too, because by now we've learnt how they advance. We want to document their tracks, the aftermath of their battles, and send the evidence back home.

The ferret asked the mule, 'What kind of work?'

'He said, yeah, there'll be an archive here, if it all works out, a place of peace, yeah, established here. An arc, yeah, archive of the, yeah, peace talks. He wanted this to be the place where the Polyarchs talk to Katahomenleandraleal, yeah, once they've overthrown the Lion, yeah, yeah. I was going to take the protocols and archive everything, yeah, because I'm a trained archivist, because, yeah, because I know about history. Yeah, yeah. Yeah-yeah-yeah.'

'Ancient history or contemporary history?' the ferret enquired, and from the look on Storikal's face it was immediately obvious that the poor creature didn't know the difference.

'Do you know about how everything changed earlier or how everything's changing today?'

Storikal looked at the jackal's eviscerated carcase and said, without lifting his head, 'I don't know why they feasted on him and tore him to pieces and took parts along with them, yeah, but not me. Piddle.'

'Sorry?'

'Nothing. Yeah.'

'We've been following them for months,' said the cob mare, 'and we've seen this kind of thing all along—they attack a pride of six leopards, leave two of them alone and slaughter four. They dragnet a lake, leave behind two little fish, no one knows why these two and no others. They burn a whole savannah. One bush is left standing. Maybe it's something to do with geometry. Requirements that we don't recognize.'

'Yeah, well yeah, that means you don't know,' sighed Storikal, as though this were worse than the jackal's death, worse indeed than cosmic entropy.

'But we know more than nothing at all,' said Huan-Ti. 'We've got part of the picture. We're collecting scraps, even if they don't . . . We've got some idea now of how the Ceramicans are constructed. Their metabolism for instance, they're very keen on folic acid and calcium. That sort of thing.'

'Yeah, but you don't know what that explains, yeah,' said Storikal, looking at the three friends, one at a time.

'We want to find out,' explained the ferret. 'That's more than most folk want to do.'

'Would you like to help us do that?' asked Hecate.

The donkey nodded.

'Then,' the tiger said, 'come with us.'

4. LOSSES

The worst thing about Hébert Ransom's death, which was bad enough already, was that there was nothing that the wolf could have done. One moment they were galloping down the slope like puppies (or piglets, or whelps), gambolling through the lush green grass together, on their way to startle the beavers, who never took a break, worked round the clock and were generally far too serious.

They stopped at the brook, where Dmitri frolicked on the stones and stood shuddering in the water, while Hébert stood on the bank watching and called out, 'Who's the pig now, Mister Wolf?'

And next thing a lance of glittering coherent heat cut the scuttling hog in two down the middle, beginning from the head.

It was days before Dmitri could even speak.

He lost weight and slept badly. He was plagued by bitter, pointless feelings of undefined guilt. If it had been him that had died, he told himself, then he would surely have acknowledged, over on the other side, in the hell most likely long prepared for him anyway, that fate was simply punishing him, for instance for betraying the Lion. But the scuttling hog, always so loyal to Livienda and then later to Lasara? (And where was she all this time, anyway? In Borbruck, as they said? If so, why?)

The beavers were so terrified, the rumours so quickly became so gruesome, that wolves were called in to restore order in the shipyards. These were different wolves from those whom Dmitri had known in his youth, taciturn tough guys, and Hébert had said that they came from the taiga, whatever that meant. Dmitri couldn't stand them at any price.

On the third day of unrest, work resumed at least partially.

In the evening, Lasara finally showed up, to inspect matters, to breathe new courage into the doubters, to show her trust in the steadfast and to organize the next day's obsequies.

When she came to Dmitri in his tent, he only said, 'I've missed you.'

The Li'l Ly'x smiled. 'Sure you have, and that's the least of it.'

'The least . . .'

'Yes. The least you can do, to love me in return, since it seems I have to love you and I can't bring myself to leave you alone.'

Then they made love, in drastic disarray, driven by fear and necessity, for almost as long as before.

When the sun came up she revealed that Hébert Ransom would be buried at sea.

'The Atlanteans liked him, I'd say all the fish did, and he liked them. I think he was happiest when he was Mother's official liaison in the Torus.'

That was when we met, thought Dmitri, everything was simple back then, even adventures. She lay her head on his chest, the tufts on her ears tickled his chin. 'Have you heard,' she asked softly, 'the Torus has been demolished, can you believe it? They siphoned off the water and used it in the field, those huge new sentient maize plantations. The armaments drive is eating up everything in its path, including Father's fondness for historical monuments. Capeside is shrinking and the arable area increases. Same in Borbruck. And none of it will do any good.'

'He'd say it's because you're working against him. If a house be . . .' He couldn't finish the quotation, and she purred, 'Rubbish. While the zander was still alive, Mother sent me some snippets of code from Katahomenleandraleal's tactical programmes, using him as a cut-out—it has all the possible configurations . . .'

'All of them? All possible configurations . . .'

'Well, all that we could adequately respond to in time, within game-theoretical limits. Even if the House of the Lion were united, that wouldn't be the guarantee of a strong home front that Father wants, not by a long chalk. The Polyarchs, the various factions in favour of surrender . . . We'd have more factions splitting off from the front, some of them totally new, there'd be collaborators expecting Katahomenleandraleal to make good on her promises . . .'

'There probably are already.'

'Yes, there probably are,' she said and laughed that beguiling, rather frightening laugh. 'But once you examine the branching paths of the stemmata, the possible factions and coalitions in the Gente high command, then my course is the safest way to ensure that at least a minority will survive.'

He blew across the little hairs that grew on her ears, but she wouldn't be distracted. 'And if there's going to be disunity however the situation stands, then the best kind of disunity is where a few of us can still agree . . .'

He licked the back of her neck, she purred.

They were silent for a while, then Lasara, restless as always, began to attack the problem all over again. 'You know, he simply doesn't realize that he's not making a last stand here. He thinks he has to fight because a withdrawal would just displace the front. He thinks, even if he doesn't know that this is what he thinks, that Katahomenleandraleal would come after us if we escape, pursue us every-where, and that in the hostile environments that I'm planning to escape to we'd have far less room for manoeuvre, fewer resources . . .'

'Is that not so, then?'

'It's a misapprehension about Katahomenleandraleal's aims. My father thinks of everything in terms of the territorial instinct—like a pre-Liberation animal. Funny. That he should think so. But she doesn't even want to expand. At least not outwards, the way he sees it. Not in four-dimensional spacetime.'

'Ah, the maths lesson,' grunted Dmitri, pretending to give in.

She yawned, conciliatory. 'Not at all. But . . . maybe this much at least. Do you know what dimension means in a topological space? Lebesgue? The covering dimension?'

'Well, it's a measure of how an object occupies space,' the wolf said grudgingly. He wasn't steady on his feet here and if he needed to know about this kind of thing he usually looked it up in the pherinfonic archives.

'Meaning?' asked Lasara, teasingly.

'Erm, well, if it takes up a lot of room, as it were, this object, whatever it is, then it has a higher dimensional number than if it . . .'

'Well, you're right, but bear in mind that some dimension numbers aren't whole integers. Not one for a line, two for a plane, three for a cube . . .'

'One and a half you mean, or six twenty-sevenths, or . . .'

'Exactly. Fractals for instance. Their Hausdorff dimension is different from their topological dimension, so we get something like a Koch snowflake: at every iteration the snowflake covers a greater area, because it keeps growing ever more fronds, but a circle drawn round the outer edges of the initial state will always contain the snowflake. It keeps growing, but none of its fronds will ever touch or cross the circle.'

'Erm. Okay. And you say that Kata . . .'

'She's growing the same way the snowflake does, yes. That indicates that if you know how to interpret the Ceramicans' multidimensional movements and patterns properly, they're limited to planet Earth's sphere.'

The wolf wrinkled his brow. 'It sounds like this is a natural process. Not a war of conquest at all, but only the necessary consequence of a previously established . . .'

'So it is. Katahomenleandraleal is such a logical thinker that she may as well not bother thinking at all—she's got no time for thinking as a voluntarist or contingent process. She doesn't hate us, or have any moods at all really, she doesn't want to destroy us as my father falsely imagines. Katahomenleandraleal knows that Gente biomass is basically negligible compared to all the other operational resources this planet offers her. She'll let us go, she's got enough here to ripen with.'

'Ripen. Sounds revolting.'

'So it may be, if you really have to use value judgements and loaded terms. But if we don't like it, we should just . . .'

'Get out of the way. I understand.'

'Then you're marvellously different from Dad.'

She got up, went to the water bowl on the low table, wet her tongue neatly, swiftly. Dmitri stretched, stared at the fire and said, 'I don't know whether you might not be doing him an injustice. Perhaps he's a little more far-sighted than you give him credit for. Perhaps more than you are.'

'Really?' Eyebrows and twitching whiskers—sceptically amused.

'Well, you say that the thing is growing inward and will stay within the borders of the Earth.'

'There's a nice old phrase. "Thou hast set all the borders of the earth, you have made. . ." '

'But what happens when it's . . . ripe through, when it's incubated, this kind of thing can't go on forever . . .'

'At the current rate of growth, Katahomenleandraleal seems to have allotted at least ten thousand years for provisional plans which don't yet include any new or further stage of self-realization.'

'Where do you . . .'

'Ceramican internal memo. Mother hacked it. And sent it to me. Months ago.'

'Ten thousand years, woof. On the other hand, from a geological point of view, it's not much time. What happens then? Shouldn't we use our home advantage, seeing as we have it . . .'

'I hope that the new challenges of life out there will help us make the necessary leap.'

'Escape as selective pressure. You want to accelerate Gente evolution.'

'Don't be cheeky.' She was impatient now, moved away when he tried to kiss her. 'My dear wolf, I can hardly believe that we're seriously discussing the idea that my old father knows what's going on. There are other points to consider, if you really think about what he did.'

'Did?'

'To your friend Hébert for instance.'

Dmitri blinked in confusion. It took him a few seconds to understand her implication. 'You mean . . . the heat beam? I thought that was Kata . . .'

'Why would she do anything like that? We're busy doing something that she either supports or doesn't care about: we're getting ready to leave. We're off to sow fields she doesn't want.'

'But why would your father . . .' It took his breath away even to think so.

She grunted dismissively, then said, 'To show me that he's in earnest. He's taken to heart something that I said, that the bat who abandoned him . . .'

'Izquierda? She's dead?'

'Not necessarily. But she's been abducted. By the . . . jungle horror, as he calls it. I tried to explain that such a precisely targeted action by an overpoweringly superior opponent ought to dampen his recklessness somewhat.'

'Ah-h, and now he's . . . showing you that she's not so superior after all? That he can be just as . . .'

'Orbital killer satellites. And the really stupid thing is that those won't stop her, they've been tried long ago, on Georgescu's orders. Did you know that he's even fired off atomic warheads? Izquierda hacked into some old defence systems, only one in forty of them even worked . . . intercepted, the lot of them. Puff of smoke, gone, just like the bat. Once again, those won't stop her.'

'But they will us.'

'But they will us, if we don't do something about it, quite right.'

'Do something?' Dmitri Stepanovich saw a new gleam in her eyes, one that he didn't know and didn't like at all, the moment he saw it. This had nothing to do with her sexy devil-may-care attitude, her charmingly outrageous ways. This was conspiracy and treachery on a scale far beyond anything he had agreed to.

He was silent, but she said something he had never expected her to say so straightforwardly. 'Don't pretend to qualms you don't have, my love. We're there already. The Lion's got to go.'

5. ENCIRCLED

The Ceramicans had conquered three contintents but on the southernmost edge of the third, for the first time their advance was checked.

The Lion had sent battalions of heavily armed badgers by balloon to the projected front. They had landed, built fortifications and dug themselves in.

Astonishingly, the front held. Their flamethrowers spat gouts of flame up to five hundred feet, they bombarded the devouring enemy with artillery and perrhobacteria. Admittedly, there were few enough direct hits (the targets blurred and smeared, could not even be photographed) but when they did land a hit, they found shell-like carapaces in the remains and organic bits that might have been the limbs of human women. Were the Ceramicans taken by surprise, did they not press on because they were caught out by the strength of the resistance? Strategic analysis was still pending. Perhaps Izquierda could have summed up the situation sooner. But Izquierda was not there.

Hecate, Huan-Ti, Anubis and Storikal had been in retreat for weeks before the hordes, until they decided to stop and wait, to see whether the new front would actually stabilize. They were on a wedge of land that had seen fierce fighting during the Liberation, a ruined valley full of yellow stones.

'They're taken aback, that's all,' Huan-Ti declared, 'they didn't reckon that we had anything left to throw at them—least of all infantry.'

The four of them had made back-up plans with those Atlanteans still surviving—the fish had had to give up great tracts of the world's oceans for lost and were now concentrated in the sea which human sailors had called the Mediterranean. The plan was that if satellite surveillance showed that the front had broken, an amphibious flying army would come to escort the heroes and make sure they were not encircled.

'Pherinfonics,' said Hecate, 'there, from the bush. It says—can you smell them?—hold on, it says . . . the fourteenth army has been overrun.'

All four fell silent for a long while.

Then Storikal said, 'Yeah, well that means, yeah, that the the that, yeah, the fishes will come and get us then.'

It wasn't a question.

They waited. The fishes did not come.

'Maybe, yeah, they're swimming, yeah, not flying? Bluntsch?' Storikal conjectured.

But the canal was also empty halfway up the western side of the valley of yellow stones and stayed that way (although as Anubis remarked, it smelt 'dreadful, as though something very large died in it, not long ago').

The horse looked at the tiger and said, 'So, no one's coming to the rescue. It's over. We wanted to be heroes. Fine. You smelt the pherinfonics too and you're better on the tactical details—how long, do you think, before they get here?'

'Two hours,' said Huan-Ti. 'At sundown.'

'I don't know how you plan to do it,' peeped Anubis, climbing up onto Hecate's broad back, 'but I'll bite and scratch to the end and my sweat and my blood will fly to all corners to tell what kind of fellow I was.'

'Of course,' said the tiger. 'We're heroes.'

The mule made a vague noise of agreement. During his time with the three friends he had learnt a great deal that the archives had never taught him, including something about duty, self-respect and history.

'Whose heroes though? Whose role models?' the horse asked of no one in particular and trotted across to one of the heavy gravestones. She let Anubis light her a cigar.

'For the Gente who sit through our broadcasts, I should imagine,' said the ferret and raised his clever little head, sniffing for the chlorine stench of impending destruction.

The air was close and oppressive, the sky billowed its hemline on the ridges and hilltops like a curtain in a blast of hot air. The ferret had the best hearing of the four heroes and soon caught echoes of the Ceramicans' ultrasound comms. 'It's their blabber, no doubt about it. I can't understand, there are bits missing and the parts that I can hear are hard to decipher. But it's them.'

'So.' The horse spat the end of her cigar onto the grave and drew up a rough order of battle, sketching in the sand with her hoof—Hecate herself would stand in the middle, at the valley's lowest point. The ferret should run back and forth as fast as he could, to throw off advancing enemy's sensors, to cause distraction and confusion in the ranks. The tiger's job was to tear apart, to kill any that left formation, if Anubis really managed to distract them.

The mule was to stay in reserve in the little copse of cedars, to trample any that Hecate's hooves might miss.

'Yeah, we can fight them that way too, can we?' Storikal asked optimistically. 'Even though they exist in several dimensions, yeah, unknown fopp to us . . .'

'They're wide enough in width, tall enough in height, deep enough from front to back and they've taken up far too much of our spacetime already,' said the tiger pugnaciously.

They had barely taken up their positions before the terrible enemy was upon them.

They're beautiful, thought the ferret in surprise. The bodies in the front ranks—could we say that, were those really bodies?—seemed made of caged light, and through the gaps the ceramic alloy of their skeletons showed like steam engines in gelatine. Their fronds burst through in swirls from the upper dimensions, the fifth, the sixth, through or upwards, downwards, in directions hard to name.

That's beautiful, Hecate thought too. She saw something like the after-image of fire, when we look into the flames and then close our eyes. An intertwinement of unmassive objects, a sideways movement through the real—the attacking forces looked like lovers embracing, an endless chain, each with his arms/her arms round her the next the other him.

They grabbed the mule from below.

The monsters reached him before the others. He fell into the underbrush, which they sliced apart.

The ferret heard his scream, bared his teeth and stood up on his hind legs. 'Cowards! Arseholes! Ratbags!'

The Ceramicans became veils, mere shells or shadows of what they had just now been and even to look at how they now moved put pain in the heroes' heads, wounded their intuitive sense. A bloody rib burst outwards from the donkey's stomach. The horse, forgetting her order of battle, leapt to his aid. Hecate even managed to hit what might have been a Ceramican head, and the poisonous, crunching thing drew back swiftly. Storikal had no hindquarters by now and twitched and swam in blood that soaked into the thirsty dust.

Hecate looked round, the white tiger was encircled by a smear of light. He was swiping his paws at unattainable targets, with no strength or assurance, but blindly, panicked. Something sharp, hot and needle-thin struck him through the right eye, a visible pain shot through him, lighting up his spine.

The ferret rolled himself into a ball and fell down the stony, rubble-strewn slope. Three flickering things with sharply wedged heads, exuberantly toothed, pursued.

Hecate beat her hooves against the earth as though to split it open.

Huan-Ti had caught a limb of some kind between his jaws and bit down hard, as though his skull were a steel trap closing. But a drillbit whined into his left side and with his good eye he could see one of the horse's legs fold beneath her.

The ferret shrieked, turned about like a flurrying breeze and dashed between the beasts that were after him; he was lightning, furred. He spat and scratched just as he had boasted, but soon enough they were upon him and trampling him into the dust. Storikal, dying, thought about what Huan-Ti had told him—these creatures are made of exotica, of incomprehensible and barely applicable techne.

Storikal wanted to cry out aloud: What are we made of?

Fine heroes we are, the cob mare thought, and felt herself becoming dizzy, guessing that this was due to blood loss from the long wound gaping on her bony brow.

Before he lost consciousness, the ferret let loose a string of filthy swear words and wished that the fish had come to fetch them. Now that it was really happening, the prospect of going down fighting was not half as noble as Anubis had believed.

The tiger gave way to his anger, slobbering with hatred as he fought, smashed his enemies together like sounding brass. Some shattered and broke. Through his own pain, he heard and felt them suffering, so yes, it could be done. He wounded them grievously and thought of the buffalo at the waterhole, of the Lion, the king in Borbruck.

They tore his ears off, dug themselves into his scalp, scorched his pelt with their burning fronds and with searing venom. Still he didn't give up. It was as though he were ten tigers.

Huan-Ti heard the horse whinny as she went down, saw great lumps of the mule's flesh flying through the air like thistledown. His closed eye burnt as though a chemical torch were scouring the socket, but the white tiger didn't roar, since that would have meant letting go of whatever he had sunk his teeth into. At last, he began to stagger, his hind legs losing their purchase. It was muddy and slippery underfoot by now, probably from his own lifeblood that they sucked and squeezed out of him.

He knew that he couldn't last much longer and so he bit down harder. Then, even though they held him fast, he shook his head briskly left and right, to break from its socket or joint the limb that he held.

Suddenly, everything whirred, yowled and clanged, and ice-cold liquid glass sprayed all about him. An elephantine strength tugged on the other end of the limb as though on a lever. They wanted to get away, neglecting now to drag him down—what was going on?

The elusive mass that pressed him down seemed to be getting lighter now somehow and points or tiny angles swarmed between the Ceramicans as they smashed into one another and ducked downward between their selves. Then the white tiger, his skull ringing like a bell bombarded with shrapnel, understood that these were beetles, bees, smaller insects, helping him, attacking the Ceramicans—hadn't reckoned with this now, had they?

A crack, a shudder that almost broke him in two, and all of a sudden, the strength at the other end of the bone or armour between his teeth let go. It was torn free now, it was his trophy, he wanted to laugh, and blood and spittle drooled through his clenched jaws.

Huan-Ti rolled over onto his back, which hurt more than anything he had ever done.

The sky above his nose had grown darker and he saw someone hovering there, dancing and flimmering, and it took a while before he realized who that was. A celebrity, a real one—every servant of the Lion knew this lady.

Philomena blinked and sparked.

Around her swarmed tens of thousands of insects, filling the valley as a living cloud, here at her command, obeying her orders. When Philomena saw that he could not hear her, she sent the tiger a dense pherinfonic package. 'Two of your friends are still alive. We couldn't save the donkey, they took his brain. The ferret is in a critical condition, needs blood. The horse lost a leg but we can replace that easily. And you—we'll get you out of here.'

They'll get me out of here, thought Huan-Ti and could almost have laughed. But he still didn't surrender his trophy. Even when the white tiger lost consciousness a few seconds later, and the insects turned him onto his side to begin to operate, they couldn't get the Ceramican limb from between his jaws. 'Leave it there,' said the dragonfly. 'He's earned it.'

6. JUNGLE FAREWELL

'Nice of you to come,' said the tree, 'haven't seen you here for a while.'

'Yeah. If it were up to me, I'd be off. Wham, bam, see my dust. It's not though. I still have obligations.' Frau Späth was wearing her hair long, braided with flowers.

'You look very pretty,' said Lasara's mother.

'Pfft. I see that you've been at the dressing-up box too,' answered Frau Späth, 'little stream there among your roots, I notice. Very perky. And new foliage. Did you get bored without me?'

THE ABOLITION OF SPECIES   193

'I have had other contacts with the outside world. The big wide world, as they say. But they became rather too . . . risky. I might have been discovered by the . . . landlady here, since I'm squatting on her dirty little property.'

Frau Späth leant on the trunk and massaged her temples, her eyes closed. Then she said, 'You know, twiglet, I'm still not really sure about . . . that's why I stayed clear of you for a while. To sort out my thoughts. I mean, what's going on here? Who are you? Whys and wherefores, and if you find pizza, begin looking for the Mafia too.' The tree said nothing.

'It might even be you've been telling me a load of crap. What if all this is just a test of my loyalty? If you belong to Katahomenleandraleal, if you're just a tree-shaped sock-puppet, telling me some more or less plausible story so that I join a plot against Fat Momma . . .'

'Fat Momma!' The tree chortled.

'Well, that's what she calls herself. Without the "Fat" bit of course. Mother, she calls herself.'

'Another honorary title worth a lot less than it used to be.'

'Are you envious? Because a machine can do what you did too, give birth? And she has more daughters than you. That Lion cub of yours . . .'

'Nothing to do with it. Family relations have been more complicated ever since the Liberation anyway, compared to the era of straightforward sexual repro-duction and . . . clear sexual dimorphism. I've got a lot of the Lion's genetic ma-terial in me as well, just like all the second-generation Liberated, so you might as well call me his daughter and say that Lasara is a child of incest . . .'

'That's your business,'—Frau Späth waved a hand dismissively—'I don't want to know about that stuff. Would probably shock me, I'm old-fashioned.'

The tree gave a dry laugh.

'What's funny there?'

'You, old-fashioned. You're the one who most of all . . . you're a pioneer . . . first generation, but unlike the other hundred and forty-four thousand you made some real use of the new freedoms—the rest were all tied up in their metamorphic games, Orphic fun and Protean pleasures, but beneath their scales and fur and chitin plates they're still the same old Adam and Eve, even those with bark and leaves. You though, you still happen to look just like the self-styled, most successful species on the planet, on the outside, but you've nothing else in common with them.'

'I sometimes think that all this flattery and these pleas for help are just meant to get me to say how I did it, back then, what I did. The know-how. Other than the obvious, I had my telomeres spliced, even before I had to fake my death. Otherwise I'd be really dead, of course. So the cell alteration . . .'

'Boring. Cells, dermis, ageing processes. The decisive factor is what happened to your neurotech. How you, how can I put it, composed your new mindstate. And when you did that, you didn't just switch off the old material, like most first-generation and indeed most of us later models did, you managed to perform some kind of core dump, and . . .'

Frau Späth dug her toes into the ground, belched, stretched her arms, rubbed her bare backside on the tree and asked,

'How's it even supposed to work, this blind spot? She can't see you, even in her own backyard? The more I think about it, the more certain I am that you're just some kind of derived function or whatever, and you belong to Katahomen-leandraleal the way my finger belongs to me. Maybe you don't even know it your-self, so you're not actually lying to me, I could grant you that if I were being nice about it. I'm not though. Never have been a nice person. As for this whole story of yours that fungal agents are masking our scent and damping the sound, surely she'd notice that something was missing here.'

'Don't be so naive, Cordula.'

If she was supposed to be surprised to be addressed by her first name, it didn't work. She didn't even seem to have heard. So Madame Tree continued, 'This works on exactly the same principle as electronic counter-surveillance trick optics back in your day. Obviously, the fungi aren't only making us a blank black spot. Didn't you use to tap in and feed the system a repeating loop? It would show an empty corridor or something such, totally ordinary, unmoving. So the fungi show . . . Momma's sensors . . . a tree, where there really is a tree, and sometimes they even show her you sitting here and meditating. It's edited, that's all. Filters, random noise generator, glitches where they should be.'

'I can't follow technical explanations. Never could get excited about them.'

'I know, you just exploit Clarke's Three Laws.'

Now it was Frau Späth's turn to chortle. Archaic allusions that describe me nicely—score one to the Entwife.

For a while the two of them listened to the jungle scrape, twitter, chirrup, rustle and snap.

Then the human woman said, 'I was a very introverted girl, you know. All the more so during puberty. Doggedly loyal to my German teacher ever since she marked me down on an essay, I thought that was just fantastic, nothing like that had ever happened to me before, I could write essays for German class with my eyes closed—and here she was, saying, "You can do better than that, it's slapdash, some of your sentences are only half there . . ." I mean, no question but that she was marking the class inconsistently, I knew that other girls had handed in essays way worse than mine and got better marks, but she found fault with mine, not theirs. She was right too. Slapdash. Bits missing, repetitive . . . other teachers would have turned a blind eye or been embarrassed to mention it, "Oh what a pity Cordula . . ." always so happy when one of us little brats was interested at all . . . and then this woman. "You have to ask the utmost of yourself, and expect nothing of others"—she drummed that idea into me, her kind of elitism. Harsh, and in the final analysis anything but true—but very helpful for a neurotic little bitch like I was then. She was my first, my first idol, I think, that woman, she turned me onto music as well, I mean, I already played piano, she started me off easy with records of Scriabin and Chopin, then all of a sudden, brrrumm, Schönberg, taking in Gould on the way. Glenn, that is, not Stephen Jay.'

The twigs giggled.

Frau Späth carried on.

'Leave the piano behind us, chop chop, orchestral appreciation, chamber music first though, Webern, Berg soon, then after that, oddly enough, after this first initiation everything was up for grabs, off we went together to contemporary music, Glass, Riley, and then oom-tss, by fits and starts I actually began to develop some tastes of my own, what with some parallel study in pop music—she tried to ban that, God bless the poor old dear. I even managed to impress her, twice, Frau . . . Fuchs-Stockmann was her name, my dear, the good old days . . . once with Robert Wyatt and then again with some erm nerdy nonsense, dance music, electronica—but by then we were drifting apart anyway. Found my next idol, hadn't I. That was . . . Katja. Incredible. If you never met her yourself, I can't begin to give you any idea of how . . .'

She stopped herself from speaking, wondering as she did, whom she was telling and why.

The tree was still eagerly attentive, and strange how noticeable that was, even unmissable. Her lenticels held their breath, her old split bark gave off a sympathetic scent, information flowed at speed through the veins of every leaf. Frau Späth thought, I'm talking here of something that means a lot to her, or at the very least, she thinks so.

Fine then.

'I'd had a couple of girlfriends before then, absolutely innocent stuff, Kiki and Bettina and so on. But Katja Benante. World turned upside down, it was . . . like a lens you look through, and everything—to begin with, I used to just watch her from afar, she would play table tennis with Sonja or dance at the parties, dark curly hair flying, long face smiling, and her freckles as well of course, like when a figure in a comic book is surprised and the little dots sort of dance about on their face rather than stay still . . . and luckily, she made friends so promiscuously, practically indiscriminate, I mean she could never get enough and she wanted to always be up to something, with someone, everyone, and everyone wanted to spend time with her. When she first noticed that I was trying to get close to her, she would always take me along to the janitor's little tuck shop in the break between lessons. It was open till noon, this little sort of glass kiosk, and she always bought a Twix, the other girls never much liked that, they didn't want to eat sweets the whole time, called it looking after their figure, silly geese—Katja never seemed to put on weight, I mean she wasn't a beanpole either, but she was . . . sturdy, you know, full of life—probably all the extra energy from the sugary chocolate she just burnt off straightaway with this amazing get-up-and-go she had, every day was an occasion, seven days a week. She had this way of running at things full tilt . . . Johanna liked her as well, and she said, there's no one else can run round a corner like she can, as though there were a whole new world behind each corner, somewhere you just have to get to. It was so, feh, what can I even say, it just stoked you up, you just wanted to share that warmth of hers—the first things I ever wrote, I wrote for her, they were little pop songs but they always had what Katja used to call "funny long bits" in the middle or at the end. I wrote them that way because that's how she liked them, something catchy you could whistle along to but they also had those bits, those atonal whatnots or . . . Then when we left school, I just gave everything away that I'd composed so far, it was a sort of deliberate breaking-off, I gave away the tapes and the scores and the files, all of it, so as to say, that's the juvenilia, down to you now whether it disappears or not—and the longest piece, the concept album, you could call it my first opera I suppose, I gave to Katja.'

'What happened to it?'

'Can you believe it,'—she laughed—'she lost it. Mislaid it somewhere. She was like that. By then though we . . . I mean, that was my great love, understand, not least because, at last, it was returned. I remember the evening when I first realized that it didn't have to be just me standing next to her and worshipping from afar, but that there really could be something between us. We had . . . it was a season ticket for the theatre, group subscription for the whole upper sixth, Frau Fuchs-Stockmann had organized it for us, so off we went to Basel in the bus, when . . . it was a dreadful production, some absurdist abstract gallimaufry about mankind's misery in the Fordist thingummy, they moved their hands in this set way, a lever, in the factory, they all had to operate it, all the characters, but in mime, that's to say, there wasn't an actual lever and . . . I could hardly bear it, except that I was watching Katja all evening, to see how she, I mean there I was with my elevated tastes in art and I was fidgeting from boredom . . . so how would a firecracker like her . . . and there she was, scooting about in her seat like she was sitting in a boat on the choppy waves, it was the sweetest thing ever, this perky bundle of fun trying to escape somehow from the dreadful dull rubbish on stage, till at last she even broke the rules enough to begin turning her head about—she was sitting in the row in front, off to one side of me, three seats further, and she turned round, and she looked at me, and she saw that I was looking at her, and I knew then that I was smiling at her like I didn't care how I looked, and she was smiling so all her face was scrunched up in a grin, like Johanna used to call her: the Runaround.'

7. ATTACK

Esprit, the hounds' High Holy Day, had come round again and by now was a festival that no one could enjoy. It seemed to celebrate something scorched, obsolete, unwanted. The Gente's rage and fear turned ugly—at the edge of the cities they captured humans who had not reached the designated refuge zones and many were tied up and burnt in the streets to mark the occasion. For days afterwards the stench threatened to mask even the king's pherinfonic broadcasts, which always proclaimed the same slogans, 'We will stop them in their tracks, we will drive them back.'

Who was 'we'?

Today Dmitri was visiting the king, to bring him a very particular message. The Lion had withdrawn to his sandalwood chamber, its walls now entirely covered with the pivoted mirrors. Satellite images burst forth all about him like exotic weeds.

He looked older than ever, but still far from defeated.

Dmitri found that he still felt the deepest respect when he looked upon his king, and something like love—possibly chemically induced, but it felt genuine.

The wolf forced himself to remember his dead friend, the scuttling hog, and wondered whether the Lion had watched Hébert's murder from this room, on these screens. Diagrams superimposed onto meteorological images showed how the Ceramican campaign had accelerated genetic drift. It all looked pretty grim.

In a melodic and sonorous voice, like the chorus in a classical play, the king began to explain the state of the world as he saw it.

'To use the old names, they have taken all of Africa, most of China, and the two Americas were theirs from the beginning. We shall dig in, and I find it amusing that we shall make our stand where thousands of years ago the planet's first technological civilization made its start, the human civilization that we so scornfully chose to call the Monotony. The war . . .'

'There is no war.' Dmitri had no desire to listen any longer to this bombast. He had been given a safe conduct, although he was down in Georgescu's databanks as a deserter. The shipyards, the island; everyone who lived and worked there had solemnly been proclaimed outlaw. Not him though; I'm a diplomat for life, he thought.

'No war?' The Lion smiled indulgently. He still had the knack of seeming to know more than anyone else.

'No more than in the sense that when an old crust grows mould, the mould is at war with the bread.'

The king breathed out loudly and said, 'I understand. She's talked you round. Mould. A metaphor—you could say so, I suppose, but I find that a better image is when cancer attacks vital organs. I won't insist that the carcinoma is at war with the organism. But I don't believe that the body should just flee in the face of the cancer. Or that it's even possible. She thinks so. Her prerogative.'

She: the name that could no longer be spoken in the two cities now remaining, Lasara.

'I see that you're still investing all your resources,'—the wolf looked at the data crawl in the lower third of the mirror, where numbered lists of munitions output and armies on the march trooped across the screen—'in preparing a counter-offensive.'

'I have given myself into the hands of my badgers. They fought nobly at Landers.'

'Thirty-seven million dead or disappeared, all civilians, on top of the badgers who died, and the king says it was nobly done.'

'What else should I say? You are too young, little wolf. You can't judge these things. I approve of Georgescu's new doctrine—drastic retreat, putting incredible distances between ourselves and the enemy, then an annihilating attack. And meanwhile, I get to watch them destroy all that the seed of the hundred and forty-four thousand could create. The grandeur and the glory.'

'Three cities. Then two. One soon. In the end, none.'

The king tugged at his beard, running his claws through it, looking steadily at the wolf.

Then he said, 'Well, cities . . . for our enemy, they have the great advantage that the inhabitants can't run away. In Landers . . . they found an old archive, the Ceramicans, preserving Monotony history. Nanotreated pages, age-proofed. They chucked it all into the big lake. It swelled up in the water, they used it to treat their wounds. Which means, we know that they were wounded. They are alive, they can be wounded, they can die as well. Yes, I say that it was noble.'

'I don't imagine'—Dmitri made sure that his sarcasm came through, but at the same time felt rather ashamed of it—'that hereabouts you give much thought to the fact that we—Lasara, myself, all the others working on the ark—have to finance defence measures that strain our somewhat slender budget. Not for defence against Katahomenleandraleal, but rather . . .'

The king waved his paw dismissively. 'Huh, against me, yes, I know,'—he no longer made any effort to conceal how tired, bored or distracted he was. He is a great soul, truly, thought the wolf and remembered how gladly he had served him.

No longer, now he had another and a harder task to fulfil.

The mission on which he had supposedly come, to negotiate a truce with the Lion, was merely a pretext. He owed it to the ruler to tell the truth, although Lasara had rubbished the idea. 'He's not a king, that's romantic twaddle, he's a dictator for life and he's lived too long.' Nevertheless, 'I have come here to . . .'

'To kill me, yes, I know. What are you going to do, little wolf? Attack me with micrococci, vibrions, perrhobacteria tailored to my engineered immune system? Burn me with laser beams, drench me with napalm, suffocate me, garrote me, stab me, cut my throat, shish-kebab or roast?' The wolf said nothing, clenched his teeth.

What doesn't he have, this king? *Serdtse*. Soul. He has no heart or soul. It's as though he weren't there, no, more complicated than that, as though he made himself up and is actually someone else, smaller, lesser.

The Lion began to laugh. 'Of course. That's how she is. Naturally. She has my respect. Evolution: she loves it, she believes in it, she's got that from her mother.'

The wolf was breathing faster. The Lion said, 'Why not then a duel? An old-fashioned assassination. The faster, stronger, tougher . . . the . . . better beast will win.'

'I can make it quick. It needn't hurt,' said the wolf through clenched teeth and wondered where he got such absurd thoughts from, how he had got into this and where it would end.

'Oh no, not like that.' The king prowled, light-footed, away from him, never taking his eyes away. There was something hypnotic in that gaze. 'You'll do what they told you and you'll do it as you should. We'll test our strengths. Here in my sanctum, you'll leap upon me like a goat in rut, you'll roll on this polished floor with me, we'll sink our teeth into one another's flesh. And if you manage it, my silly child, she'll come to term. If not, she'll kill it, since she doesn't like your traits.'

'To term . . .'

The Lion shook his mane, when he saw that Dmitri had no idea what he was talking about. 'Your child, you daft unsuitable son-in-law, you! Didn't she tell you? What she's carrying there, below her heart? She showed it to me in my synopticon, and you can't fake something like that in there. She didn't draw my attention to it as such, but she knew for sure that I was recording and examining everything. She stood still for quite a while under the cameras, before she flounced off with her rebel entourage.'

The wolf didn't know whether to believe this or whether it was an outrageous lie to test his resolve, to break him down—but one thing was certain: now he would have to leap at the king, tear out his throat, as though he were a snivelling human. He crouched, took two steps backwards and growled. 'Let me guess a bit more, it's such fun,' the king said mockingly, 'there's something in your blood and saliva, isn't there? Some noxious, toxic . . . made only for me, get it in circulation through the wound, it bypasses all the filters and metabolsafeguards . . . You should never have trusted the brute. Remember my words, in the time you have left to you: We run from those who made us, lest they destroy us. You should not have slept with your mother, you whelp.'

'My . . .'

The Lion roared.

Dmitri shrank back.

Cyrus Iemelian Adrian Vinicius Golden laughed. 'A wolf! You're a little lamb! How do you think she became my daughter? She was the first of the third generation, simple as that—her damned mother and I wrote our genetic signatures into her, calligraphy, and then she helped us to create the other third-generation quasispecies and individuals, the heavenly hosts, the new wolves, you yourself, the jolly painted badgers and all the other warm-blooded Johnny-come-latelies who can hardly stand upright now, they're so blasted ungrateful.'

The wolf curled up his lip, bared his incisors. Both combatants had begun to circle one another with measured, powerful steps. The wolf had trained for weeks for this moment, his muscles were doped up with pico-elastic fibres, they had sculpted his skeleton and put him into specially written pherinfonic worlds to practise every possible choreography. Lasara was concerned, but confident. 'If I didn't think that you could do it, I would have found someone else.'

'She chose her moment well, I'm fed up with looking after you rabble. I liked it for a while, a long while, centuries; I liked being admired and loved and feared, little dog, it helped me shed my daily cares. Now it's all old hat and I can't even make myself care enough to fear for all that I have made. When I look at the world, at Borbruck and Capeside or even where the Ceramicans rage and lay waste, I only see a bad pastiche running round, shadows from the old books, pale copies of the beauties and the horrors we read about when we were children. We're marooned with Doctor Moreau, we've been betrayed by John Crowley's beasts, David Brin's fish have turned their backs on us. The old books are gone now, the old films too—I was the black monolith from Kubrick's *2001*, I tried to haul you out of your unthinking deeps, I sold you transcendence at a reasonable price—and who do they send to end my life? Man's best friend, domesticated twice over. They're back, the hounds of the Lord, Domini canes, and they're looking for the Runaround everywhere as Arthur's knights sought the Grail.'

Dmitri hissed, 'I don't know who was ever interested in your blether, but I know they must all be dead.'

The king grinned.

With one bound, Dmitri was at his side, upon him. Rather than shield his throat, the king bit at his assassin twice, weakly, as though he had lost concentration, his jaws rattled like badly oiled wood. He batted a paw half-heartedly across the wolf's cheek and even so the blow was so strong that Dmitri Stepanovich saw red and black dancing before his eyes. But even in his daze, he bit down and heard the Lion gurgle and chuckle in surprise—he really didn't believe that I would dare.

The battle lasted a long time.

The badgers outside had all been paid off or blackmailed, but still had to stop themselves from rushing in, so loud was the noise, to join the fight on one side or another, to kill or to save.

The Lion's life was at stake and once he understood this, he fought furiously. It didn't work.

In the end, the eyes that had seen this world before it was born were full of blood. The floor and walls were slick with slobbered drool, the room stank of defeat. Dmitri, recovering his breath now, thought of denouncing the ancient beast: You king of gods and demons, king over all souls save your daughter, look now at the bright spinning worlds in your mirrors, the worlds that only you and I, with our hurt eyes, will see here today, all together, all assembled, in this room—what then is left of the world of the Gente, a world swarming with your slaves, who you taught to fall to their knees before you, to praise and worship you and do your bidding? Hecatombs of broken hearts beat for you, in fear and self-loathing and in sterile hope. And I, your enemy, can hardly recognize you now, but I know these worlds round you well, and you have driven me to claim a higher place, to become also a lord, and a judge, and king of my own misery.

The wolf, his muzzle smashed in, said none of this, but fell backwards, then onto his side, just as the Lion had collapsed. Dmitri coughed, groaned, he was the victor. The mirrors smoked, a curtain hung, torn to broad jagged shreds. The Lion tried to speak, grinned weakly, like a mad thing, and then stopped breathing.

Dmitri lay where he was for several minutes, feeling his traitor's heart beating in panic.

A child. Lasara was pregnant. Stunned, full of shame and a quite abstract happiness, he wondered whether he hadn't secretly known all along, whether indeed it had not been this knowledge that gave him the gumption to kill his patron. The wolf knew that, Ceramicans or not, the child would never have been safe while the king was alive. Is that why I did it, from a protective instinct? Is there any such thing as instinct any more and does it tell me what to do?

He forced himself to get up as the double doors slid apart and the bribed guards came running in with doctors. They paid him no attention. What was important now was to certify that the king was dead.

A blue badger wearing a breathing mask was already sending out pherinfones to complete the *coup d'état*.

There was already an interim leader, a puppet regent tied by strings that Lasara pulled—Stanz the ape.

Dmitri Stepanovich went his way on unsteady legs, down the broad empty steps of the long curving corridor, to the guest chambers, where he wanted to sleep, nothing but sleep. He went unchallenged, indeed they shunned him like a sickness. As his door opened, he heard the Lion's voice in his head.

It was not a memory, but a delayed-effect pherinfoplex that had infected his blood during the battle. A sophisticated paralysing agent bound to it had already began its work, so that the killer did not even have the strength left to be horrified by what he heard. 'She'll raise the child without a father, little dog. I am sorry,'— Dmitri collapsed against the doorframe, he felt sick and dizzy, and began to retch— 'after all I always liked you. I like my daughter as well—like all those who found a great dynasty, I like the idea of family. But I have established laws for myself and for my nearest and dearest,'—Dmitri tried to heave up his stomach, he couldn't, nor could he breathe—'that may not be broken. Although I admit that I am of no more use to the Animal Empire, that I have reached the end, that I must be done away with if my work is to have a new chance, nevertheless I swore that no one may kill me and live on after me.'

Dmitri, even as he slipped into oblivion, couldn't help smiling wistfully, a trace of his old admiration for the Lion.

The last thing he heard was the voice of a hawkwoman—Elektrizitas Pulsipher, who for so long had vanished from the public eye, was running up the stairs to the sandalwood chamber shouting, 'Let me through! I must see the king, quickly, let me through! We were wrong! A dreadful mistake! The Li'l Runaround, this is terrible, I know now, I know where it is!'

8. DARKENETH, COUNSEL

In the fields of the Gente there was much lamenting.

Grief for the Lion's end burst forth from every house.

Here a civilization had been struck to its heart, its inmost workings shaken. After its passing no archaeologist would recognize how advanced this civilization had been, since machines ran almost nothing nowadays and hardly anything left could be identified as a machine.

The wind awoke by cool whitewashed walls behind gigantic cathedrals of archives, realizing that the endless prologue was over, the heirs of the Monotony could now begin the internecine war, the kinslaughter of the spiteful and the simple.

The afternoon that had stretched out for decades, the costly peace, now gave way to restless evening, and the wind, awake again now, knew of the night that was to come. The Gente began to wonder whether they were indeed anything more than wild beasts and went into their houses that now were no more than caves and laid themselves down on their beds, worn with weeping.

The reawakened wind blew through architectures that had lost their nerve. Where there had been earth, the Gente had built with earth, polymerized the walls, made safe their lodgings, covered over the roof. Where there had been forests, they made buildings of wood, and the pre-existing human towers or halls built by the van-quished were sometimes left where they stood, sometimes gutted, to be used as quarries.

None of this mattered any longer.

The storm came forth from its chambers and from the north came the cold. Ice came on the breath of a forgotten god and the Atlanteans' wide waters froze where they lay. The vengeful god made heavy his clouds with water and from every cloud lightning broke forth. Sticks and kindling no longer cackled into flame in metal barrels placed round the mouths of rusty rainy drainpipes, those fires had died of fright.

But from one of these drainpipes, the Fox dripped out in an oily silver flow and or-dered the orang-utan Sdhütz Arroyo to respect the news he heard from the Gov-ernment Quarter, that grew into a great clamour on the streets and in the alleys.

'What do you mean, respect, I'm already going about with my head hung low.'

'If you wore shoes I'd tell you to take them off. If you had a hat, you should doff it. Since the murder, your feet walk on accursed ground and your head is raised beneath a harrowed sky.'

'Why,' asked the ape doubtfully, 'just because there's no Lion any . . .'

'There never was any Lion,' said the silvery oil and writhed on the accursed ground into an exactly circular puddle, 'you ought to know that by now.'

'It was you, boss, wasn't it? There never was a king, only you, the financier and a few of your personae.'

'Personae,' said the disc of gleaming fluid, 'doesn't really sound right. There were no masks involved, rather . . . partial personalities, let's put it that way. There were very few actors in the show we inhabited here—a small family, basically, and their partial personalities. Father, mother, son, daughter, wet nurse. Not all het-erosexual, not all married, not all . . . well, anyway.'

'If a badger can become a whale, and I've seen that happen, then this shouldn't surprise me either. What am I supposed to do, what do I still owe you?'

Ripples on the disc, like an ironic smile.

'What?' asked the ape, irked but keeping the challenge from his voice.

The puddle answered in the tone of a devil who feels sorry for the angels, 'Lay your weapons, last of heroes, from the hands that held them last . . .'

The ape scratched his back. The clouds overhead were crashing together now and the thunder was loud.

The Fox said, 'It's all a case of mistaken identity. Haplography, copying errors . . . unthinking conflation of Leviathan and Behemoth. Both monsters are descended from single-celled organisms, you see. But their hunting behaviour and methods of killing are totally different.'

The ape shrugged.

'Good,' said the Fox, 'down to business. You'll make another journey for me.'

Lightning flashed and the mossy walls shone with an algal green light.

Solemnly, and not without awe, the ape said, 'Of course. Where to?'

'To the new worlds. To the next attempt. We'll see whether my investments don't pay off in the end after all.'

Sdhütz Arroyo nodded, bent down over the puddle and, flaring his nostrils, inhaled his new marching orders, while the bloody rain began to foam all round.

third movement

DIGONOS/DIGONOS

(ADAGIO)

Iz: So it was probably a tactical and didactic move when Darwin found it surprising that teeth might remain fairly similar within a particular species, even though when we compare across species such characteristics actually . . .

Cy: Well, there's no great secret here. Natural selection transforms variation within populations into differences between populations, so that after the event you can always say, look at that, isn't it marvellous how uniformly . . .

Iz: I only meant to say that it is surprising how, without really needing to, we've taken over various features in the Three Cities, right down to the fine variations of political party, faction and forum.

Cy: I think that it was naive from the beginning to believe that we could just leave natural history behind. If you're to be so entirely different from everything that has come before, then you need to take whatever you want to leave behind you and make it your own, and to own something like this means to repeat it. Even if we're doing it quite consciously, voluntarily, to make a point: we understand this. That's how we can live it.

From the *Conversations with the Lion*, V/51

X
THE CHILDHOOD OF FIRE

1. A HEADSHAKE

The most important being on the planet lived in a place that was not a cave, but had been carved out of the warm rock as though it were, to protect its inhabitant. Inside, the bulkheads, ramps, corridors, doorways and portholes were of gold, glass and silver. The furniture in the rooms were of synthetic pinewood or woven palm, the instruments of plasteel, obsidian, marble.

Visitors from the poorer regions often saw all this as more like a mausoleum than a nursery, but such thoughts counted for nothing. The place looked imposing from the outside. Walls reached up to the entrance like a giant staircase as steep as those of Mycenae, back then, on the old world.

The vanished race of Man had once believed that one-eyed giants had built the walls of Mycenae. No monsters though had hewn the cliff faces here, but the friends and guardians of the most important being on the planet, working with mighty tools before they woke the child from its long sleep, a sleep that had itself lasted longer than the whole glorious history of Mycenae.

Set into the high staircase of cliffs that led to the place that was not a cave were great green opalescent discs of light, visible from twelve miles away, twelve in each row and each a dozen yards across.

These served the navigation systems of the ships that still occasionally came in, bringing raw materials, water and seeds for the planthouses, arriving from orbit and from a time before history. They never landed, they only ever crashed. Near the staircliffs posts and a wire fence enclosed the crash sites of the first ships. Here there were graves, resting places for the ancestors of the friends and guardians of the most important being on the planet. Very near here, this being's genetic material had reached this world, falling as cooling clumps of aggregate.

Earlier yet, the probes sent by Man had landed here. They were called Venera 3, Venera 4, Pioneer, or Venera 11 through 14. They had not been carrying anything that had language.

The most important being on the planet, by contrast, had all conceivable languages.

As soon as the most important being on the planet understood that it was the most important being on the planet, it shook its head.

'He's shaking his head,' said the guardians and friends. They did not know whether that was a good sign or a bad one.

2. FURRY FRIENDS

When he was still small, the furry friends called him 'Fire' so often that in the end he understood that this meant him.

Through a thousand small gestures, sounds and shows of honour they let him know that they thought it a very great thing indeed to be entrusted with the task of bringing him up. They played hide-and-seek with him until they could no longer find him. Then they were pleased at first, but suddenly decided that the game was 'too dangerous' and dissuaded him from playing it. Sometimes they said that he was a prince. He thought that he would always be Fire though, willy-nilly prince or not, since they always called him Fire when he had done something right, alive in the moment. 'Prince' was only a name for when he needed watching, if he had smeared himself with food, burnt someone, broken something.

Fire looked made for fast running, high leaps and great speed. His diaphragm felt the change in the air when the sevenfours had not done their work. Then he would climb the warm stone of the cliffs as high as he could, to spare his heart from the cramps and angina from the thick air down by the ground on such days. His spine, the lumbar and sacrals, the whole design of his hips, all was more limber and flexible than it had ever been in man, whose skeleton provided the historical model, the blueprint for Fire's frame. His arms and legs, heavily muscled, could turn in their sockets and at their joints at angles which would have baffled human expectation.

Fire's brain could think effortlessly about matters utterly inaccessible to his senses: nameless tenses for pasts that had never taken place and for improbable futures, higher geometries through which he could wriggle, at a pinch, in hide-and-seek or in earnest.

This was the legacy of the Ceramicans, developed from stolen secrets. His skin was bronze, except for his back, armoured with little diamond-shaped plates, his upper arms and the top of his skull; the hair on his back, colourful and tightly curled, grew in interlocking chevrons, the hair on his head shone copper-coloured. He never needed a trim since it never grew any longer than the sharp toenails on his cloven feet. Sometimes, when he was concentrating, deep in thought, the tips of his hair glowed like glimmering points of coal. His face was handsome and thin, the nose fine, the cheekbones high, the lips full; the almond-shaped eyes gleamed, white–gold, with black pupils like a cat's. His furry friends thought that the cutest thing about him in these young years was his long, pointed ears, shot through with a fine network of blood vessels like those of the lynx and jackal back on the old world.

When blood flowed very fast through these, heat was dissipated and his head could cool down. This was important up there on the warm rock, 'in the hot heights', as Fire liked to say, there where he liked to be. His ears stayed this way for the rest of his life, though later they lay closer to his head. His voice though changed when he was forty-five days old. Where before it had been soft, high and querulous, afterwards it was rougher, rounder, deep.

He did not learn to sing until after his voice had changed.

He ate meat only rarely. Creatures that had no language, and were thus lawful to eat, were scarce up here on the plateau and consequently shy, only a very skilful hunter could catch them. Besides which, he didn't much like their taste. He could only be persuaded to go hunting because his furry friends told him that he must eat meat from time to time for the proteins and because hunting would prepare him for his 'Great Task'.

This Task was the most baffling thing in his life, sometimes the most exciting and then again the most boring—it had something to do with a journey, his friends told him, that he must undertake, to do with a certain Temple of Isotta which he must seek and find, for there was 'the weaker half of the Runaround' and 'no one here but you has a right to it.'

Later he asked himself—who told him that?

Was it the nursemaid of glass, the furry friends, the salamanders or the ants, the voices in the long nights, which might have been in his head or his head amongst them, he never knew (or neither of those, or both at once)?

Rather than meat, even white boiled chicken, he liked to eat vegetables such as lightbeans or the black clewcumbers found among the grasses and horsetail ferns between the volcanic channels, to the north of his place that was not a cave. Nor did he refuse to eat the grasses themselves, and when his friends had baked, he would sprinkle mint and liquorice onto the broad, flat loaves, or crumble them into the sharp mushroom stew that the salamanders had taught him to cook, in their amphibian colony on the shallow lake. Fire learnt a lot from everyone, but most of all from his furry friends—he learnt nearly everything that they knew and had to offer—that when colours change, an observer will often think that light levels have also changed, which is not at all the case (they showed him how this worked by shining lights onto screens, large and small), that evolutionary changes in living creatures could not be reversed, even though this may sometimes appear to be the case, that natural history had come to an end with the dawn of language, that muscles, glands, breathing, heartbeats and neural reactions made music as they worked, that someone like Fire, who had all languages and lived in the moment, could hear this music in his body.

They taught him what kind of planet the world was on which they lived: smaller and less dense than the world from which life had come, and which was called 'the old world' hereabouts. Fire thought of this old world as dusty, inhospitable, even uninhabitable, he wrinkled his nose at the news that the world forced its dwellers to live with a very short diurnal cycle and a much extended year. How could they have known when it was time to do anything?

Volcanoes were the most ordinary thing in the world here and they had had them on the other world too, though much more short-lived. 'That has to do with plate tectonics,' explained one of his furry friends, 'The crust down there is broken apart and the pieces push against one another. So the hot spots are covered.'

'How,' Fire asked, 'had they ever known where they were, when nothing stayed in one place, not even the places themselves?'

When his friends noticed this line of thought, they chided him, saying that he should 'have more respect' for 'the cradle of life and language,' after all the world on which he lived had only very recently been populated—thanks to the technology of the Gente (a word denoting creatures which, like Man, were no longer around and apparently a synonym for another quaint word, 'the forerunners'), striving for three thousand days against heavy odds to bring a world to life, 'even when they pursued several strategies in parallel.' Artificial blue-green algae housed in shallow lakes and seas, now pumped dry or drained away into the earth, had scrubbed carbon dioxide to oxygen, while the seventwos and sevenfours siphoned excess pressure from the atmosphere and pumped it into space. In the third phase, solar-powered freighters had shunted back and forth from a world called 'Saturn' bringing hydrogen. These freighters had been several miles long and for weeks could be seen plunging one after another, day after day, into the boiling new seas, like meteors.

Either there were no historical records of these momentous events in their entirety or no one dared to tell Fire about them, thinking him too young to understand. Yet, he dreamt about them as though he had been there: look there, the impact, the enormous waves, the hissing, the foam, muffle your ears, cover your eyes.

The furry friends spent many hours, whole days, in thoroughly teaching Fire the local geography. Soon, he came to believe that he had made this world himself, so feelingly did his feet, his belly, the roots of his hair know the highlands, the jagged volcanic badlands and plains, the valleys that spread out endlessly to all sides, the high regiones, 'which they would have called continents back on the old world': Ishtar Regio in the north, where Fire lived, not far from the Maxwell Montes and Aphrodite Regio on the equator. There were two smaller terrae, daughters to the regiones, 'remark especially the island plateaus', one of them compact, Lada Regio, the other split into Beta, Phoebe and Themis.

'Regan, Goneril and Cordelia would have been better names,' said one of the furry friends.

Fire didn't understand this and asked for an explanation. Came the confusing reply: 'Oh, these old names, you know, worn down by use and some then put to new use—the shallow sea has a different name from the old-established name of the flooded crater, so the contents change the name of the vessel. These are all female names from really old myths, from a time even before the Gente, the time called the Monotony: Four-Akka, for instance, something like that, was the name of a fertility goddess from Lapland and Vellamo, on the map over here, that was a Finnish mermaid and here, Xochiquetzal, that was the Aztec flower goddess.'

'Azte . . .'

'Human tribe, died out long ago.'

The furry friends knew so much, almost too much for Fire's tastes, and sometimes he needed all his self-control not to ask them snarkily what use this knowledge was.

The old world: you could look through a spyglass and see it.

It had a moon. 'What does it need that for?'

It must have been an amusing question, because the furry friend at the spyglass giggled, 'That's what the Ceramicans thought—what use is a moon? At any rate they bombarded it once they found out what our forerunners were up to, up there. It was the most important staging post after all—that's where Lasara's rockets flew to, that's where the bases were, where they processed, on the dark side of the moon, the material for the second stage of the Exodus.' Fire had heard about this again and again, he found it hard to hold on to, it was all an age ago. Not wishing to seem ungrateful, and because he hoped that hearing the story many times over might give him some threads to make sense of the whole tangled story, this time he asked for an explanation: 'The Gente lived on the moon?'

'Yes, for a while, some of them at least. They took Lasara's conclusion very seriously—the Ceramicans would be satisfied with ruling the Earth. Off to the moon, then and there, with their disassemblers and assemblers, they dredged raw material from the dead rock and dust for all the stages to come. The Ceramicans though—machines that were not just machines, that were something like human beings as well—had their eyes and ears in orbit and in the end attacked the base and the . . . well . . . the mines. Too late. The work was nearly done by then. They were only able to kill about one-third of the refugees, the other two-thirds were already on their way to their next stage, to the space stations, to settle two new worlds.'

Fire still could not fit together what he knew. He lost interest and asked instead about conditions on his home world: 'Atalanta, Niobe, those are the areas where none of us are allowed, right?' He pointed top right on the Mercator projection radar map of the planet. The furry friend who was teaching him topography nodded and winked: 'That's where the mad folk live. You know, the Gente were right about everything,'—again it seemed impossible to talk about the here and now without broaching matters of ancient history—'but they underestimated the ravages of time, erosion, entropy . . . The mad folk up there, in Atalanta, Niobe, call themselves . . . men and they build machines—but they're basically degenerate Gente, not *Homo sapiens*. Not even the women that Katahomenleandraleal restored, all that while ago, would recognize these folk as human, any more than they would you by the way.'

'But . . .'

'Exactly, but. They have this religion, this ideology . . . they believe that the purpose of settling the two worlds was to bring the history of terrestrial intelligent life . . . solar life, they say, they set great store by that . . . back to the point where Man went under. A second Earth, a third . . . "to conquer the animal part of us", they mean their legacy from the Gente.'

'What were they like, the Gente?' Fire wanted to be able to imagine it, at long last.

'Like us, I suppose.'

'Like you and me?'

'No, like us . . . not like you. Your furry friends, as you say, and the salamanders down there and the birds up above. Not human, not machines, but having language.'

'Mmpf,' said Fire, to show that he thought that wasn't much to boast of having. Fire did not understand how anybody could want to be human. He would rather have been one of the furry friends and then, he reckoned, Gente.

There was a lot to learn.

'I can see,'—the oldest of his friends, his whiskers trembling as though he had caught the scent of something tasty—'that you have been wondering what we can really learn from all that we know about the past. You'll be surprised: I don't know. No one knows—we simply have a hunch and must work from there. For myself, I have simply discovered an iron law hidden in the chronicles: that it is very dangerous to sweep aside a way of life—even the Monotonous way of life— before you have made your peace with the idea that there is no point in missing this life once it is dead and gone. Events in Atalanta and Niobe are a fine and fearful example of this principle. We can only show you and tell you the implications, but you must understand it for yourself. You are more intelligent than us, but we know rather more than you. For now.'

Fire learnt how someone like Fire could do what others couldn't—walk through the lava streams and not get burnt, flex the coloured hairs on his back and shoot them out like silver needles, sometimes even know what others were thinking, sense how folk were put together from other folk and drew ever-increasing circles, spirals built from what they were and thought and dreamt. Fire learnt what patience was: they still haven't told me anything more about my Task and I have to put up with it.

He knew: once it gets to that point and I set off, perhaps I will never come back. This was painful, just a little bit, in a way, a way that he rather liked.

One of the furry friends always talked about the 'Plan' when Fire asked about the Task, 'You are a boy, then you will be a man, then a woman and then a girl, that is the plan. All that will happen as you go, in the course of your journey.' This friend had a pelt as grey as ice, but for his ears, fringed with tufts of fine green hairs sticking out to all sides.

3. THE FASH

On set occasions, at regular intervals that nevertheless seemed to Fire to diminish as the weeks went by, the fash came to visit him in the great hall, which had most of the lightscreens.

His furry friends had enormous respect for the fash. And Fire learnt to respect him too, since the fash knew everything there was to know about cooking, eating, health and living.

The fash was called Vempes. He was long and sleek, with muscular legs, and propped on his powerful thighs his body lay almost parallel to the ground. His eyes were rimmed with black, his mouth broad, the sharp little teeth within it gleaming. All the fash that Fire had ever heard of lived on the other side of the old landing ground, on wobbly ground, in the lead-grey swamp that belched muddy bubbles.

Everyone liked the fash, even the salamanders.

Once Vempes the fash had shown Fire the morphology of the old species, Fire worked out independently how the fash had been designed. 'Your body, torso and such—leopard seals, weren't they, in the colder seas, back on the old world, right? And the legs are a more robust variant of bird legs. Large flightless birds.'

'Ostrich had legs like I have now, that's right.'

The fash visited Fire as a "visiting tutor in biology", the furry friends said. Sometimes they cooked a meal together as well, meat from the unspeaking animals that lived in the tunnel systems below the final volcano.

'First thing you have to understand is evolution,' chided the fash, while Fire, rather than listen to him, was playing with the plasteel models of Gente and humans that the fash has brought with him.

'Understand evolution, frrrp. We can't do anything with it anyway.' Fire meant that a lot of Gente knowledge had been lost—outpatient breeding programmes, metamorphic and protean nanotech . . . Anything that had hauled evolution from natural history into history itself was, admittedly, still there in the databanks, but barely practicable in the world where Fire lived because—yes indeed, because what?

'A-ha, can't do anything with it anyway, quite right, young fellow. But why is that the case here, on our world?' asked the fash inquisitorially, curling back his upper lip.

'Ah well erm because there's not enough alive, here, and that's why we need to work out ways of making do without improving upon ourselves.'

'Right,'—the fash bowed his head forward a little, smacked his lips and said, 'it's a question of available biomass and wealth levels—back then the Gente lived in a non-scarcity ecotecture, they'd achieved a self-correcting homeostasis. That is, shall we say, a desirable condition in itself, which is why the two of us, you and I, will once again turn our attention to evolution and her laws.'

He activated a couple of the lightscreen surfaces and put two hologram cubes in the middle of the room, which soon showed dancing configurations, animated illustrations of his lecture.

To begin with there were bubbles, spheres, eggs, 'Chemically active units, spatially circumscribed, their internal processes and interaction with their environment directed by genetic information.'

'Right: cells,' said Fire.

'The evolutionary theory of the Monotony, which is to say human evolutionary theory,' began the fash and blinked happily, enjoying the ambiguity of his phrasing, 'began from the wrong end. Top-down, beginning with the higher taxa, focused on the struggle for resources in the fight for reproductive success, with species, the antagonistic principle, the chance events of competitive behaviour. Starting from these premises, humankind necessarily concluded that although species developed along an axis of increasing complexity, this tendency was neither universal nor unavoidable. As far as diversity of species goes,'—beams of light shot from one model to the next, genealogies traced and swept away again—'that was absolutely right, but on the level that they should have been considering, we must acknowledge that there actually is an internal logic to the whole process that has nothing to do with romantic notions of Providence or orthogenesis. They made the first steps towards understanding this during the end phase of the Monotony—they studied the genetic material, genomics, the proteins, proteomics and the metabolic process substrates, metabolomics. But the Gente were the first to get things the right way up, beginning with the chemical systems themselves, the whole array of molecular components. Structures, thermodynamics, kinetics. Think about life as a chemist would think, not a dog-breeder. Even the humans noticed ordered structures back when they were drawing and painting, but form doesn't just proceed from these, it also comes from the inherent limits of dynamic flow, from organization. The origin of species didn't only lead to a happenstance parade of . . . let's say, anecdotal organisms. Rather, the oxidation of the biosphere led deterministically to which chemotypes would give rise to life and which would dominate, right down to today, on three planets that we know of so far. Never mind random variations at the level of speciation, the evolutionary process has a direction and it's logically founded in a planet's large-scale chemical structures—the whole ecosystem, any ecotecture at all, is driven by energy degradation, which runs in one definite direction. Oxygen levels increase—you get anaerobic prokaryotes, then the aerobic ones, then eukaryotes, then the first interesting multicellular organisms, then animals, then humans, then the Gente, the Ceramicans ...Two million years before natural history comes to an end, as you know, in the birth of the Gente, the bacteria made the first revolutionary change in the terrestrial mechanism when they began to excrete oxygen, changing the proportion in which certain elements were reactively available. These upheavals are the deciding factor—not some imaginary state of equilibrium that humanity used to call "Gaia". There's no cosy all-encompassing truth which we can all feel good about living in.'

It became cooler in the room, the beams of light shrank together to a single point, that flared brightly for a moment, then vanished.

4. ABSOLUTE IDIOTS

His furry friends taught Fire how to run faster than the silvery stream that sprang down the rocks below his home, how to read the clouds for the coming weather and when to crouch down low, flat on the ground, for safety.

'Beware,' said his furry friends, 'all those who want to be human at any cost, and beware of their machines, and of the parents of those who want to be human, and beware the parents of the machines, and beware of the children of those who want to be human, of the children of the machines. Beware all that comes from Atalanta and from Niobe and from the colonies round Lavinia. Those who live there will want to kill you if ever they learn of your existence.'

'Why? And what does that even mean: "kill"?'

They said, 'It's hard to explain. They see you as something that should be so thoroughly broken that no one can ever put you back together again.'

'But I'm not an object that can be . . . I'm an arrangement, a paradigm. That's got nothing to do with whether I'm here in the flesh, flesh and blood . . .'—he struggled to explain why what these fabled persecutors apparently wanted was, in fact, meaningless—'you can't just destroy a para . . . it can simply be transferred to another substrate. Something that lives and speaks can never really be. . . . irrevocably destroyed.'

'Quite true. But they don't know that.'

'And? They can't go ahead and do something, just because they don't know that it can't be done. If it can't be done, you can't do it. Full stop.'

'They're not concerned about destroying your pattern. These people want to destroy the self-aware part of the paradigm. They'll remove you, so to speak, from your . . . from yourself . . . and they'll hide you, if they can, where you can't find yourself and there won't even be anyone to look for you.'

'So they'll take away my language and make sure I can't find it again, that's their plan.'

'You know something . . . back on the old world, in the Gente age, they would have had a much harder time carrying out their plans. In those days your parents would have made sure that from the day you were born you'd be saved to the pherinfonet, as copies or partials. Not that everyone got such treatment, but someone as important as you . . . Life was lived cheek by jowl, back there in the old world, and the Gente arranged things so that everything was connected by scents, even where scent molecules couldn't move so quickly, deep underwater. Here though the distances are too great, the planet isn't densely populated enough and in many regions it's too hot, too hostile to life to support a pherinfonic system. Which is why nutcases like we're warning you about can move freely here. And the few, the rare, face threats to their lives and their language.'

It changed things when they told him that. Now Fire wanted to know more about what had not interested him before—about humans, machines, about children and parents.

They could at last show Fire the humans, by taking him to the lightscreens inside the old life-bearing ships. There were moving images here, performing strange actions. 'They're absolute idiots,' said Fire, the prince, decisively, and laughed, and squatted down to see the pictures from closer up.

'Later, when you're grown,' said one of his friends in a warning tone, 'you'll see things differently. The creatures you see here certainly lack the gift of reason, but that's no laughing matter.' Fire had an inkling of what this meant—they didn't know what they wanted, didn't know what they should do, didn't know what they could do and what was impossible.

Fire watched while a human demonstrated his incapacity to think. Clearly, nothing in him corresponded to what Fire meant when he said 'I'. There were simply urges, such as drove him to pick up objects from the table in front of him and sniff at them.

There was nothing within him saying, 'A-ha, what's that?' Just an appetite, the desire to suck on the smell, and a blank expectation in his eyes, can my tongue lick this thing, and a hope that if the tongue can lick it, perhaps I can chew it. So he would pick up something inedible, chew on it for a while, then spit it out. Then he would bend over and test it once again with his nose, is this something worth trying. Smells good. Pick it up in the mouth, chew, drop it again. The human could do this four or five times without learning or giving up. Other humans on the viewscreens here showed similar behaviours. Incorrigible. Sniff, chew, spit.

Fire laughed.

The oldest of his furry friends growled, he found the Prince's merriment a poor substitute for fear, horror and pity.

There was a human, sitting, with matted hair and pendant breasts, ghoulishly investigating something that lay there on the table—'Mark this well, a document of human folly, naked greed, the violence and misery of humans reborn at Kata-homenleandraleal's behest, evilly cradled, without language and without a world.' The human had been snuffling and chewing at the unborn form of a human infant, a dead, half-finished thing. The human clearly had less of the gift of reason even than the lice who had infested Fire's hair and the fur on his back one long autumn and which his furry friends had only been able to remove with great effort.

Fire raised his eyebrows. If that wasn't funny, then what was it?

5. FROM MYXAMOEBAE TO MYXAMOEBAE

'Are there still humans? Where are they? Where will they come from, if they want to kill me?' Fire inquired.

'On the old world, whence comes everything that you know. I suspect that there are many of them there, by now, although once, they were nearly exterminated,' said one of his younger furry friends.

'Why were they nearly exterminated?' asked Fire.

The friend led Fire to the smallest viewscreen in his house. It was much lower-definition than those in the old ships, but you could still show a few things on it.

At first it stayed blank. The friend said, 'The first theories, back when it . . . happened, and humanity was . . . nearly killed off, conjectured that mankind had not known love. No instinct for beauty, no . . . But research revealed that beauty and its lack caused the same feelings and . . . impulses in humans as they do in us and indeed in any being that has language: the ecstasy of creation, the concern to preserve what had been made, holding it dear, desire and the urge to own something precious, even the lust for destruction because treasures had a magnetic pull of their own, that brings on ruin too.'

'But if it wasn't the lack of love that led to mankind's downfall, then what . . .'

The friend waved her hand at the lightscreen and said, 'Look, there, that mass of bubbles, it's a mould fungus.'

'Looks like a slime,' said Fire. His friend licked her long tongue across her nose, sat down on a wooden stool and said, 'That's what it is. A very special kind of slime, though. The old name was *Dictyostelium discoideum*. Very interesting life cycle, just watch. Do you see?'

The film's colours were worn and faded, something twitched there, melted, gooey.

'Mankind,' continued his friend in a warm, coddling tone, 'only discovered what you see here quite late, at the end of their dominance. They never truly understood it. Now—look here, at the close-up: this is the vegetative phase of the life cycle. Single cells. A random collection of unconnected units.'

'They look like, I don't know . . . amoebae?' He thought of the fash's lessons.

'In a way, yes. Mankind called them Myxamoebae. They live on bacteria. As long as there's any round, as long as that food source is available, the cells grow and reproduce. But now, have a look—we take away their microbes.'

'Ah-hmm. Oh-ho! What's all this then? They . . . the single cells are budging together, tottering towards one another. They're jostling . . . clumping. Kneading one another.'

'Yes. Odd, isn't it? They are taking another form. Like living tissue. Mankind called that pseudoplasmodium.'

'It moves, by itself! I can't . . . is that a new organism? distinct?'

'Hard to say. Single cells organizing together . . . what should I call the result? If I observe it, I can soon see that it's looking for food, clearly independently. A tiny little slug. It's attracted by light and reacts to temperature differentials, to moisture . . .'

'Hunts for food. Like we do.'

'Quite right. Here, let's speed up the process. Look, a new food source. It's feeding. And next . . .'

'Another metamorphosis! It . . . what is that now, a plant? It's got a stem, a stalk, then a fruit up there . . .'

'Spore capsule. And then when the spores are dispersed, the whole cycle restarts. We can see, scattered about the place . . .'

'More Myxamoebae. Fresh single-cells.'

'Right. Do you understand?' Fire thought about it in silence for a moment.

Then he said, 'Because they couldn't do anything like that. Mankind. That's why what happened to them, happened. That's why we overtook them. Because they couldn't do what the Myxamoebae . . .'

The friend shook her head. 'Nonsense. Their downfall was not because they couldn't form a slug. Rather, because they constantly tried to do so without being properly equipped. It's a confusion: people are not Myxamoebae, whether these people are humans or Gente.'

The lightscreen went blank. The 'cosy all-encompassing truth' that Vempes had spoken of so dismissively, thought Fire, humankind missed their shot at that, too.

His friend said, 'It's not about discovering what life really is. It's about what you do with it.'

Fire took this to heart and from that point on asked the fash to teach him only practical matters, such as concerned Fire's own body. Vempes knew all these things, he knew more than anybody about Fire's physiology.

Thus Fire learnt how he could mix his urine with his own spittle, which was of a highly unusual chemical composition, and leave it in sunshine to react, making something drinkable, so that even on long marches in the heat he would lose little fluid despite sweat and evaporation. Fire learnt too how to sleep with open eyes, only waking when his eyes registered something that his brain had to deal with. Fire now learnt how he could elongate or compress his limbs, his arms and legs, for a limited while.

'I am strangely made,' said Fire, once he had understood all this.

The fash didn't contradict him.

6. LARGE AND SMALL MACHINES

'And the machines?'

'You know plenty of machines. You couldn't breathe, drink or eat if not for the machines—even if you don't often see them close up.'

'You mean the skyscrubbers? The sevenfours, flying along the geodesics and leaving chemtrails behind?' Visiting Cleopatra's basin, a crater beneath the eastern slopes, he had seen them far up in the sky, cruising, sifting the air, ensuring that the dawns stayed blue and the evenings cool.

The clear, cool evenings were rare hereabouts, since the days were so long. Nevertheless, Fire had already been able, three times in his short life now, to sit on the cliff edge by his home and search the skies for sevenfours. When he couldn't find any, he would lie on his back, wait for the slow sunset and make up stories about flying—today I was up there, in my favourite place, the sky, and I flew in a circle, always circling, up above the world so high, and I thought how beautiful it is up here with the drifting clouds, and now and again to shriek out loud, and trust in my little wings. Then I met a sevenfour and it forced me down, so I had to land, and the sevenfour landed too, looked me in the face and said, 'Prince Fire, I don't know why you bother, I don't know where you want to fly away, I don't know how you expect to fly for any distance with just those little wings.' 'But I don't want to be a skyscrubber,' I told him then and there, feeling misunderstood, 'I just wanted to be a firebird, didn't want to tear apart the dirty patches in the sky, just sing my song a little while. I don't want to be the most important, I don't want to travel from here to there in the twinkling of an eye, I don't fly because it's the shortest path between two points, I always fly in circles. I only want to be a part up there of all the beauty, the watery blue, high up above the ancient fires and the new fields. I don't want to be a flea or a bug or a louse, nor the hero of the crazy circus that my furry friends always stage when they find that I'm infested, frightened as they are of the machines—nanomachines, teeny-tiny Ceramicans. In fact I don't even want to be a prince, at all, don't want to be part of this story that I can't understand, I want to be a songbird. I can decide my fate, no one can tell me where I can fly, what I can sing, and if in the end I am lost and all alone, then at least I know that wherever I land, I came there on my own little wings.'

Later he said to the oldest furry friend, 'The sevenfour is a machine and does me no harm.'

'True. It was built by the Atlanteans.'

'The fish.'

'That's right, fish. There aren't any here, no water for them. There are the fash, but they aren't fish.'

'And what's it like on the other new world?'

Recently, Fire had grown keen to bring every conversation round to the other new world. Of all the worlds he knew about—his own world, the other world, the old world—he was most interested in the other.

'On the other world,' said the oldest furry friend, 'you'd have got to know more machines by now, if you'd been . . . born there. Digging machines, building machines—they had more mechanical help there, not soft, flowing tools such as we use. *Top-down*, as they called it in the Monotony, rather than *bottom-up* like on this world. They rely on *bulk technology*, as we rely on *assemblers* and *disassemblers*. Meaning that there, they don't have the bloodscrubbers that help you, or the tiny spiders in your spittle, or the salamanders' million-faceted eyes, or the sleep clouds of the fash.'

'I'd like to go there.'

'Perhaps you shall.'

'Is that part of the Plan?'

A wave of the right paw was all the answer he got.

7. PARENTS AND CHILDREN

'Fine then, I understand now about humans and machines,'—Fire became impatient—'but what's this about parents and children?'

'Parents . . . we all have them, even if yours are closer to you than mine are to me.'

'Yours?'

'Rather than parents, we might call them "forebears". The line leading from them to me is longer than the line from your parents to you. Mine were called badgers, they fell in the last war, before the Exodus.'

'Fell? From the skies, like the . . . progenitors' ships?'

'They died. Killed by things half-machine and half-human. We were sent away to live on here. And your parents did the same to you—your mother, first bride and then widow, and your father, first hero and then villain.'

Fire wrinkled his brow, thinking of logic trees and what Vempes called 'inferential branching'—each term divided into new terms, escaping further from his understanding, parents were father and mother, father was hero and villain, mother was bride and widow . . .

'Explain it to me,' he demanded.

'The father, as the humans say, is the man and the mother is the woman. So I could be your mother but not your father.'

'What was my mother like?'

'How do you mean?'

'Think yourself into the role, tell me what she would say if she were here. What would you say if you were her? What would she have told me, what would she do, if I'd been with her on the old world, the way I'm here now?'

'I would . . . that's a hard game. I would remember his last words and wonder whether I had to accept his fate, or whether I can creep away from this dreadful place, somewhere where I don't have to think of the terrors that have passed, not the naked greed or the folly, the violence or the misery. I would . . . on the day when the Three Cities fall . . . I would hear a bell ringing the alarm, in one of the fortress towers. I would hear a little bird singing and I would know that the poor wolf has no choice, he wants too much. And I would do my duty to my son and to my daughter.'

'Your duty.'

'With the other women, rise above the scarlet flood that washes round us, that divides the widow from the bride.'

'The man left you? My father?'

'The father, the wolf . . . overreached his own discernment, was duped by the plots of charlatans who set themselves up as his kings and patrons, his Lions and Foxes, who can turn everything into money and turn money into everything else, and the darkness of the night shall have him, until it shall have passed, and twilight shall come and I, the mother, remain all alone and must ask: why did I want him, if I had to lose him?'

Fire didn't know what kings and Lions and Foxes and money, were.

But he understood that his mother's life and his father's life had been sad.

The furry friend turned away and left Fire standing by the warm stove.

8. HIGH POINTS

When Fire was fifty-two days old, Vempes the fash paid a visit, saying it was 'for the last time, for the time being.' There was, Vempes explained drily, 'still one biological matter that I haven't yet taught you—your sexuality, which is rather complicated.'

Fire already knew a little about it. He had experienced nocturnal emissions and the pleasantness of an erection, as he clung to the warm rocks. One of the furry friends had shown him what he could do if it made him too hot under the collar. He could do that on his own, but the salamanders helped as well, and as Shikibu the salamander said, 'A little coitus never hoitus.'

Now the fash used holocubes to show the prince women and girls, boys and men, phenotype-human as well as the old Gente species. Fire had to lie still with polygraph discs taped to his chest, his groin, his penis and his temples, which he found both embarrassing and amusing. At the fash's direction, two of the friends had put a neurostimulating strap about his neck.

'We'll just calibrate a bit. It's early days yet, but we want to prepare you properly for successful mating, when you find the Temple and find your bride, your bridegroom there.'

The calibration wasn't unpleasant but it was demanding. It lasted three hours and yielded seven high points. The most intense was a simulation with a female lynx ('Oedipal pattern, very deep-seated, you see,' Vempes whispered at that, but one of the furry friends retorted, 'What does it count, they simply encoded it in, back then. Hardly proof of the collective unconscious.').

There was also a strong response to a lizard creature with unblinking eyes and a melancholic gaze.

'Who was . . . what was that?' asked Fire, breathless.

'Your bride,' said the fash, and at the same time his furry friend said, 'Your bridegroom.'

Fire didn't understand the joke but resolved to remember the punchline.

9. THE GOOD MACHINE

When Fire was fifty-five days old, a large machine came to visit.

At first the prince was afraid when he saw what it was. But the furry friends weren't afraid, so he decided to wait and see, to stay on the alert.

'Is this him? The prince?'—asked the machine in a querulous, tinny tone and inspected Fire with seven bulging eyes on long, flexing metal stalks. Fire clapped his hands and turned about, as though he were being filmed for a viewscreen production, but the oldest furry friend sent him outside to the clifftop, out of the room. 'No joking about in here, we have serious business.'

'I've come to see whether he's ready, and if he is, to keep him company,' rasped the machine, who wore a ragged yellow overcoat. The furry friend said, 'He cannot seek the Temple and he cannot find the Temple. Geography has changed since Venus was first settled, even if the physical substrate remains unchanged. He will have to face many dangers if he undertakes the Task and he is not yet ready.' Speaking like this, he saw that Fire had edged back into the room from the cliff, and threatened him, from afar, with his claws. Fire laughed, but shuffled backwards all the same. Outside the wind whistled, so that Fire could only catch odd scraps of conversation. 'Emptiness . . . shameful and . . .'

'Abused, hounded, squandered', 'unwholesome', 'duty'.

'I couldn't care less what the lesserlings are up to,' the machine shouted in the end, so loud that Fire could understand the whole sentence from where he was outside, along with the furry friend's answer, 'You might not care, but by now you can see it from orbit! Three sevenfours have taken pictures, they have full-scale cities over there.'

'On the Plain of Sedna . . .'

'This is not like the domes on the Plain of Sedna, They were greenhouse plantations. I'm telling you that Niobe has cities—fourteen districts each, humans who . . .'

'Lesserlings. Not humans. They're lesserlings, caricatures, an insult to the very name . . .'

'But they're building . . .'

'Even if they're building Niniveh and Ur and Babylon and New York and Landers and Borbruck and Capeside, twice life-size, I'd still say, he has to find the Temple and he has to go through the gate. The heat signature back on Earth is unambiguous! It's died down—everything down there has died off! We have to go back, we have to investigate! Twelve hundred years! Do you know what that means, with an exponential technological . . .'

'Grimbart . . .'

'Twelve hundred years, damn it!'

In the end the machine was sent away, even more rudely than Fire had been sent from the room. It shuffled away without looking back.

'It looks annoyed,' said Fire, almost sympathetically.

'He'll come back. Forget it.'

It seemed though that the machine had said something that had an effect on the furry friends.

From now on, Fire's lessons were above all physical training in this or that skill needed for his Task. They had him leap over the widest of the lava streams or wade through them until he sent off steam. They made him jump from high walls and tumble in the red-brown dust, they attacked him from all four sides at once, so that he had to defend himself with weapons, with a stave or with his bare hands and feet. They thumped him and roughhoused him, called him up and chased him down, had him lift weights and tug ropes, throw heavy objects, catch fast objects. They watched his diet, his weight, his muscle mass. He did all this sport down in the plains and he would also climb the cliff walls, alongside the great green eyes of the floodlights, exerting himself, toiling away, and spies from Atalanta watched all this with their optical devices and were distraught to see how well he mastered each task.

The loveliest moment in all of Fire's childhood came a few minutes before it ended for ever. He was just coming back to the clifftop with two friends, they had been training sprint, grapple and dodge. The training had taken them far from home, up to the lichens. Now they were coming home the long way, the road that curved round the edge of the swamp. Fire could feel every muscle, every sinew in his flexible limbs, a sort of mild pain that felt good. He looked round to all sides, as though to draw the land and the sky into himself, and discovered that he loved it all, the cliffs, the twilight stars of the long gloaming, the creatures, everything that he knew, and Fire was happy.

Then, in a ditch to his right, he saw a dead fash, murdered by the lesserlings.

At first Fire didn't in the least understand what it was, it looked to him like one of the splendid meals sometimes dished up in his home, on the rare occasions when all would feast together—plump, roasted to a gleam, carved open and tender within, full of amazing colours.

Once he understood what it was—he walked round it until he saw the dead creature's face—his strong legs went weak and a feeling that he had never known before knocked him to the ground, an inward collapse, as though he needed now to forget who he was and where, if he was to keep breathing.

A paw touched his shoulder and he shoved it away ungraciously—and was sorry to have done so, in the same moment. The friend who had laid it there said, 'Bad news.' Fire saw the other friend using one of the primitive comtech devices that they always took on longer journeys. He put the little microphone to his mouth and the headset to his ear, and talked and listened, nodded his head this way and that, gestured to the others to show what he had heard—raised his paw—away—waving something onwards—what?

'They've . . . the people from Niobe, they've . . . attacked your home. We have to get you away. They're . . . burning the place down. Killing everything.'

'Away . . . where . . . where to then?' asked Fire and felt a sinking dullness in his belly, a fear.

'To the machine. The one who wanted to take you anyway. Do you remember?'

The chassis. The bulging eyes. Fire nodded, stood up.

'Right,' said the one with the radio, 'let's get going. No, not that way.'

Fire felt ashamed that they had to bid him come back—he had set off on the way back home, with long strides, the way they had been going. Now he stood still and realized that he didn't know where they were going. Where did the machine live?

'Come along. Into the reeds, the swamp. We need to make sure first of all they haven't got our trail.'

That is how Fire's long escape began.

XI
PADMASAMBHAVA

1. RED

Her own blood was on her feet and on her hands, a gushing dark syrup, highly viscous, running quickly between her little claws, the black dots of spintronic blockers visible in the flow, tiny ladybirds. The reptile slid her way into the eternal battle, round the other lizards struggling towards the central nodes, cutting one another away, biting legs, shooting at one another, stabbing or slicing. She slithered her way through the narrow ford, full of the screaming and the dying, northwest from Gledhill towards the Plain of Hellas.

The lizard girl, as she went, felt neither fear nor pain. She was happy and eager to learn.

This very young soldier could, when she wanted to know something, call up books in her head, and guardian angels turned the pages for her, so that she could learn all about the signals given by the battle horns, probable outcomes to the battle and missile ballistics. Soon she began to make her own entries in the books. True, she was so small that her teeth could hardly tear at others' flesh, she could only use blades, slicing and stabbing, since her bones could not yet survive the recoil of shooting a projectile weapon. Yet, she knew that one day they would talk of her as a great hero, who took to the battlefield so soon after her birth, who survived in the trenches, who went through the shadow of all the castles and yet lived, who amassed knowledge that would echo though the pages of many books.

For thrice two of the red years, she fought her way, from Vishniac, Liais and Rayleigh in the south, up to Tikhov and Wallace, always westward, always northward. The older males liked her, one reason why she survived. When these big fellows met the other females, they mostly bit them to death, took off their heads or tore off limbs. When they met the little lizard though, the males, older than her, liked to have some fun. 'You're nice and red,' they would say, 'and young and smooth and strong.' They would couple with her and afterwards, they'd often be so exhausted that the younger little lizard could kill them, or at least steal something from them. If she took weapons that she couldn't herself use—recoil projectile weapons, a plasma rifle, spectral caster or one of the heavy riot guns that could play a polycrystalline metal-oxide sheath across the target's body until he suffocated—she'd sometimes take her wares and store them in nests, in niches in the steep rifts, or on the slumped rubble of the cliffs, sometimes she'd take them straight to the dwellings of the orespiders, the drakbears, the solitonists and the heart-hounds, to the border regions where the rhinoxen grazed the flutterfields in huge, unruly herds, and sold them whatever she could carry with her.

By such means, she soon accumulated a wealth of weapons of her own, bionic machinery and other gear that improved her chances of survival; orespider pressure regulators and valves protected her muscles and her joints, she traded shockers to the solitonists so that they upgraded her eyes to see in ultraviolet and infrared, and equipped them with refined diffractive lenses, as found on a heart-hound's third eye. Solitone close combat diode lasers sat snugly beneath her jaw. She had been born with wing sockets and over time had these built up with fine-control flanged units, and soon she had two large gas discharge lamps on her hind legs, to blind her enemies with a short burst as she swooped on them from the skies, before she stabbed or sliced.

'You know the world well,' said an older lizard, a female whom she had caught giving birth on a dry riverbed. It was a curse rather then a compliment.

The little red lizard gulped down the newborns, spared the mother and explained, 'I've eaten now, why should I kill you? We might meet again and then perhaps we'll form some temporary alliance, since you'll remember that I only took as much as I needed.'

'You know this world well,' repeated her victim, 'you talk like a heart-hound.'

The poor dull monster, thought the little red lizard, she doesn't know anyone cleverer than the peripatetic heart-hounds. She doesn't know that up there in the castles are robots, fish and other beings that make the wisest and most experienced heart-hound engineer look like a simple warrior lizard.

The little red lizard licked her chin and said, 'I know the world well, that's true. And I know that there's more than one world, which is why I keep an eye open all round, even upwards, only to be sure that another world doesn't fall down at some point and kill me.'

'You mean the companions, Phobos and Deimos?'

Darkness fell and behind the willowfoams the giant crickets began their dreadful sounds.

The little red lizard drew in the cool night air through her nostrils, her head clear, and replied, 'Those aren't worlds though. Two lumps of dead rock, nothing more.'

The poor bitch wasn't convinced. 'Couldn't we live there?'

The little red lizard spat and said, 'Why would you want to? Deimos is only ten miles in diameter, Phobos barely seventeen, and they can't even muster up the gravity to hold on to one of us—even a rhinox would hardly have any weight, it could jump in the air and take minutes to drift back to the rock.'

'Minutes,' said the other lizard, wide-eyed and dreamy. When no further answer came, she crept into the shade of a splintered pylon, so as not to be found and eaten by anything else once the little red lizard had left her.

The little red lizard leapt up high, as though on steel springs, then ran onwards and hurled herself into the unending war.

Sometimes, she was strangely happy to think that Mars lived with her and with the best specimens of all the breeds involved in the *experimentum crucis*, the way she lived with her home planet. The more Mars learnt of those he suffered to live upon him, the more he understood what it felt like, to be Mars.

A world named after the god of war, the god of the sacred wolves—wolves like my father, thought the little red lizard proudly—a scarred fruit, red and orange, white cap and white socks, gushing streams burst free from the permafrost, great dark seas and volcanoes too, networks of chasms like scars crammed in between the craters and the light plains, half as large as the planet of origin, twice as large as Luna, the old moon, the first stage of Gente emigration.

Hardly any gravity here, only thirty-eight per cent of old Earth's. A year that sprawls across six hundred and eighty-seven old Earth days, each day here just a little longer than on the planet of origin, twenty-four hours and forty minutes.

Did Mars know all this, the way she knew it, the way the books knew, the Book of Life and the others? Did he know what she had learnt about herself; that the blood in her hands and feet didn't change temperature on its own to keep her alive, but needed solar heat to warm or the cold of ice to cool down, and that it had been different for her parents, the lynx and the wolf?

She wrote down in the Book what she saw and how she understood it.

'Other lizards, not so clever as myself and not so red, have filled the trenches between the castles with their corpses, and the hungry heroes lie where they fell, and become sand. They wanted to play, not knowing that it is in earnest. I know this and thus survive. They act as-if and then they're gone. They run blindly along the fissures and the fences, biting at anything round them, raised from the cradle with the taste for blood to kill whatever they can catch hold of. They're dead and gone, because they wanted only to be slaves, not true folk, not Gente, not really red. Child soldiers baked from the clay, now mere empty shells, not ten years old, each an only child, in duty bound to the *experimentum*, taught to bite and rip and not to think, doing all that they are told, and now it's over, foolish Death, take him with you, he was nothing special. Back to the frontline, carry on, for reasons that can't be named, no more than can our instincts, back to the frontline, you'll die if we, your forebears, tell you so.'

The clarity and urgency with which she wrote her world impressed the Book of Life. Already she knew so much, and something of the truth. She saw, she heard, she smelt and she understood. He wondered whether to reveal her name and tell her who she really was.

Bathed in oil and blood, she slipped through the passageways, never taking more from her enemies' flanks than she needed for her health, sometimes breaking from the ranks, making no friends, seeking no comrades.

Once, driven by an inexplicable whim, she talked to the Book directly.

'Listen, Book. Be good to me. Give me just enough wisdom to wonder whether I am still free, even though I belong to the *experimentum*, grant me still that I may be amazed, for I can think and speak of myself, unlike the legions that struggle here and fall, sink down and never even know who they are. Give me the strength to raise my head high, though they scratch and bite, though they mock me and seek to thrust me from the battle, thinking as they do that I am too young, barely hatched, not red enough, yet give me the strength to spit their mockery back into their face. I need no other aid, you need not give me a key to open the door of days to come, and I know that I will climb the castle walls, that they will open to me, nor beat me with rods nor shock me with current, they will not kill me, but the castles shall be my home, and I will be counted among the Aristoi, and I will tell them of the battles in which I fought, the battles I survived. Amen.'

Of course, she had to be careful when deep in dialogue with the Book. She devoted part of her attention, and several spintronic support platforms, at considerable cost, to observing and reacting to the course of the battle.

It was not uncommon for her conversations with the Book to end when she came to herself with a lance in her shoulder, arrows in her back, scales torn away, flesh laid raw.

She fought the way others breathe, but just as there is rapid breath, shallow breath, rasping breath, there is a scanty way to fight, a fight that does not sustain you long. She was always annoyed then to have to leave the battle behind for a while, to leave behind the hand-to-hand and the great continental drift of the frontlines, when she had to spread her wings and rise above, as high as she could, up above, below the silver clouds, gliding, when she had to regenerate missing parts of her body.

It was lovely though, even if rather humiliating, to bathe in the gentle breeze above, to feel the tug and the stretch as two loose ends of muscle knit back together, to feel a new eye slowly bloom in the socket to replace an eye gouged out. Healing, new life: an idea of peace.

2. HER NAME

At one point, the little red lizard found herself in one of the few cool, calm, stable moments of the eternal flux. She was marching a little way with two standard bearers, their backs aflame, near whom no one came, patrolling the sector boundaries, marking and fixing the lines by which the orbital stations followed the course of the endless war. In compliance with the original programmed conditions of the *experimentum crucis*, the orbitals corrected the battle fronts when needed, with a rocket attack or surgical laser strike.

The Book asked, 'Don't you have a question more important than any before? A question that would give you some overview of everything you know so far, over old and new, Dmitri Stepanovich and Lasara, your parents, the Gente cosmonauts?'

'I know where I come from, I know where I have to go, I know what I have and I know what I need. But when I come to think of it, that's not enough, is it, to know who I am?'

'It's not. You need a name.'

'What for? When I speak about myself, I say "I". And when you speak about me, or to me, you say "you". That's enough, surely.'

'What about when others talk about you? How do you know that it's you they mean and not some other "she"?'

'Good point.'

'So?' The Book liked to tease.

'A proper name, as in the old stories, how about that? In the beginning was the Word.' She giggled inwardly, thinking of the joke that the Book had told her, back before the last scuffle, at the crooked crater—how, long ago, a doctrine had arisen among the humans, which had rightly prized the word above everything else. Clearly stated premises and valid inference, above all else. A particular collective, a tiny population called 'Greeks', living in some flooded crater, had rapidly established a whole culture based on this philosophy and had come to have enormous memetic influence over all the neighbouring populations. And then all of a sudden—for even on the old world, the tide of battle could turn in a trice—an utterly unforeseen offensive had begun. It arose from within a competing group with their own meme-pool, predicated upon the idea of a first cause, not inference and causal reasoning but a basic law: 'Hebrews'. The belligerents had managed to adopt the Greek memetic weapons into their own arsenal by simply declaring that the Word, the Logos, had been made flesh, that it was God Incarnate, or as they expressed it, still bound by mammalian biology: God's Son. Their opponents, fairly flabbergasted, had had no possible reply—the little red lizard could just imagine it. 'What, hey, how, you can't just say that our Logos is now a man, I mean, you just can't do that . . .'

The little red lizard loved moments like this, when the Book's lessons gave her a glimpse into a world of wars far older and more complex than here, than this war she had been born into, raging across her planet's whole southern hemisphere since time out of mind.

'Your proper name then. Good. It has existed for a long while now, I know your name. Lasara chose it.'

'Then tell me and stop tormenting me. They'll attack soon, I'll leave these standard bearers. It's beginning again, iron and torches, flamelances. I've no time for games.'

'You are Padmasambhava. I'm glad to have been able to help.'

The little red lizard felt something dangerous come into the world with these words.

Her wings beat strongly, she licked her black teeth as though they had suddenly grown, and took flight, instead of heading back to the fight, laughing.

So great was her joy that she forgot to confirm receipt of the Book's message and sign off. As she flew, her claws ripped apart one of the banners, unintentionally, but she was not ashamed; rather, she laughed, and beneath her the standard-bearer was immediately borne down beneath a wave of looters, and he glanced upwards with horror in his gaze at her, at Padmasambhava, the new thing, the monster.

It was as though Padmasambhava saw the spectacle below her for the first time now, the circles, the trenches, the food chains and the marching graveyards of mass death, bodies piled into heaps on the vast lowlands, orgies of copulation and victory and defeat, that even affected the planet's albedo. A wedge of brown-beige youngsters had formed a momentary alliance against the older troops, surged forward into a bay, overflowed an intersecting chain of valleys, then some-one shot off a ground-to-ground missile and the whole huge trench shuddered with its cleansing impact.

White pillars of smoke stood where the day had been won, positions were taken, others were lost, the shrieking from raw throats was heard above. Pad-masambhava watched all of this as though it no longer affected her.

She climbed further, closer and closer to the silver-bellied clouds, until at last she was inside them. There she sailed through the skies, baptized with her new name and thought, I always knew. Only a very few have wings, only a very few are as fast as I, only a very few survive as long, who dare such journeys as I have made. But it was never only that, I was always waiting for more, always eager to know, but also afraid, what that might be.

Only once had she experienced directly how it really was to be one of the others, to know battle the way they did, driven by instinct and unthinkingly. She had got involved in some slap and tickle, it began as sex and then became a life-and-death fight, and when she bit down at her defeated opponent her jaw slipped and she locked her teeth, not in his Adam's apple but in his face. Some self-repairing conduit in her spintronics had formed a short circuit with his, and sud-denly, for a few seconds, she was thinking with the dying male's brain even as she squatted there above him. She found his thoughts immediately repulsive, far looser than her own, his decisions slipshod, his language nothing but stammering, and the Book of Life that he thought he could consult was a pitiful mess—pages missing, muted scents, poorly tinted colours, a worm-eaten, crack-spined appa-ratus. She felt sick from the time spent stumbling and clumping round in there. It was as though she could see the logic gates straining and creaking on their hinges, the circuits that supposedly regulated this blockhead's qubit spin photonic interaction.

That's when I knew that I was not like that and I never will be.

And now I know not only the world, but myself, Padmasambhava, a name that describes the path I will take, the path that leads not only from the trenches to the castles, but further, yonder, to the other world, even to the old world.

I am the cause for terror and rejoicing.

And in that moment everything dropped away, her beloved battleground below, the clangour of metal upon metal, the hiss of flames, the cracking of bones.

She climbed higher, up through the silver cloud layer. Up above, it was cold and clear, greenish blue.

When she reached the orbital stations, the gloss-black spinning satellites up in the night, Padmasambhava laughed.

The stations recognized her in return and sent her greetings from the past and from the future, from everywhere and allwhichwhen.

3. AN EMIGRANT

Saint Oswald knocked his wooden knuckles on his leg, also wooden. He wanted to know how rotten he had become.

There was a new shipment due today, as every hundred years—well, roughly every hundred. He had never got round to using the Martian calendar. Like most Aristoi, that's to say most true survivors of the Gente Era and those who claimed, with more or less good reason, to be their direct descendants, he still thought in Earth days, months, years, lustra, decades and centuries.

As agreed, the new wood would have been cut from the trunk grown from Livienda's last seed. It stood in the great fortress at the North Pole, a sort of cross on the imperial orb.

Saint Oswald hoped—in vain, he already knew—that the woman who was to bring him the wood would not discomfit him too much with errands to run and with her indiscreet questions. He had firmly resolved only to let her replace those parts of his run-down body that absolutely could not last out any longer unrepaired.

Sometimes, in a melancholy mood, he spoke of himself and the other Aristoi as 'the emigrants'. The woman with the wood was a good friend of his, on the one hand and on the other hand, she was a trial to him. He sometimes wished he could forget her at last. She was no emigrant, but not born here either.

Saint Oswald fairly often wished that he could at least forget something or someone.

He scrubbed his memory regularly and again and again some crap would turn up, caught in the filters of the centuries under traumatic circumstances. Sometimes this dreck would set up hallucinatory echoes in the mannikin's everyday life—recently, that's to say since his last spintronic overhaul, Saint Oswald would even hear the poodle bark. The curator of the museum where he had found a home would bark at him in his hypnagogic and hypnopompic phases and even Storikal the donkey stared him in the face from a cup of coffee, now and then, a dumb, yearning stare.

Saint Oswald had decided a while back that really, no one should grow as old as he had.

With these weary thoughts in mind, he waited for his replacement parts and for news and let his tired gaze wander up and down and across the copy of the copy of the copy of a painting by Stanz the ape, restored thousands of times, here and there, looking for the golden section.

After all this restoration, there can hardly be a single atom left of the work that the artist put there when he created it. And yet, thought Saint Oswald, it is the same work and I am the same, replaced and repaired far too many times, my head and all my limbs, the same that I was so long ago.

The tall grandfather clock in the hallway struck twenty-seven, horribly slowly.

Saint Oswald wondered whether he had gone mad, because he talked to it as though it struck for him alone, as though he had to mollify Time.

'Now mmm-hmm-hmm, stop that, it's fine, old clock, poor silly old clock, you with your time running onwards, running out, eternally, nonsensically, you with your aeons and your epochs, bearing all your sums away, gnawing away. Me though, brrr, here I sit with a smile carved into my face, no, mustn't grumble, I'm all right really. Maybe I didn't even mean it that way, what do I know, silly old clock, silly old time, although, in fact, yes, that's just how I meant it, had I better be quiet? Should I flatter you, Time? That might suit you. A speech, a panegyric in praise of almighty Time, murderer of all mortal creatures. No, sorry, forgive me, that was mean. Though, maybe, being mean is what I need, now and then, you understand. Just imagine, I haven't had a good dirty laugh for at least two hundred years—time was I lived for nothing else but a dirty laugh. I'm not laughing now, but I respect you, Time, because if you were to laugh, it would be the dirtiest laugh of all. You're a dirty great sow who could roll over and squash me like I-don't-know-what. No, wrong, I love you, unless of course you don't want that, in which case I fear you, because I hate you.'

The clock completed its twenty-seven refutations of his point and all fell silent.

Saint Oswald gazed abstractedly out of the window, which put him in a better mood.

He liked that mob down there, even if hardly any of them thought that they were Gente any more and very few indeed thought they were Aristoi. But they had—what was it called?—style.

He'd grown up in prehistoric times, so he saw the ferment down there as a good sign, as heedlessly pagan as ever ancient Rome had been, driven by a vigour that you could absolutely call 'animal', acknowledging its distant origins in the Gente genome—not a trace of melancholy or apathy, none of that unhealthy decadence in the last days of Landers, Capeside and Borbruck, not a trace of the strained good cheer in the lunar colony's twilight days.

Cultural vigour in full bloom—a remarkable breed, an uncommon age.

The Gente who supported Lasara's plan had assumed that they would be remembered as gods. Did the Aristoi have gods?

If so, they were not gods who demanded that their worshippers forget themselves. Gods of prosody and ritual calendars and laws? None of that, no one wrote epics here, not even novels, they were writing a long natural history instead, a branching and intertwining second version, now that the unnatural epic of the Gente had reached its unnatural end.

'Is she there yet? Has she come through the archway?'

The robots said nothing and Saint Oswald knew that this always meant no (since he had programmed them that way himself, to save energy). She was a good three and a half hours late, then—an extraordinary lack of consideration in a person who was, after all, not constrained by time's usual flow.

To shame her, if that was at all possible, Saint Oswald was still sitting at his breakfast; tungsten filaments, the news sheets, music from the Monotony, so that she might not notice that he had nothing better to do this morning than wait for her. But he had slowly eaten himself to a standstill, ingesting any further nourishment would be ill-advised, possibly even harmful. Before he could decide what to do with the rest of the time he had to wait, the little glass bells rang, at last, below the roof beams, beside the quicksilver mirrors and even above the wine bottles on his table. He waved his marionette hand, disgruntled. 'Fine, great, holy shit, what is it now?'

A conical servant rolled up close at hand and said, 'We've had a message, an entry in the visitors' book—Raphaela Dictioniga Römer and Eon Nagegerg Bourke-Weiss have announced their arrival, they'd like to spend some time here to play about, let rip, talk and . . .'

'Fine, I think I'd rather go puke,' said Saint Oswald, belching in annoyance. He loved the Aristoi as such, but he hated these two particular families, with their fortress mentality about anything outside their castle walls, their constant peevish silence about the *experimentum crucis*. Basically he hated that they were Aristoi; in fact, he realized, he couldn't stand anyone calling themselves Aristoi rather than Gente, just because of a couple of footling redesigns which they primped about so much. Just now he had loved them all and now he hated them, that's extreme old age for you. He was disgusted that they'd begun to call Mars 'Ares', he shuddered at the mythological mishmash dressing up their attempts at high culture— revolting, the way they performed plays and programmed films and wrote algorithms that wrote literature about Aphrodite and Ares and how Hephaestus the smith came between them.

What was all this hogwash?

Was it meant to drown out the dread all Martian residents felt? A fantasy to trump the troubling news? Since the recent news from Earth, they all lived in fear that the harmonious and almost totally indifferent coexistence of two civilizations might be at risk; an irritable orbital non-resonance lately dwindled to very limited radio traffic with the other world's so-called sevenfours, might be endangered. Because the Earth, which is to say Hephaestus the smith, had again drawn all eyes to itself, in the worst way you can draw attention to yourself, by falling entirely silent.

Saint Oswald finally realized that he downright despised how folk like Raphaela and Eon twisted and stretched their arid moral code, pretending to refinement, actually behaving like crude vulgarians, shirking their historical and political responsibilities.

Most obscene part of all, Raphaela Dictioniga Römer and Eon Nagegerg Bourke-Weiss sought him out to drag him into their trite re-enactments. 'I'm Phobos and he's Deimos,' Raphaela would honk, or Eon would say, 'She's Aneros and I'm Eros,' and Saint Oswald would have to be the go-between, the little soulful slice sandwiched between their two slabs of meat, or the two grotesques would tell him to direct, if they wanted yet again to film one of their entertainments.

Sometimes, he was told to get hold of feral children from the trenches between the castles, lizards and suchlike, for improper purposes, lewdness, debauchery.

These would be put in cages, round the erotically entangled Aristoi, to fight to the death, their screams of pain mixing with the unconvincing moans of the two grotesques, since the damn fools thought this was decadence . . .

Feh, and the eagerness with which they asked after the woman, because according to the rumours whispered among these halfwits, she always knew what was to happen, what would be the political, the meteorological or long-range climatological changes on Mars, who would be the next to die, who was born to be a hero, which arts would dominate the castles next summer—each castle had old legends of a seeress like her, women who meddled in all sorts of affairs wherever and whenever they appeared, and only Saint Oswald knew that all the women were one woman, and he knew her.

For all their curiosity, Eon and his flibbertigibbet gave no sign at all that they believed his claim, that he was one of the few whom a seeress (so to say) would visit. But they asked him questions anyway, till his stomach began to turn. Will Prangel make more of those almost intolerable red films, will it be very hot, when will the new crystal basin be ready?

'What should I tell our honoured visitors?' enquired the conical servitor.

Saint Oswald creaked, ill at ease and harried. 'A-a-a-h craprags. Tell them, today's not good, tell them I'm waiting for . . . eh, bah, a very special guest.' A horrid turn of phrase, but accurate.

The cone clattered away and left Saint Oswald thinking: I've a head full of straw and I hardly want more.

Before he could give way entirely to his regrets, a clanging piano chord from the music room set his wooden limbs twitching—an unmistakeable calling card; the seeress, his tardy guest, had arrived.

4. W

Ageless as ever—in her early twenties, her mid-thirties—white-haired, bare-breasted—not naked however, she wore dirty trousers from some sort of uniform, even though she had no shoes. Her bare skin was smeared with soot and ashes and shone, as though she had spent some time next to a belching furnace. As usual, she wore a silver chain round her neck with a pendant, encrusted with tiny diamonds, an old symbol—the letter 'W' from one of vanished humanity's alphabetic scripts. When he came into the music room, Saint Oswald saw his sponsor, thusly arrayed, sitting at the grand piano, where she played bagatelles and humoresques, her fingers teasing the keys, eerily deft, sensitive, strong and nimble, playing tricks with music's heritage.

Today's shenanigans began with an ugly but hugely comic parody of the young Glenn Gould's approach to Bach's Goldberg variations, swept into a few bars of Debussy, then on to jazz and Gershwin, then fragments from Chopin's *Nocturnes*. Oswald, a stuffed clown, a scarecrow, cleared his throat, 'That's my piano, pardon me Frau Späth, I am the master of the house here and I would like to be at least acknowledged.' Then the composer, suddenly listless, glided into a couple of Witold Lutoslawski's folk melodies from that fateful year when the Monotony's penultimate paladin had met his end.

'How are you, old stick, still knocking at the knees?' she asked in greeting, getting up.

A robot served her a glass of iced tea, two slices of lemon.

'I certainly need more of Livienda's wood, if that's what you mean.'

'Ah, shit yeah, sorry. Fuck you, fuck your parole officer. I forgot. Hmm, er, I'll bring it—that's to say, I will have brought it yesterday, otherwise my whole itinerary gets knocked into a cocked hat—ask your janitor, that'll work . . . will have worked.'

The mannikin fumbled absentmindedly at his throat, threw a particular switch and whispered into the intercom built into his head. The device confirmed that what had just now been agreed, Frau Späth had indeed done last night. Wood and branches lay, wrapped in black velvet, on the second balcony down, here in Saint Oswald's tower.

'Well, break a leg, thanks very much,' he said, bowing stiffly, 'this will be a short visit then, wherever it is that you're coming from . . . lightly singed as you are.'

The composer downed her iced tea, wiped her mouth with the back of her hand, waved at the mannikin and said,

'Feh, you just be glad, Mr Punch, that I don't take you along as bodyguard on my tours of duty. It's still a long way off, but you wouldn't have time to prepare yourself, inwardly I mean, for what I went through last night . . . errm, if we use your perception of time, what I will go through two hundred nights from now . . . will have gone through? Time travel and grammar, where is Dr Streetmentioner when you need him.'

He wasn't actually curious, but he felt rather in awe of the woman, in a jaded sort of way, and obediently asked, 'And what did you go through . . . will you go through . . . will have . . . had to have gone through? You look as though you stumbled into the middle of the *experimentum*.'

Coming closer he noticed that what he had thought were smuts or dirt on her skin was something else, not soot and ashes but scratches, bruises, scrapes, even a couple of open wounds.

She noticed his appraising look and showed her gleaming white teeth.

'Into what? The ex . . . ah yes, your little Martians and their barmy petting zoo. I really can't decide hereabouts whether evolution is teleological or not at all, since everything that happens here is all goal-directed anyway—it has a clear purpose: to store up the seed, as the Bible said, until it brings forth fruit, since bring forth fruit it must, otherwise . . . And this time has now come, of course, the time to bring forth fruit, hasn't it, just look round you, mene, mene, tekel, or what not. Which is why I'm here, why I'm there, why I run round everywhere and take my bag upon my shoulder, be good or you won't grow much older . . . Oh, and day after tomorrow, I'll fetch her two crazy children home to Her Majesty.'

He had understood one single word. So he repeated it, anxiously, as a question. 'There? Where, there?'

'Where it's all happening, in White Tiger—a giant ape has been tearing the city to pieces and I was there to guard the two royal offspring, keep an eye open for them and if need be . . . intervene, if their lives were in danger . . .'

'The offspr . . .'

'Fire and Padmasambhava, prince and princess, or the other way round if you like, the last two shoots on the old family tree . . . which caused all this . . .'—she swept her arm about in a graceful, all-encompassing gesture—'to be, or have been, or will have been, or whatever. Mmm.'

This time he had understood not even one syllable. 'Excuse me, but where were you? Inside a tiger?'

'Come on, mate. What are you on about? I was in a city. Those nincompoops over on Venus have been trying to rebuild the three cities . . . huh, it should be four anyway, to be fair—do you still remember Storikal the donkey? The four heroes? Before it went back to being three heroes again, before the Revision, before the three cosmonauts got you all to that lump of cold rock, Gente and retinue, a stepping stone to . . .'

'Huan-Ti, Hecate, Anubis.' The mannikin nodded.

'Yup, A-starred, but tell me something, little fellow, do you have any fruit here? Or meat? Pork chop or what not, a few spare ribs . . .'

'You know perfectly well that those species . . .'

She waved her hand. 'Granted, but isn't there some . . .'

He was rather irked at her needling, teasing informality, but showed no sign and stayed perfectly polite. 'I could offer you perhaps a roast of rhinox, I'm sure we have a crust or two . . .'

'Great then,' said Frau Späth and followed him back to the breakfast table.

The servitors dished up a large meal, course upon course, until she raised her hand and declared, her mouth smeared fetchingly with grease, that she'd 'stuffed myself quite nicely. Boiled, baked, roast, fruits, desserts. You've got your own little corner of heaven here, it would seem.'

He sighed.

She waved her hand. 'Bene. Bene Gente. Can I get to the point now, is that it? Right then, the programme is underway, or rather, the last stage. As predicted, the little ones have hatched just at the moment when the whole solar system and its news networks think that the Earth's transformation is . . . over and done with for now. So now those two, Padmasambhava and Fire, have to go and look things over.'

'Look things over.'

'Envoys for the Gente's heirs, a vanguard, living arks, what you will. Listen, I explained all this to you long'—he nodded, rather too eagerly perhaps, but the story had always struck him as rather doom-laden, he didn't want to hear it any more than he could possibly help.

'Which is why, you see, I have to take care of them now—those two are going to change sex at some point, so that the whole bad-taste opera stays on course, the way the Lion and the Fox dreamt it up for me back then—they're two sides of the same person, or two persons to a side, but for simplicity's sake I'll just talk of the children the way they are right now—he, as I said, is with the badgers at the moment, with whatever's become of Georgescu's boys and girls over on Venus. But she, the lassie, she's not quite on course yet, so we have to take care of her ourselves.'

'Meaning this is the moment when I lend a hand, yes?'

'I can hardly do it myself. Too many places and too many times where I'm needed, since I struck that deal with Livienda to . . . eh . . . administer her estate, till the whole heap of crap . . . till the whole story's over. I take that kind of thing very seriously, I don't make promises to just anyone and when I give my word, I keep it, *pacta sunt servanda*. On the other hand, you have to be able to delegate, which is why I've been keeping you alive for the ages of ages, my dear Pinocchio.'

'I should . . .'—she was gazing out of the window, as though daydreaming, and he raised his voice. 'Frau Späth?'

'Ah? Present. Yes.' She blinked a little, as though just now her thoughts had taken her further afar than anyone else might dare to dream (which, he thought grimly, was probably true).

Saint Oswald said, 'You're saying that this . . . Pram . . .'

'Padmasambhava, right. A little red lizard. Listen, this is what you're going to do.' She leant forward. He admired her lovely shoulders and listened to every word of her instructions. 'You'll hire a couple of robots, so that next time you stage one of your games with those nitwits . . .'

'Not my games . . .' he protested feebly, but she spoke over his objections '. . . You'll catch a couple of lizards for the occasion. But you'll instruct the huntbots to come back with only one lizard. Her. Then you won't actually make her part of your household here—if you do that, she'll not trust you and she'll run away, she's rather obstreperous that way, comes from her mother—but you'll give her as a present to one of your highborn friends . . . give her to that muggins—what's he called—Eon, is it?'

He pulled a face, a rictus of disgust, and she nodded curtly. 'That's the one, thanks. And he'll make a complete mess of things, of course . . . I mean, he'll quite quickly realize that she's too good for his circus nonsense, she's something special, so he'll get the idea of bringing her up as his own, introducing her to Aristoi society, it's happened before . . .'

Saint Oswald heaved a heavy sigh—yes indeed, that was a favourite theme in the castles, for a lot of kitsch and bad art: how we save the precious chaff that flies upwards from the *experimentum crucis*, from the sea of flames, how we turn lizards into Aristoi . . .

'And then she'll give him the slip. That's where you come in. You catch her. Bring her in. And then you bring her up, teach her, but properly, following a curriculum that I'll set for you.'

'When?' he asked, to show a little independence of thought, even if it was only impatience.

'Everything in its time. My time, that is, it's rather like music,'—she smiled—'all in the tempo. *And I'll be a friend to my friends who know how to be friends.* And now, I'd rather like a shower—unless these fabulous castles of yours somehow don't have running water?'

'Water, ultrasonics, perfumes and toiletries,' he told her, all smiles and grimacing sourly.

'Splendid, my old sawhorse,' she replied, smacking her lips in anticipation. Unfathomable, this woman! She got up and slapped him so hard on the back with her right hand that he thought he'd fly apart in flinders.

5. ENTRÉE

The official sources later painted the story in marvellous colours, saying that Padmasambhava arrived in the most splendid of the Aristoi castles by her own efforts, fighting for recognition and winning the right to gain entry. There is no reason to swallow this story, even if she, conditioned by years of killing to see life as a contest, naturally accepted such an interpretation.

In fact, there was no point at which you could say she was doggedly fighting her way towards Castle VII on the Plain of Hellas. It was much more that she drifted in that direction.

At last she arrived before the castle gates, in temporary coalition with about seven other lizards, confronting an overwhelming onslaught from forty-two others, reinforced by half a dozen opportunist heart-hounds who had run with the pack. When Padmasambhava and her companions had fought valiantly but, as in most such engagements, pointlessly, for three days, nine gleaming, black battlebots suddenly swooped from the castle battlements in a deafening clatter of rotors. They laid down a barrage of fire on Padmasambhava's enemies, until the pitiful remnants left the field.

Then they opened fire, swiftly and efficiently, on the little red lizard's companions, whooping in triumph just a little too early. They collapsed, torn to shreds, but the robots from the castle fired with such lethal precision that Padmasambhava was unscathed. She wondered whether she should flee, considered her options, even opened a connection channel to consult the Book of Life, a particularly daring move in the prevailing chaos. For the first time, it did not reply.

Padmasambhava's right wing was broken.

The left, injured in enemy action, hung down from her shoulder in bloody tatters. Her left leg dragged, and a sword pommel had smashed out a few teeth on her left side, mostly from the lower jaw. It would take hours for the missing teeth to grow back, and meanwhile she couldn't bite. So she threw down her arms, stood up, folded her wings before her face and her breast and waited for what may come.

The robots cleared out the rest of the trenches and the other fortified positions. Only then did Padmasambhava understand what was actually happening here. She had thought that it was merely a mop-up operation, unusually brutal perhaps but merely intended to remind the soldiers in the trenches not to come too close to the castles. But no: they're not shooting at me. The machines are flying in a circle, they're deciding where to land, to pick me up. They want me alive.

'Are you proud that they want you?' It was the Book.

'I don't know. Is this . . . an interim finding for the *experimentum*?'

'You tell me.'

'Well, I've survived so far—"survival of the fittest", as they used to say. Likely they're bringing me in to examine me and learn what they can.'

'So you think that the question of which school of thought is right, this, that or the other, can be decided from the life and times of one little red lizard and her fortunes of war?'

To answer that, Padmasambhava had to delve into an old spintronic folder and comb through to recall what she knew of the three theories submitted to the *experimentum crucis*.

The first two schools of thought represented Darwinism, as developed during the Monotony, a theory of replication, variation and selection, and the first of these two schools had thence derived the principle of adaptive complexity. Traits or characteristics can perpetuate themselves in a material or software substrate by forming an evolutionarily stable strategy at the ontogenetic or the phylogenetic level. All such successful traits, following the path of least resistance, cumulatively contribute to an irreversible process of specialization, manifested as the constantly increasing complexity of newly occurring species.

The second school didn't believe in any such progress, but emphasized a rickety equilibrium, punctuated by the occasional catastrophe. Here, a synchronous comparison of various species' evolutionarily stable strategies would always find equilibrium and the theory held that new traits resulted not from adaption but from exaptation, whereby individuals or populations made use of variation arising from entirely different, mostly random causes, and that this process was not in any sense goal-directed, merely a matter of good or bad luck.

The first school called the second blind to Time's directed arrow and to the fine mechanisms of selection. The second called the first orthogenetic Romantics and perfectibilists.

Then at the very end of the Monotony a third school arose, promising a synthesis of biology and computer science that raised the debate to a level where it was actually worthwhile to conduct an enormous experiment to decide the issue, 'and the best place to do it is Mars, since if we're going to be populating virgin planets, we may as well learn something while we're about it' (said the plan's instigator).

The third school held that selection was not, in itself, the inevitable result of either adaptive or exaptive complexity, but basically a marginal phenomenon. Its proponents believed they had discovered a few fundamental computational principles in simple automata which, applied to the rules of reproduction, would necessarily bring forth certain highly organized complex forms.

The original impulse which led the third school to secede from mainstream Darwinian evolutionary theory came from mussels.

A smart proponent of one of the first two schools had attempted a mathematical proof that there were potentially thousands of different shapes for mussels, believing that the fact that only six of these shapes existed in reality showed the power of selection. Whereupon another human, later the main founder of the third school, had run a mathematical model on their primitive electronic computers in response and found that his colleague had made an error, that there were in fact only six possible forms, all of which existed in nature.

This led to the argument that selective pressures were an unnecessary addition to the logic of development that had led to the robust physical forms known to science. The third school argued that organisms evolve sideways, forwards, backwards, to occupy all possible available morphologies generated by the automaton rules of which they are concrete instantiations.

Do the third school's arguments also hold true for my path here to the castle?

Is this one of those forms, one of those generated patterns?

Padmasambhava decided not to get bogged down in this debate.

Two of the nine flying machines laid down fire across the plain to fend off a new surge of warriors, while a third, swaying gently, settled on the sand before the little red lizard, like a sweet chariot come to carry her away. It opened its maw and blinked its lights, to tell the survivor that she should step inside.

Padmasambhava accepted the invitation.

XII

IN THE BELLY OF THE WHALE, TO THE WICKED CITY

1. ZAGREUS

It was a long road to reach the bug-eyed machine, and as Fire travelled, groups of salamanders and his furry friends joined him on the way, only to leave again immediately, or fall behind, following a plan clearly laid long ago. 'We're laying trails, this should confuse matters.'

Unsettled, the prince thought of what his pursuers could do to him if they caught him. Certainly he knew how hard he was to wound, nor had he forgotten how hard it was to hold him even when caught. But none of this served to calm or comfort him. He thought how they might roast him until he screamed aloud, how they could break his bones or remove body parts, even his head, and he did not imagine that he would survive this.

Above all, he had seen what they would do to living creatures with language. They could easily do to them what his friends or the fash would do to the unspeaking creatures that they ate.

To take a thinking being and turn it into a mere, broken thing: it could be done.

Cliffs and stars and living things; darkly he remembered how, a few hours ago, his soul had overflowed with love for all these things, for his home, and he knew that his home was no place of safety any longer.

'Where are we going?'

'Wait and you will see. Don't talk so much. Save your strength.'

The machine lived in a mud-smeared dome that Fire would loathe to call a hut.

The device hurriedly waved in Fire's last accompanying friend, and gestured to the two of them that they should take what they needed from the table; grass, grapes, water. 'Drink and eat, I'll pack myself with whatever we will need.'

'What do you mean "we"? How can you help me?' asked Fire stubbornly, 'And where are we going anyway? If they've come from Niobe, then they've a long reach. Where could we hide? Hey, machine, I'm talking to you.'

The machine fumbled with a number of bulky instruments, and packed, grabbing from dusty metal shelves tools whose use Fire couldn't begin to guess. The device took these items and jammed them into slots, gaps and clips on its exoskeleton, obviously designed for the purpose. Now one glass eye swung away from this work, turned to look Fire up and down, bobbed back and forth on its trembling stalk. The machine voice spoke, 'If you want to talk to me, young fellow, you'll address me as you should. My name is not "machine", it is Zagreus.'

'Zagreus, fine then. Where are the three of us headed?'

'Your friend the neo-badger will stay here. He'll protect my observatory, the sensors and distance arrays, and he'll watch on my screens as the attack unfolds, and try to predict the consequences. You and I will climb down, behind the last two volcanoes south of your . . . home, until we reach the isthmus there. There we'll be met, and lifted clear of your enemies' attacks. I'll brief you a bit, and then you'll go to look for the Temple in the last two places where we haven't already looked ourselves. I should mention that I always thought it pointless to try to spare you the work of finding the place, although that was the neo-badger's plan.' Three of its bug eyes glanced disparagingly at the furry friend, busy in the farthest dark corner of the hut. 'They thought that if we find the Temple ourselves, we could simply point you to the place and then . . . pull the trigger, as though you were a loaded gun, when the time came. Which happens to be now . . .'

The prince gave a dry cough and said, 'I think the whole thing's nonsensic . . .' and this time his furry friend, gulping, cowering at the panel of instruments on the wall, interrupted Fire. 'The bunker's out. They've blown it, now they're on the march.'

'How long?' asked the machine.

'How long what?' asked Fire, a last attempt to have some say in events fast escaping his grasp.

'How long till they get here, is what I need to know,' said Zagreus—not to Fire, but to the beast that he had called a 'neo-badger'.

'Half an hour. Forty minutes at the most.'

Spindly fingers grasped Fire by the arm; he only had time to shove some sheaves of roasted grass into his mouth and grab a belt hung with water canteens. Zagreus was already dragging him from the humble hut, and barking orders at the same time to the furry friend who had stayed behind. 'You know how to work the anti-aircraft guns? There's one on each side of the hut, under a hatch in the ground. The activation switch is next to the . . .'

'I know. Then when I run out of ammunition, I'll blast this place to smithereens as agreed . . .'

Fire guessed that something of the sort had happened to his home.

Zagreus was a confusion of arms, legs, spinal column, pincer hands, spikes and stalked eyes arranged somehow round a dark, bundled, hairy lump that swelled and shrank rhythmically; obviously something breathed at the centre of the machine. It dragged Fire after itself, away from the hut.

It swayed and tottered over the hot, hard ground but, nevertheless, moved faster than anything or anyone that Fire had met so far, faster even than the racing salamanders.

'We'll be met and lifted clear'—what was it that Zgreus had said, where were they running to and what good was it?

When they reached the lowlands, the long clouds overhead had turned green and orange-bellied. It seemed that even the upper atmospheres were uneasy.

Fire whined, 'Are you still talking to me? Am I least allowed to know your plan? Or do you think I'll just obey you blindly? Who's meeting us? Why's the ground thrumming and trembling like that?'

The last question finally had an effect—one moment all restless haste, the machine now froze dead in its tracks, turned all its eyes towards Fire and asked, 'Thrumming? The earth?' A funnel of wind was forming round them, whistling and moaning, ever louder, almost drowning out the question. 'I know that your senses are very acute, but . . . are you sure?'

'It's trembling,' said Fire, shoving out his lower lip stubbornly, but less certain now: could Zagreus really not feel it?

The exoskeleton thrust a long arm down to the ground, and stuck in a fine needle. Lights blinked within the casing, where the hairy thing at the centre moved and breathed.

'Quite so,' Zagreus hummed, 'Something's approaching. Probably tanks.'

'Is that good? Are they the ones who will be meeting us?'

'No. They're hunting us. If you have strong gods, pray to them now that our transport will reach this valley sooner than these . . . whatever they are . . .'

Zagreus left the rest unspoken, hurrying onwards, lengthening his stride. Fire reckoned this wasn't the time to complain, but rather to follow as well as he could, keeping pace.

He felt the restless, queasy, gaudy sky weighing down upon them, as though coming closer every minute, as though the clouds were too heavy to support themselves and the sickly light a fluid that steeped the horizon's every pore. With an effort of will, he made his legs longer and his arms shorter, just as his furry friends had taught him. He came abreast of the machine, would almost overtake him soon, and then threw himself at Zagreus, grappling him down to one side. They tumbled over and over, clinging tightly to one another, while behind them clumps of earth and shrapnel clouds burst upwards from the ground where the first shell had struck.

Covered with dust and splattered with earth, Zagreus raised two eyes and looked backwards at what had attacked them. Fire lifted his head from the mud and looked the same way; the two fugitives were lying in the middle of the valley now, and three vehicles were approaching from the ridge above; the first was already over the crest, speeding down the slope, faster than even Fire could run.

The things had huge cannons from which they spat flames.

'You've got very handy reflexes,' said Zagreus, impressed. Fire grabbed hold of the thinking machine's filigree frame and tried to pull it upright.

'What are you trying to do, young man?' protested Zagreus in its tinny voice, and Fire replied, 'You tell me where we have to go. I'll carry you, it's faster that way.' The device said, 'Forget it. If it comes to that, I'll fold myself onto your shoulders.'

Fire resolved to call upon his reserves to run faster, and knew at once that these would not be enough to outrun the tanks for long. Further shots crashed now to their left, to their right, with a noise that was first a whistle and then the thunder of a collapsing cliff.

'It'll work,' said Zagreus. Its joints cracked, the exoskeleton settled about Fire's frame, like a cloak, tall shoulders and collar and a broad flat cape. Fire stood up, shaking his arms free. Then he ran, zigzagging, dodging the shots, and none hit him even though they came ever faster, the cannon ever closer, their aim ever more precise.

Where next?

Dead ahead, here in the open, the middle of the plain. That was it—hold on though, how did he know? Fire understood that the machine had chosen this direction for him, these were its thoughts, and that it knew that he knew that it knew.

The furry friends had called this talent 'telepathy', and Fire knew that other creatures such as the salamanders or the fash had only weak abilities or none at all, but Zagreus seemed to assume automatically that Fire—a shower of flechettes tore the thought to shreds.

All of a sudden, there was a dreadful pain in Fire's left side, numberless stabbing thrusts, sharp wounds slicing. He knew that he could heal these faster than any other living creature, but it hindered him in running.

He stumbled, recovered, raced onwards, lurched and toppled to the right. 'Stay up! Upright!' yelled Zagreus, but it urged in vain, only physics was at work now—oscillations and gravity—and the prince missed his next step, slipped, sliced open his right heel on the sharp volcanic glass, deep into his flesh. He fell, headlong, banged his head on the hot rocks. Three seconds before he came to, and he knew that was too long—they'll aim true now, a direct hit here where he's lying, and not even his healing and regeneration could knit back together whatever might be left. But instead of a hammer blow to squash him, came a roaring from above.

Tornadoes poured down over him and Zagreus, a booming voice shoved the clouds aside and a wedge of blue light thrust downwards, clasped onto the tanks. Balls of azure lightning flared and in their midst something white as bone scribbled an ashen scrawl. Fire was blinded, and when he looked at the tanks again, two were not there. A shadow sank across the plain.

'Above! Look up above!'

A sevenfour landed, almost totally silent—Fire had never seen one from this close up; a large, long, blue-green teardrop shape, its belly white, its hindquarters young and strong, stabilizing fins—it's a fash, without legs, the prince thought at first, in the updraught of dust and scurrying grit. Then the machine's voice spoke once more in his head. 'The chassis is based on the whale shark. Huge animals, in the ocean on the old world.'

'Fish, yes of course.'

'My word, the things you know.'

A loading hatch opened and gaped where the whale shark, the sevenfour, the flying fortress, was widest. Two dark buttons to either side of this hatch, eyes, and the stark light shot forth from these once more, though it seemed more diffused than a moment before, no longer so coherent. It didn't destroy the tanks crawling across the ridge at the top of the valley, the bottleneck, but they stopped in their tracks and their gun barrels dropped.

'Get ready,' said the machine voice in Fire's head. 'Hold my struts.'

'Why?'

'He'll let down steel hawsers with hooks, to draw us up.'

They were held and lifted up and saved.

2. ON BOARD

Small robots tended Fire's wounds.

He drifted off for a bit, after the recent exertions, staring dreamily through the window in the belly of the whale at the landscapes passing below; until now he had only seen them as projections.

He soon discovered that the lesson timetable that he knew from home was to continue here, as were the extracurriculars, since, as Zagreus explained, 'All relevant data were transferred the old-fashioned way, by laser, before the fortress was destroyed. I've got them, the sevenfour's got them—all of us who care for you, have all the information you might want, and more.'

Food supplies were also adequate; on its back, the un-beast carried a greenhouse, where swootpeas grew, and peppers, melons, all shapes and sizes of vegetable; also the grasses that Fire liked so much.

'You'd have liked it back on Earth. The Tepper Plain; a huge sea of grass . . . you'd have scoffed it all down.'

'Have you ever been there?'

'No. And unlike some here, who bimble about founding cities and nonsense like that, I don't act as though I had. I mean, your retinue and tutors all want to be badgers as badly as the lesserlings want to be human, straining at the old ways. And even our sevenfour, he might not be conscious in the old-fashioned sense of the word, is trying to mimic Georgescu, his primary—ancestor of us all, all who have fur, at least.'

'Of us all . . . ?'

'Your friends. The whale shark. Myself, as well—yes, don't look at me like that—under all this cybernetic scaffolding beats a perfectly ordinary heart, there's a lung still breathing in here, you've seen my body—I'm cloned as well, from the genome of the Gente's great defender: grey back, little bit green, black belly and legs, originally evolved as a specialist in deciduous or mixed forests, near the water, plenty of undergrowth, for preference, nocturnal or twilight hours. Meaning that this planet is sheer hell for my breed. I prefer however to discard the ancestor cult—I have my own name, unlike your friends and the sevenfours.'

Fire shrugged his shoulders, shoved a carrot as far into his mouth as it would go and grinned. If Zagreus had a head in the conventional sense, he knew, it would be shaking its head now.

'The smell of blackberries gets to you after a while, doesn't it?' reflected Fire.

The strong smell was coming from a glistening something inside the belly of the whale, not from real fruit as such. Rather, the smell reminded Fire of the black-berries in the greenhouses in his fortress more than of anything else.

'I mean, if we really have to travel this way, of course I'm glad that it's all been set up comfortably. I don't think I'd like to live out my old age inside this fish though. Zagreus, how does it even work that we can sleep and eat here and watch the world go by? Do the sevenfours take many passengers?'

The furry knot at the centre stirred and breathed.

Fire had learnt that this meant the machine was sulking.

Zagreus said, 'Passengers my foot! We warned him in advance, is all, your friends and myself, and he had a few amenities left over from the old days—the neo-badgers used to sit in here and see to the instruments, that sort of thing—but anything gone kaput or missing in . . . years of neglect, washbasins, plumbing, the hammock you sleep in, he just grew from within his bodyform. Your old age? Just be glad and thank your Providence, like the other bloke in the whale thanked his Creator.'

'The other bloke?'

'I went down to the bottoms of the mountains; the earth with her bars was about me for ever: yet hast thou brought up my life from corruption, O LORD my God.'

'Sounds harsh,' Fire grumbled, biting into a juicy cabbage.

'Hold still, you accursed child.'

It didn't help. Fire had to laugh; this white stuff, these rags that the machine was winding round his head, was just ridiculous, and then it dribbled some sort of rust-red soup on the front—'It has to look convincing! We have to make the bandage seem real'—that is, the bandage holding down Fire's pointed ears.

'Why do we even have to do all this . . . mummery?' Fire asked, wheedling, doing his utmost to keep his face muscles under control for the next couple of minutes, not to disturb Zagreus' clumsy, earnest ministrations.

'I don't say this lightly, young fellow, but it's because there can be no other location for the Temple than these three . . . so-called . . . cities, one in Niobe and the other two in Atalanta. The Temple of Isotta stands for sure in one of these places, and only if you are as . . .'

'. . . convincing, hur-hur-ha . . .'

'. . . disguised as convincingly as we can possibly manage, can you go amongst the lesserlings and find out where it is. Three cities. Makes my gorge rise.'

'You always say that . . . you always have that tone, and I can see that you feel—angry. Three cities, you really don't like that at all.'

'It makes my brain hurt, that's why!' barked Zagreus. 'And because they're called . . . Three Cities, they just had to have three cities, and they called them White Tiger, Cob Mare and Ferret—how hidebound can they get?'

'What does it all . . . ow, hoo-ha! . . . What does it all mean?'

'Done.' The job was finished, and Fire looked in the mirror; the disguise was fast in place and really did disguise his ears.

'As you really ought to know, the Gente civilization was based on three cities. Now that was a civilization, good Lord! Not a jumped-up, self-important, delusional . . . Anyway, the names; they were Lasara's poster campaign for the First Exodus, to get folk to come to the Moon. Three poor bloody infantry whose escapades had somehow earned them a reputation as heroes. You see, not everyone could get onto the . . . arks . . . not in person, anyway. Most were stored, as genetic information in the first instance, and then secondly as whole-brain emulations, personalities, memories, algorithmic prints of the empirical person; Gestalts, or as they used to say in those days, seedlings . . . but a few flesh-and-blood creatures were allowed along for the ride, and the first three . . . cosmonauts your mother . . . Lasara, that is, sent off as a vanguard, blast-off, countdown . . . it was these three: the white tiger, the cob mare, the ferret. Their job was to supervise the building of the selenodomes and radio back to Earth from time to time, to the cities under Ceramican siege, and report that everything was going according to plan, the escape route was functioning. Well, anyway, these lesserlings get the whole story mixed up. They've founded three new cities and they've named them after exactly those three Gente who had excellent reasons to flee the first Three Cities, the true cities, and abandon them. A misunderstanding, and the birth of a myth. As if myth is what we need, rather than knowledge, discovery, clarity, truth. I wish we'd . . . well, what the hell. We didn't.'

Once, after he'd spent a while blister-sealed into a biotech hammock, dosing and regenerating his injuries, Fire went for a stroll, his limbs still weak and jittery, and found Zagreus furiously at work in the greenhouse. It was dibbing, potting, transplanting, mulching, rushing from grain to grapes to anther to stamen, a storm of metal.

'Are you abreacting to something? Where's the fire?'

The machine came to its senses, trembling faintly.

Once its breath was back to normal, it said, 'We could have made ourselves another Eden here, with, I don't know, oceans of orchids, a new Tepper Sea, but for this mean-minded treason they call the reconquest of history—what happened to the wisdom of our ancestors? Did you know that they didn't even begin the terraforming for seventy years? They looked at everything'—it swept one of its coat-hanger arms to the nearest oval porthole—'down there, in minutest detail. They ran every test there was to be sure that there wasn't some life form lurking here, since back then we believed that we had no right to destroy a whole habitat and ecosphere with our colonizing crap. It was the Atlanteans who insisted most loudly, knowing from their own experience how unsound it was to argue that there could be no life under Venus' hostile conditions. As they would have said, the argument didn't hold water. They had shaken hands with creatures living in bathic trenches, at boiling fissures in the Earth's crust, under conditions hardly more welcoming than prevailed here, back then. When we came here . . . when our ancestors came . . . there were still lumps of glowing metal lying about where your home would be built. They examined everything, combed over it and only loosed the spore capsules once they were damn sure they had overlooked nothing. And now? Ritual, cargo cults, half-remembered . . .'

'You're trembling. You're trembling all over,' said Fire and held the machine tight. He had come to like it, to enjoy its company. Zagreus hummed gently. 'Fine. Let's drop it. Come along, I'll show you your clothes.'

'My what?'

'For the lesserling streets. They all walk round like that.'

When Zagreus showed Fire what this meant, the prince couldn't even laugh. It was the saddest, most ridiculous, repellent, ugliest mess he had ever seen. If these people won't walk about naked, why don't they at least grow fur?

Fire flinched when Zagreus laid something like a claw on his shoulder.

The machine-badger said. 'Two things.'

'Two . . . things?'

'I've got two things for you, to keep you from lying in your hammock all day, wanking off to thoughts of your mother and other long-dead bits of fur.'

'Two things,' the prince repeated, sceptical.

'A book and an experience. You'll get both once you know how to read. Get learning.'

It threw three storage crystals into Fire's lap and said, 'Get started. Now. Not later. You have to be able to do it by the time we reach . . .'—it spoke the words unwillingly—'. . . White Tiger, over in Niobe. We'll arrive at night. They don't watch the skies, which is good. You'll be let down on a rope like a thief in the night, steal your way in over a roof or over the walls, like the Israelites in . . . never mind. Learn to read.'

Was reading something like woodcarving, or archery, that the furry friends had always tried in vain to get Fire interested in? He had tried it a couple of time, so that they left him alone. They soon had to acknowledge that it was pointless.

Once he had downloaded the learning programmes, he found that reading was rather more demanding than that.

A few hours later, he went and found Zagreus in its quarters, back in the sevenfour's tail. There was meteorological equipment installed here, synthetic tanks and actuators for the climate control systems, so that Fire's tutor was always busy with something. Without a word, the prince set down in front of the machine-badger a vine leaf, taken from the greenhouse, on which he had written in charcoal. In three of the ancient languages: I can read, can you?

'Very good. They weren't exaggerating when they called you quick on the uptake.'

Zagreus handed Fire a small sheaf of papers, gummed together and protected by a waxy protective layer on each side; a book.

'Contains the *Conversations with the Lion*, as written by the bat. A few fundamental truths and a whole lot of half-truths and the recension has hardly been impeccable either—this is the latest edition, as used by the lesserlings in the . . . Three . . . Cities.'

'Okay, the book. And the other thing your promised me, the experience?' Fire pulled a face as he asked and spat ostentatiously under an engine.

'Hmm?' Zagreus was already busy at the instruments again.

'You said you had two things for me; a book and an experience.'

'Ah yes. Quite. Further study—now that we've taught you about sexuality, from what I gather, and . . . the rudiments of . . . love.' Fire remembered his time with the salamanders and for the first time felt something like homesickness. 'Now you should know, that's to say, experience, I mean, hrrm, via the medium of a holosensory simulation that is, what the Temple is all about.'

'The Temple.'

'The Temple of Isotta. Where we're . . . where you . . . which you must find.'

Zagreus fumbled its leather bag out from under one of the steel workbenches and produced a holocube with seven more storage crystals.

'Have a look later. In peace and quiet. And not all at once, perhaps. And re-member, hmm, be aware of your responsibilities, that . . . that's to say, if the lesser-lings get hold of this . . .'

'Why are they even after me, these creatures? Why did they . . . ?'

Zagreus made a noise like a snort; since it was a machine, this sounded fairly odd. Then it twirled three eyes on their stalks and said, 'The simple answer is, they're stupid. To complicate things a little, it's because they haven't understood the book.'

'This one?' Fire spun it about three times on the workbench and put his hand upon it.

'Yes. There's a great deal in it about evolution. They swallowed that the wrong way. They think that once a niche is occupied . . . well, they think that once you exist, and since you're rather more evolved than they are, along an axis of . . .'

'Complexity,' said Fire, remembering what Vempes had taught him.

'Yes. Once that's occupied, they can't get at it. You've spoiled their chance at greater perfection, which for them always means being more like the ancient human race. Which is why they left alone the areas beyond their plains for so long—they thought these were full of . . . subhumans, they would say. Your friends, the salamanders, the fash, the hishers, all slimy things that crawl with legs, the birds, the wild beasts . . .'

'They're afraid of me. That's what you're saying.'

'That's it.'

3. AN OLD SONG

The voices, the smells and the flickering flavours on his tongue told him that in this body there was no sin. He could only agree, since for all he knew there was no sin anywhere—inasmuch as he even knew what 'sin' meant. Marble arrived overland, marble arrived by water, it was brought in bulk and Fire felt what it was to be built, as a temple, from the finest stone. A connoisseur told him a good deal about the decoration used in building; the stone-carving, reliefs, bas-reliefs, then a stone sarcophagus, flanked by elephants of stone, the goddess Diana in her moon boat, bearing her sickle in her hand and gazing with blank stony eyes at stone musicians that seemed to breathe, stone putti playing in the water—for Gemistos Platon, the Neoplatonist philosopher whose hushed voice conjured this whole richness, telling it how it was to be and why, the deepest whisper, comes from far yonder, not from the old world, nor this world, nor from the other world, but from Neptune, in truth, from Altaforta; and Sigismondo's and Isotta's initials entwined, which the cherubs bear as blazon on their shields, an emblem of this furthest birth, a memory, imperishable, but worn by the passing aeons, the sure and certain hope of reunion, a resurrection of love and of the flesh, in which there can be no sin, nor shall there be any sin elsewhere, for marble, stone and iron shall pass away, but the word shall never pass away, though it is fragile and may toss in the wind like any flower, like the grasses, a rose in Sharon and a lily in the Tepper Valley. As the lily among thorns, so is my love among the daughters. As the apple tree among the trees of the wood, so is my beloved among the sons. I sat down under his shadow with great delight, and his fruit was sweet to my taste. He brought me to the banqueting house, and his banner over me was love. Stay me with flagons, comfort me with apples: for I am sick of love; and gender is always changeable: Fire became the figure of Flora in Rimini, for there stands the first-built Temple, and it is holy, for it is not for sale, no one, ever, not even Lord Nowhere, with his wealth from everywhere, can realize its worth.

The leaves rustled and fluttered, Dame Livienda's laughter, and she said, 'Dryad, thy peace is like water,' but she did not mean any trade thereby, no river used as a road, she meant something faster, more elusive, a different sort of wealth, not the Fox's. And I'm just about to fall from the crow's nest but he (she?) grabs hold of me and hauls me back; 'No, Dryad!' We sway there in the wind.

But there is no wind. We sway with the stars. They are not far. Stones and rocks and little living things. But the blood of the little living things is poured out upon the rocks, a service to the Most High, and on the steps of the Temple, and the blood is hot, it hisses as water hisses here on my world when I pour it onto stones, the hot stone, ESEMPIO SACRO ALLA BELLEZZA ETERNA. / *Le mura che'l cingean tutto d'intorno, / Mist'eran d'alabastro e di cristallo, / E di fuor tralucean senz' altro velo, / Come per l'aria a noi, le stelle in cielo.* And I look into the mirrors in the sandalwood chamber and I see the black Temple of Isotta, the young hawk-headed vestals in long shadowed robes, woven of the feathers of doves, young girls in robes with a heart-shaped hole that shows their smooth bare hindquarters, pouring out the blood of Lasara's willing victims upon the steep broad stair, and straightaway it turns to steam, so hot is the black stone. All the steps and all the pillars call on me to hear, "Fire, do you hear?" Diminuendo . . . And hark! I hear a singing; yet in sooth I cannot of that music rightly say whether I hear, or touch, or taste the tones . . .

Music? Fire didn't know this music, where was it, it did not help, where had it gone? The blood was water, *this liquid is certainly a property of the mind / nec accidens est* but an element / in the mind's make-up / *est agens et functio*, but not an abstraction, or a phantasy. No Mister This-or-That, no Mrs Both-of-Those, one building, one word and one architectonic style, not so much different from the canyon streets of the lesserling cities in the walk-in holos that Zagreus had given him.

Isotta: third wife to the human hero whom they had called the Wolf of Rimini, the lady in whose honour he had the old Franciscan church rebuilt and reconsecrated; romanesque arches outside and in, and art, Diana with his lover's face, and the builder of the church standing next to her on the stone that supports the arch, he is clothed as the sun, the source of light for all the other images of Isotta, as moon, as Mercury, as the Muse of Rhetoric, as Dance, as twins, as putti upon the balustrades.

The sun is wedded with the moon, a mystery known since Eleusis—'Wake up, wake up! Don't get lost in there, come on out . . .'

Claws of iron and tensile wire, eyes on stalks: Zagreus.

Fire shook his head, tears in his eyes. 'It's so . . . it's very . . . it's hard to leave. The Temple. Is this how it will be once I really get there, when I find the place? Is that where I belong, is that my home?'

The machine didn't answer.

But when Fire shut his eyes to massage the pain away from his temples, he saw with his inward eye the head of a green badger, nodding.

4. THE WICKED CITY

The whole city was a lumpen mass, the only beautiful thing about it the light on the stone and glass; the play of light, the sun licking along the buildings, their edges and corners, as if to see whether they already tasted of the past. Other than this trick of the light, Fire's overall impression was somewhere between mixed and awful. There were public squares, tubby round columns ringing with appeals for solidarity, urging the populace to disregard the shortages, to accept that all pioneers had to suffer hardships, that these must be borne 'if we are to build the proud New Human fortress here on this hostile terrain' (thus went the propaganda, whipping up the citizens' empty pride).

There was a public transport system, most obviously the maglev trains, stinking of the unbelievable idiocy of creatures hurtling here and there for no very good or considered reason, merely because they have consented to some scheme for the division of labour, even if none of them has ever checked that it works properly—

they travelled back and forth to the airscrubbing plants and to the factories, to the huge agrodomes at the city's edge, to gigantic laboratories where new tools were invented and churned out in the nanofabricators, and none of this from inclination, personal interest or curiosity, but to show that they belonged to the chosen people, the indomitable, the crown of Creation, a breed that could not be destroyed even by sinful Gente experiments in disrupting the taxa.

Every meathead walking these streets was endowed with all the rights and responsibilities of a nation under siege—'Hurrah, stand shoulder to shoulder now for the Demiurge has given to us a filthy broken world, which we shall subjugate.'

Meaningless conversations overstuffed with a forced optimism; anything other than such cheery prattle was probably grounds for death by stoning. Fire heard a central office speaking through every mouth, broadcasting only praise for the brave new world. 'Nah, he's dreadful he is . . . I mean you have to take responsibility, don't you?', 'Our kiddies will have a better life', 'We've all got to lend our weight, it's about big and small all pulling together', 'What's a couple of delays really, as long as the growth rate is healthy', 'They're going to renovate the whole north of the city, top to bottom, prices will go up of course but everyone benefits in the end', 'Lavers got promoted, didn't he, it only goes to show that it's worth putting in the extra effort', 'Even if you're from a disadvantaged background you can always get somewhere with a bit of initiative', 'There'll be roads soon, running from White Tiger to Ferret, and then there'll be holiday parks on the roads, you'll see, back on Earth they could only dream of the likes of what we're building here.'

How could they stand it? Did they actually listen to themselves?

Tiny minds, busy with even tinier subjects, a nation of housekeepers, their only purpose in life to get the dusting done and cook a meal, let's make it a bit fancy, why not; always busy and never thinking what they were doing or why. Their world a backyard, no wind of freedom blowing from anywhere, surrounded by these enormous ugly blocks built not as monuments to what people can dare and what they can achieve, built rather to crush them, to grind them into the routines of the stuporous everlasting busywork sold and labelled as making history, that never raised its snout, never sniffed the air, wherever there was something in the air, something real.

Everything here was about nothing at all.

Sometimes, rather than just saying whatever crossed their mind, they began to ask: what is truth? For them it was any sort of news, indistinguishable from their trivial drivelling gossip—Fire thought of Vempes and Zagreus and their doctrines of learning and knowledge; they would have screamed aloud to hear this rubbish. 'Have you heard? The Academy's got a new plan for the cooling system', 'Serger's group is going to work out an improvement to the genome to make us more like the ancients', 'The Council has given the go-ahead for excavations in Atalanta, perhaps they'll find more seedships', 'The Academy has found out how the planet came to occupy this orbit; it was some kind of collision, and Jupiter . . .'

Benightedly blabbering out results without even the faintest idea of how these things are actually discovered. This peculiar society certainly celebrated its scientists, acclaimed their deeds and discoveries on the columns and on public screens, with hideous graphics and clumsy animations dumbed down to the simplest terms so that the gossip could go on as planned. They might just have been telling fairy stories here; it was knowledge without consequences. The same triviality prevailed in the one-dimensional, simplistic lesserling approach to sexuality, getting a little of what they fancied from the viewscreens, from posters, even from printed material which they bought and read in public, chuckling, gawping.

Big boobs or broad shoulders, vacant expressions, bashful suitors or idle sluts, a sickening leering complicity that made Fire's gorge rise, threatened to sour his memories of his sensuous escapades in fur, the ecstasy he had felt in the holosensory Temple.

Even more ludicrous than the huge viewscreens full of propagandist science and dumb grunting sex, even more pointless than the overcrowded maglevs, was lesserling road traffic.

They called their vehicles cars, though they were simple metal cages stretched over with canvas, propelled by pedal and chain; Fire's furry friends had drummed enough technological history into him that he could tell the difference, knew that they were in fact bicycles.

The deluded occupants of these 'cars' sweated and pedalled their way up steeply sloping ramps to the central circular roads. At the junctions stood tall yellow cranes of heavy iron that swayed and turned about, their lamps controlling the smooth or fitful flow of traffic. People cut in on one another, cursed, raged, became desperate or caught colds. Fire wished that he were back in the sewer, full of steaming turds, that had led him into the city; the original plan to let a rope down over the walls had proved impractical, night being no longer night hereabouts, with no cover of darkness, artificial lighting had taken off in a big way here in just the last couple of days. He wished he were back in the graveyard at the edge of the city, where he had washed in a fountain, getting ready for the moment when he must take the costume from his backpack and put it on.

No one had seen him arrive, so he walked about looking for clues in the damp cold. His fingers felt stiff and numb and he held in a clumsy grasp the book, their Scripture here. He hardly dared lift his gaze to the buildings whose high windows reminded him of the spies sent to Jericho, in the story that Zagreus had told him (where no red thread hangs, Rahab does not live there). He had to keep his chin tucked into his chest so that the icy wind didn't whistle freezing down his collar. How could they live like this, how could they breathe?

They were as proud of the unnatural temperatures as they were of all their other nonsense and dressed up in caps, long coats, baggy sleeves; look how cold we keep our city, it's like autumn, winter even, in the temperate zones of Old Earth. Clearly no one thought that the enormous expenditure of energy for this absurd deep freeze was in the least obscene. What else could be expected from creatures with such a gurgling, glibbering language—it had taken Fire forty torturous minutes to learn it thoroughly, helped by the memory crystals and by painful visual and sensory stimuli, and he was shocked when Zagreus told him, 'The worst of it is that you now have a vocabulary several times larger than most of the lunatics in there.'

Lesserlings: the prince understood now why the machine got so worked up, what it meant when it said, 'What a bunch of cretins they are. They've cauterized their own capabilities, things that the Gente could do they have burnt out from them-selves, and then they think they're human—it's as though we were to glue shut your eyes and ears so that you could pretend you're a flower.'

   True. Photosynthesis, he could do that—not right now though, since the chevrons of cunningly contrived hair on his back were hidden under a hairy shirt. The air under his clothes smothered his skin once he had been walking for more than a few minutes, and even more uncomfortable, his feet were shoved into nar-row leather boots rammed tight with stuffing—'They'll think that those are goat's legs, you'll look like a satyr to them, a devil even.' Synthetic leather from the sev-enfour's nanofabs, produced to Zagreus' specifications; 'We're not quite there yet that we would kill a sentient creature to improve your disguise.'

At first, on board the whale, Fire could hardly keep his balance in these boots, and Zagreus grunted, 'Well, that really does look human—not a few cultures forced part of the species to bind their feet, crippling them even, since that was seen as beautiful, or to totter through the world on stilts.'

Boots or not, Fire had soon learnt to imitate the gait of these lunatics, bent forward, as if burdened by the weight of dead ancestors, only just upright enough to call it walking.

Fire wondered whether he should just give up, spread his arms like a mad prophet and yell, 'Listen to me or I'll fall apart. I have been sent to blaspheme your totem beasts, to find a Temple, to bend your twisted myths back into factual shape. And no one asked me whether I want to accept the mission, how do you like that then?'

'Why are you stalking my daughter?' A stockily built lesserling, arms like articulated shovels hanging almost to the ground, stood in front of Fire and looked him up and down, grunting angrily. He was leading a little, thin, stunted creature with him, probably the 'daughter' he was gabbling about and his mouth hung half open.

'Sorry, I'm not . . . I wasn't following you, nor your . . . daughter, we seem to have . . . we must have just been going the same way . . . here,' said Fire, laboriously, lifting his head to look round and see where his thoughts had taken him.

It was a large public square, made up of several smaller piazzettas, some raised, some sunken, flights of steps leading from one to another, decorated with fountains and richly ornamented benches of some green metal. Statues stood everywhere. Fire blinked; there was something vitally important about the way these little open spaces were arranged, something he should recognize, what is it making his flesh creep like this? Edges and corners, regularly shaped plazas, polytopes projected onto a plane surface . . .

The stocky lesserling tickled his little companion's flank and took something from his right pocket, stuffing it into her mouth. He held a leash in his fist and led the beast by a thin black leather collar about her throat.

Was there some error in translation? Daughter, pet?

The lesserling in the collar chewed contentedly and gazed up at her master in dumb devotion. He stroked her head. 'She's faithful, you know. Doesn't like strangers though, she can get a bit rowdy.'

Who's he talking to, ah yes, to me, that's horrid. 'Needs to . . . get used to them?' said Fire, in an attempt to keep up his side of the conversation.

'Yes, she's still young, you see, I only just had her cloned, she can't run about on her own yet. She'll learn to talk soon, then I'll send her off to school. I'm a very proud dad. Then after that we'll have some children the old-fashioned way.'

'How . . . nice for you,' said Fire, hoping that he sounded more convincing than he felt. The prince kept walking, hesitantly, and the man and his leashed mutt fell into a trot beside him, clearly their usual pace. The conversation, which had begun on a hostile note, now veered altogether too quickly for Fire's tastes into convivial chumminess. 'The name's Preisnitel and this little thing,'—he tugged on the leash and nodded towards his daughter—'is Pyretta.'

'I'm Moskonder,' said Fire, hoping fervently that Zagreus' studies of the local dialect had come up with a convincing personal name.

The stranger nodded. 'Not from round here, are you?' A belly laugh, and he was not far off from giving Fire a cheerful dig in the ribs. 'Oh, is it so obvious?' asked Fire, pretending shyness, and the stranger replied, 'Well, if you've got time to dawdle about here so aimlessly, making friends just like that, ha-ha, with pensioners . . . I'm an invalid you see, that's life . . . Are you on the sickie, or on holiday?'

'Eh?' said Fire, out of his depth for a moment and also increasingly distracted by the little open spaces, sunken and raised, the pattern they made. Where have I seen these edges and corners before?

'I mean, your head. Accident at work, was it? The pumps, I suppose.'

'Mmph,' said Fire, for a change, noncommittally; he could have been conceding or denying, but Preisnitel nodded, 'I thought so, had to be the pumps, I mean, the uniform and all . . .'

Uniform. Well, great. The prince was got up in something that was not, as Zagreus had assured him, 'perfectly normal clothes'; rather, these glad rags meant something to the lesserlings, something about his social status and his part in the whole division of labour—something which he himself didn't know. That could turn out to be embarrassing, or even put his life in danger.

'Myself, most of my working life, I was with the . . . oh, look, news from the great unknown!' said the stocky man gleefully and even his daughter on her leash pawed the ground and shook her blonde curls.

On a pillarscreen not five yards off, an animation of huge globes spun and tumbled in the emptiness of cosmic space.

'You'll have heard,' said Preisnitel, slipping easily into a lecturing tone. He seemed to have forgotten all about being Moskonder's new best mate and now he was flexing his didactic muscles, 'that the massive impact had entirely natural causes, of course, hrrm, since the missing planet passed too close to Jupiter at one point, a-ha, . . .' and so on and so forth.

Far too often since arriving here, Fire had already had to put up with the way these people chewed up their own semantics and grammar, tripping over their tongue to make tangled knots of speech, and this enthusiasm for the new theories of Venus' origin was just more of the same. They crashed into the limits of language trying to explain how the planet had come to occupy its current orbit, or what had caused the atmospheric conditions the Gente-descended settlers found on their arrival.

Fire's attention drifted, he looked round the square where children were shrieking, couples canoodling, older people hurrying after their own ghosts or taking a breather on the benches. Then Fire knew what he saw before his eyes; the pattern, the configuration.

'All this here . . . is that . . . was there something else here, on the square, before?' he asked, keeping his tone neutral, fearful of the answer he knew would most likely come. The thickset man was still well into his lecture and droned yawpingly, 'So that when the crusty bits, erm the planetary crust which is what we've all come to call it . . . what? Oh, here, like Temple Square here? Don't you even know that, my word, where have you sprung from, my dear chap,' he laughed, 'ho-ho, you pumpmen, always got your nose to the grindstone, up to the elbows in your machinery . . . that's how you lot are . . . you don't get much news, do you? This was the heathen temple which they built when they, you know, the first nanofabs which the Gente released . . . we were supposed to come here to pray!'

The Temple of Isotta.

Razed to the ground.

'Bestial superstition. The Academy had everything taken apart, it was all erm demolished, some of the stone blocks were reused in the Ministry buildings, look over there, and the umm cultic objects which they found were hmm . . .' He meant the stelae, the statues, all the ornament and the technology that Fire had come to find. 'What . . . happened to that? To those objects?'

The bloke went, 'Pffft!' and said, 'As far as I know it's in the, preservation and restoration of course, expert care, ample storage facilities, I mean the Academy, and the square, well of course there was a decision in council and it's a gift to the people, which is why we can stroll round and enjoy the place—isn't that right, Pyretta?'

The creature gave a long-drawn-out whimper which would haunt Fire's dreams.

XIII
THE POLITICS OF THE CITADEL

1. THROWN OUT

'Go back where you came from, back to the trenches, back from our castle walls, back where you chew and screw one another's brains out, or get lost, go north, how about Syrtis Major Planitia, or Vastitas Borealis, just go where the castles aren't and freeze your arse off! You've got no right to take your place among Aristoi, not among real people, you don't belong here, not on Earth nor even on Venus. We should send you to Pluto, put you in a rocket and forget about you!' Eon Nagegerg Bourke-Weiss was shouting furiously, furiestly, shoving at Padmasambhava in her astonishment. She was numb with shock while he aimed two well-placed kicks, like a footballer punting the ball, and kicked her out of his door.

Driven out, she stumbled to a nearby fountain, dumb with shock; a coloured fountain which ran with honeyed water, and she sat down on its edge and thought, I don't need to consult the Book of Life for that, I get what he's saying, from cold; cold, that's how I am and how I've always been, and he's right, the Vastitas, yes, or even Pluto. The archives recorded that Pluto had once been considered a planet in the solar system, back during in the Monotony; welcomed as a member, so to speak, of respectable planetary society, just as the Aristoi had been kind enough to treat her as one of their own, her, a heartless red lizard from the trenches of the *experimentum crucis*, who never gave any thought to Eon's needs, who was always chasing her own mad ambitions.

Pluto, that's me: hardly any mass compared to the other planets, a hermit turned away from the worlds, obstinately orbiting in a plane tilted seventeen degrees away from the other eight orbital paths. As Pluto moves away from the sun, its atmosphere freezes and falls to its polar caps as snow. At its farthest point from the sun, the whole atmosphere has gone and the planetoid moves through the vacuum as an unsouled lump of rock and ice.

As I move through my—what do they call it? Life?

Who would want me now? Who could I go to? Raphaela will be telling him now, 'I warned you from the beginning not to treat that monster like a daughter.'

And why did he even keep me as long as he did? To watch me grow up? (A soft voice whispered into her thoughts, a bitter little voice sounding like her Book of Life in italics: 'To watch your breasts grow, to watch your hips as well, watch them fill out, to do with you what his loathsome friends always said they liked to do with lizard girls, to "break you in" for his own pleasure.') To keep me company? To teach me, raise me? But now I'm grown and I'm abominable.

Raphaela saw this; she could never stand me, from the beginning.

What do I want, here among the Aristoi? Their favourite adjective is 'noble' and mine is 'red'. I'm from the valleys, I'm from the gunsmoke and the blood.

Self-reproach wasn't helping. Her left hip hurt, somewhere in the bone.

For Eon's sake she wanted to deny that the hard separation had even happened, but with each passing minute the pain made it ever more evident. She heaved a deep sigh and faced the facts. It was how it was. She shed a tear and gave voice to her fears with a threnody. 'Eon too is . . . like the other Aristoi, who wooed me and soothed me at first, stroked me and tickled me, made me gifts, took me in their arm; we were seen together at feasts where they passed me round like a costly cloth from the northern citadels. Even Eon proves them right, the trench-dwellers, who told me that the Aristoi are faithless, inconstant, superficial? Must it be so cruelly proved that I was beguiled, blinded by their charm, thinking these masqued monsters grand and kind? Oh Eon! My lidless eyes, why do you tear them open so wide? No, it cannot be. It was not you, I was dreaming. Spread your arms, as I spread my wings! I will come back to you!'

With these fine-turned words, in the high style beloved of the Aristoi, still on her lips, in her rapture she tried to stand, to throw herself 'upon his bosom'; but she couldn't get up from the fountain's edge—her crippled hip pulled her back down so sharply that she cried out with pain.

To deepen her misery, she saw the faithless Eon standing at the window straight across from her, half covering a second silhouette, most likely whoever it was that he had spurned her for—was it Raphaela, already? Had she come over the roof, in a chopper? He was mocking her, laughing at the little lizard, revelling in her shame; at least so his laugh seemed to say, to her. Yes, him, she admitted to herself quietly, it was him, the heart-hound, the rhinox! He broke my hipbone, he managed what all the fighting and the battles could not: he's crippled me. She carried on in this vein for quite a while, pausing only to gulp down some water and rub a little on her skin.

A man and a cylindrical robot were headed straight towards her now—two figures that she hated from afar, since the man wore such a blissful look upon his face that you'd think he was blood kin to Happiness herself. At last she recognized him as the clown, the mannikin, Saint Oswald, who came to dine with Eon from time to time. He gave her a friendly hello and it was as though time stood still then, or held its breath, while something nudged her thoughts in a curious direction (was it the Book of Life?); You're Pluto? A planet with an eccentric orbit, icy, forever removed from the rest of the solar system? Then who's he? He's not of the Aristoi, but moves among them. Is he Charon, your companion?

She smiled, the first time for weeks that she'd had reason to.

'Have you had breakfast yet?' asked the mannikin, coming closer, beaming and cheerful. Padmasambhava noticed that he had new arms and legs—where on earth does he get those all the time?

2. HOW TO TRAIN A RAT

'Aargh', she said, 'oh' and 'yuck' when he showed her the worst pieces in his collection, 'that's really red.'

By now he had learnt to translate that adjective for himself. Day by day, the new housemates learnt one another's quirks, so Saint Oswald knew that the phrase was meant in praise of the monsters in his preserving jars—boggle-eyed, hunched, wizened things, smeared with their own tallow, not a few of them nothing but guts and stomach, bristling with claws like a giant dandelion clock or spiked with eight crooked legs. 'That was an early form of the species you know as orespiders. They cloned themselves into a better sort of shape, and these days walk upright. Ah, and these skingliders here—no offence, but I always found a thing that has wings where it shouldn't especially horrid.'

All these specimens had been brought up from the trenches over the years, by robot collectors sent out for the purpose, and stood now on long shelves in the uppermost room of the mannikin's curious tower, inaccessible to outsiders.

Had they been allowed to enter this uppermost room, the Aristoi would have quickly noticed that it was the lowest room at the same time, thanks to one complete rotation in the fourth dimension and a half-turn in the seventeenth, which his architecture machines had learnt from his patroness, Cordula Späth: 'What else am I supposed to do with this technology, if not make a gift of it to put you folk in my debt? So, get this: if you walk out at the back there, you're in the lowest floor but one—ground level, just as if you'd come out of the cellar—and if you walk out there, in front of us, you're up in the attic, second highest floor. Fun, isn't it? Ryu bought the technology, back in the day—not on his own, but he paid the, umm, Lion's share, ha ha. Those Pentagon people developed it as some super-dooper camouflage technique—which is where the nutty computer in the jungle got hold of it, wrote a beta version, and that's how the Ceramicans . . . well, anyway, I've been carrying the knowledge round all the while in my cerebellum, because I took a rather different view of the Great Transcendence from the Lion's, and his folk. So just before I left his . . . sad little civilization, he flung all sorts of accusations at me: "Please, Cordula, we've just transformed the whole of biology, surely that's enough of a revolution, do you really want to begin tinkering with physics as well?" Same old blinkered ideas, just like the early opponents of biotech, as if to say there are things we should not know and certainly shouldn't interfere with. I mean yes, of course there are, *quod erat demonstrandum*, but the limits to knowledge aren't set by some political bandwagon or dynastic drama . . . Well, that's all water under the bridge.'

Padmasambhava swallowed, her mouth dry. 'And that's me.'

'You? Well, . . .'

'That's the template for . . .' She was standing in front of a tall tube where something with spines and savage jaws was sleeping the endless sleep.

'Hoo-ha, that . . . it cost more to get hold of that, than anything. I had to dicker with the heart-hounds, who by the way are descended not from wolves but from foxes, hence the name, hound . . . yes, anyway, this one is only an evolutionary branch line,' said Saint Oswald, taking her by the arm and steering her out. 'I just wanted you to see so that you know why I don't think much of the *experimentum crucis*.'

She'd known that for a while, but this gave her the chance to ask a question which had been preying on her mind: 'How is the *experimentum* actually . . . maintained? I mean, the Aristoi who have decided that it has to continue, how do they prevent contaminants, how do they keep the *experimentum* erm . . .'

'Ah, you're asking how you could put a stop to it if you wanted?'

Her grimace said: you've seen through me. 'Well then, I think,'—he pondered for a moment, tugging and twitching at his shirt, where the collar never quite sat right—'. . . hmm . . . first thing to do would be to reduce the hormone feed, cut it right down, let the stuff work its way out of the water and the food chain you all eat from . . . sorry, not all of you of course, you're here now, yourself,'—she waved away his apology, he carried on—'. . . and then there's the stones, the rocks, the ground beneath your feet, which—you'll have noticed, up here it's much easier going, you're not . . .' it was true, she nodded, every day up here in the castle was like walking on cotton wool or on clouds compared to her earlier life, but she had never asked why—'. . . we . . . the blue-bloods, that is, have induced a sort of creep stress, in the ground, the cliffs and rocks, it's all been metallized and then . . . you get the odd jolt of current, all of you, quite often in fact. And in the air, there are active agents, substances which act as a mild pulmonary corrosive—so that the *experimentum crucis* subjects, whoever's born to it as it were, is . . . deliberately subjected to certain stimuli. So it goes. Here I might . . . must add, it's certainly worth mentioning, that the lizards . . . your teeth . . . well, also, that is, the long-term genetic . . . and there again, it's . . . As for food—you buy extra . . . you buy your . . . side-orders from the rhinox, don't you, for the victory feasts?'

'They have the time to plough and plant, up on their strip fields, so yes, we do,' said Padmasambhava, feeling very stupid when he confirmed what she had already begun to fear.

'The rhinoxen, the cows that is, they're, well, not directly in our employ, but we do give them fertilizer and supply artificial solar lamps and . . . and in return, they ensure that the fruit and veggies you buy, everything the lizards get from them, will tweak at your metabolism if you ever happen to show too many co-operative traits . . . The cell nuclei are subjected to some rather complicated bio-chemical . . .'

'Thank you, that's enough.' Padmasambhava leant against a bookshelf and pulled a dreadful face.

Saint Oswald grunted, then became unexpectedly sarcastic. 'So, that's enough, is it? And the earthquakes, you reckon they're down to natural causes?'

His student opened her eyes wide. 'You mean . . . there were tremors the whole time, of course, mostly when . . .'

'When the frontlines became easier to deal with, wasn't it?' He raised his brows. It would have been funny, except for the dark undertone to his voice. 'They got that from the God of the Hebrews, who confused the tongues so that no one could ever form a lasting coalition and threaten His omniscient rule— no sooner do they gang up together to build a tower, have a look at Him, up there above the clouds, than something like that . . . As soon as you begin to show signs of wanting to run your own lives, such as they are, if it looks like you might settle down, build a village, hammer out a truce, boom, you're all shook up.

Something like that sticks in the memory and sooner or later, you've got a tradition which . . .'

Padmasambhava knew all too well what he meant. To found a city or set stone upon stone was a grievous sin for her people. And now she had to wonder whether, given the answers from the Book of Life to her questions about Martian geology, it was even remotely plausible that there were such frequent quakes in the crust, and she had to admit that it was not. The suggestion had simply been there, in the infosphere, as though the analogies with Earth's plate tectonics were unproblematic. 'That . . . that's despicable. Really.'

Saint Oswald agreed. He shuddered as though to shake a poisonous dust from his limbs and said, 'My words exactly. The waste! The hours of work involved, the computer runtime, installing the Marsquake machinery within the planetary mantle, and for what? A simple test to check the theory that aggression is an evolutionary accelerator. Pfft. What is this crap? You consult your Book of Life, you'll find they were saying the same thing in prehistoric times, Futurism. Mafarka. Marinetti.'

The way the mannikin said it—'your Book of Life'—it was as though the source was not quite to be trusted, at least he didn't speak of it with the respect that Padmasambhava had expected. Her faith in the Book and its omniscience was already shaken; her host had already transferred a flood of missing data from his spintronics to hers, things she had never quite missed but that explained a lot, now she knew them. By now she saw the Book as a compendium of half-truths. She was especially dismayed never to have noticed before how the whole thing simply didn't hang together. How could I not have been interested in the breathable atmosphere? How the planet became inhabitable in only a few thousand years? What were the mental blocks, the censor mechanisms that stopped me from finding the yawning gaps in the Book's data? The dark dust strewn across this world that sucked up the sunlight, the orbital mirrors, the polar caps melting to provide gaseous carbon dioxide, the atmosphere puddling at first in the deeper craters, the tents, the photosynthetic phase, the food chain, the citadels built upon the traces of the first successful local ecotectures, finally the *experimentum crucis* implemented in the trenches, a sort of ornamental finish on the whole edifice.

Futurism? 'I'll look it up,' she promised him, her housemate and host.

Saint Oswald waved it away and then seemed to remember something. (While she looked about, behind her; there that spiny, savage creature, isn't that my mother, rather than the lynx, as the Book claims?) He spoke: 'What do we learn from all this? As a wise man once said, "Sure, you can train a rat. If you work with your rat for hours, days, weeks, months, years, you can train a rat, but all that you have at the end of it, is a trained rat." '

3. CHORDS, NOT STAIRCASES

At the house (or 'at the court', as she liked to say) of Eon Nagegerg Bourke-Weiss, Padmasambhava had led a life of excess and indulgence. Saint Oswald put a stop to that.

Certainly, he took part in the obligatory orgies and hosted some from time to time himself, as befitted his status as a sort of Aristoi lateral affiliate, but these played a subordinate role in his life. She was happy with this, she'd had enough of 'this nonsense' anyway and now simply took a young lover. Saint Oswald had said, 'Yes, get yourself one of those lads in doublet and hose, moist black nose and hairy shoulders, then you won't have to worry about others setting their cap at you.'

The chap was an 'ursuform'; so the Book of Life told her, meaning that he was humanoid with ursine tendencies. He turned out to be a good lover, a generous host, a happy companion at concerts and museums. He took her to see the other citadels but otherwise didn't take up too much of her time, and his name was Lodas Osier (she had to look this up again and again in the Book of Life, since she kept forgetting who he was exactly, what he was—a bland, almost faceless figure, rather too slim—back on the battlefield she wouldn't have given him a second bite).

Lodas Osier had an airship, for leaving the citadels and watching the frenzy in the trenches. He never quite realized how eager she was on these observation flights, for he thought it was simply a rather mordant decadence on the part of his darling girl.

During these tours, she even let slip a little of how life looked from the face of battle, so that the poor chump began to pretend that he too was a fighter like those in the trenches. He threw his weight about at galas and banquets, took up martial arts and cultivated an irksome and totally unnecessary jealousy against his lizard lady's other lovers, especially poor Eon, whom she only ever indulged if an orgy was utterly boring. In the end, Osier revived the ridiculous custom of the duel, in abeyance for four hundred and forty years in their citadel. He fought Eon Nagegerg twice under the primitive code of the duello and was killed both times, was revived and, luckily, then lost interest in the whole idea, although by then it had spread to countless followers in the other citadels. Padmasambhava was repulsed but also rather turned on by the idea. If he hadn't come to his senses, I might have eaten him after all, she thought.

Every minute that was not frittered away at her gallant lover's side, she devoted to study, under Saint Oswald's tutelage and his robots.

He soon enough revealed that everything they taught came from his seeress and his friend, Frau Späth. 'You should fear her. She lived cheek by jowl with the liege lady of Old Earth; she knows Katahomenleandraleal personally.'

A lot of the syllabus, in fact most of it, concerned music and mathematics—Euclidian and non-Euclidian projections, how they are perceived optically and how they could equally be perceived through corresponding auditory patterns. Counterpoint. The infinitesimal calculus. Whalesong and birdsong, from Earth's extinct species. The lizard (no longer a lizard now) learnt how to translate chords into staircase-like structures. The morphic correspondences of sound and architecture were the very heart of her schooling. What Saint Oswald called her 'journeyman work' was a canon encoding the shape of the tower where they dwelt, in all its dimensions, fourth through seventeenth. She learnt to see harmonic frequencies like woven cables (and vice versa), she learnt to dissect the ancient tonal rulesets of the past, from sonatas all the way to the tone clusters that drove the Aristoi so wild, and how to write the stemmas. She had to encode musical instruments into the abstract concepts of a non-linear oscillator and to understand how strings vibrated, she practically had to rewrite the laws of physics . . .

'I don't like to ask you what this is all for,' said the lizard, 'but it would be kind of you, for my pains and racking my brains, at least to tell me some of the other stuff I want to learn, even if that hasn't much to do . . . at all . . . with music and mathematics.'

'What would you like to know then?' he asked, teasingly.

'History.'

And so, with the help of a deluge of old footage, images and sound stored in his spintronics, the two of them retraced the whole course of biotic history from the Liberation of the Gente genome from the shackles of Monotony onwards—first a rough outline: how the Lion got hold of his Protean techniques and why he had wished to follow such Promethean aims, why it had taken so long to cleanse the ecotectures of the human infestation, although Mankind was already defeated, the circumstances surrounding the attack on human hands, the role her father had played there, how he had met Lasara, the lynx, the great Ceramican conquest, the exodus to the moon, the next genetic self-sculpting that ran parallel with the terraforming of Venus and Mars, and at last, the seed that was sown and nurtured— herself, and her sibling—when continued surveillance of Earth revealed, from a safe distance, that events had taken the course long hoped for.

Next they went into details, looking above all at the strategy and tactics of even the smallest of fate's twists and turns: 'So the fact that the four of them— well, except for poor Storikal—escaped death by the skin of their teeth, that was all Ryuneke's doing, wasn't it, that was why help arrived late but just in the nick of time?'

'Even Katahomenleandraleal was in on the plan, yes,' explained Saint Oswald, and she heard in his voice his admiration for how well the planners had pulled the strings, back in the distant past, 'and the whole point was'—

Padmasambhava could supply the rest herself—'the idea behind it was that everyone watching on the pherinfonetworks could see what heroes they were, Anubis, Huan-Ti and Hecate; they had dared the Ceramicans in the cannon's mouth, fought as we fight in the trenches here. Meaning that it would not be cowardly to follow them to the moon. The message was that the Exodus was a bold move, a deed fit for ...'

'For heroes, yes,' the mannikin whispered. His tone said, it was a long time ago, but if you lived through it, you still live with it.

'One more question.'

'Yes, my little fangtasm?'

'The wolf. Dmitri Stepanovich Sebassus. I don't understand why ... I mean, why he let Lasara talk him into it, a suicide mission, off to kill the Lion, when after all he—I mean, he clearly didn't do it from love. And he had no idea that she was pregnant.'

Saint Oswald smiled, enigmatically, almost maliciously. 'And why can't he have done it from love?'

'Philomena's fourteenth chronicle. It's backed up by ... various commentaries on the *Conversations with the Lion*, especially in recensions Epsilon and Tau, and the documents in the wolfsong collection, especially Britt's paper ...'

Mercy me, thought the mannikin, this little lass can't be beaten at bibliography.

'... It's perfectly obvious that Lasara didn't, well, that this faithless hound ...'

'When I look through the sources and hear Apis Olmy Seer's opera about the Flying Cats, the one she wrote on the moon . . . If I understand correctly, a sizeable proportion of researchers are quite sure that he wanted to, that when everything . . . that when the danger had passed . . . that he wanted to go back to her. To Princeton. If so, why did he let the lynx talk him into regicide?'

'You're not grokking the psychology. There are very powerful emotions, such as remorse, guilt, gratitude, trust, hope, passion, which . . .'

'Who for? For Lasara?'

'Perhaps. The long-lived heart is no less strange than ever-mortal man's; you know your Shakespeare. And you know, as well, the Countess' cryptic sentences that survive; "Won't imagination save us? I've built and built and built. I collect everything to do with it." Pietism, quietism . . .'

'It sounds to me as though she walled herself from the world long ago. And went barmy in her anchorite's cell, shut away with . . . whatever she'd collected. Perhaps he wasn't with her because she simply didn't want him there. At arms' length . . . perhaps . . . "imagination" . . . it sounds as though she didn't know that the thoughts and feelings of sapient sentients don't really matter at all to the erm . . . cosmos, if all we do is think it and feel it. On the other hand, it's the most powerful force imaginable if you live by it . . . act upon it. If you, well, kiss and cry and laugh and run risks and argue, rather than only collecting dreams, hiding yourself away.'

He smiled again. 'Now you're talking about yourself, the risks you take, not Dmitri or Alexandra. Why didn't he go to her again, why didn't she keep him? Did he find some other happiness with the Lion's daughter? My dear girl'—Saint Oswald swept his arm round in an expansive gesture that took in the whole virtual storage capacity of the synergspintronic system—'there are discussion forums on the topic and major research projects, there are tomes written and refuted—here in the citadels, we go at this sort of prehistory the way Monotony scholars of kung fu history went at the question of Bodhidharma's journey from India to China, or possibly the other way round. However it was. Back in the day.'

'Bodhi-who?'

'Dear child, not even Frau Späth knows the answer to that one.'

When it came to dodging a question, this was his big gun. Padmasambhava shut up.

Saint Oswald though guessed, correctly, that it didn't mean she was ready to drop the subject. She'd just decided to ask Frau Späth herself, in person, one day.

4. BENE GENTE

Two days after Esprit, and not a breath of air in the sacred grove (mixed tree cover, several species).

Lodas led his red lady love to the hill where, on the eve, the sharp wine had been poured, to show her what travellers from the other citadels so lief came here to do. It was early in the morning, cool, a clear light lay around, and the lovers shivered deliciously as a shower of rain tiptoed past them. They lay down between two Judas trees, on the green grass, below the shimmering pink blossom, and began to lick at one another, as the indolent panthers were wont to do, on the steps of the temple at Capeside, so many years ago. A musk rose from their pores that soon enough triggered the old holographic response and the Lion's cold high flame appeared, on a carpet of leaves, in puddles of alcohol, by the ashes of burnt-out fires, within a circle of stones, and he spoke in a voice of thunder, a warm voice, full of his ancient, undying power, to those who made love there before him, since the living image had been programmed only to appear when the scents of love hung in the air. 'Think not to say within yourselves, my distant seed: "We have Cyrus Golden to our father." For I say unto you, that God is able of these stones to raise up children unto Cyrus Golden.'

Lodas held the lizard down, his right paw pinned her at her left buttock, he rolled her over to the right to get where he knew he wanted to go; she hissed lasciviously, telling him not to stop, her need.

It seemed to her that the dead lord was looking her directly in the face as he recited what remained, after the long ages of diaspora, of the doctrine of Bene Gente. 'Cursed be they who fear incest, who shun clones, who run from making plans: for theirs is the Monotony. Cursed be they who know not what they want, for others must pay their debts. Cursed are the indolent, for they shall reproduce themselves without ever having lived. Cursed are they who seek to crawl back into the follicle of their birth, for they will devour the future's wealth, before the cock upon the ramparts has spewed three times. Cursed are those who raise up nature conservation, for they shall end as the cotylosaurs they take as their model. Cursed are the timid, the quietists, the opportunists, for they shall entangle in the tentacles of yes-of-course, and there shall they die. Cursed am I, myself, above all, for I speak to those who come after, and unto them I say things that cannot be spoken but must be learnt. But the lame is condemned by her lameness, and the liar is trapped by her lies, and the coward's heart dies of its own poison.'

Lodas Osier laughed out loud, not liking the show, which he didn't understand anyway.

His lover did not laugh. She grew thoughtful.

5. THE DAMNED

Padmasambhava asked again and again what Frau Späth was like, what she was
planning and most importantly, 'When is she coming?'

'She comes regularly,' said Saint Oswald, as though he had just looked at his
watch or his diary. 'I'm expecting her in a couple of decades. But I have a nagging
suspicion that she might show her face rather sooner this time.'

'The reason being . . .'

'Your good self. She'll come and fetch you, I think, or she'll send you off
somewhere, once your . . . education is complete.' The answers were always the
same and they always just about sufficed to stop her from asking again, for a couple
of lesson hours at least.

Padmasambhava tried not to live in expectation, too much, of all the great deeds
that Frau Späth had planned for her and she looked for other ways to use her time.

The most daring of these was politics.

It took only a few hours to analyse and understand the general principles of
government in the citadels and only seconds to learn by heart the fine constitutional phrases of these city states. ('We reject the principle of the plebiscite. Whoever is satisfied with the right to say merely yea or nay, has surrendered any right
to speak', 'A system of representation bound to primitive number-crunching
would be inadequate to any system of self-government worth the name; therefore
we have agreed, that . . .') It took two tiresome weeks though to grasp the structures of the governmental organograms; steering committees, general assemblies,
the Congress general secretariat, regional committees, grassroots conferences, the
supraterritorial General Congress in Citadel I, the virtual assemblies of the various
federations and associations, some of them organized along lines still called the
'professions' or the 'guilds' (which had not existed, as such, for a long while). Once
Padmasambhava had learnt all this, she confronted the reluctant teaching software.
At first vociferous and then ever more meekly, pianissimo, her teacher's expensive
teaching machines told her, at last, what she had suspected from the beginning:
since she had been living in the citadel for four years now and had visited all
of the other cities, and since she contributed to the production, circulation and

consumption of their wares, and since she exchanged both opinions and sexual favours with the Aristoi, she enjoyed, de facto, full citizenship, even if this had never been formally granted.

In cobwebbed forgotten corners of the constitutional documents, in poorly encoded hypertexts, she found customary law that declared her right to found a political platform and to launch a campaign. So she did.

There were ethical considerations, she argued, and resource economics, aesthetic arguments and other reasons too. Padmasambhava launched a forum group and surprisingly quickly, many of the local Aristoi, even Eon and Raphaela, joined her in demanding that the *experimentum crucis* should be ended as soon as possible.

The aim was not to persuade the blue-bloods to open the doors of the citadels to an unending horde of refugees and walking wounded; rather, Padmasambhava said, it was her 'sacred goal' to ensure that the trench-dwellers were not simply engulfed by the civilization of the citadels, but rather, that they should have the chance, at last, to build a civilization of their own. Once the Aristoi understood this and understood that this whole bit of fun was not really going to cost them anything, her victory was assured.

The discussion only picked up a bit shortly before the relevant Congressional decrees were to be ratified. At that moment, someone produced a study which declared that switching off the earthquake machinery in the Martian mantle might lead to instabilities, for a while at least, threatening the stability of those citadels nearest to the trenches.

Earthquakes, here, in our homes?

An uproar broke out and luckily Padmasambhava had been ready for this for a long while. Her reply was a magnificent speech to the supraterritorial General Congress. 'That's how it is then. The same consternation that we always have when they get cold feet in the committees and corridors of power. We are lost, aren't we? Done with. We're damned as blue-blooded individuals, damned as communities, damned as citizens of the citadels and damned as a civilization. We must act immediately, by urgently dropping the actions we had planned to take. We must take tough decisions. Meaning, we must appoint a committee and draft a report; we must prepare a plan and use millions of hours of computer runtime to ensure that everything is back to normal, meaning, just as it has always been. The suggestion that we might, only once in a thousand years, actually hold ourselves accountable even to the most basic ethical standards, is messing everything up, giving the forces of destruction free rein. We'll be crushed beneath the wheels of some dreadful disaster. So we must comb the archives for accurate data on earthquake frequency back on old Earth, we must draw graphs, we must step back and consider the whole matter objectively, from a distance, for as long as is needed, for as long as we can spin it out, we must consider our duty to future generations . . . No, my friends, we must do none of this. The voice that speaks here is only guilt, fearing punishment. We begin to realize—some of us, and very late—what injustice has been done here, and the disaster that we fear is, in truth, nothing other than the punishment we believe we have earned. But evolution is not a moral instance, as all of you should know, and this parliament is not a school, with grades given for good behaviour. All that we must do, is do what can and should be done. The proper thing, the right thing, the reasonable thing. And if this brings costs and if these costs include checking and improving the solid walls of our citadels, then this brings benefits as well—for instance, that we will in future be much better protected against any possible meteor strikes. There is no reason to be afraid. We are not hampered in our free choice even by the judgement of poster-ity—we are, after all, our own posterity. Some seem to have forgotten this. Most of us still have several centuries to live! So why should we not do what is right and then be proud of what we have done for a long, long time?'

In the end, it was her use of that little pronoun 'we' that made her speech such a success and crowned the whole campaign—a turn of phrase that said that the trench-dwellers and the blue-bloods in the citadels were already reconciled, though in truth the process had not even begun.

'Nicely dodged,' said Saint Oswald, who still detested politics, even if he ap-proved of Padmasambhava's goal.

Bernsteller Kurppheijn Tisla and others who had been the loudest voices warning against earthquakes now did a sudden volte-face and, to keep hold of their hangers-on, shared the widely held view that the end of the experiment would have benefits far beyond those that Padmasambhava had predicted, that the re-sulting enormous gains in computer runtime could be put to use, for instance, in urgently needed improvements to energy meteorology. 'For decades now the need for more detailed information on insolation topography has been growing, by about two hundred per cent each year. We must plan new collector arrays and now we can. The satellites used until now to observe and record the experiment can be adapted for solar measurement, supplying data which will allow us to increase sunfall above the level of the natural radiative balance.'

'Well, you can if you like,' Padmasambhava reckoned. To Saint Oswald she said, 'I don't even know whether they believe any of that themselves, but they're saying it to make it look like they support my programme, lest they sink into obscurity. And that tells me what I really want to hear.' She couldn't wink as she said so, not having eyelids, but he understood just what she meant.

'You play a good tune, Pied Piper.'

Not very nicely put, but good to hear.

6. QUAKE AND AFTERSHOCK

Triumph, fame, honour and high office—the only real loss then Padmasambhava had to endure from her political career was that she and Lodas Osier separated. At some point along the way, the 'whole mad bloody business' got too much for him.

He came to her in tears, piling on the reproaches. 'I was only ever a stopgap for you, something to fill the hours until Eon and Raphaela and that whole snobby crowd took you up again,'—well, yes.

That much was true; she had grown now, reached adulthood and an age which most of her fellow hatchlings would never have attained while the *experimentum* endured. And she went to the high-society feasts and bacchanalia, where the etiquette was to arrive unaccompanied and to be ready for anything, untroubled by the ties of sentiment.

'If only we could arrive together and leave together,' he bleated, feeling sorry for himself. 'If I only had that little place in your life . . .'

She laughed at that. 'Lovely! And while everyone's rutting and swiving, we could hold hands, couldn't we, and if it's not too noisy we could drift off to sleep together. No thanks, sweetie.' He sulked and looked out of the revolving window, at the waterfalls of Citadel IV's art museum and the forest round Citadel II, and other beauty spots.

She laid her hand on his shoulder and asked, rather gentler now, 'What's really bothering you, hm?'

He didn't turn away from the revolving panorama. It was six times the size of the two of them together and looped round their tilted bed, so that sometimes the window slanted towards them and sometimes skewed away to the back. 'What bothers me is that you make such a song and dance about it.'

'It's a song and dance, is it?' she asked, nonplussed. 'It's not perhaps the greatest reform in . . .'

'Well, great! Yes! Wonderful!' He turned away from her and flew into a real rage now, threw off the covers, sat up and then turned a little towards her, half-profile, and screamed past her ear. 'The greatest, the best, the most—what, why? You're a hypocrite. You want to have your cake and eat it too. You just abandoned your people in the trenches, you never went back—you could have, could have, gone to the keeps, at least to the new outposts built on your orders, where they, errm, huh, establish fair forms of trade between the citadels and trenches—but I've seen you looking down at them from the airship, you're even more disgusted by them than the Aristoi—Aristoi, who you want to be one of, except you don't, except you like feeling exotic here . . . bah . . .' He ran out of breath.

She tittered. 'Who else is going to help the trench-dwellers,' she said, in a sing-song voice, 'if not someone who was never quite one of them? They noticed that my Book of Life was different from theirs—and the Aristoi noticed as well. The only one who wants me to always be what I used to, or what I seemed to be, the only one who seems to care that I'm exotic and don't belong in his world, is you . . .' but then the window toppled past them, the chandelier tinkled, the baldachin trembled: an earthquake, not a strong one, but very sudden.

When it had passed, Lodas and Padmasambhava looked at one another, in silence and astonishment.

Then they had to laugh. Then they had to tussle, and at first were surprised by how friendly it was, then it got more serious, and since they already knew, had already said that they would most likely not stay friends, the sex that came next was good—a way of saying goodbye, and something untouched by the resentments, the suspicion and secrets of recent days.

A couple of hours before dawn, they were woken by another, stronger quake.

Padmasambhava's house (she could afford one now) stood atop a cliff in the citadel walls.

Gifts from Saint Oswald fell from the shelves, and ancient books. Glass broke. There was a long pause, when they tried to think what to say to one another, woken like this.

Nothing came to mind.

Another tremor. It seemed best to get out of bed, quickly, and leave. She got dressed. He asked, 'To the garden?' She laughed softly, no longer friendly, and said, 'Certainly not.'

She called a taxi and sent him away.

Sat down. Stayed sat. Cried a bit.

You have to stand in the place that you are, she thought, most of all these folk, the Aristoi. The whole heart of standing is: you can't fly.

I myself chose the place I am in, even though I can fly, and then I did what I had set out to do, and now? Tell me something, Book, tell me about the suffering in the trenches, the farms they're starting, about the drought, the flash floods. Tell me.

But she hadn't sent the right recognition code with her request, so the Book said nothing.

She lay down on the bed, sent a command for the ceiling mirror and looked into it.

Right away there it was, the bad news that had been troubling her for weeks: she'd sent him away just now, probably for good, and what if he just didn't find her pretty any more? What if what she suspected when she looked in the mirror, when she felt her hips and her breasts, was true; she was losing her female shape, every day she became more angular, more muscular, almost gaunt, and not all the medicines and supplements could change this, the diagnostica and the therapeutics to which the Book referred her. Granted, Saint Oswald had prepared her for this, and when her name had been revealed, there was a definite subtext there as well. Both had told her, do not set your heart on gender—I was a girl, I became a woman, I am becoming a man, and a young boy—but now, now that the prophecy was becoming physiological reality, she realized that she had always wanted it to be a metaphor, an image for a process of growing up into a second transformation of innocence, a naive transcendence. Instead of which, my breasts are sinking back into my ribcage. Is this fair? Is it tolerable? Can I live like this?

Do I want to be her, or him?

7. NOT EVEN SHADOWS

'You won't do anything daft, will you?'

Saint Oswald realized that the question itself sounded rather silly, but it was too late to rephrase it more directly. The soap-bubble taxi cruised at a moderate speed towards the square where Livienda's descendant tree stood, where Padmasambhava was due to hold her speech to mark the official end of the *experimentum*.

There were to be delegates from the lizardfolk (Saint Oswald hoped that they wouldn't have some horrible relapse and go for one another's throats), Aristoi from all the citadels, spiders, heart-hounds, even cyborgs from the polar ice caps. Padmasambhava stared dead ahead, her eyes red; she was laden with some heavy intent that her housemate could not guess, try as he might.

He began again, putting his arm upon hers and whispering in her ear, 'Why not just be happy with what you've achieved? Give them a nice Sunday sermon; don't rain on your own parade, what good would that do? Tell them about the new culture, the new allies and partners the citadels now have, a new dawn for Mars, play them a tempting tune. What harm does it do? If you jink and swerve, and set off in some new direction, throw yourself into the next campaign, they'll call you ungrateful . . . maybe megalomaniac . . .'

'I can't do any damage now, though, can I?' she hissed in reply. 'It's done with. They've stopped. I got what I wanted. I needn't fear anyone, they can't take anything from me.'

'Yes they can, though. Recognition for your achievements—you can certainly lose that.'

She snorted and told the soap bubble to get a move on through the tubeway.

So far she had only ever seen the tree as a spintronic image or a hologram: for some reason that she couldn't fathom, she had never visited the square in all this while, although she was in the citadel quite often. When Padmasambhava saw it now, for the first time in the flesh (the wood), she almost lost her nerve.

Branches and twigs were woven into a canopy where sunbeams clutched through the leaves like fingers grasping a wicker basket; she saw in it a rich emblem of alternatives, growth, a vision of what was possible, many worlds, many mansions. So detailed was the image that for a moment she doubted her decision, to grab these blind minds and shake them awake, her chosen role in galvanizing this static, stagnant civilization. Was it right? Did it matter? Where was she leading them? Pied Piper, her old friend had called her.

Shouldn't they just be allowed to live and think and do what they want, like the fowls perched in the branches? For they sow not, neither do they reap, nor gather into barns; yet, your heavenly Nobodaddy feedeth them.

'You're on,' said Raphaela and ushered her towards the speaker's lectern.

Padmasambhava stepped into the light as though under the shower, cleared her throat in as ladylike a manner as she could and began her speech with predictable words of greeting and thanks and an account of how far they had come.

Then she fell silent for a moment—which they all found charming, many expecting that she would launch into soaring rhetoric, remembering the perfect rhythmical periods of her great campaign speeches. She looked upwards into the fluttering leaves and forward, at her housemate, the face of her best, and perhaps her only, friend, and began to speak, with determination in her quiet voice, on a subject that no one, anywhere in the citadels, wanted to discuss. 'We have reason enough to rejoice, it is true, for the folk in the trenches,'—a glance in their direction—no, she was not one of them and by the look of them they didn't much care—'for the Aristoi, the heart-hounds and the rhinox. But I see no Gente here, and no humans, and no Ceramicans, not even their shadows. Of course, we can say we care about the here and now, about the energy equilibrium, about the new agricultures, social reconfiguration, here on our dear planet Mars, or Ares, or however we want to call the place. But why do we care about these things? Because we want to decide our own fate. Because we know that there is a future. A future in which I too have had a stake, ever since I was made welcome here, and because of this future I have made friends and lost them, since that is my work. I noticed—for reasons in my own biography, which everyone here knows—that there were matters of vital, central importance for the citadels, which no one will discuss. There still are such issues. For what, after all, is Earth? Is it history now? Does it have nothing to do with us, any more? And it is my biography, too, which pushes me to ask this unwelcome question; I came into this world—Mars, Ares—because information encoded into my genome and my spintronics was activated in the lizard gene pool—I call the spintronics my Book of Life, since many lizardfolk traditionally see their spintronics as books, though this is, naturally, only a metaphor. This information was activated . . . well, I was born, or to be precise, my particular characteristics were awoken in an already fertilized reptile egg, because something had changed on Earth. I only exist because Earth is not history, it is the present. News from Earth changes what happens here. In recent days, it has often been said in the citadels and in the trenches that without me, the *experimentum crucis* would be continued for a long time to come. Without me, meaning, without the news from Earth. And nevertheless, no Aristoi and no heart-hound and no lizard, none who have come here today, are interested in the news from Earth and its consequences—it seems to be of interest only to robots, machines, satellites, relics of the past, only to the late, mute, no-longer-sentient executors of my parents' legacy, who were alerted to the news and came down here, to Mars, to cause me to be born. It's been asked where I found the self-confidence to set out to do what I did, to build a consensus, to end the *experimentum crucis*. The answer is that I believe—I have always believed, I have been taught—that a great deal depends on me, that I have to set things right. The joke is that my success in the cause that has brought us together here today, has turned my head. This whole Messianic delusion (look it up in your spintronics if you don't understand the word) perhaps set things in motion, but I did not achieve this on my own, I would never have managed it on my own. Saint Oswald, Eon, Raphaela, and Lodas, and Parigi, Hjemer, Hillary, Biegar, all the Aristoi and non-Aristoi who took part in the campaign, who argued with me, who strengthened my position and sharpened my arguments, who served the cause, in whatever capacity—do you understand? I no longer believe that it is my destiny to march through . . . I believe, now, something rather healthier: that I'm simply a catalyst, a person who makes easier something already . . . implicit, in my society's . . . level of knowledge and learning. And I want to carry on in this same vein, by submitting a new subject for debate, today, to the official and unofficial authorities in the citadels, to be discussed, to be decided, so that something can be done. What are we going to do about Earth? Do we send further probes, do we send messages by radio wave, do we send a delegation? Do we take up arms, do we build up our defences, do we seek contact with Venus, with the other . . . taxa descended from the Gente?'

She had been ready for an uproar, had steeled herself against it.

But what she saw in the faces of the audience, when she forced herself to look at them, was worse; indolent incomprehension, a sort of lazy impatience—they hadn't even noticed that she had veered away from the expected speechifying, only noticing that she had gone on for too long about things that were of esoteric interest at best. The worst was the expression on Saint Oswald's face, when he turned towards her and then sat back again; she saw neither concern nor anger, nor any of the expressions she knew, that she would have been glad to see, rather, she saw only sympathy.

The gathering had been meant to celebrate her triumph, and in some incomprehensible way had become her scene of defeat—she could already imagine the thoughts going through the spectators' heads: Is she still not satisfied, we've put an end to the *experimentum*, what more does she want? Standing there, flooded in sunlight, glowing like a fuel rod, she finished her speech with words that she barely heard herself. 'All that I'm saying is: the information is out there. Earth has fallen silent, and that's a message. There's no electromagnetic radiation, no radio waves, no thermic fluctuation that might indicate industry. It's mute. Seen from space, it looks like Mars and Venus a thousand years back. We'll have to behave accordingly. Thank you.'

Sparse, polite, hateful applause.

A hasty departure, silence on the drive back to the hotel, a touchingly helpless gesture from her only friend—he took her hand, pressed it, before he went off to his room—a hot shower, a sigh, and then, when Padmasambhava had lain down on her bed, when all she wanted to do was sleep, a long sleep, forever, something that had not happened since she had left the trenches: her Book of Life made contact unprompted.

'You should go home, quickly, Padmasambhava.'

'Are you rubbing salt into the wound here? I know that I'm not wanted . . .'

'No, nothing to do with that. There's a visitor. At your house.'

XIV
LESSERLINGS

1. FISH AND FLOWER ARRANGING

On the third floor there was an aquarium. Zagreus steered. Directly between the whale shark's two blue eyes, which could see and sear and destroy everything at which they pointed, and a little below eye level, stood a fishtank torus, considerably smaller but much like the ring in which the zander Westphalia Sophocles Gaeta's group had convened, the coryphaes of Borbuck.

Inside swam fish—unusual on Venus, either on the surface or up here in the higher levels of the atmosphere. A long time ago, when the sevenfours had just begun their work, they were accompanied by swarms of pilot fish, flying cod and lion's manes, but most of these, the heirs of the ancient Atlanteans, had settled on Venus' planetary surface after a time and had become the fash and the salamanders.

Zagreus, the collapsible badger, stood before the ring-shaped tank and directed tiny robots in catching a few dozen sardines, speechless creatures—he wanted to serve them up when Fire returned from his scouting trip to the lesserling city. Watching the machines at work helped Zagreus to keep calm.

He liked fishing, he went hunting from time to time, he cooked meat no less often than the fash, Vempes, who had presumably died when the lesserlings attacked Fire's home.

We do whatever works, thought Zagreus, even when it's dangerous, even when we know the side effects and collateral damage. We breed life forms for the niches we require, creatures without the gift of speech, and we take into account the suffering we will cause, but there is no other way—back on Earth it was just like this, which is how we know that it works, that you can build an ecotecture this way.

There's no way even to calculate how wasteful we're being, compared to other conceivable solutions. Not only because we use all our runtime for practical, short-term goals, there's no way, in principle.

What am I doing, as I teach the boy what his strange destiny is to be? An answer was suggested from the archive of knowledge, the store of ancient beauty in the neo-badger's mind. He spoke many languages and in one came the words, 'Open to the world in another current, light-footed, / Things drift past you, brightly coloured, confused, / was there ever a myth that could contain all this? / Was there ever a myth here / ever a myth that / speak?'

Am I talking? What am I doing? My curse on myths, all of them and may the speaking myths at least prevail against the silent myths, for only the speaking myths help us get over our myth-making. Nothing else can.

Myths that speak, historical facts whose laws I live by, I have observed, laws mostly unknown—and I'm handing all this on to a boy, as though it were quite the right thing to do. Watch out, prince, that you're not alone, like I am, when old age strikes.

Zagreus knew that soon enough he would be the very last to remember what it had been like, up there, beyond—not on the Earth, nor the moon, that history was far too ancient for him, but in the orbital habitats round Venus, as they patiently bombarded the planet with the raw material for future life. He had been born there, on the edge of interplanetary space, on board one of the long ships whose fate had been written the day they were built, the ships that would end in one last cataclysmic flight, in ruin.

The little fishes had all been gathered now into a dip net, and a round lid shut as they were brought out from the tank. Zagreus thought, I know more than Fire ever shall about the 'why's and 'wherefore's of his destiny, yet I couldn't say where it will lead him or how it would feel to be him. Does this distance between us make me wrathful? Does anyone have the right to drag another into a fate that no one truly understands?

I should be his compass and I don't know the way to go, he thought.

At least the fish looked good, there were more than enough, Zagreus reckoned, for the boy, who was not much bigger than a house-cat back on old Earth—following the design specifications which Lasara had worked out with her geneticists so long ago, everything on Venus was rather smaller than on the home-world, the neo-badgers were hardly as big as mice, and even he, his great caged exoskeleton, massed less than a small bicycle of the late Monotonous era.

Zagreus missed his hut and his garden. He had to admit it to himself, now, that after a long and not unsatisfying life as a hermit, he had not reckoned with having to take up his role as Fire's mentor and companion on the journey of discovery.

Over time, other things had become important, for instance, re-enacting Darwin's first discoveries, teasing opuntia blossoms with a wisp of straw to imitate the action of a pollinating insect that did not exist on this planet, studying isolation and targeted migration on the smallest of scales, simulating the genetic drift . . . He had never hoped to learn anything new, but this pursuit had brought him beyond himself, given him a way of being alone, yet more than a single self, and now he had exchanged it for something much less personal. He had become active executor of the Gente estate, a task which was mostly his because whatever else she was, Lasara had also been a paranoiac—Zagreus' very existence was proof of that. He belonged to a biomechanoid series that, apart from himself and those left on the poles of Mars, was now extinct—cyborgs, built for the eventuality that it might prove impossible to settle on the near-Earth planets, that the Gente arcs might have to survive in space for a while.

The metal cage and all his other grotesqueries only served to protect the organic core from hard radiation in the vacuum, so that the genetic material did not degenerate.

Zagreus shook the fish, still twitching, from the narrow-meshed net into a large pot—their coffin, now it just needs to be sealed, he thought morbidly, and he was so tired, so damn tired.

There's not much left that I can even give the boy, he thought, but at least he has the Book.

The Book: you had to concede one thing to the lesserlings, they were the first human-descended species to have discovered a totally new approach to the concept of Holy Writ, based on the idea of the monstrous example. Unlike the true humans, earlier, with their Torah, their Gospel, their Koran and so forth, for the lesserlings, the Book was not a catalogue of righteousness and truth but a compendium of dangerous depravity. Their Book, Izquierda's transcribed conversations with the Lion Cyrus Golden, was written out as a warning, a portent and a wonder. Whenever one of their academies or city governments embarked on a course that bore any resemblance to anything discussed in the Book, that course was instantly corrected, in a sort of negative reverence, a retrognosis of Holy Writ. It was the Bad News, Satan's word. In each of the cities, an organized Inquisition oversaw the testaments. Just as Zagreus tried to make sure that it came to pass, they did their pious best to sabotage each jot and tittle.

Zagreus turned aside to the oil, the frying pan, the herbs, things he could deal with. Perhaps every creature should do for itself, he thought, what the lesserlings do as a culture—write down, or somehow mark, all that you've lived through, all that's gone wrong, to be forewarned. I should tell Fire about that. And then we can—a booming, like giant fists beating a gong, startled the badger, though he was not the nervous type, even though he had been expecting this noise for hours now, had braced for it. It meant that it was night outside and also meant that the whale's lenses had finally caught sight, at the edge of the Niobe valley, a few miles northwest of the city limits of White Tiger, of Fire's signal lamp.

He'd managed it. He'd got in and he's got out again.

'Yes, yes, at once,' Zagreus said, to no one in particular, the way old soldiers do, remembering commands and warnings issued over the long years; but the lame is condemned by her lameness, and the liar is trapped by her lies, and the coward's heart dies of its own poison.

2. ANOTHER PLAN

'So. Down the crapper. Pointless. Don't even look. That's it, then. You can take your destiny and . . .' Fire tore the bandage from his head, so that his hair immediately sprang back up into spikes where it had been swaddled down. He threw the cloth up in the air, childishly hoping that it might stick to the sevenfour's inside wall.

Zagreus creaked and groaned, every joint seeming to moan at once, and then said in a clenched voice, 'Fine, so much for the designs of the ancients. Temple torn down. Stones re-used. And I'm sure that Lasara, or whoever it was thought up the whole plan, was so very pleased with their own creative thinking, making only one condition for successfully settling in Venus: that you should find the Temple, when you came into the world, this world, that you should go there and find your destiny . . . feh, as soon as the probes and the orbitals round Earth report what our astronomers have been saying for a few years already—that there's nothing moving down there, that new conditions prevail.'

'There's new conditions prevailing on me too,' said Fire, wriggling from his constricting clothes on the edge of his berth, 'a condition of kiss my bum. I'm not doing any more, going anywhere, entering any city, until someone tells me . . .'

'We need another plan,' said Zagreus.

Fire snarled, 'Yes, that's it, make a plan, be a great light.'

The collapsible badger trundled off, furious at himself, at Fire, at the lesserlings, at Lasara.

In the galley he washed the fish and fried them, cleaned the fennel bulbs, cut them into fine slices with the knives on his fingers, chopped the green cabbage and watched while the oil heated up for him to sauté the vegetables—Tear down the Temple, then? We can't conceive the depths to which this scum will stoop.

Then he put flour into a dish—flour, that's good, this is a synthetic powder; flour, real flour, actual salt, proper sugar, we don't have those things, you do what works, with the materials to hand, it all works out in the end—dipped the fennel into the oil until it bubbled over, then stirred the slices about as they crisped.

As he was scooping them out of the pan, adding condiments, the prince came to him and, in a rare and unexpectedly intimate gesture, laid his hand on the frame, about where a biped's right shoulder would be.

'We can live like this, can't we? I mean, destiny or not. We can settle in here and ...' but Zagreus twitched what was not his shoulder, shook off the hand, sullenly served up what he had cooked and then, as Fire sat down, visibly disgruntled, and began to eat, he said, 'We can't live like this. We have no choice, the price paid for your Task was too high. Do you think that they only laid waste the valley where you lived? They've swarmed out everywhere, it's a campaign of destruction and death; the eastward slopes of Freya Montes, the Lavinia Planitia, as far as they can project their power, in low-flying war machines. They're burning the grasslands with napalm, soon they'll have a real air force and everything left living, the woods and the ponds, will be poisoned.'

Fire stopped his fork halfway and just looked at the badger. The prince, uncharacteristically, had nothing to say.

'Granted, we're out of danger ourselves. First of all there are too many sevenfours, the lesserlings would never manage to find the one sheltering us from among these huge swarms. And secondly they're still afraid—still, for the moment—of levelling their crude weapons against what functional Gente technology remains, especially the parts that ensure that this planet remains habitable ...'

'So what do we do?'

'The crucial word in your question, my boy, is "we". I shouldn't have sent you there alone. We'll go and have a look at—as you called it, the loot, the actual fabric of the Temple, which they've taken to their ... Academies, we may hope only here in this city, not in ... Ferret or in Mare. If need be, we'll steal it.'

'How will you. . . . I mean, we can disguise me, but what about ...'

'Let me worry about that. As you told me I should, I've made a plan. Eat now.'

Fire wondered at that, but complied.

While Zagreus withdrew to go over his plan and prepare it, Fire went to wash—and was surprised to see that the grime round his mouth and chin, which he had already tried to wipe away before the meal, was not grime, but as the mirror showed him now, a thicket of fast-growing stubble. Something growing on my face. Since when? He couldn't say, had no way to measure, and nevertheless, Fire thought that he knew quite well: since I stood there, on the square where the Temple had been.

3. RYUNEKE'S SERVANT

And those folk who so wanted to be humans, who lived in White Tiger, they too did whatever worked. Above all, that meant that they looted and slaughtered whatever was left of the bold designs of the Gente they hated so; the buildings were demolished and used for other buildings, the genetic material was hybridized, the various ape breeds manipulated to come as close as they could to the human genome, the sites where the geneseed had landed or dispersed were turned into agricultural nodes or sedimentation plants. The city's largest industrial park was full of folk dressed in the uniform that Fire had used as a disguise, full also of huge machinery such as the cooling motors for the ground and walls, whose gigantic fans kept the whole domed city at that low temperature which had bothered Fire so much. They used huge chunks of storage ice as their accretion material. Like the sevenfours, it had originally been an Atlantean invention.

The material reliably produced conditions in which nitrogen and methane would freeze, something like the natural climate on Triton.

The lesserlings had sawn the stuff into sheets and stored it in caverns in the cliffs, so that here and there cryovolcanoes formed, a little way out beyond the city walls, aperiodically breaking through the surface and shooting showers of hypercooled particulate matter several miles into the air. At the core of these accretions was found a very special kind of ice, packed with anabolocytes and other artificial means to preserve and repair living tissue under cold conditions. Biota from the old world had been brought, in this ice, first to the moon and then to the two new worlds.

The Academy technicians believed that they had carefully separated such storage blocks from the other ice, taking them away, blowing them up, burning them or otherwise destroying them. What was left, they thought, was safe to use in the cooling devices. Yet in many of the massive blocks that they used, fine threads of storage had survived. One of these threads had been sleeping for over a thousand years, a tiny vein, needing only a simple electrochemical command to awake and become once more the organism that it once had been, the orang-utan Sdhütz Arroyo.

Fire the prince and his friend and mentor, Zagreus the collapsible badger, were headed for the city where, as recently as three hundred Earth years before, the Temple of Isotta had stood. Seven and a half old Earth hours before they entered the city, a quarter of a mile south of the city walls, the seedform of the Fox Ryuneke Nowhere's oldest servant was hurled into the air, sealed into a ball of artificial snow and landed in a shallow puddle of bubbling mud. Very slowly, the shell began to thaw.

When at last it had dissolved, the thread instantly began to suck up minerals, free radicals, microbial carbohydrate content and other substances necessary for its rebirth, adapting them to rebuild the ape. Inferential depots opened, anchors were drawn up, markers identified, an implex made explicit, echos and outlines, my hand, my fingers, the thumb, thus and so, I take hold.

Take hold of what? Of my forgotten self, in time for the lost search, no but now, who though, or rather, on whose behalf?

4. DRIVING IN MY CAR

The wind blew onto his face, across the new fuzz on his chin, the sailcloth fluttered, and Fire laughed, it was so much fun to drive in a car through White Tiger. Especially since the car was a personal friend.

He would have loved to ask the badger how he felt, how it felt to be a pedal-driven car, whether it was such a blast for the car as well as for the driver, but firstly, Zagreus would not have heard him—it was far too noisy here on the main traffic artery of Venus' oldest city—and secondly, someone might have noticed—what's up, that bloke talking to his car, is he just barmy or is he really dangerous?

The yellow iron cranes stood at the junctions like adults surrounded by a swarm of children at play. Turn right, turn left, hand-eye coordination, arms and legs held just so, watch the signals, merge—it was magnificent, Fire was almost embarrassed to recall how silly he had found it all, last time, when he was only watching.

Before they came, he had refused to use a traffic training simulator for longer than half an hour at a time—he really wanted to learn *in vivo*, even though it had been simple enough for the simulator to reconstruct White Tiger's street plan, based on the recordings made by his microcamera implant last time.

Zagreus had agreed at last, perhaps because he too was curious. 'I only fear that they might have some kind of central surveillance of traffic patterns, motion detector hook-ups, and if we just drive about aimlessly for too long . . .'

'Not aimlessly,' Fire objected. 'Most of all, we'll be looking for escape routes!'

'Worse, then. They'll spot that too. In any case, if they notice that we have an erratic course, if we draw any attention to ourselves . . .'

'Listen, Zagreus. It was your idea to be car and driver . . . there's no way we can be inconspicuous, it's not like being a pedestrian.'

'Right then.' Agreement.

They had agreed that Fire would cruise the town centre for two or three hours, then drive to the Academy, meaning to its public area, the gigantic mediatheque, partly a museum, partly filled with galleries and cabinets closed to public view. Here, the two spies hoped to find the treasures that they had come for.

Keep clear of the red line in the middle of the street. That held for the ring roads too, all the upslopes and down and for the high bridges. Doubtless, the regulation was a memory of ancient Borbruck—this city's ribs were pre-stressed concrete box girders, mostly gently curving, cantilevered between pairs of V-shaped supports. As Fire rode upon them he felt (hoping that this was an illusion) that the roadways were rocking slightly, swinging him gently along. Making various gestures, sometimes using the raw-throated horn (when Zagreus redesigned himself as a pedal-car, he really had thought of everything, every feature of the cars that had struck Fire as so ridiculous last time), not giving an inch to the aggressive fellow drivers who tried to cut him up, always watching the tall yellow cranes and their signal lamps, really, it wasn't difficult.

Alas, there were some vulgar attempts to rebuild ancient splendours (they had copied the Amastrianon and the Iron Gate, not the benzene ring, but the forum and the hippodrome, the general division of their city into sectors, they'd even taken over the shape of Prosphorianos harbour for one of their administrative buildings, totally pointless since they had no access to river, sea or ocean). However, if you kept a sharp eye out and an open mind, you could recognize how the architects had used one or two principles that really weren't that daft—may be, thought Fire, they think they've built a city fit for humans here, and really, what else would they want?

They were implacably opposed, for instance, to any kind of unpredictable social force and thus built smooth, featureless facades. Proudly generalizing, highhanded even, they had reduced all human needs to the sheerly monumental, had made themselves everlasting, in an architecture that conquered the horizon, had designed standardized residential units that could be stacked up inside the huge grey boxes with no trouble. The distance from ground to roof would have put even the skyscrapers of sunken New York into the shade; they stretched up into the skies or away into the distance, beyond the limits of vision, but the structures were uniform in every direction, arranged in a city plan that might have been devised by a grandmaster: the gods in this city prized above all the modular, the rectilinear, the expedient, the efficient. Grids, squares, intersections, layer upon layer in rhythm, an occasional curve here or there, and Fire began to speculate how you might even improve on this. Perhaps one day they would lift their city clear of the ground, on gigantic titanium struts, so that there would be more variety in there, why not for instance modular units in moving labyrinths of ladders, for the more adventurous resident, well shielded above and below, armoured even . . .

Fire was thrown back in his seat so hard that his joints cracked and the loose bandage dropped onto his face. The prince was falling, no flying—what was happening? The car creaked and strained, left and right, the others blared their horns, above him and behind, a crescendo. Fire felt that, once again, his body had reacted more quickly and more smartly than he had himself; his legs were pedalling furiously, his arms braced against the frame which he clutched hard in each hand (the furry part of his friend's body, the part that could not be seen from outside, was breathing hectically behind his seat). Everything was swaying, the traffic below was frozen in its tracks, the street tilted—the prince realized that it must have been one of the cranes, picking him up, that is, picking up his car, with him inside it, hoisting him up and away from the onrush of shunting, blaring traffic (actually quite slow at this point)—but why?

Twisting about, the wind, the dizzying swing—they were headed for a balustrade, a balcony above a large glass door on the other side of the junction. A group of lesserlings stood there, dressed in gleaming black—was that leather? They wore protective goggles covering their eyes and nose. They were waving white staves, or bags, not quite clear yet, but the crane hurtled Fire down towards them as though he'd been shot out on a giant metal spring or by the explosion of a chemical powder. His heart racing, his breath gasping, Fire realized that there was nothing he could do—even when the tanks had been firing at him, as he dashed and dodged across the open plain, he had never been as utterly exposed to his enemies as he was now, now they'd hoisted him up high over the street. If he jumped out, he'd break every bone, and besides, if he did that, he would leave Zagreus in the lurch—could he even see what was happening? He had to be able to, even if he dared not extend his eyestalks beyond the frame. The prince thought he heard pain and the urge to escape, in the tortured creaking of metal, the urge to run, or roll, away.

Fire shook his head and then jerked it backwards so that his other eye was free. The bandage was already crooked and there was clearly no point trying to disguise his pointed ears. He didn't manage to shake off the disguise entirely, so next he leant his head against the bar right by his head and rubbed it. At last the rags came free and fluttered, in tatters, from his head, across the street, over the bridge. The crane's pincers opened abruptly and Fire and Zagreus were dropped two yards, with a crash. Straightaway strong hands grasped Fire and pulled him, struggling feebly, from his counterfeit car.

They wrenched his hands together behind his back by the wrists and snapped a metal shackle round them; the same at his ankles. Then they laid him on the floor and brought long sticks—were they probes—and jabbed him with them till he screamed. There were, maybe, ten lesserlings; three of them held tube lamps, blue-white light, something like the light that the whale shark had shot at the tanks, and they played it across the car, the badger, his disguised cyborg friend. He flared with light; Fire saw it from the corner of his eye, from beneath twitching lids, for they were kicking at him now, one eye was already swollen shut, the other filling with blood. He saw his friend curl up in the crackling St Elmo's fire and he heard him scream and then heard nothing but the thudding and booming in his ears.

And then the tumult and the tremors, the rage, the fear and regret fell in shards round Fire and upon his head, and gathered within, at the focus of his skull, behind his brow, and he turned and curled up like an embryo. What's happened, am I no longer invulnerable, can't I shrink my limbs and vanish, they're tearing off my shirt, can't I burn them with the hairs on my back, why can't I read their thoughts, they're hurting me, why couldn't I read last time I was here in this city, what's wrong with their thoughts, their feelings, their images of me, don't they see me, this isn't so, am I dreaming, but if I am, why does it hurt so?

5. THE APE ESCAPES

Dusty with heat, cloyed with marsh gas.

His back bent, his feet were clumping, clumsy, clogged, as though melted together and fused. His skin, his hair devoured the mud round him and turned it into fat, twitching like jellyfish. The whole thing grew muscles, *nolens volens*. It stretched, it lengthened, it hurt like hell.

'Go over the sea to America, come back again, watch the slaughtering monsters invade, get yourself shot to the moon and shot into orbit round Venus; let yourself be frozen for a few centuries, travel the world, meet interesting people, that's the life for a lad like you, you'll grow and you'll learn.' So the arch-villain had told him, the oldest devil of them all.

Sdhütz spat and there was blood, Sdhütz stood bent double beside the jiggling, gelatinous mess, red as a wound, that had fallen away as he fought clear of it, placental material, the afternoon tea of eternity.

'I wish I could . . . break off my . . . contract with the old bastard,' spoke the unformed mouth, but the brain behind the thought knew too well that the contract would last for the ages of ages, for as long as Sdhütz still was Sdhütz. Something hairy, cold shivers from within, his system slowly finding its way back, the cardiovascular stutter and judder and then it's ticking over nicely. On his feet: nothing he'd like less, but it has to be done, it will be done. A violet sky. Look at that. A new world.

A mighty revelation, an enormous weariness. This rebirth began and he was drained, disgusted. Whatever else you could say for it, Sdhütz bared his teeth, chewed at the inside of his cheek, sucked on nothing at all, rattled breath through his throat and thought, really, one thing's for sure, it's a good beginning.

'Hey there? Who is that? Badger? Fire?' The voice was unsure, since the fash could only see a smear of orange hair. The fash was called Vempes, and Fire, had he been here, would have been overjoyed to see him again—together with three other fash, a couple of barracuda, walking wounded, and various salamander. Fash had not only escaped from the inferno the lesserlings had made of the fortress by the volcano, he had even joined this little caravan and set out to cross Niobe and reach the Twin Mountains, where the sevenfours flew through the ionosphere in their greatest numbers. He had set out on the journey in the not unfounded hope of being rescued by the sevenfours so that he could make a new home beyond the rift valley where the greatest of the three cities stood. He wanted to seed a new ecotecture and help it grow.

They had travelled at night and hidden, as much as they could, by day and now they had arrived at the puddle where Sdhütz Arroyo was coming, if not to himself, to someone. But something had gone wrong.

'Fire?' The others, gesticulating and murmuring their disquiet, tried to hold Vempes back, but the fash, a scientist and rationalist to the bone, was simply too curious, stilting forward a pace or two on his muscular ostrich-legs towards the slimy, bristling confusion of hair and muscles, mouth, teeth and world-weary eyes. 'Who . . . are you, if you please? Can we help? Are those . . . are you in trouble?'

'Losh!' said the thing that was supposed to become an orang-utan and felt, in the muck, worse than ever in his life. It sloshed and slopped. It came closer. It looked at the fash. It felt sorry for him. Why? Because of cruel necessity and because we do whatever works.

The fash didn't even have time to regret his meddling, it happened so quickly, the thing leapt up on its haunches and pounced. The envoy of an age long gone, a misgrown thing, engulfed the poor fool. It swallowed him whole, so that it could grow.

The others didn't fare much better, their caution in vain.

Of course, they ran, then, in different directions even and of course, they screamed and ran about and shouted to warn the rest of the scattered caravan. But it didn't help, the hungry thing's legs bounded too swift and strong, its appetite was too great. Evolution: we do what works and take what we can get.

6. IMPRISONMENT

'You wanted to see the museum, spy out the Academy? Here is the museum. This is the Academy.'

Fire knew that voice. He was in a lot of pain, his ribs, his back, his temples, the leaden bonds upon his wrists and ankles, all hurt, but most of all his pride was wounded. When he opened his one good eye, he saw straightaway that he was stretched out on some kind of frame, as though he were a canvas, or an animal hide waiting to be scraped and tanned. He also saw that he was naked, not as he used to be earlier, among friends, his furry friends, but as a sign of defeat, that they had taken from him what they, in their barbarian way, considered central to identity, his clothing.

'Look at me when I'm talking to you.' Against his will, Fire had to turn his head as a meaty hand grabbing his chin directed it. The light from the ceiling was as bright as daylight; he recognized, standing in front of him, Preisnitel, who had met him on his stroll. If it hadn't been so obvious, so predictable, Fire could have laughed. He grunted, 'Where's Pyretta? Your daughter? Have you knocked her up yet?' Preisnitel spat on his face and grinned. Two thugs standing behind him also seemed to find it funny.

'And Zagreus. Where is Zagreus?'

'He means the brassneck. The cyborg,' one of the heavies told Preisnitel, who had wrinkled his brow. 'Ah,' he said, 'your vehicle,' and he narrowed his little eyes in a meaningful wink, peering at something unguessable. Once again Fire tried to catch some thought, something that his interlocutor knew, or wanted, or was. Nothing. Silent as the grave.

Preisnitel said, 'We dismantled him and incinerated it. Not a spark left of him. You're on your own and you should realize what that . . . fuck!' he screamed out, spitting with rage, since Fire had bitten down with all his strength onto two of the stubby little fingers. Blows and kicks followed, his chains were tightened.

Once the general rage had run its course, they threw him into a cold and dark room 'to cool off'—did that mean him, or them, those who were hitting him? Fire fumbled his way round the floor with swollen hands, feeling only the cold, sharper and more piercing than outside, in the traffic, on the bridge, beneath the cranes and towers.

He had a lot of time to reflect before they shone a torch into his cell and dragged him out into the harsh light, where they asked a number of questions.

His thoughts were very shallow, very small, almost zero-dimensional. It was as though this city killed all ideas, as though here it was no longer possible (necessary?) to form and frame a thought.

'Who are you?'—holding his head down in icy water.

'Where do you come from?'—a shock of current, electrodes on his nipples, his testicles, his arms and legs, beaten green and blue.

'Where were you headed?'—meaningless questions, as the torturers themselves admitted. 'We know anyway,' Preisnitel said, 'who you are and what you want and where you come from. We know far more than you do—we know about the partials and the seedlings, about inferential layering of many memories into one head. We simply want you to realize all this and then we can talk.'

Talk—they made the offer with a curious, courteous leniency and after every seventh or eighth excruciating act, Preisnitel clearly found some bizarre pleasure in presenting himself as a basically friendly and approachable chap, fond of conversation and loath to use violence. Fire didn't know what to say to all this. Now and again, he tried laughing, or weeping. Once he spat out one of his teeth at Preisnitel's feet, shod in beautiful boots, much more elegant and less clodhopping than those Zagreus had persuaded the prince to wear as part of his ineffectual disguise.

Now and again, they gave him something to eat—dry knots that might have been dumplings, tasting of sand and soap; lumpy, sour sauces, stagnant water; no bread, no herbs, nothing that he would have chosen as food if his wishes had counted for anything. He could chew at it, he could suck between his burst and swollen lips, he could swallow, whether it gave him diarrhoea, or not.

The lesserlings showed him bits of equipment. 'This is a pick-up head, from your Temple.'

'What does it read?'

'Where's the software, in your head?'

This is a speculum, this is a spring, this, a whatnot.

Glowing balls, the blue-and-yellow striped bodies of dead bees, bunches of flowers, powder, ceremonial eyeglasses, six-armed candelabra, fragments of broken frescoes, he knew none of it, he recognized all of it, there was nothing that he could say. How could he explain that he felt that he knew, but didn't have the words to explain to his interrogators, not in a way that they could understand, that would have satisfied them, so that they would let him go?

They sat him down, laid him upon a bench and chained him down, they hung him from the ceiling and plunged him into open pipes, they showed him a complicated mechanical clock that they called psappha, telling him to alter its tick with his mind. Once they had got to work on him with pincers and willow rods, that actually happened, but it didn't help—they simply became more curious and brought out more apparatus, one was called dmaathen, one komboi, one cassandra and one oopha, one okho, one persephassa, and all of them had cogwheels and springs, tensors, torque, escapements, he had to tip and tilt and push at them, they set up weak electric fields, refracted light through prisms, glass domes lit up, and every one of these experiments succeeded in some meaningless way. Fire listened uncomprehendingly while Preisnitel and the other goondas whispered to one another at length or to pallid, old lesserlings in different uniforms, green lab-coats, perhaps Academicians.

Not one thought that could be eavesdropped, no purpose in the whole thing, that he could tell.

Nothing but pain and moronic concentration exercises, cogwheels turning, filaments glowing, cards flipping, keys and levers up or down, then more beatings, hosing down with ice-cold water, shocks, starvation, hours on end spent penned into round tanks lit with a glaring light from some unknown source, filled with wan globes—in the end, Fire came to think that this must be like imprisonment inside an atom, the microcosm of Hell, and sometimes they tilted, turned, threw him this way and that in the searing light, so that he collected new injuries, coloured patches blossoming beneath his skin, his bones singing. Once, in the mirror-smooth plastic shell of one of the devices that he had to strain at teleki-netically (was it Okho or Akrata?) he caught sight of his face, hardly recogniza-ble—the stubbled growth on his chin and upper lip had become a full beard, darker than the hair on his head, gleaming, like a badger pelt. He thought of Zagreus and his friends at home and the fact that none of them, nothing was left—not his home, not his companions or teachers.

At last, in the utter darkness, in the cell where he had first been held, he heard a small voice, gentle, sad, mildly accusing, perhaps accusing him. 'Why do you want so many people to die? Why don't you help the humans here, in White Tiger? Aren't you their cousin, with arms and legs? Why this hatred, why the insistence on plunging two worlds into a senseless war? Why do you want to destroy what we're trying to do here? Why meddle with the technology in the Temple, to pro-voke the Ceramicans, who have never done anything to us? Why should you care about scores settled so long ago, vendettas that have died away?'

Fire didn't know what the voice was talking about and wanted to say so, but he was drained and battered. He felt a hand, cool and soft, laid on his fevered brow. Here at last were thoughts that he could feel, even if he could not understand them—laws that the speaker of this voice had been born to observe. 'Cloning is permitted for population growth, but the ideal remains that the female embrace her destiny of continuing the family line with children, and the male take up his duty of fathering them. This dual duty, which man and woman share, is holy, for it is not spoken of in the *Conversations with the Lion*. Which crime is to be called the worst—murdering an Academician of the fourth grade or higher, drinking spirits, seducing the woman of a direct superior? A court of the Academy shall follow the Code that is written and condemn such criminals to death or to other corporal punishment. One who has seduced the woman of his direct superior shall be tattooed on the forehead with an image of the female pudenda, as a sign of shame, the drinker of spirits shall be tattooed with the picture of a still, the murderer of an academician of the fourth grade or higher shall be tattooed with the sign of a headless body.'

Although he could not see her and only heard the voice as a low murmur, he knew, before he slipped again into unconsciousness, who this was, who they had sent into his cell: Pyretta, the daughter and spouse of the torturer-in-chief. The greatest wonder, he began to realize as he lost focus and went under, was that he could hear her think, he could feel her thoughts and all that she thought or felt was that she was sorry for him.

7. SDHÜTZ ENRAGED

The process took some time, not least because Nature first had to overcome her astonishment and disgust; never before now had she even dreamt of building an ape, poor old thing, from mud and grunge and light on the planetary surface of Venus.

In any properly run world, a naturally occurring animal of the sort that Sdhütz Arroyo was, would have spent its time eating, sleeping and fornicating in the tree canopy. In stark contrast, Ryuneke Nowhere's valet, if brought back to life according to plan, would have been charged with observing the course of political and economic events and the upheavals thereof. Now, however, nothing was running properly or going according to plan, since the awakening monster lacked an important, a crucial check on its growth. The brakes had failed, thanks to radiation damage caused by an infinitesimal subatomic particle in a cosmic-ray shower. So it grew, it gathered, it shook the ground, it split and gyred and in the process broke everything, including laws of physics, such as the cube-square rule, well known to the Gente from the heroic days of their engineering and biotech. Under this law, when an object undergoes a proportional increase in size, its new volume is proportional to the cube of the multiplier and its new surface area is proportional to the square of the multiplier—among other implications, this means that living beings, beyond a certain limit in size, will collapse under their own weight, since the increase in mass exceeds the increase in muscle power (gigantism). Sdhütz Arroyo's reincarnation, failure though it was, did not collapse under its own weight.

This was not at all due to the weak gravity on Venus, only ninety per cent of Earth equivalence. It was, rather, down to the fact that the new ape had been given, for safety's sake, a dose of the same antigravity technology that kept the sevenfours soaring and flying. The bigger and stronger he got, the higher his backside rose up into the seething skies.

Thunder and lightning.

The orang-utan, increasingly unhappy with his lot, saw the city of White Tiger trundling towards him from the horizon, since he was trotting towards it. He didn't much care for it. He decided to express his displeasure as soon as he could.

8. THAT'S NOT AN ANSWER, IT'S ANOTHER QUESTION

When Fire noticed the physiological changes taking place in his body, at first he was ready to put them down as the first effects of his imprisonment—they had after all stretched him on the rack to test the limits of his ability to grow or shrink his own limbs. Weren't the swellings, at his heart, and next to it, marks left by the beatings, the cold drenchings, the hot iron, and hadn't his skeleton been beaten and abused, which is why it was now widening at the pelvis? The hairs of his beard, which had just begun to grow, were now falling out again, and something in his throat shrank and tugged, it began to feel smoother.

He tried speaking a few words, here in the dreadful dark, perhaps they were listening to him. 'I'll do what you want. I want to,'—how had they called it, ah yes—'cooperate, I want to . . . help the cause of peace . . . no more war . . . no more provocation . . . I am . . . I was suborned, misled . . . I'll answer all your questions, if you only . . . ask them . . . so that I can understand. You give me too much credit, I don't know as much as you think.'

The door really opened.

Preisnitel, Pyretta and a couple of others came in. The woman gave him something to drink, helped him sit up, stroked her fragrant hand across his brow, while he wondered at the sound his voice had made: higher, softer, not what he had expected, and when he swallowed, and clutched at his throat, coughing and hacking to get hold of himself once more, he felt that his Adam's apple had vanished. The cartilage had shrivelled, the vocal chords had shrunk, how could that be? Fire had no time to think about this; they brought him, so weak that he had to be propped up between two of the bully-boys, into more pleasant quarters, they washed him, dressed him, gave him good food, fruits that he didn't recognize, a flatbread strewn with currants; and to his shame and rage, he couldn't keep down what he ate.

He was allowed to sleep. At breakfast, eating worked rather better.

He stood by the window at the back, in a mild flood of daylight filtered to a nicety by the beautiful windowpanes, and looked at the Academy's courtyard and recognized that here in White Tiger there were, in fact, some glorious buildings—'courtyard' was a ridiculous understatement, it was a city within the city, with tall glass residential towers for the elite, sheathed in glass, curved and twisted in biological shapes, there were laboratories and libraries, not blocky, blank edifices like the buildings in the Academy's outward ramparts but made up of modular bubbles, under many-angled cowls bejewelled with solar collectors, overgrown with grass. Fire, remembering his lessons with the fash, recognized that many of these buildings imitated Old Earth molluscs: the tall towers were the upright *Cerithia*, others were *Rhinoclavis* or *Terebralia*, and a snail-like structure was a mollusc that, appropriately enough, had been called *Architectonica nobilis*.

Dotted here and there between these splendours, as though placed by the gentle hand of a God who loves both reason and art, were open auditoria, plazas, harmonious gardens and streams and bridges, little lakes, a theatre like that in Epidaurus . . . Could the folk who lived in such pleasant parkland really be evil?

Fire bit into an apple, probably from one of the trees down below, and felt a gratitude that sickened him a little.

They had even allowed him to have a little bath, tiled sky blue, and his own toilet—if he had had any idea of what surrender might achieve, he would have given up many weeks back what he didn't have anyway: his say in the matter.

His penis had shrunken and shrivelled, he could hardly even pee with it. His testes, he remarked rather disinterestedly, had withdrawn some way upwards into the abdomen—was this a result of imprisonment, or was something else happening? He felt the little mounds upon his ribcage, symmetrical, apple-shaped, covered with smooth, taut, milky skin, veined with the finest blue—did they do this, or did I do it myself, or is something else going on?

In the new interrogation room, his chair was admittedly not upholstered but it was ergonomic and comfortable and on the table next to him a cup of coffee was set; across from him sat Pyretta, smiling after sleep.

'Good then,'—she set the Book down on the table, well-thumbed, crinkled—it was his personal copy—'you've asked for some easier questions. Do you know what inferentialism is?'

'Yes. It's the late Gente theory of consciousness. Izquierda developed it, building on work from as long ago as the Monotony.'

'And what does it teach, this theory?'

'It develops . . . the thought that a sememe—a mathematical symbol, a word—derives its meaning not from reference to an object, or from the intentions of the person who uses it, but from its role as a link in an inferential chain. A word means something, or a sentence likewise, because the word or sentence is the premise or conclusion or vehicle of an inference, a calculation.'

'Quite right,' Pyretta nodded and smiled. 'And do you know how the theory applies to the seedlings? How it was possible that a consciousness . . . a person . . . that is, a semantic bundle with its own freedom of action . . . could switch substrate—someone who had been a brain could become a computer, or another brain, or,'—she winked (did I really see that, did she wink?)—'a liquid and, nevertheless, retain their identity.'

'That's all in Izquierda's *Conversations with the Lion*, isn't it?' he replied.

'A question isn't an answer, my friend.' She used the words, still smiling, to remind him that he was at her mercy—a threat.

'They . . . it says that they were hesitant at first, they thought that this sort of transfer was a simulation at best . . . that the results were machines, or brains, that mistakenly believed they were such-and-such person without actually being them. But then . . . then Lasara's work in attribal accidence . . . her . . . her contribution to Gente scholarship . . . the switching of bodies, gender, species, even taxa . . . laid bare the actual function of cognitive drives such as perception, memory and testimony, the three drives underlying not only . . . cognition, but individuality too. That was the end of all . . .'

'One moment. Identity: what does that even mean, technically?'

'Errm . . . who am I, if I'm not that which I want, to which I can bear witness, or which I remember? It was believed that these three functions weren't inferential. In fact, it was only a matter of the difference between truth and probability, the degree to which you could depend upon it. Since these three drives also . . . form the premises for certain conclusions, once they actually apply. If testimony is false and perception deceives us, or memory plays us tricks . . .'

Pyretta raised her right hand, telling him to be quiet, and listened to something relayed to her via the earbud in her left ear.

She spoke into a small microphone on her mouthpiece. 'He . . . where? And from . . . yes, I know, Niobe has none of our . . . ah. Ah, fine. Yes.' She shook her head, wrinkling her brow. 'Yes, right, I'll ask him. Yes, what else? Quite. Straightaway.'

She looked at Fire in silence, while breath went in and out, oppressive.

He knew that she was suddenly afraid and that no one was speaking into her earpiece now, but he did not know what she had heard that had frightened her—since the moment in the dungeon, when she had touched him so unexpectedly, he had not been able to read her thoughts clearly.

She breathed out once more, as though defeated, and then, raising her eyebrows as though she herself could hardly believe what she was asking, she said, 'What do you know about a giant red ape?'

fourth movement

MAKE IT NEW

(FINALE)

Cy: Look straight into the sun. Your eyes can do that, as can mine. People's eyes . . . human eyes, earlier, couldn't manage it.

Iz: I know what you mean. Fundamentally, the humans never suspected what the sun really is.

Cy: There were a lot of things they didn't . . . it was all so murky, like a twilight, for them, for . . . us. I was also human.

Iz: I remember, even if I wasn't there. I saw you for the first time much later, in Hamburg, on the rubble, glowing, with ashes in your mane.

Cy: We freed apes from the laboratories. It was the best of times, the most . . . righteous. Not because of any guff about ethics, we had nothing against science as such, but because . . . these experiments were such a total waste of time—they were showing chimpanzees videos of humans solving problems, puzzles and so forth; then set them behavioural tasks to see whether they'd understood what they'd been shown. And because they performed so well, the humans thought that they'd been . . . analyzing the mental processes of the human brain, that they had what was called a model back then, a theory of mind. And all the while the humans themselves had no such thing, at least none that the apes could have taken as a model for their behaviour, a standard. It was a long time ago.

Iz: Mindreading across species. Back then, one blind alley among many: today . . .

Cy: Today . . . look into the sun. Look up to the skies.

Iz: The sky is full of light.

Cy: Yes, do you see it? Everything that seems dark is . . . the whole black expanse is really white, once you believe. The age of the Three Cities is coming to an end, but still I am the king. I can take away your doubts, all of you. There will be a better world, and a twilight more lovely, more true.

Iz: You never looked better than with the ashes in your wild hair. Never more like a king.

Cy: The cities will burn. The skies will glow more brightly. Ashes will rain down once more.

Iz: The sun . . . is . . . swimming, the light is water.

Cy: The light is water, indeed, and the water is light. That's our theory of mind.

From the *Conversations with the Lion*, VIII/21

XV
BEFORE LEAVING

1. FRAU SPÄTH'S FANFARE

'Why have you come? What do you want?'

The red lizard had learnt this approach in politics—begin from the most hostile position possible, so that you can smooth things over afterwards. The naked woman with the 'W' pendant round her neck was sitting on the sill of the open window, as though readying herself to jump out. She smiled guilefully and stirred with her index finger the freshly brewed hot coffee in the green cup (my best china, she's helping herself, just as if everything belonged to her, thought Padmasambhava, more impressed than riled), and she spoke placidly, as though stifling a yawn, 'To teach you what you need to know. Then send you off on your journey.'

Her finger in the coffee, no scalds or burn—that's as much as to tell me that she's not human, even if she looks it. Perhaps she's even less human than I am, than anyone here, than anything on this planet. Padmasambhava snorted as though to give up the ghost through her nostrils, and snapped at her long-awaited guest, 'I know everything that I need to know! And I'm going on no journey for the moment. I came back here to creep into my room and taste every drop of the journey I've just made from the limelight to—whatjamacallit? Derision.' The coffee, she thought as she spoke, she's not drinking it. It's steaming, hot brewed, her finger's fine, but maybe this woman is not so heatproof on the inside (her throat, her belly). Or is there some other reason she's not drinking it down? Never mind, I'll send her packing. 'You've got the wrong address. Wrong house, wrong person, wrong moment.'

'Puh,' a sound that meant nothing, and then a fanfare, of six thousand notes, ultradense accretion of sound, its geometry incomprehensible to any organic brain, bypassing the ears and the spintronic system, sent directly into Padmasambhava's auditory centre, so that the red lizard collapsed under the onslaught of sensory data, sat down on her backside and gaped open-mouthed at the woman who had transmitted it. It took Padmasambhava five minutes to get her breath back into its rhythm, and to find the beat of her own pulse. Then her chin felt like the bulging windchest of an organ carved from damp soap, her pelvis felt like a thrumming glass harmonica. She looked from somewhere deep within herself at the world outside, turned upside down, it even felt good in some dreadful way, or hurt her deliciously. Padmasambhava gulped, was afraid, was glad.

She breathed in, out, in out in out. Then she felt her forehead and realized that she was sweating in rivulets, her scalp, her temples, her cheeks. A reptile sweating? What was this? It dripped from her chin, ran down into her collar. The wings on her shoulders twitched, wanting to unfold, which would be utterly pointless here indoors—they strained for their full span, urgent to escape.

'What . . . did you do to me?' she asked the composer.

'Oh, music. Something you still have to learn. First you learn that, then you learn to dance.'

Padmasambhava shook her head. 'All those . . . hell's handbells . . . you really . . . I don't know. I had no idea.'

'Oh well,' Cordula Späth shrugged her shoulders and put the coffee cup down on the table (what, the table? Why was she sitting on the lizard's right, now, on the metal stool, instead of on the left, in the window? And why was it dark outside and why was the window closed? What had happened, in the five minutes, the twelve hours, the two years since Padmasambhava came through the door?). The composer went to her, discombobulated as she was, and helped her to her feet.

'That wasn't really fair of me, given that you had no idea. If someone really knew nothing about music, about the old arts, the new arts, the timeless arts, then I wouldn't have hit them . . . her . . . him . . . I see you're well underway with your transformation, as it happens . . . whatever, anyway, my little demonstration wouldn't have had such an effect on someone who really had no idea. Credit where it's due, pi pi pa po.' She took the lizard in her arms, gave her some body heat, held her tight until she stopped shivering.

While Padmasambhava was still busy trying to understand the warm fuzzies of gratitude tumbling round inside her, the coffee piped up. 'Hallo? Ladies? Am I simply to be left sitting here, out of the picture, ignored? Typical women: you pay for their fun, they suck you dry and then dump you in a cup and put you to one side. What am I, a joke? Or am I the one you prayed for, prayed to, even, as though I were a God or a priest who knows the right sacrifice at the right time, who sets aside treasures for the victim of the sacrifice, the real chauffeur to the other gods, the lightbringer in darkness, the universal solvent, the self-igniter, wreathed in flame . . .'

'Oh, shut it, Ryu,' the composer grunted, 'You'll cock up all our confidence-building measures with your brabble.'

Padmasambhava didn't shake her arms from round her, but she did look over her shoulder at the blackness within the coffee cup. 'Ryuneke Nowhere? Is he here? After a thousand . . . more than a thousand years?'

Cordula Späth led her to the table, helped her into a scarlet seat that dutifully moulded itself to her contours and said conversationally, 'Well, they're all here, as long as your definition of "here" fits. Presence is simply a temporal problem and not a very complicated one at that.'

'It's a problem of integrity,' the coffee snarled, 'I mean, most of them, apart from Cola and me, forgot who they were a long time back, they've split off into partials or they've integrated several personalities into one—what can you do, a thousand years of migration will fray even the most tightly woven . . .'

'And history. Don't forget,' the composer smiled apologetically, 'that at least here on Mars, history is underway again, has been for a generation or two. For long-term personal integrity, that's more dangerous than even the longest stretch of empty time.'

'You should know. I kept pace longest, in any case—go with the flow, that's the secret. Most folk's concerns don't change much, whether they're humans or Gente, Aristoi, lesserlings, badgers old or new, they all worry about their solvency, natch!' Smugness seeped into the fox's nasal drone, while a tiny cloud formed, clearly visible, above the cup, and drizzled downwards. It was raining from cloud to coffee.

Raining into himself, what is that?

Padmasambhava struggled to contain a laugh, knowing that if she let it out it would be a shriek. Instead, she forced herself to do what she had always preached in politics—she channelled her confusion and perturbation productively, asking Cordula Späth, 'Tell me. What do you mean by the . . . definition of "here"?'

'She's got guts,' cackled the coffee, and Cordula Späth replied, 'Space. Time. The two most fundamental lessons, aren't they? Causality, the mortar of the universe, is just a third in their sequence. Cause and effect—how the whole influences the individual and vice versa—you were getting close in your speech beneath the tree. If it could still speak—if she—tch, Livienda made a conscious choice to forget speech and language. I don't blame her. These things happen. She's happy, I think.

Her children are alive, her seed prospereth. But the dynamic of individual and history is rather like gravity, you see, spacetime tells matter how to move and matter tells spacetime how to bend and twist. The collective and yourself; lineage and yourself; the future and yourself—you were floundering a bit, in your speech, but what you wanted to say is that these are reciprocal relationships, there's nothing unilateral about it; I mean, looking at it logically, you can just as easily say that the Messiah died for our sins as you can say that we commit our sins out of our desperation at His sacrifice. Logically—not morally.'

'Pardon me, but I really don't follow you at all. Nice that you know what I wanted to say, though. Even if I don't actually recognize it when you tell me.'

'You will, don't worry.'

Don't worry? It sounded more like: you'll have to.

2. FIRST INDUCTION

There were lines in space and lines in time.

Sometimes, they were pulses from oscilloscopes, sometimes, marks on notepaper, and always, there was a hook to it—'What you heard on the first day, what bowled you over, was the complete works of Gustav Mahler, collapsed into a femtosecond. The ancients called this the *nunc stans*—the given moment, in its entirety. I wanted to show you how I exist. So you had to get to know the first of the two poles I'm stretched between. The other pole is, that it's not only time but space as well which can be collapsed this way—down to a tiny sphere, with the Planck length as its diameter. Macromusic and micromusic. Listen to this!'—and always a hook, to draw her through the consonance and dissonance of many voices, to organize the contrapuntal progression, beneath the earth, above the clouds, leaping from one orbital station to the next ('It looks like the belly of a whale in here, if the belly were lit up,' said Padmasambhava, and Cordula nodded, 'And you don't even know how right you are and how that confirms everything I've taught you about non-local holographic memory and about resonance').

Plains, spheres, Klein bottles, one thousand thousand topographies and always hooks and eyes as well: 'A camel through the eye of a needle, now that was one of the smartest topographical images ever,' and Padmasambhava became the camel and Cordula Späth became the needle's eye, and then the scene flipped about ('Involution, make sure to keep your eye on a couple of reference points in the grid, so you don't feel sick,' warned Cordula), Padmasambhava became the needle's eye and the composer was the camel. 'You see, whether I'm the person in the room or I'm the room round the person is simply a matter of emphasis—just as if I count the stresses or the unstressed syllables in scansion, or from one general pause to the next in a . . . look, that's where the twistor equations come into it.' The lizard often wondered what kind of processors the composer was using, that she could run all this thought. Her own spintronics generally ran at about six per cent capacity. If she was running some large computations in parallel and consulting the Book of Life at the same time, it might run as high as twenty per cent. Now that she had to work through Frau Späth's set exercises, she was nearly running out of spin capacity.

They were relaxing in a bubbling fountain below the Museum for Gente History in Citadel V when the lizard finally asked straight out, 'What are you working with? What's your substrate, what kind of processors are those that last for thousands of years? Is that actually your original brain, teaching me to wriggle myself into multidimensional knots?'

'Okay,' said the composer. 'I notice that you're not really listening, kiddo. Who are you, even? Who is it wants to know what you've just asked me? Close your eyes. Listen to . . . how did they use to say it? Listen within.'

Since the pupil–teacher relationship demanded it, Padmasambhava did what she was told and saw herself hooked to the floral spur of a touch-me-not, or growing as a forest on the river bank, heard a rustling high in the branches (weren't those Livienda's leaves, across in the other citadel?), saw herself as a lantern spider, glowing gold, climbing between the bell-mouthed blossom, searching out ways to compromise the data she had spun into her webs, saw herself as the zander, drawing up his catalogues of permitted gamete pairings and snapping at a worm, which hung on a hook, which was the hook, and always that hook, which hooked her in, seduced by the lures of metonymy, heard out, seen through, fish in a tank who can't see the glass, get me out of this torus, give me a chance, bring me to land, into the trees, the Amazon jungle, up in the clouds, cutting the gas to ribbons, rattling at identity, 'Give me the world, I want to . . .' what? What was the word—know it? See it? Hear it? Be it?

'I am . . . am I all those?' asked Padmasambhava in astonishment and looked down at herself—certainly she was no longer who she used to be. 'How . . . what happened, even?' for he understood, new-born as he was, far too late that he shouldn't even have been able to shut his eyes, no eyelids, after all—he, she, no, who?

'You see.' Cordula raised her eyebrows in amusement, as the newborn fell back into the warm water and simply drifted, exhausted, as though he had just climbed a sheer cliff. 'Now you're beginning to understand what it is, music.'

'A . . . a means to build something, isn't it?'

'Quite. But what?'

'Me.'

'Right again. You, as a memory palace for the many minds from which you're made. And you need music . . .'

'. . . not as a means of expression and not a method of communication, but as a spintronic . . .'

'Careful. In more general terms, please.'

'No, not spintronic . . . as a computational converter, since my brain is a pattern-recognition instrument and has to learn to process certain types of inferential processes to do with the fine structures of spacetime and how to move through them, and without this help, without music that is, wouldn't know how to formulate these.'

Padmasambhava realized, as he heard himself speak, that now he sounded like the Book, and when he tried to contact it, it didn't respond, but its every field, every file, every pathway, suddenly lay open to him. 'I'm . . . inside my Book. It's inside me. We're one.'

'Yes. You see? We've made some progress: first, integration. And now, alloplasticity.'

Padmasambhava laughed. 'That's a bit like saying, I'll tell you what your hands are and then I'll teach you how to pick things up.'

'Or play piano. But your analogy is faulty—I'm teaching you how to change things and also how to change place, I'm teaching you the movements, not by telling you, "look, here's you and here are things," but by showing you that you can be these things, or people, or conditions. And when you are they, then you can change them, by changing yourself.'

'Sounds straightforward.'

'But living things, and machines, never would have learnt the trick, if it hadn't been for Ryu and his buddy, who called himself Cyrus afterwards . . . too soon to tell you all this, though. That will come in the second induction. Let's do something else—is there a park anywhere, can we play badminton?'

3. SECOND INDUCTION

In the warm summer wind, on the brink of the coming tasks.

'Can I go anywhere in time or space?'

'Nonsense, What I'm showing you isn't magic. Solve your twistor equations, that will always be the best approximation. Or make yourself a cellular automaton to help you envisage it, like Izquierda did—you can go anywhere we've set up eyes for your hooks, or where we've given you the hooks that fit the naturally occurring eyes and built them into your music. So to speak.'

Cordula Späth harrumphed. 'All the usual laws of conservation apply, you can't get away from those: energy, mass . . . those fuel cells built into your brainbox, back in the day they'd threaten wars for world domination using that kind of technology, though they could never have actually waged them without destroying half the biosphere. Seriously, little lizard, if we were to convert your inward kitbag into mass, you could blow a nice dent in Mars here, or shunt Phobos and Deimos'—they'd been on both moons, in old stations abandoned for centuries—'out of their orbit like billiard balls.'

'And the same's true for you, I suppose, you're just as powerful, even worse indeed.'

Frau Späth laughed. 'I have more hooks. My reach is longer than yours.'

'Because of those naturally occurring eyes that you can . . .'

'You, for instance, can load your, personality, let's call it, like the basic software for a universal Turing machine, onto any animal and quite a few plants knocking round this solar system since the new genetics was introduced, that is since the Liberation. Which doesn't mean that there aren't a couple of beetles scuttling about somewhere, or newts ducking and diving, to which you don't have access . . . erm, since there must be a recessive genomic form, as it were, clinging on in its niche. And you can't travel to the past that way, meaning as a simple datastream, since after all the animals and plants that existed back then, before the Lion, don't have pathways that you can travel on.'

'But all these architectures were first found in nature, before we . . .'

'No, you see, that was a classic triadic argument. They began by imagining that the principle "buildings are metaphors for memory" could be transferred to fit a consciousness entire. The methods of the loci, the *ars memoriae*—mnemotechnology from the middle ages.'

'Middle . . . during the Gente?'

'No, sorry, I'm still speaking in human terms . . . during the middle period   of the Monotony. Humans used to have trouble, because they were such good storytellers. So that the stories didn't just spurge out all over the place, they needed some statics, some starch, backbone, scaffold—as you might notice, I'm very much in favour of that myself, possibly because I've worn human shape so long that I really don't want to change my habitation. Stories: you're always between Scylla and Charybdis there, since every good story has to be very personal, meaning that there are no universal rules, and has to aim to say something to others as well, to find an audience, since without them a story is not a story. They built cathedrals inside their heads, palaces where every memory had its place. Then towards the end of the Monotony they discovered the principle of computational equivalence, in simple terms, that the dreary old dualism of spirit here, nature there, was nonsense all along, since programmes can be run to describe the phenomena of consciousness just as easily as natural events, they're simply computational processes within a framework of set rules, which was always obvious, it's just that they had to find the—let's tip our hat to relativity theory and call them the Lorentz transformations—right then, they had to find the Lorentz transformations to move between these . . . frames. Which, by the way mustn't include any of the so-called psychophysical laws, since they've been passé ever since anomal monism—epiphenomenalism, emergence; these were all fumbling attempts to approach the mind-body problem and what they called intelligence, but they always came at it by fetishizing intelligence instead of beginning with the body, corporeal spacetime. Then the Gente turned things the right way round and the prophecy was fulfilled: once you have the right epistemology, then by inference, you can simply peel it open and get at the right ontology—they reached this point once seedling tech was invented, thanks to Izquierda, may she rest in . . .'

'And the Ceramicans?'

'Ah, there's the rub, isn't it? No one knows how much they're capable of. Not even me—I haven't been back to Earth since and I've only spent a dram or two of time on Mars and Venus of the future, where I didn't . . .'

'Was that abstemiousness on your part? Did you decide not to, or is it that the erm sockets there in the future aren't suited for your plug, from a certain point onwards, the locks won't take your keys, the eyes don't fit your hooks, the way it is for me and the past?'

'Why don't you find that out for yourself? Whether I deliberately never sprung into the next millennium, or whether it simply doesn't work? You'll presumably still be round, in one shape or another.'

Padmasambhava would not be distracted. 'Back to the Ceramicans . . .'

'We were never able to eavesdrop on them with enough precision—not even Livienda and myself, back then, back in the jungle, cheek by jowl with Katahomenleandraleal. Katahomenleandraleal and the Ceramicans managed to just cut loose from anything that we understood as communication . . . or pattern processing . . .

let's use a more general term, from anything we would call music. Izquierda was terrified, I never saw her so . . . How was it before? Most animals that lived in any kind of social group had the capacity to send at least a couple of specific signals, be these auditory, visual or chemical—whalesong, birdsong, gesture, colour signals such as an octopus varying her pigment, pheromones. At first, we thought the Ceramicans might be a kind of elephant—it was only in the Eighties of the last human century that they discovered that elephants communicate, acoustically, at frequencies well below the range humans could hear. But the joke was that Ceramican communication used—uses, if they're still round—not some substrate inaccessible to the natural senses, not something that's merely beyond the range of what humans or Gente can see or hear or smell, but that they use something beyond what we can think. There's the pinch, the organ that failed us wasn't the ear or the eye, it was the brain. The situation only changed, improved, once we developed seedling substrate, the first real high-capacity quantum computers, with embryonal spintronics . . . and because I did a little self-analysis, a bit of self-reflection, being on the next level myself by then, though I don't like to brag about it. At least not too much, ha ha—anyway, introspection revealed that   . . . Livienda, Lasara and myself, we really were a first-class team.'

'The three of you invented me.'

'And your sister. Brother. Whichever.'

4. PRAXIS

The composer taught him to swim, to really fly, to instinctively know the moment when the air round stops being safe to breathe, and to stop breathing, but also to know when to need to breathe again, when it can be done, when it tastes best.

They became friends—he came to call her 'Cola', a nickname that Ryuneke sometimes used when he joined their talk, a name she pretended she couldn't stand, but secretly enjoyed.

In the end she slept with him as well.

At first he had trouble seeing his new 'wiring', as she flippantly called it, as his own body. How did that work, being a man? Once, after sport, she kissed him a little longer than normal, a little softer, a little moister and better, and he got an erection, which she left him with, so that he could work out whether he liked it. It happened again and again—sometimes just the sound of her voice was enough, when she laughed a 'good morning' into his ear, spintronically, while she was out and about. The first time though, he was too confused, too happy and too much in love, to get stiff straight away, the way he did when he simply smelt her scent, or held her close to him.

The sleeping together felt very different from what he knew. No games, like at the Aristoi feasts, but rather a bold seriousness, not unfriendly but often hungry, brusque, as though in her fifteen hundred years of life (or thereabouts) Cola had learnt not to joke when it's no joking matter.

'You think you're a reptile? Ah-h, you're just a snugglebunny.' And kisses, ever again.

'Be glad that you're not over there on Venus. Sheer barbarism, which has nothing to do with the productive labour capacity, they probably have more than we do, since their terraforming was more extensive: it's down to the transport infrastructure. They're still a little way from their Renaissance. You, at least, have your enlightened absolutism, with the Congress and its central spintronics standing in for the king. Citadels as nation states. And all those antique usages in your speech, the Roman numbers, the Greek names . . . the avant-garde in the French Revolution used to think that they were Greeks and Romans too, not to mention dear old German Classicism.'

'I have only the patchiest idea of what you're talking about, Cola, sorry to say.'

'Ur and Babylon, basically. Wagadu and Ecbatana. Atlantis and Mu. Forget it.'

5. HATRED AND PROGRESS

'I was truly devoted to you and you made me a laughing stock, you dragged my devotion through the dirt.' Lodas Osier was talking to a picture he had made for himself, an image of all that is wicked. 'But I'm not afraid of you any more. I was too blind to recognize the truth, I didn't want to know how much you had stolen from me. I still shudder now when I remember how you killed any innocence that was in me. Do you want to know what will happen to you? I will not rest from the fight. You forced me to lie down in the grave before I had died, I wanted only your blessing, a stranger's benediction, from the trenches, and forgiveness of a sort for what we had done to you all, and now I am more shunned and despised than you. I cannot join in the feasts, I cannot sleep, I cannot recognize myself. Now I know what I must do. If I don't prevent it, you'll be a goddess, a god as well. So I must prevent it, before they place more faith in you than you deserve.'

If Lodas Osier had been anything more to Cordula Späth than a tiny blip on the radar, at the farthest edge of her involvement with Padmasambhava, she would probably have called him a 'poor hound', though a bear's pelt grew on his arms and his chest.

He shaved this pelt every day now, ever since he had parted from the red lizard, the red dragon now, and he took pleasure in imagining that he was a throwback of some kind, or a throwforward, catapulted here from some past millennium, a human. He pored over the history of *Homo sapiens*, their arts and their sciences.

And so, at last, he hit upon the idea of being a tragic hero. Tragic heroes, after all, were blamelessly guilty, and his guilt, he had decided, was to have not talked Padmasambhava out of her political lunacy while there was still time. He believed too that she had left him, even though he in fact had left her.

He should have defused the bomb while he could, but it was as though he had been dumbstruck—maybe by some banal instinctual drive, or maybe some greater, more abstract circumstance had lured him into smoothing her way, opening the gates for her destructive charms. At first, he had simply stood by and watched, he had done nothing, and then, when he was no longer with her, he had taken from her the support that might have kept her sane, kept her grounded. He was guilty.

Her first onslaught against the established order, the powers that be in the citadels, had succeeded, but now that Pandora's box was open, she couldn't let it lie.

Now Lodas Osier saw change and decay in all round him (and within himself).

For centuries, fixed amounts of the citadels' total productive capacity had been earmarked for certain purposes, and now these were suddenly diverted from the runtime pool by the newly-founded 'Committees for the Preparation of Possible Defence Measures', whose members were a rum lot (young merchants, discredited scientists, religious zealots, even lizards immigrating from the trenches); with the runtime gone, fora broke down, cliques shattered and even intimate relations juddered to a halt.

The calendar of festivals was thrown into confusion when many citadels wanted to make the official end of the *experimentum crucis* into one of the High Holy Days (which would have been the seventh, or in the case of Citadels II and V, which still celebrated Esprit, the eighth).

A wave of enthusiasm had founded a number of new Societies for Improved Energy Budget Research, but many of Padmasambhava's admirers and acolytes who had joined, found that their fellow members still harboured resentment about the earthquakes (which, slowly, were coming to a halt), and the societies were falling apart. Qualified geologists and ecologists left their ranks, while cranks with weird ideas about 'military meteorology' joined instead, further polarizing the members who remained.

But it was not only the general decline that made Lodas Osier feel sick, not only the squabbles over the spoils. To his mind, what was almost worse was that in midst of the chaos could be seen the seeds of a new and a different order, an evil awakening, hinting towards (he spent hours combing through his chronicles before he found the process described, found the word for it) the formation of parties and of states—the four citadels on the equator united into a new political entity, the First Martian Republic, apparently led by a triumvirate, headed by an individual called Drower Bogdanov, formerly a robot-wrangler in the service of an Aristoi grandee who had just now split apart into two virtual partials and been absorbed, permanently, into the spintronic net (these and similar forms of eccentric, self-chosen disembodiment came in waves every fifty years or so, but seemed to have picked up more than usually of late).

The fellow was already saying that Padmasambhava had been right, that social life in the citadels needed a revolution or at least a rejuvenation, to be ready for the inevitable conflict with Katahomenleandraleal and Earth, and that if no one else was ready to take up the task, since the other citadels chose to 'fritter away the decisive moment in their trivial games', then he and his folk would . . . In the citadels of the south, a light background murmur of paranoia was heard, claiming to know that Bogdanov had expansionist aims, that he was an usurper, a 'dangerous parvenu'. It invoked the tradition of megalomaniac conquerors, which Eon Nagegerg Bourke-Weiss, a leading Bogdanov opponent, recalled had found expression back on Earth 'at different times in the monstrous forms of Alexander, Caesar, Rhodes, Hitler and Cyrus Golden.'

Most of these bogeymen, except for the Lion, were believed to have been figures of myth. Soon enough, only the entertainment industry was really interested and used them as before it had used Odysseus, Herakles, Jason and Oedipus.

Padmasambhava, on the other hand, was hardly seen in the nets any longer, she seemed to have helpers who deleted her images and covered her tracks. The fact that she was now male-gendered served, for a while, to entertain the frivolous and the gossip forums. Lodas Osier took due note and was not amused. Even though sex changes were hardly more unusual in the citadels than, say, a firm commitment to hetero- or homosexuality, he took it as a belated personal affront, especially since the reports had it that this new male formed no liaisons with other males but had taken up with a woman.

'So I must forestall your future, before they place more faith in you than you deserve.' Lodas Osier repeated his mad new oath to the travestied image he had made, of the lizard that he had loved.

Then he went on, 'You walk amongst us, in our citadels, and turn your face from us, as though you were in pain, but you are not. You are venom and I must suck you from the wound that you have dealt us.'

Lodas Osier had decided, that he was to blame for what had happened.

He wanted to do penance, which demanded that he must do away with both Padmasambhava and himself. So he began to build an infernal device.

Later, once it had exploded, and the communication network on Mars chattered and hummed for months on end about the aftermath, the arguments, how had he built it, where had he got the components and materials, Saint Oswald found the *mots justes* to judge the events in aesthetic terms.

'The ancients would have called it an outstanding performance. My dear children, a parton bomb, that takes a lot of thought—virtual particles, fluctuations made up of quarks, antiquarks and gluons, and then a sort of judo throw . . . never mind the optomechanical fuse: a head that . . . blows its top, as it were, when it sees Padmasambhava strolling down the street. What an emblem of jealousy that was. Sheer spite exploded there—and not much less thought and planning than went into the Liberation itself. Just think of it—the same quantity of grey matter; one creates an entirely new biological and moral cosmos and the other only wants to punch his ex in the face. What delightful forms intelligence can take. I simply can't get over my astonishment.'

'Then stay where you are, numbskull,' said Cordula.

6. YOU SAVED ME

Now Cordula Späth had more time for her ward.

Padmasambhava quickly suspected that this new attentiveness meant that soon they would part.

On the day that everything went to hell, they spent the morning together.

They had already lain with one another all night, sometimes indulging in indolent rumpy-pumpy, then with their arms round one another, exhausted, happy, held together, much loved. In the morning they went to the largest swimming baths in Citadel II, recently part-residential. The inhabitants called themselves little mermaids or Poseinids and had made themselves into fishlike creatures, convinced of their cause.

Cordula and Padmasambhava swam with them, until they had learnt all their songs.

Then, without drying off, they went outside in the sun, to the great blue meadow.

Padmasambhava recognized the madman at once, as he stepped out from the bushes like a halfwit bandit, coming closer, arms spread, arms shaved, who does he want to hug here, wondered Padmasambhava, me, her, both of us?

Sickeningly, because he was sick, he sent a file to her Book of Life, because he knew that like most of her spintronic gearings, unlike her meat body, it would probably survive the blast. In the last quarter-second before the explosion he sent an enormous load of snapshots, imprecations, scenes of the two of them arriving at grand parties together, squabbles they'd had at the edge of the crowd in an exhibition, bickering about their last attempt to manage a joint runtime account, as though he wanted to justify himself, show that he was the jilted lover, for all those admirers, Padmasambhava's acolytes, for whom his deed would also be a ghastly beacon.

Padmasambhava didn't have time even to skim this huge gobbet.

Even before the light flash from the explosion could reach them, and the many cosmic veils were rent, micromantles, macroscreens, she felt Cola's hand on her arm and felt a tug, as though someone were pulling her sideways out from the text. Outside, events took the form of a grid, with a deep well into which the spurned lover vanished, trailing blazing sparks of hatred behind him, diving down into the shaft like a comet that sits upon its tail of burning dirt.

Cordula and Padmasambhava though stood on a prominence, and Padmasambhava's beloved teacher's voice explained calmly, 'You know, we really don't need to get riled up over all the shit that happens to be going down in local spacetime. We cloak ourselves, or unwrap ourselves, just as we please—the way I taught you. We dance, or we stand still to let everything else dance on past. He could burn up everything that shares his spacetime, but he can't touch us, for we are guarded by the arts. I couldn't have wished for a better closing lesson.'

Padmasambhava bowed her head and said, 'But I did nothing. You did it. You saved me. You cut the causal chain between his act and my death.'

'I didn't cut it. I put a kink into it and then I used the unbroken curve to only slide the cause-and-effect away, hoppla, out of your subjective-now, permanently. He's still blasted himself into the planetary crust and the meadow is nothing but ash, the swimming pool has gone up in steam. Most of the mermaids and Poseinids are dead. There'll be an almighty investigation, I've just had a peek at it over in the future. All the hoo-hah will clutter up our evenings for a little while yet, but there are hardly any other consequences. Except, as mentioned, that you've now graduated.'

'Again though, I did nothing.'

'No. That's true. But if you couldn't do it, just as well as I can, then you wouldn't'—she swept out her arm in a movement that encompassed the grid and the well and the prominence—'be able to perceive any of this.'

7. A LONG TIME AGO

'When you have become as old as I have,' Saint Oswald said, when Padmasambhava visited him for the last time in the topologies of the dreamtower, 'you realize who was really important, simply because you notice how much you miss them. I mean, no one has died, in the old-fashioned sense of the word, since the Exodus—back then it was megadeath, though, and I saw part of it. These days folk just go into voluntary dissociation, or unite into entities, as the citadels are doing. What else should they do? No one wants to die any longer, snuff out, but every body realizes after a few decades or a few centuries, that true immortality is simply unobtainable—entropy, the course of events, the fine structure of the universe, everything's against it. Everything stops sometime, so it would be better to just one day seize some opportunity to stop in a way that . . . changes things, for the better, to some extent. Hrrmm, well, they're gone, or they're no longer the same, since that's how it has to be. But still you miss them, him or her, if you outlast them.'

He sat on a chair woven of tightly meshed happiness.

'I can only give you the vaguest idea of who we were and how we came to be that way. But it's still easier for me to tell you, now, than it would be for you to have told me, then, who you are, today, if somehow you were to slip through a hole in history and back into my dim and distant past. Just think what it must be like to talk about something which, for you, is the present, and for the person who's listening, is the unimaginably distant future—you have third and fourth and fifth natures here, spaces which scaffold your quotidian, and they contain so much knowledge that he'd probably see you as some kind of scientist, think that your whole world is engulfed by science, that it takes all your time, like a wall overgrown with ivy. The technical terms that you'd use to describe even the simplest everyday aspects of your life—it's simply not true what the cultural jades say, our Aristoi's worst offenders, when they think that you can translate any concept into any language. A great many words are not only parts of speech, they're also the objects of speech-acts, and the perspectives—uh-h in this hypothetical past that I've suggested, if you had to explain your world and your time, then anyone listening, myself for instance, a silly young woodentop that I was, would always be asking, is she talking about herself or about others, from within or from above, is that authorial narrative, is it internal monologue, is it the omniscient billiard ball—and only because you keep on saying things, totally naturally, that simply couldn't be experienced, back then. The only kind of progress that I can recognize, that sometimes makes it almost make sense to keep hoping, is that thinking creatures don't just have a growing understanding of nature, and of all the constructs on top, that thinking creatures have made, but most of all of themselves. They understand cursewords and blessings, shit and transcendence, they understand the capacities of the languages that they have, that they can share, each a god to the other, like Romeo and . . . The Monotony had only the most rudimentary understanding. Rather helplessly, they called it empathy. They could only reveal it very slowly in their literature. There was hardly anything of it in the epic, maybe more in the psychological novel. Today . . .'

His fingers played piano in the empty air, an absent-minded tinkling, wanting to shrug off the thoughts about the gulf between then and now, that made him melancholy.

He spent ever more time sitting down, since he wanted to spare his legs, now that the northern citadels had seceded and cut off his wood supply for the time being. It would be two hundred years before the material would need replacing, but Cordula Späth had already frankly told him that she wouldn't be coming, and the mannikin had his own not terribly optimistic views of whether the citadels might have become states by then and how far they would trust one another. The ancient puppet ran his hand, dry as dust, through the hair just beginning to grow on Padmasambhava's head.

Frau Späth's pupil had now taken on some human affectations, so as to be a little more like Cordula, who in her turn neither encouraged nor dissuaded him; hence the hair.

'Really important . . . And who would that have been, in your long life?'

He smiled. 'Oh, once I get going on that topic! I knew nearly everyone who was anyone, did you know? The top nobs! I dined with Dmitri Stepanovich, the old mutt, when he came to our museum investigating the murdered zander—he was always so concerned to seem ascetic and he gave a banquet to thank us, the staff, as they called us back then, for our help. He had this marvellous way of looking quite the rogue, but only if you weren't watching or if he thought no one was watching; it was almost like a facial workout for his muscles to make up for all the po-faced seriousness that he had to show in the king's service. Your father, of course.'

'And my mother?'

'Ah, well, you know . . . it wasn't so easy to gain access to her circle, not even at the end when so many former loyalists, myself included, had gone over to her party to save our own skins, which didn't actually happen in most cases, not literally . . . well, be that as it may. No, I had my own little pool of women, obviously, and the ladies were most welcome at Lasara's soirées, even one from the Temple in Capeside, would you believe? Her name was Abykhail, a hawk-maiden, we spent some most galvanizing time together on the cushions in my bachelor pad, she was . . . she'd been P.A. to Elektrizitas, the great priestess, guiding spirit of the quest for the, ha ha, the Grail, the Li'l Runaround, with the sermon she'd given on the Temple steps.'

'The Runaround . . .'—earlier, Padmasambhava might have consulted the Book at this point, but now he just knew. 'That was this . . . soteriological whatnot, that the citadels are once again . . .'

'Yes, it sank without trace, seemingly, two or three hundred years ago,' Saint Oswald said, regretfully, 'since no one could agree whether that had just been some kind of encephalopathy—a fever perhaps, affecting the Gente once they were destined to fail, an aberration—or a useful instrument that Lasara, perhaps, had wrought, using it to lead the Gente towards the idea of transcendent, metaphysical, very long-term goals and projects, so she began with something which meant hardly anything, only a sort of thought exercise. There has to be something bigger and greater and more important than ourselves . . . and as soon as they'd got used to that, she could air the idea of the Exodus . . . or maybe it was both at once, the irrational foreshadowing of a rational plan to transcend the limitations of Gente society—well, the whole hair-splitting debate turned on this point, whether . . .'

'. . . whether the Runaround, seen in this sense as a symbol of transcendence, has actually been found or whether we should seek it anew.'

Padmasambhava pulled a rather sour face, since he knew that even a few acolytes of the Padmasambhava cult claimed that her speech beneath the Livienda tree had been merely 'a reminder that we have not yet found the Runaround,' in the words of the leader of this dubious sect-within-a-sect, a spiderrhinox hybrid called, crassly, Little Kennedy Cyrus Georgescu Atlas Dmitri Summers.

Saint Oswald, sunken in his regrets, looked at the copy of a copy of a copy of a copy of a picture that Stanz the ape had painted. Padmasambhava was just about to ask him about it, when the mannikin spoke.

'You should have seen them . . . on the ramparts at Capeside . . . how they worked together, forming chains, while banners blazoned with the Lion snapped in the wind—most of them had already had their ticket stamped for the Exodus, as copies, seedlings, partials. It was glorious, there's no other word for it. The flags, the oaths, and working up their courage, the honour of defeat, their dignity as the axe fell. They knew they would die there, only a small fraction of Gente were ever sent to the moon in person, bodily. They knew that they would not survive, but they were reconciled to that, their souls were already halfway to Heaven—and so they laughed in the enemy's face, bared their breast, bared their teeth, the great pandas with their flamethrowers, the wild yaks with their horns, who made the first sortie and even managed to cut a swathe through the Ceramican ranks, stampeding through them. The tigers, the beautiful gazelles, the elephants . . . I was there during the battles, before the third rocket was launched. I saw the explosions, I heard the earth tremble and then I was fetched out at the last minute. I even fought alongside them, can you believe that? I helped load the big guns. It lasted weeks, almost two months, even when they were already in the city—on every street corner, at every doorway to every building, we didn't . . . the Gente didn't give an inch without a fight. It sounds childish, but you know, I spent so much time with the Gente, with their old books and data storage, and only then, when Capeside fell, did I realize: the losing side isn't necessarily the wrong side, only because it lost. The Ceramicans were stronger, but that doesn't mean that they were right. We . . . we Gente,'—and at last he had brought himself to admit what he had always felt— 'we Gente were . . . more splendid. We were beautiful, we fought well, we showed courage, we didn't simply lie down and die or let ourselves be eaten. We knew how to defend ourselves—even after the king died, for whatever had been kingly in him was never his alone. The Etruscan shrews with their needleguns, firing off their flechettes that exploded on impact like a star, the sportive lemur who would load the ground-to-ground guns for hours on end, battery upon battery, in the clamour of the battle, without tiring, without going deaf, hither and yon like the wind, grab and load and shoot, the spectacled bears with their classical Greek helmets, their magnet lances, storming out of the rubble of the cellars on the seventh day after the city was already occupied, driving the Ceramicans back from many of the eastern districts, the snow leopards, the eagle owls with their radio beacons, the forest salamanders and red-eyed frogs, the armadillo lizards, bald crows, little auks, otters, elephants, hummingbirds and . . . that was us, all of them, the Gente.'

They were silent for a while.

Then the mannikin spoke. 'You know what I'm talking about, more than all the rest round here. That does my old heart good. Is she sending you off tomorrow?'

Padmasambhava didn't need to answer.

'You'll miss her, I've often found myself missing her, that's the way we love her.'

'Why is she so different from all the others here?' Padmasambhava enquired, amazed at his own question. 'So different from the humans, the Aristoi, the lizards, the Gente . . . who is she? What is she?'

Saint Oswald shook his head gently. 'Cordula Späth . . . I think she's the only one who doesn't need to believe in God, since she knows Him personally. For her, God isn't something to be accepted or rejected, who insists that you're either a believer or an atheist—she knows all his tricks. She's a saint and a scapegrace.'

'God?' Padmasambhava asked.

'We rarely talk about that, since the Gente. We've become rather more circumspect than the humans used to be—it's so easy to lose control, to commit trespasses not easily avenged.'

'Avenged by . . .'

'Stir up the fire there. Make it hotter. I think I'll get rheumatism if I'm not careful. One thousand years, umpteen illnesses, survived them all but do I get any less susceptible? I get no less susceptible. I only get ever more ungrateful. I've tried to be friends to my friends who know how to be friends.'

He bent down and kissed his old friend on the brow.

They looked at one another, knowing that this really was goodbye.

8. DEPARTURE

No coffee cup this time, but a lab flask. 'That's an old joke, Ryu,' Cordula snapped, 'you really could give up all these Jekyll and Hyde gags, you know.'

The Fox simply shimmered, a pale leaf green, saying nothing.

'What should I . . .' Padmasambhava began hesitantly, but the composer simply nodded. 'You have to drink him, of course, for the final boost. The information, and more than that, the ridiculous amount of energy . . . which is where the heat comes from, you see. He's concentrating an immensity into a tiny little space, his volume here gives you only the . . . teensiest idea of what he really is. The final push, Padma. Before you can make the great jump, on your own, without me.'

'Where to?'

'To go get your sister of course, on Venus, where else?'

1. OUT FROM PRISON

What do I know about a giant red ape?

Nothing here could surprise Fire any longer.

Look now, he had to confess that he had been just on the verge of hoping that he and Pyretta might, perhaps, be approaching something like an arrangement. But now that they were talking about a giant red ape, that had, obviously, been a misunderstanding, as hideously incomprehensible as everything else hereabouts.

'Nothing. I don't know anything about a giant red ape,'—perhaps it's a translation error. What did you put in my food, why am I growing breasts, why is my penis shrinking, why is my chin smooth and hairless? Maybe the giant red ape knows, I don't know, I give up.

Pyretta looked down. Fire saw in her what once he had seen, eternities ago, on the lightscreen in his home—the whole foolishness, nakedness, violence and suffering of mankind, and he thought, I like her but, really, that doesn't help us much. Then, with a gesture that he had come to know well, she brushed a strand of red-blonde hair from her face and looked at him as though she knew that now Fire could see her thoughts, as though she had opened herself before, as once already before—the prince shuddered; he saw the soldiers, the firing keys, the ramps and the cruise missiles, saw how her headset and microphone crackled with a bright fire of electrons, from the communication, now more hectic than ever, among the ruling powers in the cities, Ferret, Mare, White Tiger. The two junior cities in Atalanta had, by now, an image of what had just breached the walls of the oldest of the Three New Cities, where Fire now sat captive. Pyretta was thinking of a decision tree that became the set of real options for Fire's fate; if the government in Ferret or Mare decided that the long-feared interplanetary hostilities with the Ceramicans, or the Martians, had finally broken out, if they assumed that the ape had come from the fifth, or some higher, dimension, then they would punch in the launch codes and feel no pang of conscience at destroying their sister city. The sevenfours would relay this panicked decision, just as they had always routed communications between the new cities, even before the lesserlings, since the first stone was laid, in silence, committed to non-intervention. If Fire knew anything though, anything at all that might explain the giant ape's rampage, perhaps help to drive him off, then for both their sakes, for the sake of all humanity (lesserlings, thought Fire, she only calls them human), who will otherwise be burnt up, blasted, squished, then he should say so now and not get hoity-toity about it.

She waited for Fire's answer.

It was all wrong, the question was based on false premises, he even had trouble thinking of himself as 'Fire', as 'the prince', as 'him', it was as though this had nothing to do with him any more, with her, with the two of them, slowly but irresistibly losing relevance, to do with whom, when?

Besides which, there was more to see than Pyretta wanted to let him see that she wasn't asking out of genuine concern but because that was her chance to rise, to shine, to escape, get free. It was her chance to climb the highest rung of the ladder in the Defence Department hierarchy, which in turn was the most important executive arm of the great organization called the Academy hereabouts, which earlier, back on Old Earth, had been just called 'the government'. Fire saw that she was truly Preisnitel's daughter and that only a few weeks ago he had still been leading her round on a leash. And he really intended to have a child by her. Fire. Flame, Fiamettina (what kind of names, memories, are those? Who is thinking me?) felt sorry for the life of humiliation that Pyretta had endured, from the nose job to 'balance her features better' (Preisnitel's words, even though it was his crooked face that she'd inherited) to the regular liposuction when he had been feeding her too many chocolates and meat treats; the ear pinning, the breast enlargements (twice), the whole misery endured for the sole purpose of entertaining the repellent lesserling, persuading him not to withdraw the shelter of his hand from her, for folk like her still, after all this time, didn't count as free-born members of this society, even if like Pyretta they had found work (Preisnitel thought this was 'cute')—a well-paid, prestigious post in the Defence Department.

Pyrettta's only chance to escape this stifling bondage and avoid falling prey to her dreadful father was to try to turn to some higher power, a power which outranked him and could command his obedience—meaning the Defence Directorate, the Academy itself.

Fiamettina recognized that this was the real reason why the poor woman had opened her soul to him (her?), the prisoner: never mind any sympathy she might feel for hypothetical victims of some possible act of war; that had nothing to do with it. Only this yearning had allowed Fiamettina's weakened, almost deaf telepathy to hear what was in Pyretta's head.

In this brief moment, while they waited, Fire, Fiamettina, looked directly into Pyretta's recent past, at her last and so far most promising attempt to win the favour of the powers that be. For weeks Pyretta had worked with doctoral assistants and researched on her own, always learning, always studying one of the great puzzles of the machines and artefacts recovered from the Temple of Isotta; what was meant by the term 'music', by 'rhythm', 'harmonies', 'tone rows', used in so many of the stelae texts—were they merely decorative? Were they instructions?—in so many glyphic inscriptions and in the schemata.

She almost discerned something that she could almost understand, but it looked like nothing that she or her fellow researchers knew. What were melodies, what was counterpoint and fugue, tempo, a symphony, a sonata, beat, what technology was being described here, or what art?

Fiamettina, Fire, read a text with Pyretta's eyes, a text that she had painstakingly decrypted until her eyelids drooped, long before the prince (the princess?) had appeared in White Tiger, the man (woman?) who might have the key to this mystery, a text that seemed to say something about the Gente and about humans and about the way both races related to music (were related by music? Were inter-related through music?), something that Pyretta did not understand, because the term 'music' meant everything and nothing at all. For her it was like the names 'Kafka' and 'Mahler' in the text, signs with no referent. 'The music comports itself like animals: as if its empathy with their closed world were meant to mitigate something of the curse of closedness . . . as in Kafka's fables, the animal realm is the human world as it would appear from the standpoint of redemption, which natural history itself precludes. The fairy-tale tone in Mahler is awakened by the resemblance between animal and man. Desolate and comforting at once, nature grown aware of itself casts off the superstition of the absolute difference between them.'

That was certainly shorthand for something, it described a transfer or an equation or an inference, but what kind? Where? How? What substrate could run something like this?

Fiamettina knew that she had a faint and foggy idea of what the answer might be, no, perhaps not an answer as such, but another puzzle bound up with this one, that Fire had first noticed (whoever Fire was, or would be) for the first time at the square of the ruined Temple of Isotta, a discrepancy, an aporia . . . but of no interest to Pyretta any longer, it seemed. Her long study of this Sibylline fragment and the other dead remnants was over and done with in a trice, once the ape had appeared to threaten the city.

There must be an answer to this, what do you know, help me, tell me, give me some weapon.

The doors in the longer wall of the interview room glided apart.

Preisnitel bustled in, accompanied by two of his nastiest thugs, and put his right paw onto Pyretta's shoulder; he fixed his eye sternly on Fiamettina and said, 'I think we've spent long enough watching and listening to this dickering about. There's serious stuff happening outside. People are dying. White Tiger is in turmoil. I know that protocol dictates that we try the soft approach from time to time . . . only for a change . . . to winkle out this creature's secrets, if it has any,'—he nodded at Fiamettina—'But given how things are and considering that we need results right now rather than some time soon, I think that no one will be too concerned if we depart from protocol, isn't that right, girlie?'

Flame knew straightaway that the ogre shouldn't have used that last word. It was more than enough, it was the last straw.

Which is why the three men in the room were astonished but neither of the two women when Pyretta rammed her left elbow into her sire's crotch, grabbed the weapon that he wore at his hip and shot him with it. She felled his two henchmen with well-aimed roundhouse kicks and then shot them, one in the stomach, one through the throat. They lay there, twisting and writhing, taking their time in dying. Pyretta grabbed Flame by the arm and shouted, 'What are you just sitting there for like a . . . we've got to go! It's over! The whole city . . .' She tore her comms system from her head, threw it to the ground and ground it beneath her heel, so that it died in a crackle of static.

'Yes,' said Fiamettina, standing up, 'I'm free, that's true. And so are you.'

2. MYTHQUAKE

Errors were made in the attempt to stop the great ape, who, like Moloch, Behemoth and Leviathan, the more he grew the less he knew about who had made him or what his purpose was.

If the lesserlings, who tried so hard to be human, had known the myths of mankind a little better, then they would certainly not have attacked the monster with such useless weapons; ground-to-air missiles, anti-tank mines, gunfire. The terror swept through their city, snapping their bridges with its knees, trampling underfoot their yellow cranes, snatching their maglev trains from the rails, crushing their cars with debris torn from the towers.

If they had known about King Kong, they would have known that when such a creature falls dead, the consequences are barely preferable to having it rampage unhindered. If they had known about Antaeus, the legendary hero who drew strength from his mother the Earth, growing mightier whenever he touched her, so that his enemies could never cast him down for long, then they would not have shot grapnel-lines at the ape and tried to drag him to the ground with their high-tension winches. The giant snapped the cables, swallowed the winch trucks whole and, the one time that they actually managed to make him stoop a few yards, scooped up people and machinery from the ground and shovelled them into his mouth, immediately becoming even larger, wilder, more wrathful and indomitable. All the while he screamed aloud. If they had known something of the Hydra, they would never have thought to attack him with rotor blades, saws, swords and lasers, cutting off his fingers or carving lumps from his thick skin, for where these fell to the ground, they shuddered and twitched, wriggled and changed, and soon there were new apes—whatever had gone wrong with the storage ice, the cold crypt where the monster had been born, was also wrong with the whole huge orang that had struggled free of the cold womb to lay White Tiger waste. A catastrophic replicator, an avalanche of copies, a runaway growth pattern. They fled from it and called on the other cities to help.

Every radio message sent strengthened the others in their resolve to have done with the problem once and for all.

The new orang-utans, Sdhütz Arroyo's myrmidons, swarmed afar and marched through the districts and neighbourhoods of the city where they had fallen, until they had formed a cordon, and gradually drew it tight. The bizarre army came ever closer, ever faster, while the city's defenders fought furiously and with no plan at all; from the Forum Tauri and from the farmfactories' heat tanks, from the Mokios cisterns and the Pege gate, from the inland harbour and the Middle Way, all converging on the square where once the Temple of Isotta had stood.

For the invaders heard the ancient echoes more clearly than ever the lesserlings had.

3. PULL DOWN THY VANITY

The city collapsed horribly; a failed cake in destruction's oven.

Huan-Ti would never have wanted his name to be given to such a place, his fangs would have turned yellow with shame. Two women ran aimlessly beneath collapsed bridges, across burst sewers which poured the city's subconscious onto the street, between the fires; one who had, only a little while before, worn chains, and one who had just then been entrusted with watching her. The differences between folk melted away, as always happens, not only when Landers fell, and Capeside and Borbruck, but even when they ran panicked through the burning streets of Nero's Rome, when they ran to escape Pompeii's engulfment.

Machine guns rattled in the distance, sirens howled, glass shattered and tinkled. The lesserlings were only mortal, like the humans and the Gente; they fought in the open street, they toppled blind statues, and as always happens, there was looting, there was heroism.

Red apes leapt through the rubble everywhere and, where they landed, did more harm than ever the citizens could have done for themselves; here, we'll show you what destruction is, make room. The woman who was a flame, who barely knew any longer whence she came, who burnt but was not consumed, spoke stumblingly, as though in her sleep, 'A tumult almost like ... music ...'

The other woman had been looking for an escape route, feeling responsible for them both, wishing for a bolthole or a way out, but now she spun about and grabbed her companion by the shoulders and screamed loud enough to drown out the uproar all round, the clamour in her head, 'What, music? There it is again: music! How much do you know! Do you think I'm stupid, like Preisnitel, like the Academy? Is it true after all, what we ...'

A wild flickering danced, almost ceremoniously, across the face of the woman she held, who didn't understand, saying, 'What did they ...'

'That you're a cover for a ... cluster bomb! That they're all inside you, partials, an invading army, that you are as legion as ... these apes, at least ... that there are thousands of Gente within you, and the key ... bah, always the same old shit, always the same blind alley wherever we turned, however we searched, and ... We were able to crack some of the archives and we scoured the long-term memories of crashed sevenfours, and in the rubble of the ruined ships we found the same, the key, the key is music! And no one here, no one, do you understand, not one of us, knows what that means, music, whether that's a name for something in your language, for a ... how should I know, the Gente partials steganographically encoded into your brain or for some fucked-up old-world witchcraft ... Tell me, what's music, how much do you know, who are you? We're screwed anyway! Can't you at least show me that much respect, tell me the truth? Music?'

'That's it though, I . . .' Fiamettina groped for the words, 'I know and at the same time I don't . . . you have to understand, I can imagine what music is, but I've never . . . heard . . . music.'

'Right. So. You hear it. It's something that's heard. Is it . . . something to do with orientation? With the inner ear? A whistling? Something spatial . . . the sense of balance? Which is why our cameras . . . when you visited the place . . . you were swaying, tottering . . . on the square where the Temple . . . ?'

'I can't tell you, Pyretta. I make it and I am it, but I can't name or define it. It's what I have to do, it's the way they made me, engendered me . . . my mother and my father, the lynx and the wolf. That I know music, that it's in me . . . there's no such thing here, on this planet. There are notes and sounds, there are voices, there is speech and noise, there's the way you spoke to me in prison, there in the cell . . . but all of us, all of you, the lesserlings, the neo-badgers and the sevenfours and the fash and the salamander . . . none of us has ever heard a beat or a note or a bar of music. It's as though it's been deliberately burnt out of us, as though there were a biologically fixed taboo, as though this whole civilization, the terraforming, the colonies, were set up from the very beginning with some purpose in mind, not like on Mars, set in motion, or . . . planted . . . to stay well clear of this technology in particular, until at least I was awakened, until I went at it, my Task . . . I can hear it, I can play it and if only I have the time and the occasion and the place . . .'

Pyretta opened her eyes wide. 'You really want me to lead you there. You still want . . . you never abandoned your task.'

She shook her head at being talked to like this. 'Don't cast aspersions. I don't want all this, I'm not to blame for . . .'—a jerk of the head—'for this. And my Task . . . I'd have foresworn it a hundred times, long before you killed Zagreus and kept me prisoner, tortured me. If only I could have! At any moment I would have taken an oath, put it behind me, made no more trouble, embraced any other fate as long as it kept me away from the Temple of Isotta, kept me from hearing music or thinking about it . . . but I can't turn my back on it. As long as I breathe, I have my Task.'

She knew what she was saying. If Pyretta was serious about stopping her, about doing what the Defence Department had trained her to do, then she would have to kill Fiamettina.

Did she want that? Would she do it?

'Oh faddle, stop that,' said Pyretta, smiling, unsure, beautiful. 'What's that about? Who's got anything left to lose anyway? Come along. I'll get you there. I know the city.'

4. LIZARD

Padmasambhava, who had been a girl and a woman, who now was a man, clad in black velvet, went like a breath through the walls of flame and, walking over the dead, found that White Tiger was a rather lovely city which he would have quite liked to visit under more pleasant circumstances.

It shouldn't have been.

Another world, and onwards to a third. Although Padmasambhava was walking on paved ways and tarmacked streets, the scene of continuing disasters, he had no trouble seeing the past ages on which he truly trod. You were here long before me, poor ghosts of Venus, I respect you. All cities are geological events, like the citadels and the trenches at home, the volcanoes and the quakes. Padmasambhava saw those still alive go at one another's throats, or save, help and protect one another, and knew that he could not take three steps without meeting those who would soon be ghosts, who already carried with them the glamour of all the legends that one day would be told.

'Shame,' thought the tourist, 'something could really have been done with this city.'

Without looking round he crossed strange quarters, rich neighbourhoods reserved for the better sort, fine and tragic quarters for children who have been good, historic abattoirs, museums and schools surrounded by statues that reared up from the ground like scorched antennae straining for transmission that would never be sent. He went through sensible streets laid out round hospitals and technology parks, he found dark corners and kept on in his intent, keeping none of this in his memory, it matters not what gate or bridge or crossroads is here, soon it will be gone while I go onwards, as though I were the tipstaff, interested only in seeing the sentence carried out, the judgement of the flames, the riot and the turmoil, the fights, the stampede and the trampled underfoot, the fireworks here on the ground—when all of this is past and gone, one who walked here will live on: myself, Padmasambhava.

He was headed for the square where the Temple of Isotta surely stood, but he didn't go straight ahead, rather walking in a sort of *détournement*, like a sightseer in the storm. Padmasambhava felt as though he were playing a game; unfold the map, take a glass and stand it on its rim, somewhere on the map, then walk the line of its curve, following the circle as closely as you can, mark what you see as you walk, as though you were a camera, filming, taking pictures, a noteblock to be scribbled with impressions.

On a tall, broad stairway Padmasambhava finally met three apes, utterly enraged, gnashing their teeth, drooling and spitting, ready to kill. Padmasambhava smiled and spread his arms as though to say, my errant children, stop now, don't fight over nothing, stop your foolish behaviour, come to my breast, kill no longer, dear apes, leave your troubles and your folly.

The lesserling witnesses, among them a family who had been in danger of being torn apart by the three apes, saw the dark stranger standing, like a rip in spacetime devouring the light around. They stumbled away in terror. The three apes, stuffing their maws with rags and dirt, growing and roiling, pullulating with boils and vivid tumours, slurped and slapped their hands, chattered, grunted, spat blood and mucus, gall and drool, and then stretched their crooked, clawed fingers towards Padmasambhava and opened wide their fanged mouths. But they never touched him—from his skin there wafted towards them a light, a scent, a shadow, a music older than the three worlds together.

And where the three bloodthirsty beasts had stood, a shimmering flurry of insects burst into colour—umber moths, mud-loving beetles, grasshoppers, scorpion flies, fleas, ants both winged and wingless, soldier beetles, malachiidae, fireflies, moths, digger wasps and sand wasps, hornets, painted ladies, red longhorns, greenfly, long-horned grasshoppers. Chirruping and chirring, trilling and buzzing, humming, whirring and scrabbling, their sound flooded down the broad stairs, yet none of it breached the curtain of other air, finely aquiver, in which Padmasambhava stood mantled. He did not need to tell the hexapods his commands, they knew it from the beginning: they were the partials of a failed reawakening and they had to banish what had given them birth. They would find him, each and every orang-utan, screaming and flailing and hating, find him in every back alley, high on the rooftops, in White Tiger's deepest tunnels, they would swarm him and shred him and sting him, spray him with poison and he would dissolve into a myriad of forms, just as they had arisen. A great and joyous swarm would arise, leave the town, on the ground, in the air, through the sewers, and outside on the plains, the volcanic heights, the slopes of the craters, in the mountains and the chasms, the ridges and the cliffs. They would sting the bleak ecotecture of this world into action if they could, perhaps they could heal it.

5. ESCAPING FORWARDS

Pyretta barged her way brusquely through the knotted, raving crowd, swinging her pistol, kicking like a mule, clearing a path for the two women so that Fire thought, I'll have to note all this—how she walks, what she says, how she makes doors and passages where there were none, I mustn't forget. Fiamettina was inexplicably certain that soon enough she would leave Pyretta and never see her again. Perhaps her guardian's boldness, even rashness, the way she boxed and kicked her way forward, revealed that Pyretta herself didn't intend to survive tonight, the best night of her life—why would she? To report for duty again, report for re-education?

'We'll be there soon,' Pyretta called back over her shoulder, again and again.

'We': a word for a friendship that should not have been. 'So,' thought Fire, 'we can make friends with the lesserlings, I wish I could have shown you this, Zagreus.'

Not far from where Pyretta helped Fire through the wreckage of a wire fence, two young men were beating an old man's skull with iron pipes.

'Territorial behaviour,' thought Fire, that's what Vempes the fash had taught her when she was still a boy—when individuals, or small homogenous social groups (gangs, battalions, bucket chains: Fire saw and heard all of these round her) are separated by distances greater than might be stochastically predicted, they manifest territorial behaviour. They avoid one another, but they also form groups and thus get in one another's way. They defend the places where they want to die.

A bright light fell from the skies, between the rooftops. Pyretta sighed, 'Ah-h-h!' amazed at the glint, pointing up. At first Fire thought that some miracle had happened, even greater than her escape from prison, her friendship with Pyretta, for it seemed that the gods or the goddesses were shaking down upon her all the herbs that she had missed so much since she was taken prisoner, her favourites, her food—rosemary dancing with angelica and fennel, chives with mustard leaf, but they had legs, they had wings, and Fiamettina saw soon enough that these weren't plants but insects, who, like the lesserlings, clumped and swarmed, formed flocks, stretching and slicing the spaces of the air, flying in formation, patrolling; and each swarm, it was clear, was not made up of one species but of many different insects, in complex coalitions, like the neurons clustering in the brain to dream or show the world to the thinking being they are.

Silver, gold, Delft blue—'Where are they . . . what is that?' asked Pyretta, not expecting an answer. The two women, friends, standing shoulder to shoulder in friendship, looked up at the spectacle and paid no mind to the looters and the killers, who were finished with the old man and entered now, stage right.

'They're . . . they're not doing anything. Nothing's happening. Why not?'

Pyretta was right. They had stopped, up there, as though waiting for something, waiting to be called, commanded, waiting for a sign. The suspense was unspeakable and it was broken by the dull thud of lead striking a skull. Pyretta collapsed, dead in an instant. Fire ducked, not in fear but readying herself to leap; her mind was still in shock that something so dreadful could happen, just so, and time still flow on—her friend, alive one moment, no longer now—but her eyes blazed and the second ruffian hesitated for a moment, his arm still raised, grasping the piece of drainpipe.

For the insects, this was enough.

They shot downwards at the little group like bullets and formed sheets and layers, wrapping themselves about the killers' faces, leaving Fire untouched, they hovered round her like a mist. She felt a gentleness enfolding her, wishes perhaps, and benedictions. It lasted only a few seconds. Then both of the lesserlings lay, not a breath in their bodies. The insects swooped upwards, back to their height.

For me?

Fire stood, shocked, weeping; knelt down by her friend and touched her, here, there, on the arm, on her brow, saw the blood puddling onto the ground without seeping away, the street was well tarmacked here. For me? The beetles, the bees, they protected me, is everything happening here happening according to some plan, by order, is there a guiding intelligence—did my mother know all this in advance, is some law at work, unfolding?

Lasara, mother, *lux in diafana, creatrix*. All the old and the ancient languages reached, by their roundabout ways, an understanding in Fire, a comprehension that had learnt and spoken all, long before that child called Fire had been born, all that lived within her now, that came to her, that came now to themselves.

Mother, you're sending me on. You're playing your game and I am one of the pieces. How many boards can you play on at once? What stakes are you playing for, where have you set them, in which field, which houses?

Fire bent down and kissed the dead woman on her lovely brow and said, 'Pyretta,' wanting to make a promise, pledging that she would not forget the name, a vow that went unheard.

Only a name, and I have too many myself; Fire, Prince, Princess, Fiamettina, and I know that my parents had many, and their parents, and that at the end of the Monotony most humans had more than one name, and titles, masks, *personae*. Fire supposed that the lesserlings had only one name each because their civilization was still young, only a few generations, so that it was unlikely that names would be confused. (She was wrong here, the lesserlings had vaunted their will to know that each and every one of them was unmistakable, irreplaceable; a civilization drew its vigour from the tension between this uniqueness and the common cause they all served—so, at least, the first regents of the Academy had thought—and to ensure that no name was ever repeated, they used onomastic computers, working with a fixed number of historically attested human morphemes, making combinatorial constructs that expressed a person's genetic profile and, as far as possible, sounded nice. A name's meaning arose from its difference from all and any other names; the computers drew on an ancient, secret doctrine, inherited from the Monotony.)

Fire shut her eyes for her friend and thought, I believe that she died in freedom and that this must count for something.

Flame stood up. She needed no guardian, no guardswoman to lead her, she knew this now. She would go where she must.

6. FROM THE MOUTH OF ETERNITY

Padmasambhava reached the place as though whirled there by the winds and he found none there left alive. In the middle of the city, which also seemed the middle of the world, omphalos, the tumult had fallen silent, and Padmasambhava heard, felt, smelt his sister approaching, his lover, the other half of himself. Only a little while yet and she would be here, in the patterns, in the *temenos*—he felt her thinking about biology, about territory, about something called Vempes, that had been a fash, that had taught her, and Padmasambhava spun her thoughts further, while he paced slowly, calmly among the corpses and the ruins, beginning a most secret dance. Humans, true humans, not these—what were they called, lesserlings? Not these, but the real members of that ancient species, *Homo sapiens*, had once set up experiments with other kinds of animals to test dispersions and distances. Remove an animal from its own territory, in the wild, and soon enough another came to take its place, defended the habitat as though to the manner born; the boundaries remained, and only the regency had changed, unless and until they mimicked the continued presence of the old ruler (the true-born ruler? Royalism, loyalism, Lionism . . .). For this they used 'playbacks', mocked-up sounds, and visual and olfactory traces. Something very similar had happened here, though it was far harder to give it a name; and this was why the terror that stalked White Tiger, the violence and rage, had spared this place. The true-born was here still, but it was no denizen or guardian of the square that drove the fear away. It was rather the square itself, as potent as a curse spoken from the mouth of eternity.

Where are you? I will be drawn to you, even if you want nothing other than to sleep, there on the breast of your gentle friend, who herself now sleeps deeply. Put one foot though before the next, find me, so that I need no longer seek you.

7. TO NAME BUT ONE

Norferd, Academician third class, found his immediate subordinate Preisnitel, together with his two bodyguards, in Interview Room III of the Criminological Research Centre (and prison) in the Academy's eastern wing. He was shocked, of course, but he also, very pragmatically, began to think about how he might escape the city, perhaps through the sewers. The academician was one of the very few people in White Tiger who had not lost his head when the ape appeared, or when he heard about the danger that the other cities would launch an atomic strike— rumours of which had seeped down from the elite, via their chauffeurs, nannies and factotums, through to the populace.

In sticky situations Norferd always took care not to lose his head, since he was very fond of it and knew that as heads go, it worked very well indeed.

Those who were not busy with urgent tasks had been making their excuses and 'popping out for a moment', while the technicians on watch at the consoles had broken into ever louder arguments. Tempers were rising. Seeing this, Norferd had ducked into his desk like a tortoise into its shell and rummaged round a little in those rudimentary electronic networks that stood in, here on this barren world, for the constant hum and flutter of news and wonders that had been the pherinfonet, in olden times. Before Fiamettina, elsewhere, realized the same thing, Norferd had noticed that the territorial instinct was shaping all these events. That will lead to some unpleasantness, he thought. He sat down on the chair where a few hours ago Fire had been interrogated. The neon tubes above him flickered, not quite as though they were about to go out, not yet at least, but there was clearly something wrong with the power supply.

Territoriality; Norferd didn't know it but his efficient and enviably well-trained brain was now busy following the same paths and patterns that Padmasambhava and Fire were thinking through. Indeed, tonight, in the worst and longest night in the city's history, there were many who were following the same trains of thought—though he was a scientist, of course, so even if he had known this, he would never have let himself fall prey to esoteric nonsense about the interconnnectedness of all souls.

There was nothing spooky about such coincident thoughts, obviously; it was down to factors which the scientist could very easily have grasped. The whole thing was due to the reconfiguration of local event-patterns in the higher-dimensional space that the city occupied, a reconfiguration which set up field effects in the electrical and electrochemical processes of the four-dimensional organic brains thereabouts, suggesting certain thoughts to any creature who could think at all. Given time, Norferd could have worked that out for himself. But now he was thinking of something that he had learnt from the archives—towards the end of the Monotony, humans had appeared on Earth demanding what they called a 'Pleistocene rewilding' in the regions that would later, much later, be Countess Alexandra's home. Rewilding was a trend, back then, in ecosystem design, that's to say in the earlier stages of ecotecture—various species which in previous centuries had been driven out of certain regions, or brought close to extinction, were resettled there by the humans, under expert zoological supervision ('Dear Bolson tortoise, welcome back to New Mexico'). Pleistocene rewilding wanted to go one step further. The idea was to identify descendant species of the megafauna which had lived in these parts way back in the Pleistocene epoch and herd them into special nature reserves set up for the purpose. Norferd knew that the ecosystems in question here had hardly withstood the shock. New parasites and epidemics appeared, the fences and other enclosures swallowed up astronomical sums of money and the human inhabitants had to cope with consequences that seriously harmed the reputation of all the ecosystem planners, individuals and organizations, round at the time. The only sign of any progress to come out of the whole thing was a small pride of lions, which finally provided the substrate for an experiment far more ambitious than the Pleistocene rewilding, when a human created the Gente. He, or his cognitive self, took up residence in the pride's alpha male and became a king.

Was not the plan that had led to the founding of the new Three Cities to recreate mankind here on Venus as lunatic, in the final analysis, as the ridiculous Pleistocene rewilding had been? 'A bad joke,' thought the academician, and stroked his shaking chin with a trembling hand. 'We wanted to recreate what had existed during the Monotony and we managed it—all things considered, we are now a species that walks upright on two legs and poses a greater threat to its own survival than anything else could.'

There was a basic console at the longer wall of the rectangular interview room. Norferd got up, sat down there and called up a net connection. Most of the local forums were no longer talking. A very bad sign, this; folk had other things to do and only the bots and automata were still going, computer-driven, and amongst these, hold on a moment, let's have a look, he'll have them soon—the meteorological observation cameras. A-ha, that's what we'd been missing.

The sevenfours.

They were gathered above the city, higher than their usual flight pattern, at the edge of space. Dozens. Hundreds. They wanted to watch as the city burnt, to remember. Norferd nodded, nothing more to be done now. He thought sadly that there were one or two things he'd still have liked to have known, such as how it all began, life, that is.

Had the replicators come first, or metabolism? Did evolution have a telos? You'd have to test that one out empirically, set up some kind of *experimentum*, prepare a great arena. He got up to look for a candy machine.

8. FOUND

Padmasambhava saw her coming up the stairs, dazed, delighted, happy, eager to see him, just before the bombs fell. He thought of what Saint Oswald had said, that 'we hear music with our muscles.' He saw her climbing towards him and his sinews sang.

It had taken a great deal of work to create the place where the two of them were to meet.

And they too had been hard at work—in the space of only a few hours they had made true what had been idealistic nonsense, back when human and Gente thinkers had wanted to believe it, that thought alone can change the way things are, without needing action to mediate. Their brains were folded and built just so, working not only in the usual four dimensions but in many others, faster than light. Certain ideas that they entertained cast mighty shadows on the lower world, the real world, fresh hues lighting up the things, linking or splitting images and times.

Fold, and loosen, and something moves in the inner ear—a way to keep balance in time and space, called music, so that Fire can continue the dance that Padmasambhava had begun in these last few minutes, barefooted, in the dirt, in the ashes, while he stood silently by, waited for her and greeted her with an ancient gesture, his right hand raised.

No one could see the barriers behind which the apes died, or became insects, and the lesserlings killed one another as fast as they could, and far too late the floodgates were opened so that the citizens could flee, so that the city could empty somewhat before it burnt. A Defence battalion had fought their way, reluctantly, against heavy opposition, to the edge of the square where the Temple of Isotta had stood, should have stood, soon would stand once more. The soldiers had brought weapons and they took up their positions on a lawn a safe distance away and saw the two strangers and decided to shoot at will. High above, the whale sharks with their long-focus lenses saw quite well what was about to happen and kept their counsel as they always had.

Insects that had not yet reached their goal, gave up and swarmed from the city.

Only the first giant ape remained and a few of the smaller ones, perhaps two dozen.

The Defence soldiers on the lawn took aim, but before they could fire the first shot, time stood still.

'I'm Fire,' said Fiamettina.

'I'm Padmasambhava,' said Padmasambhava.

'Strange kind of name,' said Fire.

She looked about and completed the thought. 'Strange kind of place.'

He nodded. 'Yes. And it's not even the true place, only a model. Come, take my hand.'

She did so. He showed her, with a glance, with a gesture, how they could get away from here in no time, without time. That was his share of the work. And hers, she chose their destination.

The children of the lynx and the wolf vanished.

Light fell from heaven, devouring the ruins, the wreckage of the city.

1. BREAKFAUST

'That's it! Enough! I'll start with a can of beer this morning then, from the super-market over there!'

Herr von Schnaub-Villalila reckoned that he was anything but irritable. By and large, he was right. Instead, he was something else, which didn't help much either. Although the slings and arrows could hardly shake his equanimity, constant irritations would wear him down so much that, after a while, he just had to rant and rave. The young lady serving at the bakery counter couldn't do a thing about it. It was more to do with capitalism, in particular, and stupidity in general. She stared at the handsome young man as though he had threatened her with a gun. He was German, but looked Asiatic, wore an expensive Milanese suit and was waving his paper bag as though he wanted to bash her brains in with the bread roll inside. He shouted for the whole station to hear. 'Beer! Or nothing at all! Nothing would be great, that tastes BLOODY LOVELY!'

The problem was that he simply didn't want, couldn't bring himself, to explain every damn thing to everyone. Not at breakfast, not when he was buying bread rolls. His unpleasant profession began soon enough after breakfast, explaining, convincing, persuading, as soon as he'd bolted his food. A bottle of water, was that too much to ask? Mineral water. Perfectly ordinary, *non*?

But what did Herr von Schnaub-Villalila have to put up with, for weeks now, ever since the nice little bakery nearby had closed? He lived in a spacious penthouse flat, in a pre-war building, but now he had to come over here, before he could go to his no less spacious office at the other end of the town. And what did he get?

It was this:

'Three-grain bread roll, please, and a bottle of water.'

'Still or sparkling?'

'Sparkling.'

'Fizzy or tingly? Classic? Medium?' As though this were a wine tasting.

Next morning:

'Three-grain bread roll and a bottle of sparkling water.' And another woman at the counter this time, asking him, 'Fizzy water then, dear?'

'Yes, that's right, fizzy.'

'With gas?'

Oh dear Lord, sure, yes, gas, mineral oil from the plasma gun, whatever. 'Yes, yes, with gas.'

'Lot o' gas then, love, or jus' a bit?' Please repeat until this shit hurts your head.

'Whatever.'

'Wha's that mean though, "whatever"?'

Third attempt, twenty-four hours later:

'Three-grain bread roll and a bottle of fizzy water, lots of gas.' This time it was a bloke, who got stroppy. 'What's fizzy? Carbon dioxide? Classic or medium?'

Mondaytuesdaywednesdaythursdayfriday, and there was no way to phrase it right, probably the training for the job drilled this into them: customers wanting water, no matter how precisely they ask, are to be asked at least once what kind they want, so that the patient then suffers from existential doubt.

Raving and waving his arms, he'd already forgotten what exactly today's bloody stupid question had been. He only knew that he couldn't take it any more, not for anything, not for a bottle of water, not even if it was the living water that Jesus had promised to the woman at the well, that he knew for sure.

The same nitwitted idiocy every day, not only when he was buying his bread rolls. That's what made Herr von Schnaub-Villalila mad, all the time, every time.

For instance, the business about his name. Again and again in the course of his job, which was quite interesting as it happened, he would meet some halfwit who couldn't let it lie, who had to ask, in the following words or something grindingly similar, 'Ryu von Schnaub-Villalila, that's a very unusual name, where's it from?'

From Harvey Nick's.

Won it on eBay.

The Emperor granted it.

Where is a name usually from, you noodles?

But with the patience of an angel, Ryu would always trot out his little speech about his Japanese mother and his German father, a nobleman in the diplomatic service, about his far-flung Italian ancestry . . .

Thirty-six years old, working for an international financial service provider, responsible for their cultural sponsorship, for corporate art, prize juries, foundations law, anything else?

They didn't actually want to know any of this, of course, they were just bored, bored with themselves, understandably. Why do I put up with this? Because I'm paid to. Scandalous amounts.

Ryu wasn't one of those who, in such situations, begin thinking that there had to be more to life, who knew . . . He preferred to blow his top at the bakery counter in the railway station.

Anyway, this girl—strong build, peach-red cheeks, fairly pretty in fact—was not totally numbed by her work, yet, and could actually put up some protest at his behaviour. 'Well listen, what do you want then? I only asked you what else it would be. Say something or pay for your roll.' Muttered agreement from the queue behind Ryu lapped up and down his spine like a wave of shame, and for a horrifying moment he didn't know what he should do. Then a hand wearing valuable rings (he saw that straightaway, he had an eye for such things) reached past him and put a five-Euro note on the little glass tray. A man's voice, rich and round, spoke in his left ear, far too close really, 'Come along, come to my place and have a drink,' and then, louder, in a tone accustomed to obedience, to the girl, 'Keep the change.'

Ryu didn't know the man, about fifty, dark winter suit and a light overcoat, with his paternal smile and his rather boozy but limpid eyes, who murmured, 'Shall we, then?' and—shoved? Pulled?—Ryu through the station hall: but all of this told him that he really should know him. This was someone important.

'I've got errm meetings to get to,' Ryu said weakly, like someone pretending to fend off advances, while wanting to give in. The huge concourse was suddenly a parade of horribles—that child has snot running from his nose, the air smells of dead maggots, those two selling cutlery there are murderers, must be, the teenagers laugh like lost souls, the train staff were card-carrying fascists.

Ryu discovered that he had become very sensitive to this sort of horror in the midst of the everyday.

Once, reading Peter Weiss, *The Investigation*, he had felt suddenly sick at the scene where the former Nazi bigwig tells the court that he collects 'porcelain paintings and engravings / and old farm furniture'. The thoroughly unwelcome question had popped into Ryu's head as to whether that wasn't his clientele, whether today's connoisseurs might not be tomorrow's mass murderers and money men, just as yesterday's aesthetes had been mass murderers and money men the day before yesterday.

Look closer; one of those two men selling cutlery didn't have a natural jaw, but an artificial something hanging down his neck (porcelain paintings engravings) and the screeching girls were pale, as though partially filtered out of the picture, and the snot on the child's upper lip looked bloody. 'Do you see it too? We should get out of here, quickly,' the man said, and Ryu suddenly thought about him, My boss. My . . . king? Sounds right. Why?

Certainly, we should get out of here, but what's 'here', in fact, and who are 'we', am I Faust, is he Mephistopheles, is he the Whisperer from the great Darkness who'll show me secrets I might rather not know? 'Business,' said the stranger. 'I need you to help me cut a deal. I want to bring someone on board for my project, who knows how to . . . hide things in sound. This person doesn't speak to scientists though, since they've made a lot of money from her research by taking out their own patents and setting up start-ups. She won't talk to me, you understand? She only talks to money, directly, or with money's authorized representatives. That cuts down the dickering, and she loves to cut things down.' It was a long explanation, Ryu thought, notably open and straightforward, which set out the rather complicated circumstances in a few clear words. He walked as though in a dream, astonished at the people they passed, or who walked past them, astonished too that some of them seemed not to be people at all, but were women wearing huge muscle suits, encased in exostructures with too many arms and legs, like the computer-generated images from a science-fiction film, and astonished that from time to time the concourse roof vanished, giving way to a clear sky, half of it bright blue day and half, deep night.

What am I so surprised at, in fact?

I'm surprised at what's going on round me and at my kidnapper and at his astonishing speech, but most of all that I didn't even hear this speech, since when I think about it I realize that I perceived it rather differently, unconventionally, in fact, through my nose—he speaks with his aftershave, he speaks in scents.

Walking along, Ryu took the bread roll from his crinkling paper bag and chomped on it, mostly to find out whether bread rolls taste the same when you're going mad.

2. PLOTTING THE CURVE

There had always been incidents like this, not only during the Monotony but before, and since. Humans were the only creatures who steadfastly refused to recognize them as true events, when they ran across them, unless perhaps the event in question played out in their brain, as happened in the case of the mathematician and physicist Theodor Kaluza when he introduced the so-called fifth dimension into space-time continuum theory.

Rains of frogs, fish in the desert, the talking ass, dragons at the edge of medieval swamps, werewolves, vampires, incubi and succubi, spontaneous human combustion, all these reflected higher or lower-dimensional realities, hawk-headed gods, unicorns in the shopping centre, dwarves, giants, figures we joke about, who really were no joke, and there was even a pinch of the real truth hidden somewhere in spiritualism.

A loyalist deputy, at the height of his tirade against the Jacobins, looked at the spot where the arms of the true King of France should hang and saw the blazon of Cyrus Golden, the Lion. Instead of trying to understand what the world was trying to tell him, he began to laugh like a madman, which made a great impression on Maximilian Robespierre, who also happened to be present. The experience shaped many of Robespierre's later decisions and thoughts.

The Apollo 13 mission's failure to land on the moon before returning to Earth was not because of those well-known technical problems. Rather, the astronauts had spotted a Gente construction team on the moon, from a distance. The squad was at work building the first moon base—was an echo, sent backwards against time's arrow, which NASA couldn't find again with their survey satellites, meaning that (in the words of the secret inquiry commission's official concluding statement), it had been 'not really there'.

A good percentage of late-medieval witch trials were connected one way or another to Ceramican sightings. Consistent with the worldview and expectations prevailing at the time, they were mostly thought to be demons.

British Prime Minister Margaret Thatcher published her memoirs under the title *Margaret Thatcher: The Downing Street Years*, with one awkward passage excised. In the first draft, which understandably never reached publication, she wrote in the chapter on the Falklands War about 'our very own aquatic UFO scare' and claimed that during the war against Argentina over the islands' sovereignty, high-ranking commanding officers had told her about creatures swimming in the Atlantic. They moved 'too fast for biological entities . . . and were somehow powered by an unknown sort of energy', a teeming, swarming pod of submarines. At first, it was feared that they might be 'secret weapons of the kind that Hitler's madmen claimed to possess during the final years of the Second World War'. Whatever the truth, these objects had not taken the Argentinian side in battle—as Thatcher wryly commented, 'So they decided that the phenomenon did not exist—because in war, just as in politics, you only acknowledge things that help you or hurt you and let everything else fall by the wayside.'

In the Monotony's final phase, an Australian ethicist and animal rights proponent spent years considering the utilitarian principle of the greatest good for the greatest number. Serious thought, strenuous moral consideration, deep reasoning; could we build upon Bentham's and Sidgwick's work to extend the principle to animals? For a while he was taken seriously and his ideas were much discussed in academic circles and scrutinized for their practical applications. Next though, he made even more outrageous suggestions as to how human-animal relationships might be improved and his campaign to 'protect dogs and cats against the dangers of traffic by encasing them in ceramic armour' left him totally isolated, whereupon he unexpectedly announced that an 'envoy from the future' had revealed the idea to him. He was put on indefinite academic leave and cut off from his broader intellectual basis, and socially ostracized. He ended his days as a drunken madman.

3. MADAME LIVIENDA, THREE PARABLES

Therefore the true eternity of the eternal people must always be alien and vexing to the state, and to the history of the world. In the epochs of world history the state wields its sharp sword, and carves hours of eternity in the bark of the growing tree of life, while the eternal people, untroubled and untouched, year after year adds ring upon ring to the stem of its eternal life. The power of world history breaks against this quiet life which looks neither right nor left. Again and again, world history may claim that its newest eternity is the true eternity. Over and against all such claims we see the calm and silent image of our existence, which forces both him who wants to see and him who does not, to realize that eternity is nothing of the startling newest. Force may coerce the 'newest' into an identification with the 'final', to make it appear the very newest eternity indeed. But that is not like the bond which obtains between the latest grandson and the earliest forebear.

—Franz Rosenzweig (translated by William Wolfgang Hallo)

'We will live forever tonight.'

—Chastain

'Today shalt thou be with me in Paradise.'

—Jesus of Nazareth

4. THE COMPOSER

'That's comedy gold. I think I'm going to piss myself.'

He would have believed it, too. He'd never heard such a scornful, condescending, obscene laugh. She chuckled for a little while yet, snorted, made guttural noises, was much amused. The woman couldn't be particularly old but Ryu found that she had a lived-in look. Her studio flat was smokier than a rock-music club (granted, that was an assumption; Ryu von Schnaub-Villalila didn't visit rock clubs). Even her white hair had a yellow tinge from the smoke, the banker decided—was it dyed? It had to be, even though it looked quite natural. She was lanky, well-muscled, wearing black leather trousers, black boots, a man's shirt and broad braces, and she sat at a mixing console between full ashtrays, scrawled notepapers, books, piles of minidiscs and CDs, twiddling with the buttons. From time to time, the woman looked at his face and found something colossally amusing there and whickered with laughter. 'Brou-ha-ha-ha-ha. A shrine to love. Brilliant. A festspiel. For a—what did you say—a biotech mogul? And he's sent you along to talk numbers? And they're supposed to be so impressive that I'll just jump right in? Even though your little pitch reveals that you have not the first idea of who I am or what I do?'

'Frau Späth . . .'

'Don't you Frau Späth me, you little nerk.' Hardly had she lit her next huge cigar, than she was blowing the smoke more or less straight into his face. Comedy cigars, ridiculously thick. What a carry-on.

High time now to get to work, use his contrivances. Step one: stubbornness.

'Frau Späth, I may not be a particular connoisseur of new music, but I know how we can come to an arrangement, a mutually congenial partnership . . .'

'Mutual. Not the first idea who I am,' she grumbled and burrowed into a heap of newspapers and scraps of paper that was in danger of tumbling over. 'Not the foggiest, the silly goose.'

'You don't much like me . . .' Ryu began again, and the composer took a tuning fork from a heap of old *New Yorkers*, struck it on the back of her chair, held it up in the air and said, 'Now that's a good pitch,' then threw the thing negligently into the back of the room with all the other rubbish.

Lovely, right then, step two: time to bring in Ryu's phenomenal memory, which could absorb last-minute crash briefings on potential grant recipients, so he always had the details off pat even in the toughest negotiations.

'He's told me that of all those working today you're perhaps the only person to have really learnt the central lesson from the seeds that Iannis Xenakis planted . . .'

Cordula Späth sat down in her upholstered office chair, leant backwards, crossed her arms behind her head and said, sucking at her cigar, 'Mmmmhhhh-boash and the central lesson of Iannis Xenakis, my goodness me, what might that be then?'

'Music is not a language.'

Ryu had had to look that up and didn't entirely know what it was supposed to mean, but it seemed to have been worth quoting, since for the first time he actually saw a spark of interest on her face.

She lowered her eyelids just a little, as though aiming at a spooky parody of come-to-bed eyes. 'The full quote is: "Music is not a language. Any musical piece is akin to a boulder with complex forms, with striations and engraved designs atop and within, which men can decipher in a thousand different ways without ever finding the right answer or the best one. By virtue of this multiple exegesis, music evokes all manners of phantasmagoria, as would a catalysing crystal." Pretty, isn't it?'

Ryu narrowed his eyes. Now she was testing him. Pulling his leg. Time for step three: serene honesty, burnished in the fires of business negotiations. 'I have no idea whether it's pretty. I don't understand it and I don't think about it . . . much.'

'Good for you,' said the composer, approvingly and sucked in a lungful of smoke. Ryu cleared his throat and began again. 'But I can tell you what my client wants you to consider and he says that it's taken from your favourite philosopher: If music isn't a language, then what is it? Since it has . . . errm . . .'—he had to think for a moment, then he had it—'it has language-like attributes. We tend to think, don't we, that certain musical elements might stand for other things, such as emotions.'

'Go on, it's getting funnier,' said Cordula Späth. Now he had her. He knew how to move on this terrain of, well, mutual interest. 'Good, so my client says: perhaps music's non-linguistic nature is actually a kind of para-language, as mathematics is—after all, maths isn't only a language, it's also the subject area for language—the number "1" is a mathematical expression which doesn't have any sort of . . . ontic status beyond mathematics, at best you can have one apple or one war or one human being, but you can't have one one.'

'Mathematics . . .' She looked as though she were tasting the idea, like a tab of LSD on the tip of her tongue.

'Yes, or perhaps even more fittingly—my client says, again referring to the same philosopher . . .'

'He's called Bobby Brandom, looks like Santa Claus. His thing is quite new and I like his style, he calls it inferentialism.'

'Okay, so, more fittingly: perhaps it—music—is something like logic in its vocabulary. Logic after all is much less an object language, that is a language describing things and facts, than it is an instrument for making explicit the . . . fundamental semantic and pragmatic structures of a discursive practice. And by analogy, music's function might be to make explicit the fundamental structures of the spacetime that we experience. Since after all music unfolds within time, it depends on time as no other art does, and on the other hand it very easily can produce the illusion of space, place, spatial volume. In which case, music would be the one truly dimensional art and we could use its capabilities and functions to . . .'

'He wants me to write music which lets us travel through time or leap through space, so that . . .'

'Honesty compels me to say that he wants to, if I may use his words, "set up a defensive weapons system with your help". In the form of a sacred drama, a love-opera. An artwork that aids escape and evasive measures, to complement an offensive weapons system he has already developed, a . . . biochemical system.'

'An offensive . . .' She smiled, nodded as though about to begin making notes, as though there were no going back now to respectable ignorance.

'I can't tell you very much more except that he considers you sufficiently . . . well-educated . . . to appreciate that if I tell you that one of the most important, errm, components of the . . . offensive system . . . is an intelligent mutagen which can tap into the phylogenetic memory and retrieve a . . . living being's . . . phenotype . . .'

'Who is this guy, Doctor Moreau?' She got up, went to a shelf, got down a Filofax and chucked it into Ryu's lap. 'Write down the amount there now. And a telephone number—don't give me a visiting card, I always chuck that crap away. Then I'll think about it. Don't call us, we'll call you.'

'Good . . .' and now step four: the sweetener, '. . . there's one thing I must add. He's offering you a bonus which has no corresponding cash value.' Ryu was glad that he could leave this dive soon, he had whipped out his ballpoint and, still talking, began to write down what she needed to know.

'Spiffy, ideals and values. This kind of stuff sends me right to sleep . . .'

Step five: talk right over your negotiating partner, if there's no other way to assert your authority. 'Immortality. He's offering you physical immortality, Frau Späth.'

5. THE LION, THREE PARABLES

No, single persons cannot decide. The decisions of single persons are always, or nearly always, one-sided decisions. In every collegium, in every collective body, there are people whose opinion must be reckoned with. From the experience of three revolutions we know that, approximately, out of every hundred decisions made by single persons, that have not been tested and corrected collectively, ninety are one-sided.

—Joseph Stalin

If a group achieves enough togetherness to exercise agency as a group, over a period of time, perhaps we should, on just those grounds, conceive of it as a living individual whose life extends over that period of time. I claimed that the continual existence of a person requires the continuation of an individual life. I never restricted the required individual life to the life of an individual human being. There was always a need to leave room for the possibility that, say, Martians or dolphins might be persons in the Lockean sense. So one line I could take, in defending my so-called "animalism" against Rovane's appeal to group persons, would be to stress that the idea that does the work, in the position that is only awkwardly so called, is not the idea of an individual constituted as such by mere biology but the idea of a kind of continuity recognizable as the continuity of an individual life.

—John McDowell

There are bright senses and dark senses. The bright senses, sight and hearing, make a world patent and ordered, a world of reason, fragile but lucid. The dark senses, smell and taste and touch, create a world of felt wisdom, without a plot, unarticulated but certain.

—John Crowley

6. FELIX CULPA

She was easily tempted by immortality and by other, more dangerous, temptations.

In the past few years, too few for comfort, she'd been asked far too often to abstain.

Just half a year before Ryu showed up in her studio, she had finally realized that she and Katja, brisk little Katja (whom she called her 'Little Runaround', a name dreamt up by a mutual friend), didn't really have what might be called a future together.

For one, Katja was unfortunately 'just not lesbian enough' (Cordula's diary)—the brisk little thing's current beau was called Stefan. He was a decent, clever chap but, Cordula reckoned, you had to concede that he wasn't actually a woman, and that was a very bad sign. Secondly, Katja was prone to let the sorrows of the world weigh on her shoulders to an extent that no artist could be expected to put up with, and Cordula, because she loved Katja so, was always somehow involved, so that in the end, although she was usually a very strong and principled person, even she felt her backbone wilt a little.

This was because even though a trouble shared inevitably leads to shared intimacy, this didn't mean that they became intimate physically—now and then a little kiss, now and then some clumsy sweet caresses in a bed here or there, but no appetite, no greedy feasting.

Never.

All that with Stefan's parents for instance.

They were a meek, unassuming couple with not much money. He had spent decades in an insurance company, slogging away dully and then, all of a sudden, he was unemployed, while she was a pensioner, having worked for the Catholic welfare system.

Stefan hadn't lived with them for a long time. His elder sister, who was mentally 'off her trolley' (Katja), had been in residential care for a couple of years, and her child, Stefan's nephew, lived with his grandparents, Stefan's parents. The two old people weren't hugely keen on the system in place, but they didn't oppose it either—'averagely complicit', Cordula decided, meaning that these people had never actually done anything very wrong and therefore (she quickly realized, since she knew tragedy just as well as she knew music) they were quite clearly among those hit hardest when they least expect it.

The mother had just begun drawing her pension and money was tight since the father had been knocked flat by unemployment and wasn't earning anything on the side. Then she was diagnosed with a horrible form of leukaemia. Her husband, grandson and son all supported the therapy suggested, as did Stefan's girlfriend, and saw her through it even though it very nearly killed her and had to be broken off twice, before it succeeded in a shaky sort of way. Hardly had she recovered than they discovered that her husband had a galloping cancer of the lungs and oesophagus.

They took him in to operate, unsuccessfully, on the rapidly growing tumours, and within a few weeks, he was a wheelchair case, sent back home with a respirator and unable to take solid food. He became a burden for the woman who had barely escaped death herself—all told, 'it won't . . . last long . . . however it happens,' as Katja told Cordula over the phone when she called up telling her to break off the concert tour and come back to their small hometown, to be there for Katja.

'How long is not long?' asked Cordula, regretting the question instantly.

'Look,' Katja said, exhaustion in her voice, almost catatonic, 'if you want to see him one last time, you'd better take the next train.'

How to answer that?

Cordula didn't get the chance. 'By the way, since we're proclaiming the good news,'—the composer could hear the grin in her lover's voice, sexy, sarcastic, she could see it clearly—'Stefan and I have news too.'

'What,' said Cordula flippantly, trying to lighten the mood amidst all this horror, 'are you pregnant?'

Katja laughed humourlessly. 'How did you guess, honeybee?'

The night that followed the phone call was full of pain and jealousy and lurching, lunatic loneliness, and Cordula Späth felt like the worst kind of heel. How can I

get mad at the news when the child's poor grandfather will never see it, has problems so much worse than mine? What kind of monster am I, crazily pretending
that I have some kind of claim on her?

So she really did go back on that next train they'd talked of and she was there
as a support for her sweet girl and she was properly sympathetic to Stefan, but
one week later she wrote Katja an e-mail about the whole stinking situation, an
uncontrolled scream of concentrated yearning and despair.

Katja's answer came soon enough. Cordula had to understand, it just wouldn't
work, or it was painful and confusing, because she, Katja, loved Stefan, even though
'I like you very very much. But even the thought of anything more breaks my
heart, I'm so happy and frightened at once.'

Cordula, who wasn't stupid after all, understood as soon as she'd read it that
the sentence with 'very very' was about the loveliest thing that anyone had ever
told her, and given the context, was also the saddest. Love scared of itself, scared
it could be too strong.

So beauty and sorrow were so close together, they embraced one another like
fighting crocodiles sinking in their powerful jaws, which told her something
dreadfully simple about the human race. So the artist took what little human
strength she had and set out single-mindedly to make art, something that would
outlast the way things really were.

Obviously she could expect no help from the other humans. They weren't any
better off than herself, each unhappy in his or her own way, of course, but all of
them unhappy. Their imaginative capacity was also dangerously deformed, since
they generally thought that the real had to be more important than the true.

Cordula knew that she couldn't expect anything from the likes of them.

So she took the Lion up on his offer.

7. METAMORPHOLOGY

'What kind of animal, Frau Späth?' the Lion asked, on one of the few occasions
when they met face to face, on his estate in Boleskine, Scotland. They were in the
conservatory where he tended his rose garden, a scented gallery in which to walk
and think. 'What would you choose to be?'

'I'm not telling. As for you, well, I know that already.'

'Ah?' He smiled, breathed in the scent of a yellow bloom, turned to face her. 'What else do you know of me?'

She stuck her thumbs into her broad studded belt and looked him up and down fondly, this man who was soon no longer to be a man. She said, 'You don't always strut about like you had a poker up your bum and you don't always show such an aristocratic bearing as here, now, with me, I know that much. Even if I haven't seen it. There are times when you've put in long hours in the lab and you just crawl up to bed like a careworn old woman.'

'Up?'

'Or down. Not here on the ground floor, anyway.'

He nodded. 'What else?'

'When you have meetings with your people, you never come with an aide or an adjutant, such as that Schnaub-Villalila. You always arrive alone, to savour the moment. No, to let the people you're meeting savour the moment, so that they can feel the thrill. A kind of motivation technique. And then you sometimes give them such an epic bollocking that they fall like ninepins, it's a massacre. After which, you just turn and leave. You go among the sleepers like a bloody typhoon and then next time you'll be like some kind of saint, giving them all your blessings whether they like it or not, forgiveness, redemption. You're persuasive and you're cunning. You're as queer as I am, if not more so, and you have considerably more success when you go a-wooing. But when it works out, soon enough you don't know what to do with your success. You're fairly cold-hearted, but to make up for it you have a red-hot brain, so much so that steam sometimes comes out of your ears. You're working hard on becoming a lion, so that you don't have to stay a snake.'

He took her hand, she let him. He said, 'If I may ask such a stupid question, how do you know so much about what I am, about what I do?'

'Because we're very much alike, of course, and because I'd do much the same if I didn't prefer art to . . . yuck, lucky me . . . politics.'

8. THE GOOD LIFE

As for Ryu von Schnaub-Villalila, he made the best of it and in the end even bought himself that lilac villa, which is to say he bought a white villa and had it painted, to outrage the starchy Hamburg suburb of Blankenese, which duly and very easily happened.

Everything was going according to plan. He had left his old firm. Ryu was weaving and unweaving a complex web of companies and acquisitions for the

Lion, as his Great Work demanded, and after a while, any auditor who looked at these might imagine that the Lion and his biopharmaceutical concern were actually working for Ryu, rather than the other way round—putting their shoulders to the wheel so that Ryu could spend his days reading aesthetic treatises and fundamental research, approving, signing off, financing.

The master as servant and the servant as master—well, others could rack their brains with such thoughts, auditors, or Marxists, Ryu simply told himself, 'Honestly, I'm making the best of it.' Sometimes he said this in the morning as he shaved, and the other Ryu, in the mirror, agreed.

He was a financier and he operated according to economic rationality, which seemed to him the most reasonable sort of rationality to be had hereabouts. He decided that the finest part of it all was that he was developing a free and easy and very fungible attitude towards his own identity. He didn't even mind, much, that he had to arrange his various globe-spanning romances round the fine nuance of *person* and *property* (Teresa in Santiago, Ellen May in Cape Town, Miss Emma Frost in the Hellfire Club in Westchester—delectable!—or the angelic Umberto in Milan, who after the act would read D'Annunzio aloud, for hours, by moonrise, on the balcony; Ryu didn't understand a word). After all, he was wealthy and getting wealthier, being the catalyst for a great change in the world, which privately he had begun to call 'the end of Monotony and the abatement of Mankind'.

What happened, belonged to him; he owned events because he made them happen. But it wasn't him at all; really, there was no such person, less and less each day. And in his private jet he read Georg Simmel: 'Ownership that is not to some extent activity is a mere abstraction. Ownership as the point of indifference between the movement that leads towards it and the movement that leads beyond it shrinks to zero. The static concept of property is nothing but the active enjoyment or treatment of the subject transposed into a latent condition and the guarantee for the fact that one can at any time enjoy it or act upon it.' Ryu didn't take history by the throat, he whispered in its ear and tickled it. He felt himself beginning to trickle away, which worried him and tickled him. He wouldn't be pinned down, he decided. He could escape from others just as easily as from himself.

His radio-telephone trilled. He picked it up.

It was the composer. 'Hello, Ryu. I wanted to tell you something I've just thought of.' To piss me off, he thought. To torment me. By now he knew her quite well.

These days she was living on a Pacific island which the Lion had bought for her, saying she could 'work better' there. She lived in a ridiculously detailed copy of a house built somewhere by some writer she admired, Curzio de Malaparte. He could see her now, lying on her balcony, stretched out, basking, probably surrounded by the young girls she picked up in exclusive clubs on America's East Coast and then sent back home after two weeks, richly laden with gifts and deeply humiliated—'*please never darken my doorstep again, baby.*'

'What do you want?'

'I was just thinking about the animals we're going to be.'

Now she would doubtless let rip with some horrible affront, such as that he was no better than a lab monkey with electrodes in his brain, pressing the button to jolt his pleasure centres for so long that he would starve without noticing. Perhaps she's even right, Ryu thought, downcast into an odd gelid mood, as always when he talked to the composer. She's right to talk to me like this, because she, Frau Späth, has, as it were, sold her soul to the Lion to lead her life of luxury, whereas I could have had the choice, relatively speaking a free choice, since after all I was born with a silver spoon in my mouth, as the saying goes, old money, I've always been stinking rich, always will be, no matter what.

But the composer surprised him. 'I thought perhaps you could be a fox, after this revolution or whatever he's planning.'

The seventeen viewscreens on the curving wall showed him a world that would have to get a grip on itself and not fall apart, if it was to play host to 'this revolution or whatever he's planning'. Ryu knew more than most people about what lay in store, and the treasures he heaped up round himself made an unpleasant contrast with the scarcities being created every hour—as far as I'm concerned, he thought, I know all too well what's in store for us: the Persian Gulf, the Caspian basin, the South China Sea, the Nile basin, water wars on the Jordan, the Tigris and Euphrates, the Indus, ever-more armed conflicts over minerals and even wood . . . We'll cut one another's throats for the simplest necessities, we'll rob and steal when we could be working together, building technology, conserving, planning populations, equitably using what we have, using reason.

'A fox,' he said.

'Yes, you should be a fox. You'd look good with a brush, believe me.'

She was teasing him and she was keeping quiet about something that Ryu never guessed at any more than the Lion did. Whenever the composer called up and began these conversations, apparently impromptu and rather aimless, she had a real aim in mind, strategic considerations. She wanted to know that the deal still held, since Cordula Späth knew quite well that she was selling for a mess of pottage. Not in a thousand years could immortality, nor all the other luxury gadgets and gimcracks they were giving her, make up for what she had put into this project.

'A fox, lovely. And you?' He didn't intend ever to let one of her volleys go unreturned, everything had to be batted back right away.

'Me?'

'Yes. What will you be? An owl, a rat, a shark?' He thought he was funny, which was his Achilles heel and would remain so for the next millennium and a half.

'Nah, I was thinking of something more ambitious. I think for a change I'll be something that the world has never seen before. A free human being.'

XVIII
PARADISO

1. ROSES IN THE FOREST

When they both came to, they were entangled in thorns.

There were bristles and tendrils, and both hurt.

They had expected to set foot on Earth by setting foot on an open space like the one they had left. No open space here, not even light to see by, only a few shards. An overpowering scent of roses flooded Fire, not only in her nose but as a taste, in her mouth. She breathed rapidly and sagged, twitching, into the blossoms, the moss roses, where some softness touched her cheeks and her hips. She turned and snagged on tangled stems like barbed wire, scratched herself new wounds, cursed, 'Shit and derision, what, where is here and what is it?'

Padmasambhava didn't answer, because he had no answer. Where is here and what is it? Everything's all over the place.

He tried to break free of his own confinement by thinking away the spines and thorns that tore at him whenever he shifted, moved. Scratching and scraping, he reached downward, where rough-hewn, mossy, dark green stones were set together. But he couldn't wish away this thicket, it wouldn't obey his commands, in some way it exceeded the skills he had learnt from his teacher Cordula Späth. As he sent out his thoughts, the hedge raced away from them, turned a corner, another, into a higher realm.

Of course, the home world, with its too many dimensions. The Ceramicans must have planted this garden, this rose bower for their cold goddess. At her bidding.

Padmasambhava could hear Fire snarling herself up in the thorny snares and zip fastenings, hear her struggling, spitting, yelping gently. Overcoming his initial terror, he resolved not to lose his head: Fine, I might not be able to turn all this to dust like those misshapen apes on Mars, but it has to obey the laws of physics and chemistry like everything else we experience. So I'll be able to burn it. 'Fire? Sister? How much heat can you stand?' he called across. She was still struggling and laughed fiercely, to say, a great deal, of course.

We know all this stuff about one another anyway, Padmasambhava thought, surprised and happy and why do we? Because each of us is not only ourself, but somehow each is the other too.

We are one another, if you can say it that way—he felt his old wings straining, wanting to unfold and felt his claws finally take hold on the wall beneath him. He grew warmer by an effort of will. Soon he was glowing and then the briars and the thorns were glowing too until they were aflame. It spread, devouring the hedge, a small, controlled firestorm, swiping about itself, collapsing into ashes, a breath that slew.

The children of the lynx and the wolf fell through the soft ash into a small dip in the ground, which was sifted black, over the next few minutes, with the tinder of Padmasambhava's burning.

The dip was linked to other dips or pits and to platforms, to stairs, and enclosing everything were walls, some collapsed, some slumped, some crooked, but some still standing upright—the Temple of Isotta.

Padmasambhava breathed in, cooled down, and raised a chill breeze, so that round him the flickering, dancing heat died away on the terraces and slopes.

'Look at that, how beautiful!' said Fire, standing up, pointing at the cloisters to the south and north, that the blaze had not reached before Padmasambhava called it back. Round the pillars, on the ledges, on every wall still standing, more roses blossomed in the yellow-gold sunset; crimson flowers that smelt of pepper and oranges, clear and pungent in the evening air despite the echoes of the fire; pale-pink chalices, brimful with their own pleated petals, earthy, sweet as violets, thalassic, dark as musk, others in cremerosa, coral, a silvery cherry red, hundreds, thousands, sweet-smelling, spicy.

Padmasambhava raised his hand. Then he did something quite lovely with his nose: sniff again!

Fire nodded, happy. He could see now that her cheeks were red. The roses guarded the temple and lifted it up above the jungle around and had pherinfonics in their scent.

They were as old as the great trees; fragments of the archives from time out of mind, torn to shreds, and now smelt, scented, and finally reconciled, wafted onwards by the interplay of cool evening air and the swirling scurries left over when the fireball had died. 'The Garden of Yima on Mount Hukairiya,' said Fire, reading out one of the messages. 'Europa,' answered Padmasambhava. 'For, behold,' said the flowers, 'I create new heavens and a new earth: and the former shall not be remembered, nor come into mind.' A tapestry of messages, a harmony unconfused. 'Wilderness is Paradise enow', 'There shall be no more thence an infant of days, nor an old man that hath not filled his days: for the child shall die an hundred years old; but the sinner being an hundred years old shall be accursed', 'I have tried to write Paradise / Do not move / Let the wind speak / that is paradise. / Let the Gods forgive what I / have made / Let those I love try to forgive / what I have made.' 'And they shall build houses, and inhabit them; and they shall plant vineyards, and eat the fruit of them. They shall not build, and another inhabit; they shall not plant, and another eat: for as the days of a tree are the days of my people, and mine elect shall long enjoy the work of their hands. They shall not labour in vain, nor bring forth for trouble; for they are the seed of the blessed of the LORD, and their offspring with them.' 'Communism is the riddle of history solved.' 'We also have machines which produce heat by movement alone. Further, we capture strong solar radiation at selected points. On the other hand, we have access to certain subterranean sites where heat is generated either naturally or artificially. According to the nature of each task we set ourselves, we may choose the most suitable from among all these various sources of heat.' 'And I heard a great voice out of heaven saying, Behold, the tabernacle of God is with men, and he will dwell with them, and they shall be his people, and God himself shall be with them, and be their God. And God shall wipe away all tears from their eyes; and there shall be no more death, neither sorrow, nor crying, neither shall there be any more pain: for the former things are passed away.'

How old were these messages? They were surely not from Katahomenleandraleal or the Ceramicans, so how had they been able to escape what had happened to the Gente world?

Two children from heaven, they realized that they were younger now than when they had left on their travel, though they remembered it as having happened barely a few minutes ago. They were happy at this, happy enough to go to one another and take one the other in their arms. The sun set quickly, and one more ancient message reached their sensitive nostrils. 'Almost that passage had made morning there / And evening here, and there was wholly white / That hemisphere, and black the other part'.

Wings, pennons, beating on the balconies and in the gardens and on Semiramis' terraces, thought Fire and kissed her brother, who only saw flowers, leaves, roses and briars. Together they sank into the ashes as it grew dark and they made love, bit at one another, playful, long. They took from one another and gave again, a yearning from their childhood, from each childhood, distilled to a lustful joy. But at the same time it seemed to them that they were doing important work, some task that they had to complete and transform, rebuilding and building until at last it was right. They made love until they were sullied, smeared, streaming with sweat, quieter now. Night had fallen. The forest loomed in silhouette in the darkness behind the titanic ruins and no noise came from it, nothing to betray that any creature was rousing in the night.

'We'll wait until morning to have a look round here,' Padmasambhava said, and Fire snuggled closer to him, where it was warm.

'Look,' his sister said, 'up there, the . . . North America Nebula, wider than the moon.'—and indeed the cloud of ionized gas, far away in space, near Alpha Cygni in the Swan, looked like the outline of a continent that might, for all they knew, still be on the map somewhere, or might have vanished into the vaults of memory; they had both learnt its contours when they studied the old world.

Their keen eyes made out other details in the skies, they counted a few stars and put them together in groups, they knew names and they knew stories, they murmured to one another, and told tales of where they each had come from, tales of the mountain with its searchlight eyes, the furry friends, the *experimentum*, the citadels, politics. They knew neither hunger nor fear.

At last they were tired enough and fell asleep in the leaves' grey ash.

'Ca-dow! ca-dow!' called something that might have been a bird.

The noise came wrapped in a blue-grey, iron light. Day was about to break. Padmasambhava didn't need to open his eyes, having no eyelids, but the sound awoke his brain which awoke his visual cortex and he saw Fire, standing, shaking her fists at the sky—what was this? There, on the longest transverse beam of the ruined temple, some pale thing crouched, and clearly his sister saw it as a threat.

A bird, in fact—but not where the sound was coming from, it was simply watching them both with a detached attention and there was something not right about it. All round the temple, the last place where roses still grew here on the old world, creatures were now calling 'Rack-ack-ack', 'Eli, Eli' and 'Ca-dow, ca-dow!', then hissing and bellowing too. A wake-up concert. Padmasambhava stepped up behind his sister, cautiously, prowling, and whispered. 'How long has it been here? The white bird up there?'

'I don't know,' said his sister, not taking her gaze from the doubtful guest. Its neck seemed too wet or smooth or slick to be really feathered—and now Padmasambhava, remembering his ancient zoology, whispered, 'It's . . . a crane, or . . .'

'More like a swan. But the colouration is missing, even on the beak and in the eyes. The whole thing's white,' and both knew why—whatever it was that was watching them was not of flesh and blood and feathers, but was made of some bone-coloured, cool, reflective, fired material.

A hybrid? A Gente Ceramican?

Padmasambhava looked round to see what other surprises might be aboard in the early light. They had made a hearth-like place, a little patch of warmth with their bodies in the night as they moved, which now steamed gently, and here and there across the temple's crazed topography the twilight drew up vapours from the ground.

Padmasambhava was unnerved. He didn't feel half the connection here, with this ruin, that he had felt with its equivalents on Venus and on Mars, he couldn't read its compass, didn't know how he might leave here—perhaps he could leap away, take one more step through the music, to some other place on Earth, somewhere just as important—

'No, you're not enclosed,' the Ceramican swan spoke in a sing-song female voice. 'This is merely a reservoir of dreams. Your debarkation.'

'What's she talking . . .' hissed Fire, crouching, looking upwards even more aggressively then before.

'She's . . . she knows what I'm thinking,' Padmasambhava explained, his voice low. At the same time he wondered why he had bothered to keep his voice down if the bird really could just peer into his head.

'Who are you? What do you want?' Fire was furious, and the bird spread its wings to close them again an instant later, as though for a moment to show its own blazon, to offer a formal greeting.

'You may call me Countess, *dove sta memoria*.'

Was that mockery in her voice, or a gentle warning to drop their hostile tone?

'You're not her,' Padmasambhava replied coolly and put his arm round his sister's shoulder to stop her doing something rash, angry as she was. The boy from Venus knew as much, or as little, about history and the ancient past, as the girl from Mars, and Fire now said, 'You can't be her. You're here to trick us—an imitation, a shadow.'

'Plato. Even now. Poor souls,' said the white bird, and suddenly the last children of the Gente saw it double, saw it with open wings spread wide and with folded wings at once, a bird close and displayed together.

'Said otherwise: the Countess of your stories was only a shadow—and she knew it, which is why she fell silent and vanished. She'll stay that way, she's gone forever, it makes no difference now whether her bio-lab is invaded, or if she's resurrected after a thousand years, in a Temple of Isotta that's as ruined as her lab, to help you find the Li'l Runaround at last.'

'Is that what we're to do, huh?' sneered Fire, but she dropped her fists at last. 'Vanish, meekly, as she did?'

'Shh,' said Padmasambhava. No fighting now. The bird was too wise for such things. 'We know a lot, but we don't know everything,' he told his sister, and the swan sank its head and looked to the jungle and rose in the air to glide away, northwest, on the young winds, for them to follow. 'And I'm afraid that we don't even understand half of what we know.'

She was sullen and silent, but she went with her brother, the rising sun at their backs, leaving behind the ruin, the wreckage of ages and aeons, going into a jungle of colour and growth and dew, that smelt of passing rain although the night had been calm.

They scented some last messages as they parted the draperies of rose.

The pherinfones were dreaming.

'And they sung a new song, saying, Thou art worthy to take the book, and to open the seals thereof: for thou wast slain, and hast redeemed us to God by thy blood out of every kindred, and tongue, and people, and nation; And hast made us unto our God kings and priests: and we shall reign on the earth.'

'Better a live dog than a dead lion.'

'*Bien que la plupart des sites, surtout paléolithiques, visités par nous au cours de ces deux expéditions, n'aient fourni que des renseignements stratigraphiques insuffisants (soit parce qu'il s'agisait d'ateliers de surface, soit parce que l'analyse des terrasses n'a pas pu être poussée a fond), il nous paraît utile de donner l'essentiel de nos observations, et quelques conclusions provisoires sur le préhistorique d'une région riche en espérances, mais encore difficile d'acces, et par suite trop pu connue.*'

'And I looked, and, lo, a Lamb stood on the mount Sion, and with him an hundred forty and four thousand, having his Father's name written in their foreheads.'

The moon was bright for hours yet. They followed it and the swan.

And in their following, they were resolute: we must go onwards.

When the trees stood before them, yards high, there was always a gap between two trunks to slip through, or beneath a fallen hulk; Fiamettina and Padmasambhava were like the yellow snakes that crept ahead of them on the path from time to time, like the small rodents, dark-eyed and curious, like the hunched, horse-like quadrupeds, like the chuckling apes, the scolding, screeching birds of all colours, in strange attire, in baffling temperament, all round them.

Fire wheezed and wiped her black forehead with the back of her hand. 'Why didn't we hear them yesterday, any of these animals? Why was the forest so still?'

'Perhaps the roses . . . swallow up . . . sounds from outside, or the temple precinct itself is . . . it has a field . . . once again: we don't understand Ceramican technology any better than the Gente did, don't forget that.'

'Is that what the swan is? A Ceramican?'

'Not really, there never were any in the shape of Gente back then . . . it was always human women. Shaped like, I mean.'

'Quite,' said his sister, with an air of finality and multiple ambiguity.

Now and again brother and sister tried to communicate some kind of plan by winking, or by thinking something that the other could follow but which the bird could not. It stopped and sat, always on the thickest branches, patiently waiting for them to catch up, looking down to where they struggled in the undergrowth, sometimes taking hours to fight their way free and catch up with it, to follow.

They could not stop trying to guess what exactly was going on here, since although they knew that the swan could hear or somehow sense everything they thought, it didn't work the other way. They couldn't discern who or what it was and they were afraid—not a piercing fear, but a constant, creeping uncertainty.

Huge spreading ferns and other, stranger flora claimed their place between the trees of the rainforest. Although both were well-versed in Earth botany, they were amazed by copper beeches grown to astonishing heights, with crowns up to fifty yards across; by alder, spruce and fir, on one slope even by three palm trees and by something that, if it were smaller, might be called reeds.

As they clambered across a high ridge that fell away sharply to the right, they heard rattling and clinking and they stopped, peering down. Humans passed below—not lesserlings and not Aristoi, but true human beings, men, and horses too, a small caravan; silver helmets, pikes and colourful costumes with breastplates, with heavy jewellery and bristling beards.

They started at the swan's voice behind them. It had landed silently on a branch and now whispered, in a low but commanding tone, 'Don't startle them. They're just looking for gold.'

'Humans?' Padmasambhava turned to look at the Countess, the impostor. 'Are they alive again? Did you breed them back from old genetic material, did you . . . ?'

'They've gone!' Fire shouted, grabbing Padmasambhava's arm. Her brother looked down and saw, yes, it was true—he could still see the marks where they had trod, the grass and sedge, but their track broke off in the midst of a thicket. 'An eddy, a kink,' said the swan, when the two of them pressed it to explain. 'Tiny currents in the space-time continuum. Not everything's ready yet, you see. Not even now, after seven thousand iterations—sometimes the curves overlap. The loops.'

Padmasambhava felt himself reminded of musical arcana that he had learnt from Cordula and Saint Oswald: but Fire shook her head grimly. 'I saw them. They were there. Where have they gone? That wasn't an explanation, you mad bloody bird!'

'It will all be made clear,' said the female voice, and Fire noticed that the creature didn't move its beak while it spoke—so, we're hearing this in our heads, there's no sound travelling here.

'No, we've had enough of being patient, we've scrambled all this way after you,' protested Padmasambhava, 'Now we want everything to move a bit quicker here,'—a glance to the side, to his sister, to be sure that he was speaking for them both, she nodded—'otherwise we're not budging from this spot.'

The slick creature replied by doubling itself once more—Fire took a step back and would almost have fallen off the cliff if Padmasambhava had not held on to her. Two swans, swaying, wings spread, thrust themselves at the startled visitors to Earth.

It was not that one swan had sprung from the side of the other, but rather that they had each derived from the other in the same instant—there was no one original swan, but both were taken from the template of a third (or fourth, or fifth) swan, copies from a higher dimension.

Padmasambhava, and Fire too, heard the invitation with his brain. 'Get onto my . . . onto our backs. It shall be as you ask; a bit quicker.'

They flew over treetops and cliffs to the forest's edge, where began a steppe, followed by a sandy desert; they flew through a sky with ever fewer clouds, and now no moon, but a blazing sun. Sometimes brother and sister could overhear the swans' whispering thoughts, crinkling like silver paper, for the two birds thought to one another as the two of them did also. But these were riddles rather than guidance: one thought said, 'Elder nearby', and another, 'Imagination shall save us', and another was the desire to build and build and build. Then they became songs which mixed in the wind and sped away, lovely melodies for two voices, sometimes in sad, shimmering tones. 'How fares my Juliet? that I ask again; for nothing can be ill, if she be well.' 'O comfortable friar! where is my lord? I do remember well where I should be, and there I am. Where is my Romeo?' And then these thoughts became tiny little flags, raised to commemorate names from the long-distant times in which the swans had lived before: Adeal Florence Nicolson, Anne Liser, Aphra Behn, Tsvetayeva, Liane de Pougy . . .

On the horizon they saw at last chalk-white towers, vast blocks piled up on one another like pyramids, rearing high, and now a picture, rather than a voice, spoke to tell what awaited them there; a scaffold, a cage, a pylon, crossed by struts and braces, rebuilt and overbuilt, and at last they found in their memory stores what they were reminded of—Katahomencopiava and Katahomenduende, the ancient twin godhead, now wasted away to a skeleton.

So it was a gravestone, this heap of huge white blocks.

Could this be true?

Had the terror that had shattered the Gente, now itself given up the ghost?

2. THE PLACE OF THE SKULL

As they came closer, the distance grew greater—a baffling truth. 'Before I saw them properly,' Fire said to her brother as she dismounted, 'they were less imposing, less . . . awesome. From further away, you know, from the air.'

What had looked like huge ashlar blocks were actually stylized animal heads, like the human heads that once had stood on Easter Island, more slender, scaled down in their geometry, each from twenty to thirty yards tall, ten to fifteen yards wide, raised up from the sand into the heights, as though the bodies were buried in the yellow dunes. A city without doors or windows.

The swans refused to come any further into the thanatopolis, staying at the entrance between the two badger heads. The Countesses gestured with their wings that Padmasambhava and Fire should go onwards, into the monument's vast reaches: when they turned round, once, to see their steeds, the bird was one again.

Animal heads: a lion of course, but spiritualized, refined to a Buddha's face, with heavy brow and dainty mouth; a wolf with dags of stylized hair like carven ice, a rabbit with a nose gleaming more brightly than the rest of the material—was it coated, what with? Fire was already considering climbing up on one of the heads when suddenly [they saw that] a figure was standing—they couldn't tell where from, how—in an avenue between the hare and the panther. It looked a little like a human female, a little like Zagreus, like Saint Oswald the marionette, and in its light white armour like the swans that had brought Fire and Padmasambhava here to this place. It nodded briefly, for politeness' sake, and then talked to brother and sister as the swan had talked, a disembodied voice broadcast directly into the auditory centre. 'In the name of the curatorial programme, welcome, children of Lasara and Dmitri.'

'You've been waiting for us?' Fire couldn't believe it, didn't want to: it ran clear against her sense of her own mission, the Task that the furry friends had talked of, against her scout's honour.

'Of course,'—confirmation, from whatever or wherever—'we opened an entryway for you as soon as we knew what you were, a window in the loops. Your genetic make-up, your persons—close enough to the patterns laid down before we were sealed. No harm could come of it, so we accepted you as envoys from the later civilizations.'

Padmasambhava wanted to consult his Book of Life, but Fire was ahead of him. 'You're . . . administering an estate here? Your programme is . . . all that's left of Katahomenleandraleal.'

'Yes. Servants must be mortal; we can't outlive our masters by too long, lest their memory be profaned.'

'It's talking about humans,' said Padmasambhava, but Fiamettina was ahead of him again. 'And the Earth . . . the dimensions where you . . . these loops; they're hoops, aren't they, curves, shaped time . . . you've brought history to an end? The way we might seal an arc? Earth's reality has become . . . a curve in time that leads back into itself, the higher-dimensional equivalent of a Klein bottle in three dimensions or a Möbius strip in two?'

'The construction, the monument, is held together by Ceramican work. They're diffused . . .'

'. . . through all phases of development right up to the moment of the Singularity. In the Age of Gente, in the Monotony . . . and we're two Gente partials, so that means we're visitors for you. Guests, from outside, for your museum.'

Hence the humans in the jungle, Padmasambhava thought, conquistadors, who had slipped for a few seconds through a burst seam in the Ceramican construct.

Because it wasn't quite finished yet, as the swan had said, because work on the grave site was still continuing. And this world, here, was the capstone, Earth in stasis, the End of Days.

The truth was: there was no armament programme, no great secret that the powers on Old Earth had sealed themselves away to protect, blinding the orbital probes. Instead, this was the logical, the grandiose conclusion to what Lasara had observed earlier, the turning inward. History remained, in its scope and reach, but the distance from one episode to the next could be broken down to the finest imaginable granularity—'Hold on, does that mean we can't get out of here? That we're part of your . . . stasis, your monument?' Fire broke into Padmasambhava's thoughts.

The stranger, whatever she was, spokesperson for a drone collective administering a dead goddess' affairs, gave no answer. Which was worrying.

Brother and sister did not want to go any closer to the meta-Ceramican, instead, from where they stood, they tried to register any differences, with their fine directional instruments, but they couldn't even detect a heat gradient where she stood. It was as though she were not standing there at all, as though there were merely a hole in spacetime with roughly the same shape.

'Perhaps she's, I don't know, consulting the . . . curatorial programme, or . . .' Fire suggested.

'Or with the Ceramican collective hive-mind,' Padmasambhava conjectured, admitting to herself that the envoy's blank, featureless face was quite spooky. It seemed to suggest some mysterious correspondence with the stone animal heads.

At last the voice spoke again. 'Apologies. The calculations took rather longer than good manners would allow. You have misunderstood our intentions. We do not propose to lock you in here. You are guests, you may look about, and we will open a . . . take-off slot? An exit window, as soon as we can—this does not depend entirely on us though. Eigen-time manipulation obeys certain idiosyncratic laws, so I had to compare the . . . available data, that you could give me, with our loop projections to tell me how long you have to stay here, under local conditions, before we can shoot you out again—we have to include a number of variables, the influx of solar energy, which we sort of spin about through the epochs to produce the illusion of normal days, weeks, months, years, decades, centuries, millennia, and then the magnetic . . .'

'How long?' Padmasambhava interrupted.

'A thousand years, local time.'

'A thousand Earth years,' repeated Fire, somewhat distractedly.

'Yes. That's how long we waited, in Earth terms, before we heard from you.'

Padmasambhava ignored this. 'And how do we pass this time, what do we do? Tourists in a mute world ... ignoring accidents and burst seams ... full of the monuments left behind by the Ceramicans, and other signs of their destructive or creative acts? Or are we allowed to ... tunnel through time? Get to know older epochs? The golden age of the Gente ... I mean, I've learnt a few tricks, from the composer.'

'Cordula Späth. Of course, we should have known that she ... But sadly it's not as easy as that. Tricks—of course you have, otherwise the two of you wouldn't be here. But the old art, the secret doctrine, is more than just a few tricks, and we built our tunnel system using that art itself. Moving through these demands more than you can give, more than you are.'

'Pity we have to talk to you ... lot ... collectively ... about all this,' Fire said wolfishly.

'You're forgetting the trouble with the idea—and practice—of personal authority. The chaps in charge were selected according to the alpha male principle. Mostly they knew least of all about what was going on and always had excuses. So we decided to put the world in the hands of the staff, that's us, and bury Katahomenleandraleal, who set up the staff.'

That sounded like murder. Being children of the wolf and the lynx, they didn't ask more.

'Don't fret. And don't imagine that you'll get bored over the next thousand years—you are so various, you'll bear fruit, in your own way. There are animals here too; we've created a planetary ecotecture never before seen since the Monotony began—a present moment with no speaking creatures, no one that needs language. Plants, beasts that hunt and beasts that graze—your garden, if you like. We'll help you get to know the planet. You'll explore the synchronic paths for yourselves—you might never find the time tunnels, or not at first, but you'll travel. I,'—a moment's introspection, consideration, then—'I can't tell you much more for the moment. We'll meet again.'

She was already gone.

Fire said, 'What did she mean, we're ... so various?'

3. SO VARIOUS

Padmasambhava and Fire stayed together for many years.

It didn't take long for them to find out what the Custodian had meant; they found in themselves, in brother and sister, the wolf and the badger, the zander and the ape, always just a little below the inferential surface, or in little gestures, turns of phrase from the ancient languages, and in the end they also metabolized what they needed to alter their bodies, from the Old Earth's foodstuffs, from the air. They never changed much—they never became anything other than the winged red reptile, the long-legged maiden with her long arms, but they grew a little fur here and there, other ears, better eyesight, quicker tongues, and then would let them lapse, and they grew memories. 'This was the Tepper Plain. When you went on leave for a little while back then, you stood here and you asked yourself whether you had ever been happier than serving the Lion.'

'Yes, I remember. And then I met you in the cave, where you were working on the first storage banks for the great seedling habitats. Then I went onwards, into the city, and you became Lasara.'

'And so I became your daughter too, because you weren't just the wolf, you were the King as well, can you feel that? I can hear it in your laugh.'

In the end it was hard to bear the polyphony, the history, the stories they had to live out. They parted ways, 'for a while at least,' Padmasambhava said.

Fire explored the ecotectures, and slowly fell in love with the Ceramicans' work, the fine, almost bashful adjustments they had made to the biotic structures—mutations in particular flower blossoms, such as the petunia and snapdragon families, which had already altered the basic arrangement of their organs in ways that changed the behaviour of the bees, to make new kinds of collective intelligence. Alterations to the chemistry of certain woods to prevent rainforest trees from leaching mercury when they burnt—seventy per cent of Earth's extensive forests were now of the rainforest type. New shells for the molluscs, new spines for sea urchins, new kinds of calcium skeletons. Animal teeth with wooden substrates, and hybrids of all kinds between animal and plant, animal and human—she found centaurs, on the steppes round vanished Borbruck, and butterflies with human faces. Wild strains of wheat that grew not only in the soil but even in rocks, drilling down roots, flourishing.

Meanwhile, Padmasambhava was looking at liquids. He collected rain in leaves, he sliced into plants, he let blood from animals, and always asked the same question, and never had an answer, until one morning he woke from wild dreams to find the Custodial spokeswoman there before him once more, spectral, pale, an omen in woman's shape. 'Do not seek any more, Padmasambhava. He is not here—we made a deal. Though he was our secret liaison to the Gente for the longest while, we wanted to try to do without the Fox. He agreed, and he organized the Exodus together with Lasara.'

'But there are traces of Lasara to be found all over—why is there no sign of him?'

'We have made Time stand still, and time is money, so Ryuneke is banished from our realm.'

Padmasambhava had no choice but to believe this, but since, in the long yearning of being apart from Fire, he had found nothing so satisfying as his search, he simply changed its purpose, and went in search of her.

It was her though who found him, and both were glad.

'We're ageing again, have you noticed?' his sister asked. 'Slowly, very slowly, but the process is . . .'

'I assume they have their reasons for allowing that. The Custodials. So that we have some yardstick for the passing of time.'

They travelled together to places each had visited on their own, mostly on foot, being in no hurry.

Very rarely they even permitted themselves tiny musical jumps, never through time (since they were afraid of brushing against the loops), always in space.

They were relieved to find that they got along better now than in the first years together. One evening, on the shore of a clear lake, smooth as a mirror, high in the mountains, Fiamettina mused as they sat by their campfire. 'Our parents probably intended that we . . .'

'. . . Mother more likely,'—Padmasambhava nodded—'she was always good at planning things. He . . . went with the flow, really,' and Fire agreed, going by all that they knew, in their own persons, of their parents. 'Yes. Well, they probably thought that by switching genders at . . . puberty, it would be easier for us to understand one another, but it's just not that straightforward. You can't just become a man or a woman, when you were the other before, and understand what you are straight away. A person is what she does—we had to live how we did, for a while, before we became what we were.' '*Yeah*,' Padma said, vaguely, his voice full of love, a solemn word in the ancient language.

Then she kissed him, so that he wouldn't put on such airs, just because of a little epiphany.

Sometimes they watched the Ceramicans, the latest generation, the sixty millionth, and sometimes were watched in turn. They never again saw a living totem of the past though, such as the swan had been as they arrived.

The Countess was unique, it seemed.

4. PLANETARY ABSTRACTION

Nothing could have prepared them for it, no simulations, no filmed memory, no canned scents, no lecture in the belly of the whale, no help from Zagreus the collapsible badger or Saint Oswald the marionette: the ocean, what it was, how it began far away in the distance, the sea, the first home of all living things, the mother, a gigantic planetary abstraction.

'So much water you could go blind from looking at it,' Padmasambhava said. 'So much you can leap in and swim about,' Fire replied, which was such a practical suggestion that the boy from Venus gave in. She grabbed him by the hand and tugged at him until they were running, until they could hurl themselves into the waves, beneath a sky made so much vaster for being mirrored in the sea beneath, into the green and blue.

5. A BEAVER'S EYE

One morning, far inland, while Padmasambhava was still asleep, Fire was washing herself in a cold clear current between huge mushrooms, when suddenly soldiers with rifles splashed across the river, many of them, no more than ten yards from where Fire stood. They were obeying harsh barked commands, some stumbling, some with a grim resolve, many wounded, all hurrying—a dozen, two, and when they reached the other shore they vanished again as having been.

When the noise began Fire had ducked behind a slippery grey stone to hide, and now, daring to raise her head again, she was startled to see a furry thing on the other side of the stone, an animal that had been waiting there, just as she had been waiting here.

It raised up its head and looked at her, in its eyes there was—how could there be—a sign of recognition, writing? Pictoglyphs, intelligence, the Promethean spark? The animal wrinkled its mouth to one side, as though attempting a wry grin, embarrassment. Fire looked at it and said, 'They were wrong, weren't they? The Ceramicans. They've made a mistake. It's all much more complicated.'

The beaver shrugged, just as a human would, glided into the water and swam away.

Back at the camp Padmasambhava asked Fire what she had found that so disturbed her; 'You have goosebumps all over.'

'I was just thinking,' Fire said, evasively, because she felt that what she had just learnt had to stay her secret, 'that the Ceramicans can't really control everything. They're going against everything that they know they've learnt, about how ecotectures behave over time. Sooner or later, whenever that might be in upwards of seven dimensions, they'll meet the same end as the Gente met, if they don't understand that . . . once you've seen something, you can't make it unseen.'

She was thinking of the symbols in the beaver's eye, the alphabet, the alphabeast, the indomitable alpha-beastliness of yesterday, today, the day after tomorrow.

6. HELLO AGAIN

Deep in the steppe they found the woman, the last human.

She sat up on a hill, below a tree, which held up a sort of lean-to, a little hut, half of wood, half of stone. Here, and everywhere else in the late days of Earth, there were many such little buildings, left behind by some unseen hand, sometimes taken away overnight; sometimes they were hollowed-out granite blocks, often simple shelters in open spots, shrines, uninhabited hermitages. Some inscrutable behavioural instinct drove the Ceramicans to build these things.

Cordula Späth watched as a flock of sheep grazed.

'She's become a shepherdess,' Fire said in astonishment. She only knew the woman from her brother's stories. As they came closer, Padmasambhava saw that this was not all that had changed; the composer smiled, showing sharp teeth, and lynx-like whiskers sprouted from her upper lip, a neat little moustache.

'Sit yourselves down here and eat with me,' she invited.

In a basket lay cheese, wine and other old-fashioned indulgences.

Cordula swept her right arm round in a gesture that encompassed the whole landscape. 'This is my Mount Purgatory. D'you like it?'

What Fire and Padmasambhava liked most of all was the baked thing they were eating. It was coarse, and it swept about in a circle as though drawn freehand, but it crunched nicely between their teeth, and tasted of its grains—'Ah yes, that's what old Adam had to gather by the sweat of his brow, that's what we call bread, ladies and gentle-apes. But you don't know it until you've eaten it with tears.'

'With tears?' asked Fire, surprised.

'Best just not to listen to me, I'm completely round the bend,' said Cordula dismissively, and passed her a radish. 'I live in long-dead stories from an age when there was still sin.'

'Sin, huh?' Padmasambhava said through a mouthful as he chewed, and the composer shook her head. 'I should have known better. Advised him against it, you know. It really was a great sin what he did, you don't need to have been brought up Catholic to see that—he destroyed all humankind to clear the stage for a story of his passions and his love—mine as well, to a lesser extent. You just don't do that sort of thing. Anything left alive, or brought to life afterward, was only there to play some role in the cast of . . . it was overblown, it was a work of art though, basically. We've forgotten by now, but the word Monotony for example, for what he swept away, well, it's a category judgement with a great many aesthetic connotations, it's the kind of thing a dandy would say, and he was a dandy. Or his lover Ryu taught him to be. A story with four protagonists. The hundred and forty-four thousand Gente of the first generation, with their genetic and neuronal memories of him and his love, of me and my love . . . the question was whether we could take two homosexual couples, one happy, one not, and make a planet-wide civilization on that basis. Well, we could, couldn't we? I'd just like to know what good it's done anyone.'

'And has it been atoned? The sin?'

'Feh, tricky question. He couldn't stop his little troop from making their own play from the script he gave them. They took it all to pieces, and they found every possible theme in the one or two themes that he'd lain down for them—I mean, making a theatre of the world was hubris, it had to be, saying that all things that draw breath must think and feel within the limits he set down for them. Then the thing found its own way, unfolded in all directions, in all dimensions, five, eleven, a thousand, and that was the penance, the atonement. I mean, who now still re-members what the Runaround was, what the comparison was supposed to be, the parallels between his happy love and mine, unfulfilled? Lust or yearning, life together or dying by inches for a loved one—they can both be the spur for great cultural achievement. But when these deeds are done, they take on their own life: a resurrection, if you like. And the punch line was, that humans had to die if hu-manity was to have a chance. That's what the Gente were, after all: the first fully realized human race.'

'The first,' said Fire, sceptically, and took a long drink of wine straight from the bottle.

'Of course, what else? Others had to follow, and they still do. On your two worlds for instance,' said Cordula Späth, and jumped up to fetch a lamb back to the flock. It had tumbled down into the stream and didn't know where to go next.

When she came back, Padmasambhava said, 'The hut here—we've found quite a few of these, once we even found one which was a raft floating on the ocean—are they all for you?'

Cordula put her head back and shook herself as though wanting to shake herself dry, then she bared her teeth, looked at the two of them with smiling eyes and said in a conspiratorial tone, 'I think that they don't even know that I'm here. After all, I'm not here. I'm everywhere, everywhen, or at least I'm everymore than Ryuneke, whom they don't let in at all. I know how it continues. I know the beginning, once everything ends. I took their holes and tunnels and carried them onwards, I've spun the solar system in there and more, half the galaxy, new networks—I know the third Gente, and second mankind, I've seen the Sun dying—don't look at me like that. But even so I always find myself drawn back here, since their barrier has no effect on me, you know, their rules that have put you on hold for a thousand years. The huts though, hmm, maybe Earth builds them herself, or Time or someone like that, maybe it's not the Cerams at all. Although people from my . . . people of my age—feh, as though there were any others left—would probably expect spontaneous buildings, appearing in the middle of new nowhere to house the dead or the not-yet-born, to look much more Henry Moore or Frank Lloyd Wright or errm Hundertwasser at the very least.'

Padmasambhava and Fire had to spend quite some time searching though, poring over their archives, before they could identify these names. Cordula watched them silently, amused, for a few seconds, her right eyebrow raised, then she said, 'Good for you that you look it all up in your own heads. Earlier you know, your parents, they would have just dived into the pherinfone network and fetched it from there—well, and as for myself I only conjure up these old names because I . . . because it makes me feel they were still all here, you know? The humans I lived with. The Monotonous, who were like me. Yes, we were boring, but we were quite lovable in our own way as well, noble in reason, infinite in faculties . . . Let it free. No, sorry, I meant, let it be.'

She hugged the lamb, cradled it in her arms and spoke in a friendly tone, saying, 'Don't you have any money, you little fool, eh? No one's got any money here, no one misses it, funny that, isn't it, little sheepikins! Good sheep, nice sheep! I could eat you up, but you know what, only for now I won't!'

Something in the scene astonished Padmasambhava even more than if he had had seen the lamb lying down with a lion. This woman was more dangerous than anything he had survived in the trenches—she was probably on first-name terms with the cosmos, he thought.

I hope that I'll live long enough to be able to call her my friend.

The composer held the lamb towards Fire, who began to stroke it tenderly, took it, and was just getting busy cleaning dirt and earth from its wool when, winking, Cordula Späth disappeared.

7. IF THAT'S HOW IT IS

After five hundred years, half their time allotted, they felt again that it would be good to say goodbye, to stoke their need for one another and to face new challenges.

He wanted to draw up a map of the invisible seams: where had they seen humans, what was the distribution pattern, what epochs did they come from, what costume dramas were they acting out?

She had something else to do, she wanted to go back to the river where she had met the beaver and seen his soul.

She had had the thought because, recently, she felt like some migratory bird. 'As though someone's calling me, or as though I need to follow the magnetic lines. I like it. It's good to be called.'

What she wasn't telling him was that she thought she had seen the bird again. At the Euphrates, amongst all the other birds, the one who had greeted them, brother and sister, as they arrived, at the overgrown wall of roses.

Ryu wasn't here, nor any of the other ancestors. The dead kept their distance out of respect for the living who lived here and who, by all appearances, were speechless beings without language. But perhaps there were others in the ecotecture who had never died and who felt at home here, others whom the Ceramicans had never been able to touch.

'So you're leaving the place where we lay down together,' said Padmasambhava, 'because you can hear the rhythm. Because they're calling you and you want to go deeper into the music.'

'Yes, I think that's why,' she said, touching her index finger to his nose, because he had a nose and she had an index finger and it was fun to draw attention to these facts. There were only the two of them left now, on the old world, to draw attention, to point things out, to set signs.

Dmitri's and Lasara's children had, at last, found another task, different from the one they had believed their whole lives were leading them towards. They were not needed as spies or scouts, there would be no war, the history that came after history had ended, was no such petty story.

There were doubts for the future, but they doubted much more interesting matters than mere survival.

The Gente would have been proud, the Lion would have thanked them.

Two living beings, close friends, promised one to another.

Each could be what it wanted to be, for itself, for others, for five hundred years still, until they were due to leave. They had their legacy and were not in its bond. The clouds drifted past, going nowhere much. The sun was there for everyone, for Earth, Mars, Venus and for other places where life could go on.

'If that's how it is.' Padmasambhava said, 'then I'd like to be a wolf.'

'And I'll be a raven,' said Fire.

So it was done, and then lives began such as never had been lived before.

Shantih shantih shantih